Join the readers who *love* Tracy Buchanan!

Praise for *THE ATLAS OF US*

'The **best book I've read** in a long time'

'Full of **secrets** and **surprises**'

'One of the **hot summer reads** of 2014'

'Kept me **hooked**'

'A **captivating** story'

'Will **keep you guessing** till the end'

'**Beautifully** written, **exciting** and **unpredictable**'

'A **gripping** journey packed with adventures, secrets, struggles, devastation, but also courage and love'

'Each page brings **a new revelation**'

'A **fab summer read** to take on holiday'

'When it was finished, I **wanted more**'

'I don't have enough words to describe how **fantastic** it is'

'I **totally recommend** it'

'If you **thought you knew** what was **coming next** you were **wrong**'

'A **thrilling** ride

D1165199

'**Wow**! What a book!'

'One of the **best debuts** of 2014'

'Found myself going to bed early **just so I could read more**'

'**Can't wait** for her next one!'

'A **beautifully** atmospheric **page turner**'

'I was **enthralled**'

'I **heartily** recommend it'

'Easily one of my **top reads** of 2014'

'My goodness, what a **spellbinding** book'

'I found myself sneaking off **just so I could read** the next chapter'

'Extremely **powerful**'

'Raw emotions that **fill your heart**'

'Engaging, **passionate, romantic** and full of **heart-warming** and **heart-wrenching** moments'

'I am **highly anticipating** her next book'

'One of the **best books** I've ever read'

'I simply **loved** it'

'I **highly, highly recommend** this book to anyone'

ABOUT THE AUTHOR

Tracy Buchanan is a web journalist and social media specialist who lives in Milton Keynes with her husband and daughter and their one-eyed Jack Russell. Tracy travelled extensively while working as a travel magazine editor, sating the wanderlust she developed while listening to her Sri Lankan grandparents' childhood stories – the same wanderlust that now inspires her writing.

To find out more about Tracy follow her on Twitter @TracyBuchanan or visit her website and blog www.tracybuchanan.co.uk.

Also by Tracy Buchanan

THE ATLAS OF US

my sister's secret

TRACY BUCHANAN

AVON

This novel is entirely a work of fiction.
The names, characters and incidents portrayed in it are
the work of the author's imagination. Any resemblance to
actual persons, living or dead, events or localities is
entirely coincidental.

AVON

A division of HarperCollins*Publishers*
The News Building
1 London Bridge Street
London SE1 9GF

www.harpercollins.co.uk

A Paperback Original 2015

4

Copyright © Tracy Buchanan 2015

Tracy Buchanan asserts the moral right to
be identified as the author of this work

A catalogue record for this book is
available from the British Library

ISBN-13: 978-0-00-757939-6
Set in Minion by Born Group using Atomik ePublisher from Easypress

Printed and bound in Great Britain by
Clays Ltd, St Ives plc

MIX
Paper from
responsible sources

FSC
www.fsc.org

FSC™ C007454

To Paul and Jessica,
my brother and sister

Prologue

Busby-on-Sea, UK

March 1977

Faith lay still, the rain wetting her face and bouncing off the soft skin of her outstretched palms. She heard voices, footsteps, but couldn't move, couldn't call out. She looked up at the soaking tree branches above. If she narrowed her eyes slightly it almost looked like she was underwater, floating under a submerged tree...

Wouldn't that be wonderful, discovering the drowned forest she and her sisters had spent their summers searching for? She remembered the first time she showed them the map she'd made. Three years ago. She was sixteen, so naïve then, so excited too. She'd hurried down the beach, the pebbles stretching out before her, the sky bright blue above, sun hot and hazy. When she caught sight of her sisters, she slowed down. She liked watching them when they were like this, quiet and still. Her thirteen-year-old sister, Charity – the youngest of the three – lay on a towel, chin tipped up towards the sun, eyes closed, wild black hair a tangle above her head. Her sunburnt legs stretched out from faded denim shorts, her halter-neck top matching her red knees. She was at that confusing age between girlhood and womanhood that Faith remembered so well.

Sitting behind Charity on a large white rock, her pale knees tucked up to her chest, was Hope. She watched the sea pensively as it foamed against the beach, the end of her pen in her mouth, notepad open in her other hand. The swimsuit she was wearing – an old one of their mother's, swirling colours of green, red and blue – and the turquoise swimming cap that hid her long red hair made her look more like thirty than fifteen.

Faith quickened her step towards them, bare feet scrunching pebbles, the object of her excitement hidden behind her back.

Hope peered up first, face lighting up when she saw her older sister. 'How's the poem going?' Faith asked her.

'I'm stuck on the colour of the sea.' A frown puckered her pale skin as she turned to look back out towards the sea. 'It's such a strange colour today, not blue or grey or green.'

'Ribbons,' Charity lazily murmured without opening her eyes. 'Blue, grey and green ribbons.'

Faith smiled as she sat down next to Charity, pebbles warm beneath her bare calves.

'Ribbons. I like that. You're not so useless after all, Charity,' Hope declared, scribbling in her notepad as Charity stuck her tongue out at her.

'I've got something to show you both,' Faith said.

Charity opened one eye, squinting up at her sister. 'Please not another type of snorkel? Because honestly, they all look the same to me.'

Faith laughed. 'I promise it's not.' She looked over at Hope, impatient. 'Come on, I want to show you both together.'

Hope put her hand up. 'Wait, I have one more line to write.' She finished scribbling then snapped her notepad shut, shouting,

'Finished!' Then she jogged over to them, pulling her swimming cap off and raking her fingers through her wavy red hair as it fell around her thin shoulders.

'So,' Faith said as Hope joined them. 'You know we're going to travel the world when we're old enough?'

Charity and Hope exchanged a smile. Faith always came up with fun adventures.

'As Daddy pointed out, we can't visit every single country in the world,' Faith continued. 'That would take us a lifetime. We need a *focus*.'

'I quite agree,' Hope said as Charity nodded.

'Well, I've decided what our focus will be.' She took a deep breath, looking at each of her sisters in turn, drawing out the drama.

'Oh come on, Faith, don't torture us,' Charity said, bouncing up and down on her toes in anticipation.

'We should focus on visiting submerged forests!' Faith declared. 'I was looking through the photos from Mum's field trip last week in Austria, they're beautiful!'

Charity went still. 'Submerged what?'

'You never listen when Mum tells us about her trips,' Hope said, rolling her eyes.

'They're forests that disappear beneath the sea over time,' Faith explained.

'Mrs Tate read a poem in class about a whole town that got flooded in Wales after I told her where Mum was going,' Hope said. 'You can still see the remains of its forests when the tide goes out.' She flicked through her notepad then tapped her finger on a page. 'Here it is. "When waves crashed on the sea-shore / with thunder in its wake / The bells of Cantre'r Gwaelod / are silent 'neath the wave."'

'So these forests are a bit like Atlantis?' Charity asked.

'Kind of,' Faith said. 'But minus the buildings. And they're not just beneath the sea. You can find them in lakes and rivers too.

There's one in Austria that only appears in the summer when the snow melts. The water floods the trees, and even a park bench. I found a book in the library about them, and drew a map of all the forests I could find in it.'

Faith pulled out what she'd been hiding behind her back and laid it on the towel. It was a large and rather beautiful drawing of the world map, tiny illustrated trees dotted in different locations. At the top, in Faith's pretty looped handwriting, was: 'World Tour of Submerged Forests.'

The three sisters bent over the map, hair trailing across it, dark, red and blonde. They traced their fingers over the trees then all peered up at one another.

Charity smiled. 'This is so cool, Faith.'

Faith's pretty face lit up. 'Isn't it? I can collect samples from the trees as we travel. I'll be a marine biologist by then anyway.' She looked at Hope. 'And you can write poems about them.' Hope nodded, grey eyes sparkling. 'And Charity, you can—'

'Sunbathe after each dive?' Charity suggested.

The three girls laughed.

There was the sound of crunching pebbles. They all looked up to see their friend Niall approaching. The top half of his wetsuit was around his waist, exposing the tanned skin of his chest. His face was very tanned too, his blue eyes even more vivid as a result. He looked like he'd grown up in the weeks since they'd seen him last. Faith supposed he wasn't the annoying little boy they'd first met on this beach four years before. He was fifteen, after all, nearly a man.

She noticed Charity staring shyly at him, her cheeks flushing. Clearly Charity had noticed the change in Niall too. Hope on the other hand was oblivious, rolling her eyes as she always did when Niall appeared.

'Come join us, Niall,' Faith said, beckoning him over. 'We've decided to do a world tour of submerged forests.'

4

Niall crouched down and looked at the map. 'There's a submerged forest off Busby's coast, apparently.'

Hope looked at him cynically.

'Seriously. A fisherman saw the branches of a tree during a storm.'

'That's hardly proof,' Hope said.

'But it's something,' Charity said, jumping up and shading her eyes as she looked out to sea. 'I'd love to see it.'

Niall smiled at Charity. She bit her lip, looking away. Hope shot her a warning glance, but Faith smiled. It was nice, watching the way they were together. Niall was a good kid, despite his troubled background. It wasn't his fault his parents drank too much and lived on the grim estate at the other end of Busby, was it?

He pulled a pencil from the small blue rucksack Faith always carried around with her and quickly drew a little tree over Busby-on-Sea on the map.

'If we find it, it can be the first forest we visit,' he said.

'We?' Hope replied.

'Yeah, who else will teach you all to dive properly?'

The three sisters looked out to sea, the waves crashing and receding before them. Then Niall picked Charity up, throwing her over his shoulder and running into the sea with her as Faith laughed.

The happy memory dissipated. A tear slid down Faith's cheek. She was so cold, so frightened. Her sisters would find her though. They'd see her bed was empty and they'd come looking for her. Then she'd tell them every little thing that had happened during the past few weeks and they'd figure it all out together, because that was what they always did.

No more secrets, she thought to herself.

She closed her eyes.

Chapter One

Willow

My friend Ajay reckons the Aegean Sea is named after Aegea, queen of the Amazons. My aunt Hope disagrees. She says it's named after a famous sea goat.

I know which one I prefer.

In fact, I feel like I'm channelling a female warrior when I do dives like this, all swaddled up in my diving 'armour', ready to do battle with the sea and unearth its treasures. I feel it now as the dive boat we're on bounces over the waves, the sea spreading out around us, the island of Rhodes just a shimmer of land behind us.

'Nearly there,' Ajay says, smiling at me. Without him, I'd have never got on to this wreck dive. I smile back, grateful.

One of the other divers who's with us – an Australian called Guy, all blond hair and muscles – paces the boat, frustrated. 'I might just jump off this boat and swim there myself if it doesn't get a move on.'

The rest of the crew laugh.

I haven't worked with Guy before but I've worked with divers like him, all bravado and testosterone. I can guarantee that by tonight he'll be telling me stories of all the times he's nearly died diving wrecks. Usually that's a sign of someone who puts their ego above competence.

I throw Ajay a 'where'd you find this one?' look. He mouths back, 'He's good.'

We'll see.

'You dived a cruise ship before?' Guy asks me.

'Not a cruise ship,' I reply, standing on my tiptoes as I crane my neck to see any sign of the site.

'Willow dived the Russian tanker with me,' Ajay said.

Guy looks me up and down. 'Oh yeah? Pretty risky salvage dive. Big payout though, right?'

'Not bad,' I murmur.

That was a good job. I was in between contracts in Brighton at the time, whittling away the money I'd accrued from my last gig on a North Sea oil rig. I'd seen the tanker on the news and wondered if the commercial diving company Ajay worked for would be hired to salvage it. It looked like a risky dive, lots of wielding and moving of heavy equipment…lots of opportunity for that equipment to tumble on top of the crew. When Ajay called asking if I was free to work on it, I hadn't hesitated. It wasn't just the job, it was Ajay too. We'd clicked straight away when he was my diving instructor. He's one of the good guys – and he never once tried it on with me after a few too many beers.

'This job will be risky too,' Guy says, eyes lighting up. 'Why's it been allowed to stay under for twenty years, anyway?'

'The cruise company went bust so couldn't pay to salvage it,' one of the other divers shouts over. 'The Greek authorities couldn't afford it either.'

'I heard a mystery benefactor stepped in to pay,' Ajay says.

I look at him. 'Really? You didn't tell me that.'

'Just found out this morning, Foivos told me,' he says, gesturing to the old Greek guy captaining our ship.

'How many casualties?' Guy asks.

'A hundred and eleven died,' I say.

'Rogue wave, right?' Guy says. 'Dived a ship in the Atlantic Ocean that was taken down by one of those. Must've been big news at the time.'

'Very big news.' I pick up my stabiliser jacket – or stab jacket, as we call them – checking it all over.

'The rich dude who owned it died too, didn't he?' Guy continues. I give Ajay another look. This man talks too much. 'Man, I can't wait to get under.'

Ajay shoots him a look. 'Remember to keep the excitement in check. Safer that way.'

'Yep, you won't get much diving done when you're dead,' I say.

'You didn't tell me what a firecracker we have on our hands,' Guy says to Ajay. 'Was she this bad when you were training her?'

'Worse,' Ajay says, smiling.

'I am *here*, you know,' I say.

Ajay looks contrite. 'Sorry, Willow.'

'You will be sorry when I kick your arse at table football tonight.'

Everyone laughs. This is what I've learnt working as a diver the past few years. Let them know when they've gone too far then lighten the tone, no hard feelings. The commercial diving world is tight and it's hard to fit in, especially as a woman. I manage though, I've even made some good friends, my 'tribe', as I call them.

Guy catches my eye and shoots me a sexy smile, his blond hair hanging in his eyes. I ignore him. Ajay thinks I'm too fussy when it comes to men, comparing them all to my dad. But it's hard when every time a man looks at me, I think of the way my dad looked at my mum when they were young.

One of my earliest memories is of us all sitting in our huge garden. I watched my parents gaze at each other beneath the willow tree I was named after. Then my dad noticed me watching them so he pulled me into his arms, telling me he loved me over and over.

I loved those summer days at the cottage. That memory of my parents still haunts me now.

We all grow quiet as the buoy marking the ship's location comes into view. I take a deep breath.

Finally, we're here.

I focus on the routine of preparing for the dive to calm myself, pulling the shoulder straps of my stabiliser jacket down so it's nice and snug. Then Ajay helps me get my air tank on. I check my diver computer on my wrist, pressing the small buttons around its large clock face to set all the measurements up. Then I pull my weight belt up and grab my fins before walking to the edge of the boat and looking down at the calm sea. The ship is right under my feet, right here. I press the button to inflate my stab jacket, feeling it expand against my chest. Usually that feeling sends a thrill of excitement through me: time to head in and grapple with the sea. But I'm suddenly feeling apprehensive, even *reluctant*, to jump in.

Ajay squeezes my shoulder, looking me in the eye. 'All set?'

'She can handle herself,' Guys says. 'You said yourself she's dived worse wrecks.'

'This is different,' Ajay says.

Guy nods. 'Yeah, I guess the fact no one's dived it since the rescue operation makes it more dicey.'

'It's not just that,' I say, glancing at him. 'That rich dude who owned the ship? That was my dad.'

Shock registers on his face. 'No way.'

The rest of the crew are quiet as they watch me. I've been wanting this for such a long time, campaigning the Greek authorities to let me dive it as soon as I got my first set of qualifications when I was eighteen.

And now here I am.

I turn back to contemplate the sea. It's gentle and aqua-coloured, tempting me in. I know how deceiving it can be, how in one moment it can turn into a death trap, like it did for my parents.

'Ready?' Ajay says, standing beside me as the rest of the crew line up.

I take a deep breath, channelling that queen of the Amazons, then put my snorkel into my mouth.

This is it.

I jump in before I can stop myself, the warm salty water splashing on to my face. My inflated jacket makes me bounce up and down for a few moments, then I start deflating the stab jacket and the weights around my waist pull me under.

The sound of the boat's engine, birds squawking above, the rippling sea all disappear as I descend. There's just the deep quiet, that special quality of silence that only comes with being underwater.

The colour of the water around me changes the further down I get, from aqua to green to deep blue then misty black. The warmth dissipates a little and everything seems to slow down.

Is this how Mum and Dad felt before they were eaten up by the sea? I try to picture them. The last time I saw my mum, I was so tired, I barely took it in. Why had I been so bloody tired? If only I'd held on to wakefulness just a few moments longer, there would have been more than just fragments of memory to grasp at: the red of Mum's lipstick, that crooked tooth of hers. If I'd been more awake, I could have held tight to her, told her not to go away, cried and begged.

Then Dad. I still remember the feel of his soft fingers against my forehead as he brushed my fringe away from my eyes a few days before, the smell of his citrus aftershave as he leant down to kiss me, green eyes like the sea. Maybe he would have delayed the launch if I'd begged him to? Aunt Hope said he was like putty in my hands, one of the country's richest businessmen and his daughter had him wrapped around her little finger. Would it have been enough, my desperate plea for him to stay?

How different things would have been if he had.

Ahead of me, I see the yellow of the other divers' fins. The mist disperses and Ajay swivels around, his long legs like reeds. He shoots me a thumbs up and I do the same.

At first I can't see the ship, it's so murky down here. But then it comes into view. I grab the torch attached to my wrist and shine it ahead of me. The ship is vast, stretched across the ocean floor like a white beached whale. Half its upper deck is smashed into the ocean floor's surface, the side of the ship with its name – *Haven Deluxe* – emblazoned across it is tilted towards me. What was once floating is now submerged, wood and metal as one with the seabed as it rests on its side in the foggy sea. My aunt Hope says the ship's dead, an underwater coffin. But it still feels alive to me, as though any moment it might pounce into life and spill out all the memories from my parents' last night alive.

I stare at it, feeling an unbearable sadness. The first time I saw it was on the front of the brochure. Even at just seven, I could sense my dad's excitement. Finally the cruise ship he'd dreamt of building was ready for its maiden voyage. He used to read the brochure to me like it was a copy of *The Very Hungry Caterpillar*.

The next time I saw that same photo, it was shown alongside photos of the ship languishing at the bottom of the sea the week it sank. My aunt Hope had been looking after me in the ramshackle pebbledash house she and Mum had grown up in in Busby-on-Sea. We got the call in the middle of the night to confirm they'd died.

'They're gone,' she said as she peered up at me in the darkness. I've never quite forgiven her for that. *They're gone.*

I hadn't been able to process it properly, I was so young. I remember running to my room and slamming the door, saying 'no' over and over. My aunt didn't come to comfort me. Instead, she went outside and knelt on the shore, smashing her fists into the waves as though she was punishing the sea for taking her sister away from her.

The memories dissipate. I can't get caught up in them, I must stay focused.

So I continue swimming towards the ship, trying to stifle my grief and sadness. After a while, I see the hole in the side of the ship that the rescue divers must have made all those years ago. The lights from our torches join up to illuminate the area in front of us. The hole's ragged and just about wide enough for two to swim through without snagging skin.

Am I really about to go in there?

I stop a moment, floating in the water, staring at the ship. Then I kick my legs hard and head towards the hole. Guy goes to follow me but Ajay holds him back. I know why he's doing it: I have to be the first one in there. My heart clenches at that.

Thank you, Ajay.

I slide my body through the hole and the ship's once grand dining room is right there in front of me, an eerie shadow of what it once was. I find it hard to breathe for a second, my chest struggling to take in the air being pumped from the tank on my back. The tank itself suddenly feels heavy, too heavy, and my heads swims slightly.

I try to focus on my breathing as I look around me, the rest of the divers are spilling into the hall behind me and spreading out around the area, cameras ready to take photos, to assess what needs doing. Some divers have large nets to bring items of note up to surface. But my camera stays floating from my belt. I need to see this with my own eyes, not through a camera lens.

Faded Garden of Eden murals line the walls above, a large staircase winds its way up to a gilded balcony. Nearby, a huge chandelier lies on its side, its smashed crystals glinting in the light from our torches. To my right are tables and chairs embellished with gold leaf, piled on top of each other. And in the middle of it all, now lying on its side but once lying across the dining room floor, a glass viewing pane that's splintered and thick with sea moss.

Survivors said the first wave hit as dessert was served that evening.

I imagine the whole area coming to life before my eyes as it does still in my nightmares: the tables and chairs righting themselves, silver cutlery clinking into place, fragments of glass floating back together to form large wine glasses. I pass a smashed piano and can almost hear the soft lilt of music echoing in the background, the sound of laughter and chatter around me.

Maybe Mum would have been sitting at one of these tables in her long black dress, the silver mesh purse I'd got her for her birthday clutched in her lap. Dad would be dressed in his smart tux, his blond hair swept over his forehead. He'd be whispering something to Mum and she'd laugh in response as they clinked their champagne glasses together. This would have been a big night for them, the launch of Dad's ship. In those last few months, he had worked into the early hours. Mum often waited up for him, and I sometimes watched her without her realising. She'd be curled up on the sofa in her silk nightie reading a book, glasses perched on the end of her nose. When the key turned in the door, her face lit up and Dad would walk in, twirling her around in his arms as she laughed.

A few nights later, they were here, in this very dining room.

But then the scene disintegrates, chairs splintering, tables collapsing, glass and silver smashing apart as my parents fade away until I'm back in the foggy depths of this sea coffin again, still an orphan, still alone.

This is harder than I thought. I've wanted it so long I've lost track of what it really means: I'm here, in the belly of the ship where my parents died.

The yellow of Ajay's fins catch my attention. He's filming the scenes around him for the video we'll all watch later to assess just how much work needs doing. He heads down a corridor leading away from the dining room and I follow. Some paintings are still secured to the walls, including one of a woman in her fifties with black hair and penetrating blue eyes. My grandmother from Dad's side. Like my other grandparents, she passed away before I was born. I slide my fingers over the canvas and it bubbles under my fingertips.

In the distance, I see the remains of a bar, stools toppled on to their sides. A large balcony appears on my right, providing a route out on to the ship's decking area and the sea beyond.

There's a loud creaking sound. Ajay and I both pause, his limbs floating, almost disappearing into the haze. One of the pictures falls from the wall, bobbing towards me. I push it away.

Another creaking sound.

Ajay waves his hand from side to side, the diver signal that something is wrong and we need to head back to the surface. My first chance to see the place where my parents died and I have to leave after less than five minutes here?

I shake my head. He grabs my arm. We look at each other through our masks, my eyes pleading with his to give me more time. He shakes his head and points towards the surface.

In the distance, the other divers start heading back. I feel like taking my snorkel out and screaming. Instead, I follow Ajay out of the ship.

Before I head towards the surface, I look back once more and say a silent goodbye to my parents.

That evening, I walk into the restaurant of the large beachside hotel where we're staying in Rhodes. People turn to stare as I pass them. I suppose I look out of place here among all these tourists, a lone wolf, as Ajay calls me, pale skin, tattoos and short black hair. Wait until they see all the other divers pile in.

Ajay and Guy are already here, sitting in a quiet corner, two bottles of beer nearly empty already. I slump down across from Ajay, unable to hide my disappointment.

'It sucks, doesn't it?' Guy says.

'Sure does,' I say, trying to get the attention of a waiter, desperate for a beer too.

'So you must have been young when your folks died? Did you have family who took you in?'

I nod. 'My aunt.'

I spent that first week after my parents died imagining them coming back, found and safe. Then my aunt had come to me one morning, her bag slung over her shoulder. 'Right,' she said. 'Let's see your new school'.

That's when it hit me, my parents were really gone and the wonderful life I'd had with them gone too. Waves of grief overwhelmed me and the emptiness of the life that lay before me seemed to unravel. I yearned for the huge cottage I'd grown up in just outside Busby-on-Sea. I yearned for my lovely room with its aqua walls like the sea. I yearned for my dog, Tommy, but Aunt Hope had refused to take him in. I didn't want this decrepit old seaside town with its soulless school and strange homeless woman with her trolley full of shoes.

I'd burst into tears. My aunt had to postpone the visit I was such a mess.

The only thing that got me through those first few months was imagining the grey sea outside my aunt's house was the Aegean

16

Sea. I'd envisage diving under the waves, plucking my parents to safety. It wasn't long before I begged my aunt to take me swimming. She reluctantly agreed, and would sit perched on a rock with her notepad and pen in hand as she watched me teach myself to swim in the shallow sea just outside the cottage. Occasionally, she'd look up and shout out some half-hearted words of advice. 'Kick your legs harder, Willow!' or, 'Not like that, you look like a rhino.'

'Did you get into diving because of your folks?' Guy asks now.

I nod as I order a beer. 'If the rescue divers had got down there quicker all those years ago, they might have saved more passengers. I guess I wanted to see if I could do better.'

'Why didn't you get into rescue diving then?'

'I did at first. It wasn't enough. So I did my commercial training with Ajay.'

'What inspired you to get into all this?' Guy asks Ajay.

'I used to dive the forest in the lake near where I was born. I suppose it got under my skin. You?' he asks Guy.

Guy smiles. 'Grew up by the sea.'

When the waiter arrives with my beer, I take a sip, savouring its coolness. We all grow quiet, looking out at the sea. White buildings scatter across a nearby hill that stretches out above the waves, tourists walking up a set of steps towards some ancient ruins, the setting sun casting them in yellow. Beyond, the sea stirs, flexing its muscles, ready for another night.

Ajay tilts his bottle towards mine. 'To the sea getting under our skin,' he says.

I cling my bottle against his. 'To lost souls,' I say.

I wake the next morning, eyes adjusting to the glare of light slicing through my hotel room. There's a ringing sound and I can't quite figure out where it's coming from.

'Your phone,' Guy says, handing it to me. He's lying naked in my bed, his arm flung over his head to protect his eyes from the sunlight.

I take the phone, see it's Ajay, and so I drag myself out of bed, grabbing on to the desk nearby to steady myself when I see stars. I put the phone to my ear.

'Ajay?' I say as I squint out of the window at the bright blue skies, the clear sea. Behind me, Guy rises and pads into the bathroom.

'I've been looking through the items some of the divers recovered from the wreck,' he says.

'They managed to recover stuff?'

'Only a few bits and pieces. I think there might be something here that belonged to your mother.'

My heartbeat gallops. 'I'll be there in half an hour.'

Twenty-eight minutes later, I'm standing in a large warehouse by the main port in Rhodes, looking at one of four tables laid out with items taken from the ship. Before me is a bag threaded with silver, its straps made from satin and silver leaves. It's faded by the sea and time, but it looks like the bag I've seen in photos, the same bag Dad helped me buy Mum for her thirty-fifth birthday just a few months before I lost her.

I gently pick it up and open it…and there it is, etched into a tarnished silver plate inside:

Mummy,
Happy birthday.
Lots of love, Willow x

I clutch it to my chest, emotions so intense I can hardly breathe. I remember how excited I'd been to give it to her. Dad had made her breakfast, setting it all out in our gorgeous garden. I'd patiently sat at the table, waiting for her to come out, the bag carefully wrapped in my lap. When she'd opened it, she'd been delighted.

I look inside, not surprised to find it empty. I wonder what she kept in there that night. Her trademark red lipstick, a small bottle of perfume – that rose scent of hers. Maybe a comb?

I slide open the small zipper, carefully dipping my fingers in. There's something in there.

A necklace.

I pull it out. It's rusty and twisted but the pendant hanging from it is still intact. It's a symbol of some kind, half a circle with a curved thread of gold inside.

'Was that in the bag?' Ajay asks, looking over my shoulder.

I nod. 'I don't recognise the symbol though.'

'Looks like two initials, a C and an N. Wasn't your mum's name Charity?'

I frown. 'Yes, but Dad's name was Dan.'

Ajay shrugs. 'Maybe it's not initials then.' Someone calls him over. He puts his hand on my arm. 'You okay?'

'Yeah. Thanks for calling me, I'm pleased we found the bag.'

He smiles. 'Me too.'

As he jogs away, I stare at the necklace. It's not in any of the photos I have of Mum and God knows I've stared at them enough to know.

I pull my phone from my pocket, dialling my aunt's mobile phone number. It takes a few rings for her to answer.

'Willow?' she says, voice curt.

'Hi. Are you at the cottage?' I ask.

'I am.' She pauses. 'Well, how did it go?'

'Not great. The ship's unstable, they've had to cancel the recovery. To be honest, I don't think I'll get a chance to dive it again, it's just too dangerous.'

'Good. It's best left alone.'

I suppress a sigh. We'd argued when I'd told her I was going to be part of the dive crew who'd be salvaging the ship. She had this romantic notion that it would be disturbing the dead passengers' souls, even though all the bodies had been recovered long ago.

'They found some items though,' I say, looking at the necklace, 'including the silver bag I got Mum for her birthday.'

My aunt doesn't respond for a moment. I just hear her breath, quiet and slow. 'That's good,' she says eventually, sounding a bit choked up. 'I'd like to see it when you come back.'

'I'll bring it with me. There was a necklace inside that I don't recognise.'

'She had lots of jewellery.'

'This one's unusual though. Ajay thinks it might be two initials intertwined, a C and an N?' My aunt's silent again. That silence speaks volumes. 'Did you see Mum wear it?'

'No, never.'

'Then why did you go quiet?'

'No reason.' She's lying. I can always tell when she's lying, her voice goes up an octave. 'So if the dive's cancelled, does that mean you'll be coming to clean up the cottage with me?'

I think of stepping into my parent's cottage for the first time in twenty years. 'I might stay here for a few days actually.'

'Don't make excuses. It might be the last chance you'll get to see it.'

I've been trying to forget the fact that I finally relented to putting the house I grew up in on the market. I haven't stepped foot in there since my parents died. Maybe if my aunt had taken me there after, like I'd begged her to, it might have been different. But she'd insisted it would just upset me. And the more months and years that passed, the more painful the thought of going back there became.

I look down at the necklace. Maybe it's finally time I go.

20

Chapter Two

Willow

Near Busby-on-Sea, UK
August 2016

I peer up at the large white cottage that was my childhood home until my parents died. It seems to blur into the clouds above, the green of the grass that spreads out behind it and the blue of the sea in front add the only hint of colour.

I walk the stones I used to skip up. They're overgrown with moss now, barely visible. And those large bay windows, I'd once sat by as I waited for Dad to return from work. But they're so grimy now, no way anybody could see through them. The rose bushes are still here. They used to be so beautiful, Mum tending to them, dark hair wrapped up in a scarf, lip caught in her teeth. Now they're overgrown and tangled with weeds.

I haven't cared for this place.

I breathe in the sharp clear air and remember doing the same as I set off for my first day at school from this very spot, uncomfortable and rigid in my bulky new uniform. I'd stared out towards the sea and realised, even at that young age, the perimeters of my little world were widening. Then Mum had put her hand on my shoulder and squeezed it.

'Come on then,' Dad had called out as he held the door to his Range Rover open for me. 'Time for you to break some hearts at school.'

'Come on then,' a sharp voice says right now.

Aunt Hope is standing at the door, arms crossed, an impatient look on her face. Her grey eyes – the same colour as my mum's – drill into mine. Her long red hair is loose around her shoulders, silver bits threaded through to the ends. I didn't realise she'd started going grey, but then the last time I saw her was a few months ago, a brief visit to drop in her birthday card and present, an old book of poetry I'd found while visiting Scotland for a dive. She's wearing one of her eccentric long dresses, blue-green like the sea with pearlescent gems all over.

I lug my bag over my shoulder and walk up the mossy stepping stones towards her. She pulls some keys from her bag and places them in the door. It creaks open and I pause before entering, noticing the slate-grey floor tiles, the beginnings of a long staircase. Memories accost me: me skidding down the stairs with a screech as Dad chases me; Mum greeting me at the door after playing outside.

I step into the house and the warmth of the memory disappears, replaced with the dust and the cold. The awful pain of my parents' absence hits me in the chest.

'Dust didn't have a chance with the housekeeper your father hired,' Aunt Hope says, marching down the hallway towards a small window in the middle. She yanks the yellow flowered curtains apart, dust billowing around her. The sea is unveiled in the distance, vast and blue. 'Remember her? All ruffles and disapproving glances. What was her name?'

'Linda, I think,' I say, but I'm not really listening to her. I walk down the hallway, taking in the photos on the wall. Mum and Dad on their honeymoon, all tanned and smiling, against some pretty mountainous backdrop. Mum looking down at a newborn me in hospital, face soft with disbelief and love. Another of Dad holding a tiny me curled into his arm, a huge smile on his face. Then the three of us dressed in woolly coats, huddled up together outside this very house in the snow.

I walk up to it, tracing my fingers around my parents' faces, the grief bubbling inside, almost unbearable.

'Were they happy here?' I murmur to Aunt Hope. 'They looked happy.'

She looks into my eyes a moment. 'I think they were, yes.' Then she heads towards the large kitchen as I follow. The white marble floor tiles are now filthy; the pine units streaked. Aunt Hope pulls the sheet off the marble island in the middle of the kitchen, dust making us both cough.

'Tea?' she asks, pulling a travel kettle from her bag. I can't help but smile, typical of my aunt, always needing a cup of herbal tea wherever she goes. I often wonder if that's all she eats, too, she's so thin.

I try to peer out of the grimy French windows, catching a glimpse of the willow tree.

'Still have lots of sugar?' my aunt asks.

'Yep.'

She shakes her head with disapproval, heaping three spoonfuls into my tea.

'You could do with some sugar yourself. You're looking really thin,' I say.

She waves her hand in the air like she always does when I bring up her weight.

'So,' I say, getting the necklace out and dangling it between my fingers. 'Recognise this?'

She looks over her shoulder at it. 'Nope.'

I examine her face. I can't tell if she's hiding something from me. She sits down across from me and we sip our tea in silence, the necklace lying between us.

Sometimes it's better if we're quiet, that way there's no chance of an argument brewing. The argument we had before I moved out was the worst. She'd always told me the reason she didn't have many photos of Mum from when they were young was because she'd lost them all. But on my sixteenth birthday, I'd crept up to the loft and found a photo album. Inside was a photo of Mum sitting in the sun, tanned pretty face tilted up to the camera, black hair piled on to her head with a red halter-neck top on. On the back was the year: 1974. Mum would have been thirteen. I flicked through the rest of the album, noticing blank sections that suggested photos had been removed.

When I'd shown the album to Aunt Hope, she'd said some must have fallen out. I could tell she was lying. We argued bitterly – she was holding bits of my mother back from me and I couldn't forgive that. In the end, I packed all my things and stormed out of the house, staying with an older girl I'd met at swimming classes. I still saw my aunt, working at her café at weekends and in evenings, and we settled into a strange relationship, half aunt and niece, half manager and employee. When I handed in my notice after getting a job as a lifeguard in Brighton, she'd wished me good luck. 'You know where I am if you need me,' she'd said.

Since then it's just been a case of popping in for birthdays and at Christmas, and the occasional phone call. I guess I've preferred my own company over the years. Coming back to Busby-on-Sea and seeing my aunt just brings back too many memories, not just of my parents but also those sad empty years after they passed away.

I study her thin face over the rim of my cup, take in the lines around her pale grey eyes that seem more pronounced than last time I saw her, the pinch of her lips, the pale shade of her skin.

She's definitely getting older.

After we finish our tea, she stands up. 'Well, we can't sit here and sip tea all day, can we? How about we tidy the place up a bit and you can have a think about what you want to do?'

We spend the day in awkward comradeship getting cleaning supplies from the local shops and ringing around local handymen to get some broken windows sorted. By the time darkness falls, we still haven't finished the last room: the living room, a long room divided by a pretty alcove with plaster-clad butterflies around its edges. One part of the room used to be dedicated to the TV and sofas; the other to all my toys. I remember winter nights with the fire roaring, the three of us snuggled up watching TV or playing games.

It's cold and draughty now, dust and spider webs clogging the walls. The once thick rug I used to love is dirty with dead flies and mud.

'Shall we just stay here?' Aunt Hope suggests. 'We can work into the night, get it out of the way. There are clean sheets in storage.'

I peer up at the ceiling. It'll be strange staying here again, the first time since my parents died.

'I presume you'll be wanting to get away again?' my aunt continues as she examines my face. 'If we leave now, it might mean another whole day of clearing up.'

I take a deep breath. 'Alright, let's stay.'

Aunt Hope helps me roll the rug up and we place it in the hallway. We then scrub the dark wooden floorboards, both seeming to take comfort in the repetitive nature of the task.

'Your mum loved these floorboards,' Aunt Hope says after a while. 'Your dad wanted to get a posh carpet but she insisted on stripping these down and restoring them.'

'Yeah, she used to get annoyed when Dad pulled me along the floorboards on that rug. But then she'd join in after a while.'

My aunt wipes a grimy hand across her forehead, leaving a dark streak behind. 'Put this in the bin bag, won't you?' she says, handing me the filthy rag she's been using. I pull the bin bag in the corner of the room towards me and go to throw the rag in. But something catches my eye, an envelope with my name on it. I pull it out. It has the cottage's address on it, a postal stamp from a few days before.

'What's this?' I ask.

'Just some junk mail.'

'But it's addressed to me, why would I get post here?' I say. 'And why would you open it if it was addressed to me?'

Aunt Hope shrugs. 'I didn't notice your name on it.'

I open the bag wider, sorting through the rubbish until I come across what looks like an invitation.

To Willow,

You are invited to a private viewing of
Niall Lane's next exhibition:
The Charity Collection, *a Retrospective and*
Commemoration.
10th August 2016
7pm
Brighton Museum & Art Gallery

Beneath the text is a beautiful photograph of a tree that appears to be underwater with an etching in the bark.

I look up at my aunt. 'This is the same symbol that's on the necklace. And have you *seen* what this photographer called his collection? What's this all about, Aunt Hope? Is there something you're trying to hide from me?'

'Oh, you're so dramatic, Willow. There's nothing to hide.'

'But why would you throw the invite away?'

She shrugs. 'It was yesterday, too late for you to go.'

I squeeze the invitation in between my fingers in frustration. *Deep breaths, Willow, deep breaths.* 'How is this photographer connected to Mum?'

'He was just some kid who had a thing for her a long time ago,' my aunt says, dismissively waving her thin hand in the air.

'What do you mean a *thing*?'

'Your mother had lots of admirers. It was nothing.' She stands up, wiping the dust off her long skirt. 'I'm going to put some soup on for us.'

'Why can you never be straight with me, Aunt Hope? She's my mum! It's like you're jealous of her memory.'

She shoots me a cold, withering look then leaves the room. I quickly pull my phone from my pocket, Googling 'Niall Lane'. A photographer's website appears at the top of the results page. I click on the link and a page with dozens of photos materialises, all of submerged forests, underwater trees or ghostly tree stubs littered across vast beaches. They're beautiful, eerie and atmospheric.

I click on the 'About Niall' page. The description is brief:

Niall Lane is a renowned underwater photographer whose photographs are exhibited around the world. His Charity Collection *has won a number of industry awards.*

There's a black and white photo of a rugged-looking man in his fifties. A memory suddenly comes to me of digging up pebbles on Busby-on-Sea's beach around the time I lost my parents. I try to grasp at the memory before it slips away again. There's so little I remember from my time with my parents that when a hint comes, I'm desperate to gather it in. I close my eyes, press my fingers into my temples, willing the memory to hold steady.

There! A man. Tall, very tanned, dark hair shaved close to his head. He was dressed in a wetsuit, a camera hanging from his right hand, dark tattoos scrawled all over his arm. I remember him because he grabbed Mum's arm while they were talking.

It was him. Niall Lane! Many years younger but definitely him.

I click around the site then find a map featuring all the locations where Niall Lane has taken photographs. I peer closer at the map. It's hand-drawn, small illustrated trees marking the location of various places. Another memory stirs.

I dart upstairs.

'Where are you going?' I hear my aunt call up after me.

I ignore her, pulling the loft hatch down and climbing the stairs attached to it. There are only a few boxes up here. I pull the closest one over and open it. Inside are some of Mum's counselling books – except for one book, old and musty-smelling with a green cover, a fish symbol overlaid on it: *Submerged Forests* by Clement Reid. I open it and there it is, the map folded in four. I pull it out and unfold it, laying it on the floor. It's the size of an A5 piece of paper and seems quite old. I take it downstairs and show it to my aunt.

'Why is there a picture of this on that photographer's website?'

Her brow furrows as she takes the map. 'It was your mother's. She wanted to visit all the submerged forests in the world. Silly notion.'

'Why does Niall Lane have it on his website?'

'They used to dive together. He must have taken a photograph of it.'

'Mum dived?' I ask, incredulous. 'Why wouldn't you tell me? It makes no sense!'

'We all did. We spent our childhoods by the sea, remember.'

'So this photographer and Mum used to hang out when they were kids?'

She nods.

'They must have been close,' I say.

'Back then, yes. But they were children.'

'Then why did Mum have the necklace in her bag the night she died? She wasn't a kid then.'

My aunt hands the map back to me. 'Why torture yourself with all these questions, Willow? The past is the past.'

'It's *my* past. Why are you being so elusive?'

'Honestly, the way you read into things.'

'And the way you *hide* things. Like those photos of Mum I found the day I moved out, all those blank sections.' I scrutinise her face. 'You're not being honest with me.'

'This isn't an episode of *EastEnders*, Willow.'

'Really? You'd make a good actress, the amount of times you've lied to me.'

She shakes her head. 'I can't listen to this nonsense. I'm going to finish tidying the dining room, your soup's in the kitchen.'

I don't sleep all night. I'm in my old room but it's a ghost of what it once was, the sea-themed wallpaper faded, the cream carpet filthy. So I get up and pace the freezing house. I eventually end up in the garden. It's very early, mist still a sheen over the grass, the air very still and quiet. There's a sheet of grey clouds above, one indiscernible from the other. I walk the length of the garden. It seems to go on forever, a two-tier fence running around its edges to mark it from the rest of the land.

There's a patio area just outside the house that's overrun with weeds now. A beautiful sundial sits at the centre of the patio and, to the side, a large gazebo with circular benches. The rest of the garden is simple, a long green lawn that's like a meadow now, grass shin high. Around it, beneath the fence, are tangled roses. And then, right at the end, a huge willow tree that seems to have doubled in size since the last time I saw it.

My heart clenches as I notice the swing swaying below it. Dad made that for me. No big deal for some dads. But it was for mine. He usually got other people to do stuff like that, but he'd sanded down the wooden seat with his own hands, painted it glossy white with red stars then attached the ropes.

I sit on the swing, feet still on ground so I don't break it as I sway back and forth. I close my eyes, try to imagine Dad pushing me.

Then out of the corner of my eye, I notice something in the tree's bark. I lean closer and there it is:

Willow and Daddy
1996

The year the ship sank. Sobs build up inside and I put my hand to my mouth.

'Oh, Dad,' I whisper.

When I walk back inside, I'm surprised to see my aunt standing at the table. She's usually an early riser but never this early. She's looking down at the map I found, her grey eyes glassy with tears. When she notices me, she quickly folds it up.

'Was Mum serious about visiting all these submerged forests?' I ask, more gently than before.

'She was just a kid,' she says dismissively.

'Was it the submerged forest off Busby's coast that sparked her interest?'

Aunt Hope takes a sip of her tea. 'That wasn't discovered until we were older.' She peers up at me. 'In fact, it was your parents who discovered the forest.'

I look at her in surprise. 'But I had no idea.'

'Why does it matter?'

'*Everything* to do with my mum and dad matters. That's why I'm going to try to contact that photographer,' I say, using my phone to do a web search for contact details. All I get is a generic email address.

Aunt Hope shoots me a cynical look. 'What good will that do?'

'He'll have memories of Mum he can share. He must've invited me to his exhibition for a reason. I'll email him, see if he wants to meet.'

I grab the map from her and unfold it again, taking in all the different locations.

'And maybe I should to try to visit some of these,' I say, feeling excitement swell inside. I realise then that the idea has been growing since the moment I saw the map. 'It can be a homage of sorts, doing something Mum always wanted to do.' I look up at Aunt Hope. 'Mum would like that, right?'

Aunt Hope gets a faraway look in her eyes then she shakes her head as though shrugging it off. 'Fine life you live, isn't it,' she says, 'being able to follow some teenager's pipe dream at the drop of a hat. I bet you've whittled all your inheritance away?'

How typical of my aunt, ruining a special moment. I sigh. 'Actually, I haven't. I earn decent money with the diving and anyway, I'm between jobs right now. I can do what I want.'

Aunt Hope looks around her. 'What about this place? Will you sell it or not? I need to know so I can tell the estate agent, who's due to value it.'

'Not yet,' I say, unwilling to let go of the past right now.

'Good,' she says. 'Your mother was very happy here.' We both stand at the window in silence, looking out over the overgrown garden. A gust of wind makes the long grass ripple, and the swing sways, a ghost of a past I so desperately miss.

Chapter Three

Charity

Busby-on-Sea, UK
March 1987

Charity peered out of the café's window. The sun was a soft globe as it sank into the horizon, the air no longer so cold that she had to run from table to table to clear up just to keep warm in the arctic temperatures. The spatter of sea spray now felt less like daggers of ice on her cheeks and more like the spit of a mermaid, as her dad used to say.

Spring was coming.

While others rejoiced, the improving weather made Charity anxious. She'd promised herself she'd be back on her feet by spring after being made redundant. But there was still no job, no money. Every extra day she spent back in Busby-on-Sea, dark memories pressed even closer, gaping and roaring with every sight she saw, every person she spoke to, the smell of seaweed and brine, the squawk of seagulls and the hoot of distant ships feeding the old grief again and again.

She had to get away before it swallowed her whole.

'Charity, love?'

Charity looked up to see Mrs McAteer peering at her. She was the queen of gossip here with her coiled grey hair and pearl necklace. Her daughter Addie used to be best friends with Charity's big sister. Addie had managed to escape Busby-on-Sea for good. Most people did escape now.

'So sorry,' Charity said. 'Got lost in my thoughts there for a moment. So, you were saying about your son?'

As Mrs McAteer launched into a story about her 'poor Gav', Charity nodded sympathetically. People had started coming to the café to bend her ear about their personal problems after hearing she was a qualified NHS counsellor. She didn't mind so much, it was good to know she could help. But it would be even better if they could pay her. Then she might have a chance of getting out of this town.

It hadn't always been like this. She used to love it here. Busby-on-Sea was one of several small towns on the south coast of the UK, a few miles from Brighton. It had felt like the only town in the world to her and her sisters when they were kids, the three of them its rulers. Their parents let them run riot along the stretch of pebble beach outside their house, collecting shells and rubbish washed up ashore. The town centre was too tidy for them with its smart shops circling a grand old ship; the long promenade that led from the marshes near their house too civilised with its white railings and gleaming pavements. Even worse were the new houses that lined it, all modern and posh. And then there was their mother's café which sat smart and welcoming on the opposite end of the promenade to their house. Each sister took a job there as they grew older.

Some kids walked past with a ghetto blaster, music blaring out from its speakers. How different it was now, Charity thought as she watched them walk past the disintegrating white panels of those houses. Everything seemed to be rotting now. The only thing that remained new and gleaming was the large white house that sat overlooking the town from the cliffs above, renovated just a year ago, according to Charity's sister, Hope, for a millionaire and his wife. It was glossy but it looked isolated and vulnerable up there alone, exposed to the elements.

'That'll be ten pounds,' a voice said from behind Charity.

It was Hope, her long red hair tied in a knot above her head, a bright patchwork dress with long sleeves worn beneath her purple apron.

Mrs McAteer looked indignant.

'I'm including twenty minutes of Charity's time,' Hope said with a serious look on her face.

Charity smiled to herself. Typical of her sister to be so blunt. If it weren't for Hope's delicious cakes and the arty facelift she'd given to the café since their parents passed away a few years ago, they'd have no customers. Charity could see the way people regarded Hope with wary eyes. What if one day they had enough of her sister's attitude and stopped coming? Then where would her sister be? She couldn't rely on her poetry, that never made much money. And she'd taken on the remaining mortgage repayments on their cottage.

'Don't listen to Hope,' Charity said to Mrs McAteer, smiling.

Mrs McAteer looked Hope up and down, then placed some coins on the side before squeezing her ample frame out from behind the table, patting Charity on the arm and smiling. 'You've always been a good girl.' Then she left the café, turning once to throw Hope daggers.

'Silly old bat,' Hope muttered.

Charity rolled her eyes. 'You're wicked, Hope.'

'Can't you see she's taking advantage of you, expecting a free counselling session each time she visits? We could turn this place into a café-come-therapy practice the way you're going.'

'I can see it now,' Charity said, putting her arms in the air, making the shape of a sign with her hands, the sleeves of her bright red jumper sliding down her arms. 'Shrink Shack: cakes and counselling.'

'We'll make millions.'

They both laughed. For a moment, it almost felt like old times, like Charity hadn't moved to London eight years ago with just weekly letters and the occasional visit bringing them together. When she'd been made redundant, leaving her with no choice but to move back to Busby-on-Sea, she'd worried things would be awkward with her sister. But after a couple of weeks, it felt like they'd slipped right back into their childhood routines.

The sound of screeching tyres could be heard from outside. Everyone looked up as a red sports car pulled to a stop outside the café. A woman stepped out, tall like a model with glossy caramel hair and bee-stung lips. She was wearing a black fur coat over tight red trousers, and was tottering on tall black stilettos. A handsome blond man in his mid thirties slid out of the passenger side, adjusting the collar of his expensive-looking suit and shooting the woman a smile.

As they strode into the café, the whole place fell silent.

'Dan and Lana North,' Hope whispered to Charity.

'The ones who own the mansion?'

Hope nodded, looking the woman up and down. 'So they finally decide to grace us with their presence.'

Lana North stopped in the middle of the café, peering around her. Charity wondered how it must look to this rich, privileged woman. At least it no longer had Formica tabletops and orange tiled walls. But the driftwood tables and paper sculptures made from pages ripped from poetry books hanging from the ceiling might look odd to her.

'Well, *look* at this place,' Lana said to her husband. 'Isn't it sweet, darling?'

'Quite the hidden gem,' her husband replied smoothly. Charity looked at him as she wiped the sides down quickly. He looked alien among the teacups and perms and half-eaten slices of Victoria Sponge. Tan too bronze to be from anywhere but some distant island; blond hair too perfect for the salty air here.

He caught her eye and she smiled at him. 'Hello, welcome to the Art Shack,' she said. 'What can we get you?'

'I really fancy a glass of champagne,' Lana said, throwing herself into one of the pastel painted chairs.

'I don't think they're licensed to sell alcohol, darling,' Dan said, smiling to himself as he sat in the chair opposite her.

'You're right,' Charity said. 'We have coffee though, the Busby-on-Sea special: piping hot, black and sickly sweet.'

Dan looked up at Charity, green eyes holding hers. 'Now *that* sounds like my type of coffee. I'll have one of those. Darling?' He looked at his wife.

She shrugged. 'I suppose that will have to do. And maybe one of those things too,' she said, flicking her hand towards a tray of shortbread.

'Make that two,' Dan said.

As Hope and Charity prepared the order, the hubbub returned to the café and Charity watched the couple out of the corner of her eye. They were laughing about something, Dan leaning close to Lana's ear as he whispered to her. They looked completely in love.

She'd felt like that about someone once.

Hope handed Charity a tray with the coffees on, interrupting her thoughts. 'You take them,' she said under her breath. 'I'll only pour the coffee over that bimbo's head for being so disdainful about my shortbread.'

'I don't think she's a bimbo. She managed to attract a millionaire, after all.'

'That doesn't take brains.'

Charity smiled as she walked towards the couple with their order. Her sister's view of the world was rather black and white.

'Busby's famous coffee times two,' Charity said, placing the coffees down on the table. 'And my sister's fantastic shortbread,' she added, placing their plates in front of them.

'That's the real reason we came. My staff tell me the cakes here are to die for,' Dan said. He took a bite of his shortbread and raised an eyebrow. 'Looks like they were right. You're very talented,' he said to Charity.

'Oh, I can't take the credit. My sister Hope is the cake connoisseur.'

Dan peered towards Hope, shooting her a huge smile that lit up his handsome face. 'Divine, thank you!'

Hope's face flushed. Charity smiled. She rarely saw her sister blush.

'Do you cater for events?' Dan asked Charity.

'No, but maybe we should.'

'Well, just shout if you need any financial advice.'

He held her gaze and she felt herself blushing too.

'I will,' she said, walking back to the counter and mouthing the word 'divine' to her sister.

Half an hour later, as the last customers trickled out of the café, including the Norths who left an almighty tip, Charity and Hope worked together quickly and quietly, putting dishes away, clearing tables, wrapping leftovers up to take home. They'd been doing this for three months now and it was beginning to work like clockwork. They quickly closed up then started the short walk home. Their house was away from the hustle and bustle of the town, down a lane that sloped away from the promenade and ran through long grass by the sea. There were just three pebbledash houses there, their backs to the sea, wild gardens reaching out to the pebbles beyond.

Though the houses had been battered by the salt and the grit, white exteriors discoloured and damaged, they looked charming in the right light, the long green grass and stretch of blue sea in the distance almost giving a picture postcard look.

But right now, under the fierce glare of the setting sun, they looked old and tired, like the town itself.

Hope let them both in and they walked down the small hallway into the messy living room with its red patterned carpets and tatty old chairs, dusty books higgledy-piggledy in a tall oak bookshelf, its shelves bending under the weight.

The kitchen looked just the same as it had when Charity had grown up there with its beige cupboards and dusty glass cabinet filled with old china cups. Even the thick oak table had her name still etched on its surface. Maybe Hope had done that on purpose, keeping it the same after their parents passed away? She'd never left home and had helped her father care for her mother when she got cancer, then her father when he had a heart attack not long after, the heartache from losing his daughter and his wife finally taking its toll.

She walked to the fridge, shaking the memories away, and reached in for a courgette and some peppers, throwing them to Hope. Hope caught them with a smile, finding an ancient chopping board and knife. Preparing meals had been a big part of their household as kids. One of Charity's early memories was from when she was five, her podgy hands kneading some bread dough on a speckled old wooden board as her dad stood over her, his bushy white eyebrows sprinkled with flour, his livered cheeks red from the wine he'd been drinking. Nearby, Hope would sit with their mother at the dinner table peeling carrots, the same solemn look she still held now on her face, her mind no doubt conjuring words to describe the orange of the carrot and the spiral shape its skin made when peeled for a poem she was writing.

And then there was Faith, who usually stood at the sink, singing softly to herself as she made a fruit salad, the orange glow of the setting sun highlighting the outline of her long blonde hair, her neck arched gracefully as she peered out of the window towards the school fields behind the cottage, always searching for something beyond what lay within that family kitchen. Probably one of those submerged forests she'd become so obsessed with.

Charity glanced now at the old map of the world they still had pinned to the corkboard, illustrated trees marking the location of all the submerged forests Faith wanted to visit. Her eyes settled on the tree Niall had drawn. She wondered where he was now.

Hope, Faith and Charity had first met Niall as a grubby-faced boy on the beach outside their house when Charity was just nine. He'd told them his parents were never around and he didn't even go to school; that he could come and go as he pleased. The sisters were in awe. When he taught them to dive, they spent summer days searching for the submerged forest he was so sure existed off the coast of Busby. Faith was the best diver. She'd scoot ahead with Niall, her long legs sweeping gracefully through the water. When Hope wrote a play about the submerged forest, Faith insisted on being the goddess of the sea, Charity and Hope demoted to mere nymph status. But that's what she was, a sea goddess, completely at home in the ocean.

In contrast, Niall powered through the water. As he got older, he got stronger from working at the docks. Charity couldn't help noticing how muscular he was becoming. When Charity was fifteen and he was seventeen, Hope had got into trouble one day when they were swimming. Niall had dived into the sea and saved her, and something had changed in Charity's attitude towards him. Instead of being the kid she and her sisters played with, he became a romantic figure, a *man* strong enough to save her sister.

She'd sought him out at the docks to thank him the next day, and he suggested they meet up after he finished work. She'd pretended to be disgusted at the idea. But of course, she went. They'd both walked to a beach just outside Busby-on-Sea and Niall introduced her to her first taste of oysters – illegally sourced, as it turned out. They talked until it grew dark, finally sharing their first kiss. When Faith met her at the front door coming in later than her curfew, she'd expected a telling off from her oldest sister. But Faith had just smiled. 'Don't go breaking his heart,' she'd said. 'I like Niall.'

Hope hadn't been so happy, she just glared at Charity then shook her head.

Faith had always been so kind, so understanding. God, she missed her so much.

That night, Charity pulled the small wooden box she kept full of Faith's keepsakes from beneath her bed. It was the size of a shoebox, intricate flowers etched around its sides. She opened it and gently lifted out the photos she kept that told the story of Faith's short life. She looked at each one, trying to control her emotions. One was of the three sisters standing with their parents outside the café the day her mum opened it twenty years ago. Charity was just six, her dark hair frizzy like her mum's, her knees chubby; an eight-year-old Hope stood awkwardly beside her, just a wisp of a thing with red hair down to her elbows. And then Faith, nine and already so beautiful, smiling directly into the camera, the blonde hair she'd inherited from their grandma shining under the glare of the morning sun like it might evaporate any minute. There were more photos too, one of Faith picking up a swimming award when she was twelve, another of her at her fourteenth birthday party, all legs and glossy hair. Then one taken the day she got all the A-Level results she needed to get into the marine biology course she'd applied for at the University of Southampton, face flushed with happiness as she gave a thumbs up to the camera.

The last photo was of Faith standing outside the University of Southampton. Charity recognised that nervous smile of hers. Faith used to get it the morning of her exams, or that time when her dad discovered she'd been storing underwater plants in the café, stinking the place out. Despite all her bravado about leaving Busby-on-Sea to go to university, Charity remembered how nervous Faith had been that day. Charity hadn't wanted her big sister to go.

Charity set the photos aside. Beneath them was the pale pink lipstick Faith always wore; a small Petri dish; a solitary silver pearl earring…and then the ornate silver necklace Faith had been wearing the night she died, a bejewelled anchor hanging off it. Charity picked it up, tangling it around her fingers.

She thought of that terrible evening. Faith was back from university for the Easter holidays. She seemed distant, tired. Her parents explained it away, saying the course was hard work and Charity and Hope must leave her to study. Charity remembered being disappointed. She'd envisaged days on the beach with the sister she so worshipped, even some diving if the weather behaved. The first sign something was wrong was the doorbell ringing in the early hours. There'd been the sound of shuffling from their parents' room, then the door opening, her dad's heavy steps as he'd walked downstairs. Charity stood at her bedroom door with her ear to it.

There was the sound of muffled voices then her father's footsteps on the stairs again.

'Faith?' he shouted out. There was a slight hint of panic in his voice. That had worried Charity. Her father was so calm, not easily ruffled.

'What's going on, Tony?' her mother had asked, appearing from her room.

'Get Faith, wake her up.'

Charity opened the door then, saw Hope doing the same. They exchanged a look then watched as their mother knocked on the door to Faith's attic room.

'Darling?' she asked, voice trembling.

Nothing.

'Faith, it's Mummy.'

'Oh, Mother, honestly,' Hope had said, pushing in front of her mother and opening the door, her usual bolshie self. But then she'd gone very quiet. 'She's not here.'

Her mother had run downstairs and the two sisters leant over the banister, watching as two police officers followed their parents through into the living room. Charity learnt later they'd found Faith's student card in the pocket of a woman's body they'd found near the main road out of Busby-On-Sea and had come straight to the house. A few minutes later, Charity heard her father's low desperate moan.

Charity felt as though the world was tilting. Her father *never* cried. She'd grabbed Hope's hand and they waited quietly as the police officers left. When their parents came to them, Charity could tell from the looks on their faces something dreadful had happened. She'd run into her room and buried her face into the pillow, unable to face it. It had been Hope who'd eventually said the words.

'Faith died,' Hope said into the darkness, her voice close to Charity's ear. 'We've lost her. It's just the two of us now.' Then she'd felt her sister's tears on her cheeks, mingling with her own. The grief had been astounding, making her head swim, her breath come short. She saw her sister in a quick succession of images: by the sea, hair sweeping out behind her; tucked up beside Charity in bed, reading stories to her; at Christmas, the three sisters sipping hot chocolate around the tree.

All gone.

The last item in the box was an article she'd kept, reporting Niall's sentence.

LOCAL MAN JAILED OVER HIT AND RUN FATALITY.

Eighteen-year-old local Niall Lane has been sentenced to two years for causing death by dangerous driving. He was seen driving from the scene by a witness after knocking over nineteen-year-old Faith Winchester on Ashcroft Road in the early hours of 21st March this year. The witness found the victim at the bottom of the steep verge sloping down from the road into Busby Forest. An autopsy revealed she died from a traumatic brain injury, believed to have been caused by her head impacting with a rock. Faith Winchester lived in Busby-on-Sea all her life with her parents, the owners of the Busby Café, and her two younger sisters. She was a promising student in her first year at Southampton University and hoped to become a marine biologist.

Charity looked at the clock in her room. Midnight. It was now ten years ago today and yet the grief felt as sharp, as painful, as it did then.

Charity dug her hands into her long blue coat, the early morning mist swarming around her ankles. The road ahead of her curved around a corner, disappearing over a hill. Trees lined it, dipping over the road, making it seem darker than it was. It was hard to believe the sea glimmered just half a mile behind her, Busby-on-Sea now waking to another day.

She paused as she got to the precarious bend that had caused so many accidents as cars struggled to negotiate it. Exactly ten years ago today, Faith was found in a foetal position. Her scarf was later found on the road just above.

Why had she been walking on this road alone so late at night? She should have been in bed, asleep. That question had tortured the grief-filled silences her family had shared those first few weeks and months after Faith died, and ten years later, still no answer. Their parents died not knowing.

Charity closed her eyes, tears squeezing between her lashes.

When she opened her eyes again, a tall figure was approaching from the bottom of the hill. He was wearing a black leather jacket, blue jeans, dark hair shaved close to his head.

She recognised him instantly.

Niall Lane.

He paused, blue eyes narrowing. 'Charity?'

She opened her mouth to say something but suddenly a roar filled the air.

Niall's eyes widened as he pointed behind her, shouting her name. She turned to see a small red sports car bouncing around the bend and hurtling towards her.

Chapter Four

Charity

Busby-on-Sea, UK
March 1987

The light from the rising sun illuminated the car's exterior and in a flash, Charity saw a woman's face streaked with mascara.

Tyres screeched over the road, the smell of petrol filling the air. Charity couldn't move her legs, panic flooded through her.

But then strong hands were gripping her under her arms, pulling her out of the way as the car careened past her.

She looked up, saw Niall staring down at her. His cheeks were stubbled, his face tanned, dark circles under his eyes. Her whole body throbbed from being so close to him, from feeling his warm breath on her face, seeing those lips so close. She was shocked to feel the urge to press her lips against his like she used to do again and again.

Then the reality of the situation hit her.

She dragged her gaze away from Niall's, watching the car zigzag across the road, finally coming to a stop with a shudder.

They both jumped up and jogged over.

Sitting in the driver's seat was a dazed looking Lana North, the woman from the mansion, a small graze on her head, blood dripping down into one eye.

She peered up at Niall and Charity. 'Whoops,' she said sheepishly.

Charity placed the two mugs of steaming hot coffee on the table, avoiding the intense gaze of the elderly couple sitting there. It was clear word was getting out about what had happened that morning…and that Charity had been there with Niall. By the time the paramedics arrived to check Lana over, the road was busy – it was the only main road linking Busby-on-Sea to Southampton – giving residents plenty of time to see Niall and Charity standing there together. She'd been desperate to leave but Lana had grabbed her hand, told her to stay, a vulnerable look on her face.

How could she say no?

Niall could have left. But instead, he'd hovered nearby, watching Charity as though he were trying to figure out if she was real or not. She daren't look back at him, her thumping heart betraying emotion she was trying hard to bury.

Charity peered towards the entrance to the café. Hope was at a doctor's appointment so they hadn't seen each other that morning. But she was due in soon, so Charity was hoping she could pull her to one side to break the news gently to her.

Charity wrapped her thick orange cardigan around herself and hurried back into the café. Was it her imagination or was it even busier than normal, despite spring being held off today by sharp winds and the threat of rain? People glanced up at her as she passed but she kept her eyes ahead of her, jaw clenched.

It was a small town. Gossip spread like wildfire, one of the many things that hadn't changed in the years she'd been gone.

The door swung open then and her sister walked in. Hope paused at the entrance, eyes on Charity, and Charity knew in that moment Hope had already heard. Then she slammed the door shut and strode to the counter.

'Tell me you didn't know Niall was back,' she hissed as she flung her purple suede coat off and grabbed an apron, barely looking at Charity.

'No, of course not, Hope!'

'They're all loving this, aren't they?' Hope said, lowering her voice and casting her eyes over the busy café as Charity passed an order to her over the counter. 'Nice bit of gossip to stave off the monotony. I just can't believe Niall bloody Lane really is here. It makes me sick. What's worse is people won't just focus on the fact Lana North crashed her car. They'll also be talking about the fact the man who killed Faith Winchester was with you, her sister, at the time.' She scrutinised Charity's face.

'It was a coincidence, I swear,' Charity said. 'I just needed to go to the road, it is the anniversary of Faith's death after all. Niall told me he'd gone there for the same reason. We—'

Charity fell silent as Mrs McAteer approached the counter.

'What can I get you?' Charity asked her, forcing a smile on to her face, pleased for an excuse to get away from her sister's rage.

'Just a hot chocolate, love,' Mrs McAteer said, patting Charity's arm. 'Good work saving Lana North's life.'

'I didn't *save* her. She was fine, just a bit dazed.'

'My Gav knows one of the ambulance men. Apparently she'd had too much to drink.'

Charity thought of what Lana had said to her and the unmistakable smell of stale booze in the car.

'Poor you, having to witness it after what happened to your poor sister on that road,' Mrs McAteer continued, shaking her head. 'And then to have Niall there too, the scum.' Her lip curled up. 'Bloody cheek, him returning to town. My Addie will be mortified when I tell her. Your poor sister must be rolling in her grave.' Charity tried not to catch Hope's eye. 'And then to have some drunken rich girl driving her—'

She clamped her mouth shut and a hush fell over the café as Lana's husband walked in.

He looked just as otherworldly as he had the day before. But when he stepped into a beam of hazy sunlight shining through one of the windows, the perfections slipped away. Dark shadows showed beneath his green eyes, the faint hint of stubble on his chin and cheeks and, as Charity peered closer, what looked like a trace of oil on the cuff of his shirt.

He looks better in the light, Charity thought. *He looks better with those imperfections.*

'Can we talk somewhere, Charity?' He glanced towards Mrs McAteer and smiled tightly. 'Somewhere *quiet?*'

'Of course, let's go out back,' Charity said, grabbing a bag of rubbish.

Dan took the bulging bag from her and smiled, following her out of the door. He threw the rubbish into it then got a pristine white handkerchief out with his initials on it, wiping his hands.

'Long time since I put the rubbish out,' he said.

'How's your wife?'

'Fine. I must thank you for being there, she said you were a real comfort.' He looked down at the tomato skin on his handkerchief. Then he peered back up at Charity and she noticed how very black his pupils and long lashes were, making the green of his eyes even more prominent. 'I heard you're a psychiatrist.'

'A counsellor.'

He seemed to think about something for a moment then leant closer, lowering his voice. 'I was wondering if you might talk to my wife? I'd pay of course: double whatever your hourly rate is.'

She frowned.

'I'm afraid I'm not practising in any official capacity at the moment,' Charity said. 'Your wife would be better off going to a proper clinic or via the NHS.'

'Lana will refuse, I know what she's like. But she seemed to really like you. If we arranged for you to come to the house, have some privacy, she might open up more. I can pay double, treble.'

Charity sighed. She really wanted to help but it didn't feel right. 'I'm sorry. I can recommend a great counsellor a few towns away though?'

Dan raked his fingers through his blond hair. Then he forced a smile. 'Of course. I'm sure she's okay. Look, why don't you come to dinner as thanks?'

Charity examined his face. Was this a ruse to try to get her to treat his wife over dinner?

'That's very kind of you,' she replied, 'but that's really not necessary. It's been enough for you to come here in person to thank me.'

'Let's say seven on Saturday evening?' he said, as though not hearing her. 'I know Lana would love to see you. I presume you know where our house is?'

'But I—'

He smiled. 'If you turn up, wonderful. If you don't, then we feed the food to the fish. And if you see Niall Lane, can you mention dinner to him too? I hear he was quite the hero. I've tried to track him down but I think he may have left town.' Charity felt a strange mixture of relief and disappointment. 'I'll leave you to it,' Dan said. 'But I very much hope we see you Saturday night, Charity.'

Charity watched him stroll away, his hands in his pockets. He paused a moment to watch a seagull fly across the grey skies above, then he disappeared around the corner.

'So Niall's left town, has he?'

Charity turned to see her sister standing at the door. 'You heard that?'

'Some. That's good news though isn't it? That Niall's left.' Her sister was scrutinising her face again.

Charity nodded. 'Yes, I'm relieved. Very relieved.'

'He better not come back. Now he knows you're here, he might not be able to resist.'

'Don't be silly, Hope, it's been years.'

'Why silly? Feelings grow more intense with absence, especially when someone's behind bars. They have time to think, to obsess…'

'Hope, please don't do this.'

Hope sighed. 'Fine. So, are you going to go for dinner?'

'It'll be awkward, I don't know them.'

'It'll be good for you to make new friends. I go out with the writing club lot, you ought to get out a bit too. Who knows, maybe you'll become friends with Lana North and you can teach her how to drive properly?'

'Oh, Hope,' Charity said, shaking her head in disapproval. 'You really are naughty.'

Charity went to walk back in but Hope grabbed her arm, looking Charity in the eye. 'Just remember one thing if Niall does come back. He killed our sister. No matter what spin he puts on it or how you used to feel about him, he killed her.'

Charity peered up at the ruby-coloured gates guarding Dan and Lana North's huge white mansion. This place had been a dilapidated mess when she was a kid, once owned by a duke and then left in a state of disrepair after a fire. Local kids would sneak in through the gates, smoking drugs and making out in the rooms. She'd even come here with Niall once but they preferred the comfort of the sea shore and caves near her house. It was quite something to see what the Norths had done to it since.

She paused at the marble steps leading up to the house, smoothing her hands down her cream trousers and adjusting the collar on her cerise blouse. She hadn't been sure what to wear; these weren't the kind of people she'd usually have dinner with. Back in London, all her friends and associates were other NHS counsellors. It was an unspoken rule that every dinner was a casual dinner, so Charity usually turned up in what she'd been wearing to work, jeans and a large bright shirt cinched at the waist with a belt.

She took a deep breath and walked up the stairs. Behind her, the sea rippled, the cliff the house was sitting on diving into the craggy rocks below. She put her hand out to lift the ornate gold knocker made from a lion's mouth. But before she had the chance, the door was whipped open by Dan. He was wearing a casual white suit rolled up to the elbows, a pastel blue shirt beneath it, the shirt undone slightly to reveal the smooth tanned skin of his chest.

'You came!' he said. 'I have to confess, I was worried you'd be a no-show.'

She had thought she would be a no-show too. But Dan had seemed so worried about Lana, and the vulnerable look in her eyes as she'd clutched at Charity's hand after the accident ate away at her.

The truth was, Lana reminded her of Faith a little. Beautiful, vivacious, a slight hint of vulnerability. No one else noticed that about Faith apart from her sisters. All everyone saw was confident, clever, beautiful Faith. While she was all of those, she also had her insecurities. Charity recalled an Easter holiday when Faith returned from university and was blanked by a group of girls she used to go to school with while out shopping with Hope and Charity. She'd laughed it off at the time but later, Charity saw her crying in her room.

Charity stepped inside the mansion, taking in the huge hallway and marble floor draped with a black and gold rug. Ahead of her was a long stairway that swept up to a balconied landing, like a scene from *Gone with the Wind*. When Dan closed the door, she felt stifled. It was as though the heating had been on all day.

'Your place is gorgeous,' she said as he took her lime-coloured jacket. 'I remember when it was a crumbling mess.'

'So do I. It's taken us two years to sort it out. Well, I say us. Lana's done most of the work. She found the place too.'

'I'm very impressed.' Charity held out the bottle of Blue Nun. 'Sorry, it was the only bottle of wine I could find at the local newsagent's. My dad used to say it tastes like vinegar.'

Dan laughed. 'I happen to like vinegar very much.' He led her to a set of doors on their right, pushing them open to reveal a large room with a gilded table running down its centre. She realised with a shock that on the dark walls around it were murals of couples in various states of undress. Her eyes homed in on one particular image of an olive-skinned man kissing the neck of a voluptuous woman with blonde hair and porcelain skin.

'Lana has a very vivid imagination,' Dan said, following her gaze.

'It must be interesting when the in-laws come for dinner,' Charity joked.

'Don't worry, we use our other dining room for them,' Dan replied.

'You have *two* dining rooms?'

'I know. It's a bit much, isn't it?' Dan gestured to a number of bottles sitting on a small gold table in the corner. 'Champagne? Wine?'

'Red wine, please.'

Dan pulled out a chair for her then reached for a bottle of expensive looking wine, pouring Charity a glass. As she took a sip, her mouth filled with a delicious cherry flavour and she relaxed a little.

'Thank you so much for coming, Charity,' Dan said. 'I know Lana will be very pleased.' There was the sound of heels clicking along the marble floor outside. 'Ah, speak of the devil.' Dan leant forwards, lowering his voice. He was so close, she could smell the black cherry scent of the wine on his breath. Behind him was a mural of a man's blond head dipped in between the legs of a woman, her head thrown back in ecstasy. Charity felt her face flush hot. 'I'm not expecting you to do a psychological profile,' he said. 'But maybe you can give me some advice on how I might be able to help her?'

'But I didn't say I would, Dan. Really, I—'

The door swung open and the overwhelming scent of musky perfume wafted in as Lana stepped into the room. She was wearing a short red V-neck dress with huge shoulder pads that engulfed her tiny frame. It was more suited to a society party than dinner. She blew Dan a kiss then quickly strode down the room and took the chair across from Charity's, leaning over the table and taking her hand. Her glossy curve of caramel hair covered Bambi-like eyes. She licked her bee-stung lips nervously. Charity noticed her hand was trembling.

'Thank you *so* much, Charity, you were so lovely the other morning,' she said, her words almost tripping over one another, her navy blue eyes bright.

'It's fine, I'm pleased I was there to help you. How are you feeling?'

'Oh fine,' she said, sweeping her hand through the air. 'Back to my old self.'

The truth was, beneath the glossy veneer were telltale signs all was not entirely well. Lana's movements were erratic and jittery; she was incredibly thin, even thinner than she'd been in the photos Charity had seen of her in the papers; the purple bruises under her eyes suggested problems sleeping; and, though immaculate from the front, her hair was all matted at the back. There was also a large stain on the hem of her dress and bruises down her legs.

Dan stared at his wife's matted hair then he looked imploringly at Charity.

Lana glanced at Charity's glass of wine and smiled. 'It's delicious, isn't it? We got it from this wonderful vineyard in Umbria last year. Did you know the rate of divorce is at its lowest in that part of Italy? They say it's down to the Umbrian "super" wine, as they call it. It makes couples *crave* each other.' Lana looked into Dan's eyes. 'I can confirm it's not just an urban myth.'

Charity took another gulp of wine, feeling increasingly uncomfortable.

Lana peered towards the door. 'Is Niall in the bathroom?'

Charity spluttered on her wine. 'Niall?'

'Lana managed to find him in the end,' Dan explained. 'He's been staying just out of town.'

'He's coming to dinner?' Charity asked, struggling to get her words out. Dan nodded.

'Didn't you both come together?' Lana asked Charity, a confused look on her face.

Charity shook her head. She should never have come. She looked towards the door. She ought to make her excuses and leave right now. What would Hope say? What would the whole *town* say?

Dan frowned as he looked at Charity's face. 'Have we put our foot in it by inviting him?'

Charity didn't know what to say.

'But the way he looked at you the other day,' Lana said, looking at Charity. 'I really thought you were together.'

'We weren't together,' Charity said, peering at the door to the dining room, imagining Niall walking in any minute. What would she say to him? 'We haven't been in touch for years,' she added, trying to compose her face.

'Oh well,' Lana said, reaching for the bottle of wine and sloshing more into her glass. 'It'll be good for you to catch up then, won't it?'

Dan looked at his wife, an exasperated expression on his face.

'So what's the deal with you two, anyway?' Lana asked, scrutinising Charity's face. She smiled. 'Oh look, she's blushing!'

Dan put his hand on his wife's arm. 'Darling…'

'Were you childhood sweethearts?' Lana continued, ignoring him.

The door clicked open and Niall stepped in, a bike helmet under his arm. So Niall was riding a motorbike nowadays.

His eyes rested of Charity, a frown appearing on his face.

Dan rose from his seat, shooting Charity a concerned look before composing his face and smiling. 'Please, do come in, Niall.' He walked around the table and pulled out the seat next to Charity. As Niall walked behind her, Charity looked down at the table, trying to control her thumping heart.

He sat next to her, the scent of him making her think of the sea and the summer evenings they used to spend together on the beach.

She curled her hands into fists. Damn it, why had she come?

'I'm sorry, I didn't realise you were coming,' he said quietly.

'I didn't realise you were.'

His frown deepened. She took the chance to properly look at him. He was wearing black jeans and a grey t-shirt, his cheeks flushed from the cold. The long black hair she'd once so loved was now shaved close to his head. There were fine lines around his eyes that weren't there ten years before and a small scar across his chin. She wondered if that had happened in prison, and her stomach twisted with nausea at the thought.

There were new tattoos entwining his arms too, black warped clock faces and gothic anchors, even a whole tree stretching up the olive skin of his right arm. And then that tattoo etched onto the side of his neck, the same tattoo she had on the small of her back, a black cresting wave beneath a blue moon. As she stared at it, she could almost feel the needle burning into her skin.

He caught her eye and a host of emotions seemed to run over his face.

Niall shifted uncomfortably.

She could pretend to be ill and leave, couldn't she? Say the wine had been too rich, that her tummy was fragile. What would it matter? She didn't have to see any of them again.

Dan looked from Charity to Niall and took a deep breath. He could definitely sense the atmosphere. 'What can I get you to drink, Niall?' he asked.

'Do you have beer?'

'Of course.'

Niall looked around him, brow furrowing as he finally noticed the explicit murals on the walls.

'Oh, do you like them?' Lana asked, twisting around in her chair, one thin arm elegantly draped across the back of Dan's chair. 'I had them done when we moved in. They're wonderful, aren't they?'

'They're different,' Niall said.

Dan handed his beer to him and sat down.

'Your house is gorgeous,' Charity said, desperate to bring some sense of normality to the dinner. 'You must feel a bit lost in a big house like this, just the two of you?'

'We manage to fill it with all Lana's knick-knacks, don't we, darling?' Dan said to Lana.

'I may have a teensy bit of an obsession with antiques,' Lana replied, laughing. 'It fills the time. We're off to Paris soon so I can't wait to do some shopping there.'

'You really do live the life, don't you?' Charity said, smiling.

'A very bourgeois life,' Niall said as he looked around him.

58

Dan frowned. 'We're hardly bourgeois. Lana's dad was a dustman. My father worked on ships, my mother was a nurse. My shipping business wasn't handed to me on a plate, I started out in the docks with my father, hauling equipment about.'

Niall's eyes lit up the way Charity remembered they did when the subject turned to politics. 'Doesn't matter how you got there,' he said, 'you're still an owner. That makes you bourgeois. It's nothing to be ashamed of, I'm just making the point.'

'Fine,' Dan said with a smile. 'If working hard makes me one of the bourgeoisie, then so be it.'

'What about your staff, do they work hard too?' Niall asked Dan.

'I don't operate that kind of business culture,' Dan replied. 'My staff aren't expected to work long hours.'

Niall fixed him with his blue eyes. 'But they do, don't they? Some of them, anyway. And yet you're still the one with the mansion, the fast cars, the expensive champagne,' he said, gesturing around him.

Charity noticed the tops of Dan's cheeks going red.

'Ladies and gentleman,' she said to ease the tension, 'meet the modern-day Karl Marx.'

Dan's shoulders relaxed and Lana laughed.

'Never could impress you with my political rants, could I?' Niall said, holding her gaze.

'So, Charity, what brings you back to Busby-on-Sea?' Dan asked her. 'You worked as an NHS counsellor in London, right?'

'Counsellor?' Niall asked. 'I didn't realise that was your thing.'

'It is now.' She turned to Dan. 'I was made redundant so had to return.'

'Bloody Thatcher,' Niall said.

Dan smiled to himself.

'I bet that must be fascinating,' Lana said, 'hearing about people's more intimate secrets as they lie on a couch.'

'It's not quite as exciting as that,' Charity said. 'More like a battered old chair in a stuffy office with stained carpets. People are referred by their GPs and a lot of the issues are ones many people deal with: insomnia, anxiety, depression.'

'Oh, you must speak to Dan then,' Lana said. 'He's a terrible sleeper, up most of the night.'

'That has nothing to do with my state of mind, darling,' Dan said, 'and everything to do with your snoring.' He turned to Charity. 'So what's next for you? I presume the plan isn't to work in your sister's café all your life, as wonderful as it is?'

Charity sighed. 'I'm looking for jobs but there's nothing out there.'

Niall nodded. 'Hearing that a lot lately.'

'Have you thought about going private?' Lana asked. 'Setting up your own practice?'

'I'd love that. But I don't have any capital.'

'Dan can give you money,' Lana declared, clapping her hands. 'I can decorate your office!'

Dan laughed. 'Darling, you're getting a bit ahead of yourself.'

'Why couldn't you?' Lana asked. 'It would help Charity out.'

Charity laughed nervously. Lana didn't seem to have any kind of filter. 'I'm sure Dan has better things to do with his money.'

'Like buy my wife antiques in Paris,' Dan said with a raised eyebrow. He turned to Niall. 'What about you, Niall?'

'I'm not into antiques,' Niall said with a smile. 'Don't have a wife either.'

Dan laughed.

Niall leant back, his long legs stretching out in front of him. Charity glanced at his thighs, remembering how she had found it hard to hide her feelings from her sisters as she watched him strip his wetsuit off to reveal his muscular thighs the day after their first kiss.

'I'm an underwater photographer,' he said. 'Mainly advertising jobs.'

Charity looked at him, surprised. Sure, he used to lug around an old camera, but she didn't realise that was what he'd ended up doing.

'Wonderful. How did you get into that?' Lana asked.

'Happened by accident really,' Niall replied. 'An old school friend ended up working for an advertising agency, knew I was a photographer and that I could dive, asked me to do a last-minute job a couple of years ago. More assignments came in.'

'Is that why you're back in Busby-on-Sea, an assignment?' Dan asked.

'No. I've been trying to find a submerged forest that's supposed to be here actually.' His eyes caught Charity's briefly then flickered away.

Charity went very still. Faith's underwater forest?

'Why would a forest be submerged?' Lana asked.

'They were once land forests,' Niall explained. 'But due to lots of different reasons – dams bursting, floods – they get submerged by water. They're all over the world, in oceans and lakes, even rivers. Some are quite beautiful to look at.'

'So, like a woodland Atlantis?' Lana asked. Charity thought back to the first time Faith had told her and Hope about them. She'd asked the same thing.

'Exactly like that,' Niall said. She wondered if he was thinking of Faith too. She wished he'd change the subject, this was becoming too painful.

'What makes you think a submerged forest lies off the coast here?' Dan asked Niall.

'A fisherman got lost at sea once and thought he saw it,' Niall explained. 'Became a bit of a local legend.'

Dan went quiet, a thoughtful look on his face. 'I think that fisherman may have been right about that forest, you know. I have a viewing glass on my boat and I saw something very interesting during a trip the other day.'

'Really?' Charity and Niall asked at the same time.

'Really.' Dan rang a bell by his side – an actual bell! – and an older woman with dark hair walked in. 'Those photos you had developed for me the other day, Clara, can you bring them down?'

When Clara reappeared with a bunch of photos. Dan handed one to Charity and her eyes widened. In the top right corner of one was a shadowy outline of what looked like branches.

'Where exactly did you see this?' she asked Dan.

'Across from the lighthouse. The co-ordinates are in the top right corner, see?'

She looked at Niall, unable to contain her excitement despite how painful the memories were. It was just where he'd suspected. He smiled at her and Charity's stomach contracted. He rarely smiled but when it happened, it set the room on fire, the lines around his mouth deepening, his blue eyes sparkling. It suddenly felt like something was blossoming inside Charity again; something she'd stifled for so long. Had she ever stopped loving him?

She thought of Faith. If she hadn't *started* loving him maybe her sister would be there now?

'Can I have the co-ordinates?' she asked Dan.

'I can do one better,' Dan said. 'How about we go out on my boat tomorrow. You can both dive off it, see if you can find the forest for yourself?'

Charity looked at Niall. How could she possibly spend the day with him? It was out of the question. 'I'm afraid I'll be working at the café.'

'The weekend then?' Dan asked.

She shook her head. 'Sorry.'

Niall sighed, looking down at his plate.

The door opened and Clara walked in again with a large gold tray. At first, Charity thought it was a tray of seashells of all different shapes and sizes but, as Clara drew closer, she noticed eight plump oysters in their shells were lying on a bed of seashells, a dollop of what looked like black beads on each one.

Niall's eyes lifted to meet hers. She knew he too was thinking about their first date.

Dan lifted one of the oysters into the air and looked at Charity then Niall. 'To real-life heroes and damsels in distress.' Then he tipped his head back and let the oyster slither into his mouth, his Adam's apple bobbing up and down. When Charity ate hers, it tasted just as the oysters had that moonlit night with Niall: of the sea, salty and earthy, the subtle taste of the caviar now making it even more delicious.

'So how did you first meet?' Lana asked Charity and Niall.

Charity looked down into her drink. She didn't want to talk about the past.

'On the beach,' Niall said. 'We were just kids.'

Lana leant her chin on her hands and smiled dreamily. 'Oh, how romantic, meeting on a windswept beach!'

'Don't get ahead of yourself,' Dan said, laughing.

'No. I have a nose for these things,' Lana said, tapping the side of her nose. 'You can sense the chemistry oozing off these two. I'm right, aren't I?'

Charity squirmed in her seat while Niall's neck flushed red.

'I *am* right!' Lana said.

Dan put his hand on Lana's. 'Darling, I don't think—'

'So you're not together now,' Lana said, tapping her lower lip with her finger as she narrowed her eyes at them. 'Why did you break up?'

Charity peered at the door. She should have left.

Niall opened his mouth to say something but Lana put her hand up. 'No, wait, let me guess. You cheated on Charity!'

'Lana, that's enough,' Dan said sharply.

'No, wait,' Lana said, looking between Charity and Niall. '*She* cheated on you.'

'It wasn't like that,' Niall said quietly.

Charity felt tears sting her eyes. She took a quick sip of wine and looked away. Her last meeting with Niall had been so abrupt, a few moments on a windswept dark beach the week after Faith died, the terrible incident throbbing between them. It had been horrific enough to be told by her parents the day after she'd learnt of her sister's death that she'd been knocked down in a hit and run. But then to discover Niall's car was seen screeching away from the scene of her death. It was unbearable.

Hope had been livid. 'You must never see him again,' she'd hissed at Charity.

'It was an accident,' Charity had said, so confused, still in shock and trying to process the news herself.

'He killed our sister.'

Charity hadn't said anything. What *could* she say? She knew she must talk to Niall. But she hadn't seen him since Faith had died and he wasn't in their usual spot that night either. Each night, she waited for him, until a few nights later when she saw him waiting in the moonlight, head down, shoulders hunched.

That's when he'd told her they couldn't see each other again; that she had to get on with her life. She'd been devastated. People might think him a murderer but she knew he wasn't. He was as grief-stricken as she was. He'd loved Faith too, spent many summers with her.

It was a terrible, terrible accident.

But Charity knew he was right. When she got back to the house, Hope was waiting for her.

'You don't have to say anything,' Charity had quickly said, before Hope could say anything. 'It's over.'

Relief had flooded her sister's face. 'Thank God.'

How would she feel now, knowing Charity was having dinner with him?

Charity stood up. 'I'm sorry, but I have to go.'

Niall looked up at her, brow creased.

'Oh, that's a shame,' Lana said, pouting.

Niall stood with her. 'I'll walk you out.'

'No,' she said, her voice firmer than she'd intended. 'Please don't.'

His blue eyes flickered with an unbearable sadness. She felt that same sadness well up inside her. That fateful night had changed the course of both their lives. Charity hadn't just lost a sister and Niall a friend. They'd lost each other too. Seeing him again made her realise just how utterly sad that part of the whole tragedy was. And how painful it was to dredge it all back up again. It also made her realise how much she still cared for him.

'Take care, Niall,' she said softly.

His eyes seemed to grow glassy. Then he blinked, forcing a smile on to his face. 'You too, Charity. I hope you get a job soon, yeah? Don't let Thatcher the Milk Snatcher beat you down.'

She smiled. He seemed to understand. 'I won't.' She turned to Lana. 'You take care, too, Lana.'

Lana shot Charity a flimsy smile then turned away.

When Charity got outside, instead of walking to her little car, she headed to the edge of the cliff. It was dark now, the moon above bright enough to light up the grass in front of her and the sea below. To the right, the cliff stretched out for miles, the odd light or two beaming in the distance. To the left, lights flickered from Busby-on-Sea, one road that stretched away from it in darkness: the road Faith died on.

Charity looked out over the sea as it splashed against the cliffs below. How Faith would have loved to dive that submerged forest.

She peered behind her at the huge white mansion. Over the years, she'd been unable to stop herself imagining how things would have been if that fateful night hadn't happened. Would she and Niall have stayed together? How would their relationship have evolved over the years? Maybe they'd be here together, a loving couple? Maybe they'd be at Hope's...or Faith's.

She imagined them sitting around a large dining-room table made out of driftwood – Faith had always loved driftwood – bookshelves lined with oceanography books, beautiful underwater photos of submerged forests on the wall. She saw them laughing, drinking, Faith's long hair a sheen of blonde down her back. Or maybe she'd have it cut, more practical for diving for samples. She'd still look stunning. She saw Niall relaxed, smiling; Hope happy with some man or another, the book of poetry she'd just got published lying on the side. Yes, that would be what the dinner was for, a celebration of Hope finally being published. Maybe having Faith around would have pushed her to do more with her poetry, Faith had always been so inspiring, making her two sisters want to do something special with their lives. With her gone, any real hope and ambition left them.

The scene disappeared. The truth was, she was on this cliff top alone, Faith gone, Hope a closed book. She collapsed to her knees and let out a sob.

'Charity?'

She looked up to see Niall peering down at her in the darkness, face filled with concern. He put his hand on her shoulder. She quickly stood up, brushing grass and mud off her trousers and wiping her tears away. 'I'm fine,' she said.

'I had no idea you'd been invited.'

'I know, don't apologise.'

'I shouldn't have mentioned the submerged forest.'

She got her car keys from her bag, unable to look at him. She went to walk past him but he softly grasped her arm.

'I feel like I have so much to say to you,' he said, eyes pained. 'I didn't reply to all your letters because I wanted you to just get on with your life.'

'I don't want to talk about it.'

'On Tuesday, when I saw you on the road…'

'Niall, I said I don't want to talk about it. Please just leave me alone.'

She shrugged his hand off and strode away. He stayed where he was, watching her with hooded eyes. More tears started rolling down her cheeks. She angrily wiped them away and then jumped into her car. She felt bad for walking away from him like this but she couldn't let the past infringe on her future, she just couldn't.

As she drove away, she saw Niall standing at the edge of the cliff, looking out towards the unlit road where Faith had lost her life.

Charity quietly let herself in when she arrived home ten minutes later. She was hoping she could sneak upstairs without her sister noticing.

But before she had the chance to even step foot on the first stair, Hope appeared at the door to the living room. 'You're back early.'

'I had a funny tummy,' she lied. The thought of telling her sister she had been sitting at the same table as Niall Lane was just too daunting.

'That's a shame.' Hope lifted her pen to her mouth and nibbled on it. 'So what are they like, the glamorous couple?'

'A bit strange. I think Lana gets very bored in that huge house.'

'I'm not surprised. And Dan North, is he still as charming and handsome as he was the other day?'

Charity shrugged. 'I suppose, if you like that sort of thing.'

Hope narrowed her eyes. 'No, I suppose your sort is tall, dark and murderous.'

'Jesus, Hope!'

'I can see it in you. It's happening all over again.'

'What are you talking about?'

'Niall. He was there, wasn't he?'

Charity clutched the banister. 'I didn't know how to tell you.'

'I knew it!' Hope said, sighing as she looked up at the ceiling. 'You're sullying Faith's memory by seeing him.'

'That's not fair,' Charity said in a raised voice. 'I had no idea he'd be there.'

Her sister didn't look convinced. 'And now what?' Hope asked.

'What do you mean?'

'Will you see him again?'

'Of course not!'

Hope shook her head. 'I don't believe you,' she said before slamming the door of the living room behind her.

Chapter Five

Charity

Busby-on-Sea, UK
March 1987

Charity looked down at herself as the boat she was on powered out to sea. She'd somehow managed to squeeze her curves into the old wetsuit she used to wear when diving as a teenager. Behind her lay Busby-on-Sea's small coastline, ahead the disused lighthouse, foaming waves crashing up against the craggy rocks it stood on.

If there was a submerged forest out there, and Dan's photos suggested there really was, she was determined to find it for Faith.

She'd woken that morning after a restless night, images of Faith winding her graceful body through a forest of underwater trees infiltrating her dreams. What better way to *honour* Faith's memory – not sully it, as Hope accused her of – than to discover the forest for her? So she'd called a local boat company as soon as she woke and arranged to go out to the area where the co-ordinates on the photo suggested the forest was. The next morning, she'd woken even earlier than Hope – a relief because she didn't want to argue again. And now here she was, an impulsive decision, one she was starting to regret. It had been years since she'd dived. In fact, the last time had been a week before Faith died. Charity and Hope had finally convinced her to come out diving with them and Niall. Faith had refused at first, said she was too busy studying. But then Charity had told her how much they missed her. 'Just one hour,' she remembered pleading with Faith. She'd smiled a smile that had seemed so rare since she'd returned from university for the Easter holidays and the three sisters had set off with Niall. Charity remembers sneaking a kiss with Niall behind the rocks as they'd got changed. She saw Faith watching them. But instead of smiling, she'd been frowning.

Only a week later, all their lives would be shattered.

'Right,' Charity whispered to herself as the boat came to a stop. 'Let's do this.' She shrugged on her old stabiliser jacket, pulling her mask over her face. She did her checks like Niall had taught her as the boat's captain, an old man with a grey beard, looked at her disapprovingly, knowing she shouldn't be diving alone. Yes, it was risky. But what other choice did she have? Hope had refused to even step into the sea since Faith died and Charity couldn't go with Niall, could she?

When she was ready, she took a few breaths then she jumped in, the bitter cold of the sea seeping into her skin as she deflated her jacket and descended. The tank felt awkward on her back, the wetsuit digging into all the wrong places. But as she got deeper, the shrieking seagulls quieting, the water misty and cold, a calmness descended upon her. She stayed still for a moment, taking it all in, the sea rippling and swaying, lifting her with it. She looked up, caught glimpses of the sun above, sparking off the surface. There was no sound but the gurgle of her snorkel and the deep low hush of her breath as she kicked her legs and glided through the water, trying to find some sign of the forest in the murky depths.

After ten minutes, the calmness dissipated. Emotion swelled inside her. She seemed to see Faith everywhere. She struggled to breathe in the air from the tank on her back, felt panic whir inside.

She couldn't do this.

She started inflating her jacket, slowly rising to the surface, trying desperately to control her emotions as she moved up and up. When she broke the surface, she pulled her snorkel off, taking quick gasps of breath. She'd been a fool to come alone.

She looked up and was surprised to find another boat bobbing up and down next to the one she'd hired. It was gleaming white with chrome railings, *Salacia* written down its side in midnight blue. On its deck were two men.

Niall and Dan.

'Great,' Charity muttered under her breath.

They both looked imposing, tall and broad-shouldered in their wetsuits, Niall in his token black, Dan in a navy blue one. Beyond them, the sun peeked up from the horizon beneath wispy white clouds, the air feeling more like spring than ever.

'Charity!' Dan called out to her as Niall regarded her with hooded eyes. 'Why didn't you just get in touch with me, you could have come with us?'

'I didn't know you were coming this morning.'

'Well, here we are,' Dan said, spreading his arms out as he smiled. 'You joining us?'

'No, it's alright,' she said, swimming towards the boat she'd hired. 'I'm going to head back.'

'So you saw it?' Niall asked her.

'The forest? No sign of it.'

Dan's face lit up. 'Then you were looking in the wrong place, it's another half a mile out.'

She paused, looking at Niall who was standing behind him, arms crossed, frown on his face. 'Are you sure?' she asked.

'You saw the photos,' Dan said. 'Still want to go back to shore?'

'Jim'll take me, won't you?' Charity asked the old captain.

'I have to be back to shore by ten,' he replied.

He had told her that. She peered out towards where the forest might be. Could she forgive herself if she didn't see the forest Faith so desperately wanted to find with her own eyes? But she'd been so panicked before. Would it be the same if she went down again?

She took a deep breath. No, she mustn't be scared. She couldn't miss this opportunity. So she put her hand up and let Dan pull her on to his boat as the captain handed her stuff over to Niall.

'You were diving alone?' was the first thing Niall said to her when she embarked.

'Yes.'

'That was stupid.'

She raised an eyebrow. 'And you haven't dived alone before?' He didn't answer. 'Thought so.'

'Charity!' She turned to see Lana skipping towards her. Her long caramel hair was coiled up on top of her head and she was wearing a bright red wetsuit that clung to her perfect body. It made Charity feel self-conscious with her too-tight, too-old wetsuit on and the curves she'd inherited from her mum. She wrapped her arms around herself. 'I'm so pleased you joined us,' Lana said, squeezing Charity's arm.

Thirty minutes later, they dived into the sea. As she descended, Niall not far away, memories from the summer she'd spent diving with him and her sisters seemed to flow over her even more intensely than when she'd dived alone earlier. But she felt more in control with people around her. She could do this.

She noticed Niall watching her, his vivid blue eyes blinking at her through his mask. Was he remembering those days too, the way

Faith would twist her body around like a pro, blonde hair fanning out behind her?

Did he remember how they'd sneak quick kisses, pulling their mouthpieces out when Hope and Faith weren't looking?

Charity turned away. It was all in the past.

Dan kicked his legs and scooted downwards, Lana following. Charity thrust herself through the water after them, Niall not far behind her. Niall had always kept behind the sisters when they'd dived all those years ago, letting Faith lead the way, him 'keeping the flank', as he used to call it. He'd grown to be protective of them, checking their gear after they'd already checked each other's, making them each give him the thumbs up. Faith used to call him a 'big softie beneath all that brooding'. Charity felt safe with him behind her now, just as she had all those years before.

Charity peered into the distance. It had grown so misty, Dan and Lana were just faded outlines in the deep. She felt Niall's fingers brush against hers and she turned, saw him floating beside her. He gave her a thumbs up. She did the same. Maybe he'd sensed her nervousness on the boat.

The mist dispersed a little and Dan and Lana came into view, hovering in the distance as they looked at something. For a moment, she thought it was a line of fish. But as she drew closer, she realised it was a misty branch.

The submerged forest!

She exchanged an excited look with Niall. It was like they were hovering over a foggy forest, just a hint of a branch the only evidence it existed.

She propelled herself towards the branch, feeling like she was in a snow globe, bubbles of water shimmering around her. Then the fog dispersed and the top of a tree appeared before her and beyond, several other sunken trees.

Charity took a moment to take it in. Faith would have loved this, Hope too. Beside her, Niall stared at the forest too, eyes wide. This was all supposed to be so different.

She headed to the closest tree, a great oak, surreal without the context of sky and leaf-infested grounds. Its surface was clogged with small barnacles and, when she reached for the uppermost branch, yellow fish darted out from behind it. She sank lower, swirling her fingers around at waist level, paddling the fins on her feet until she was aligned with the tree's trunk.

Faith had told her the trees in a submerged forest were petrified, meaning the conditions beneath the sea had almost turned them to stone, fossilising them. The reason she used to get so excited about them – beyond how beautiful the photos showed them to be – was that studying them could reveal so many important facts, such as how sea levels had raised over aeons. She was determined to write her own thesis on it and tell the world something new and exciting.

Charity tentatively reached out again, carefully brushing her fingers against the barnacled wood, imagining her oldest sister beside her. It felt furry with moss, bumpy beneath her fingertips. Up close, she could see crabs sheltering in the bark's knots. Charity felt emotion well inside. For years Faith had wanted to find this and here it was, right before Charity's eyes. If only her sister was alive to see it. Niall turned to her, and she could see his eyes were glassy too. Maybe coming back here to find the forest was an homage for him too, a way to make amends.

He broke her gaze and lifted his camera, the flash lighting the petrified oak up in an eerie glow. He started circling it, taking more photos as Charity watched him. He looked completely at ease doing this. He'd clearly found his calling.

She looked towards the other trees, all different heights, some broken, remnants of trunks lying on the ocean floor. She noticed

Lana floating as if sitting on one of the fallen trees in a mock model pose as Dan pretended to take a photo. Then he scooted to her and pulled her close, her legs winding around his.

She didn't want to disturb them.

She peered back behind her, noticing Niall pulling something from the pouch attached to his stabiliser jacket.

A knife.

She knew what he was going to do. She ought to stop him, it felt wrong to do such a thing to such an ancient tree now. But instead she stayed where she was, mesmerised as he found a part of the bark that wasn't clogged with sea life and started carving. They'd promised themselves they'd etch their names into the trees if ever they found the submerged forest. When he moved away, Charity could see it was their two initials – N and C – carefully entwined, just as they'd planned it to be. And then beneath it: 'For F.'

Charity watched the ripples in the sea as Dan steered them over calm waters an hour later, the spring sun warming her cheeks. Niall was quiet, barely saying a word.

When Niall took over steering the boat, Dan strolled over to Charity. 'This forest seems to mean a lot to you.'

'Yes, my sister was desperate to find it.'

Dan frowned. 'Why isn't Hope here then?'

'I mean my other sister, Faith. She passed away when I was a teenager.'

'I'm so sorry.' Dan put his hand on her arm, his green eyes filled with concern. 'What happened?'

'Car accident. She was just nineteen.'

'How tragic. Was she driving?'

'No, she was walking along the road. It was an accident.' She looked quickly over at Niall. She didn't want Dan and Lana to know about Niall's role in Faith's death. They would probably find out soon enough but she didn't want to be the one to tell them.

'Faith, Hope and Charity?' Dan said. 'Lovely names.'

'Thanks! My dad was an English teacher before he quit to run the café. That's where Hope got her love of poetry…and her red hair. He used to read *Faerie Queene* by Edmund Spenser to us before we went to bed, he named us after the three daughters in that. We didn't have a clue what it was about, but the way he read it to us—' She smiled at the memory. 'It was mesmerising.'

'And your mother? What did she do?'

'As well as running the café, she was a part-time lecturer in environmental sciences.'

'Hence your interest in submerged forests?'

Charity looked out at the calm sea. 'It was Faith's interest, actually. My mum once did a trip to visit a submerged forest in Austria. Faith was completely transfixed by the photographs she brought back. She grew intrigued by them. I guess it was her version of a fairy tale.'

Dan smiled sadly. 'And that's why it's been so special, seeing the forest today?' Charity nodded. 'How wonderful. I'm pleased I could help with that.'

'You have, thank you.'

Lana appeared from below deck and curled into Dan's arms. Charity felt awkward as they kissed each other, so she left them to it, wandering up to Niall.

'You okay?' she asked him. 'You're very quiet.'

He examined her face a few moments then sighed. 'I miss us,' he said gently. 'I miss Faith.'

She swallowed, felt tears flood her eyes. 'Me too.'

He took her hand briefly and squeezed it. They looked into each other's eyes and Charity felt as though she was underwater again, struggling to breathe the air from her tank. When he let her hand go and turned away to stare back out to sea, she was relieved.

Soon, Busby-on-Sea's harbour appeared, a short wooden jetty with four disused boats moored up to it. A figure was standing on it…someone with long red hair.

Hope.

When Dan anchored up, Hope marched towards the boat, her thin arms wrapped around her body. Niall stepped off the boat first. 'Hope, Charity wasn't—'

She put her hand up to him without looking at him. 'Don't talk to me. Just go away, please. Right now.'

Dan and Lana exchanged raised eyebrows.

'Well, I guess I'll see you around,' Niall said to Charity. He took one last pained look at her then jogged off towards his bike.

'Unbelievable,' Hope said as she watched him, shaking her head.

'I was diving alone and bumped into them all, I swear,' Charity quickly explained. 'They found the submerged forest – Faith's forest, Hope.'

'I don't care about the bloody forest,' Hope said. 'You and him on the road where Faith died. Niall happening to be at the Norths' for dinner the other night. And now *this*?'

'I don't know how to convince you,' Charity said. 'I swear I—'

'What is it about him?' Hope said, interrupting her. 'Is he so amazing you're willing to overlook what he did?' she asked, watching him jump on his bike and rev his engine up.

Charity grabbed her sister's arm, making her sister look her in the eye. 'You have to believe me, Hope, *nothing* is happening between us.'

Hope reached into her bag, pulling out a newspaper and thrusting it at Charity. 'Try to tell the rest of Busby-on-Sea that.'

As Charity read it, her heart sank. On the front was a grainy photo of her and Niall from the morning Lana drove her car off the road: *Lana North saved by hit-and-run killer.* Then beneath that, a smaller headline: *Sister of hit-and-run victim Faith Winchester once dated the man who killed her sister.*

She looked up at Hope. 'How did they know about me and Niall?'

'If I could figure it out, why not the local newspaper?' She shook her head again, eyes glassy with tears. 'Now everyone will know how you've betrayed Faith's memory.'

Then she turned on her heel and strode away, long skirt swishing around her thin ankles.

Charity closed her eyes, her head buzzing with it all.

Hope was right, the whole town would now know.

Chapter Six

Charity

Kerala, India
April 1987

Charity dragged her suitcase down the wooden pier towards the hotel, stopping to wipe her brow as the sun beat down on her. Boats bobbed up and down on the aqua waters of the lake, lush green trees lined its banks. It was certainly a contrast to Busby-on-Sea's rotting jetty. But it was also completely different from what she had imagined India to be. She'd seen the hustle and bustle on the way from the airport out of her taxi window. But now she was here by this beautiful lake, it was calm and quiet.

She pulled Faith's map of submerged forests from her bag. When she'd disembarked from Dan's boat the month before, she'd gone looking for Hope at the café. As Charity entered the café, the place seemed to go quiet, people contemplating her with cynical eyes, no doubt thinking of the newspaper report…and, as far as the photos suggested, assuming she was dating her sister's killer again. But all Charity cared about was Hope. She eventually found her at the back of the café scrubbing tables, clearly seething with anger.

'I don't want to hear it,' she'd said before Charity had a chance to speak.

'Fine,' Charity snapped back, unable to contain her frustration. She'd grabbed her apron and got to work, sneaking looks at her sister and hoping she'd calm down.

But she didn't, the silent treatment continued that evening when they got home. The next day at the café, Niall turned up, only making things worse. Charity even heard Mrs McAteer gasp in outrage. Charity had grabbed his arm, marching him out of the café. 'Are you crazy?' she'd said to him.

'I'm sorry, I just wanted to check you were okay.'

'By coming *here*?'

'I didn't know how else to find you.'

'We can't be seen together, Niall. It's too much. I can't lose the only sister I have left over this.'

He nodded. 'Of course. I just needed to know you're okay.'

'I am. It'll be fine. I just need to get on with my life, like I was trying to do before you came along again.'

He flinched when she said that and she felt terrible. But it had to be said. She turned away, unable to look at his pained expression any more. 'Goodbye, Niall,' she said before hurrying inside.

Over the next few days, as Hope's silent treatment continued and two more rejection letters for jobs Charity had applied for landed on their mat, Charity got out Faith's old map of all the submerged forests she'd wanted to visit. It was faded now, one of the corners torn. She lay it flat over her bed, breathing in the faint trace of Faith's floral perfume that still remained on it.

She'd been saving money from her earnings at the café the past three months. That's when it occurred to her: she could get away from Hope, give her some space for a while – *and* visit another of Faith's forests. It would give her time to gather herself and try to work out her next steps to get out of this awful situation.

So she booked a trip to India. When she'd told Hope, her sister had looked shocked. In a way, it was a welcome relief from the dispassionate way in which she'd been regarding Charity lately.

'But why?' Hope asked.

Charity showed her Faith's map. 'Seeing the forest off the coast here has given me the bug. I want to do it for Faith. Come with me!'

Hope's eyes had hardened. 'No. I have the café to think of.'

So now here Charity was, alone. The small boat that had transported her here from the main jetty on the other side of the lake motored away. Charity took a deep breath and then walked down the wooden pier, the new backpack she'd bought chafing at her shoulders. The hotel was made up of white villas of all different sizes with red tiled roofs. She felt a little out of place among all the exotic surroundings: the dark latticed wood at the front of reception, the huge exotic flowers spilling from wooden vases all over, the saris worn by the staff, the framed pictures of Hindu gods on the walls, the scent of spices drifting in from the restaurant.

Once she got to her beautiful room, Charity sunk down on to the bed, holding her sister's map close to her chest. 'I wish you were here with me, Faith,' she whispered.

The next morning, Charity was sitting on a large rickety boat with six other tourists, heading out on to the lake. She felt a sense of trepidation. Faith had told her about this forest. It had become flooded after a dam was created by the British back in the nineteenth century, the minerals in the water preserving the trees eerily in that moment.

'Oh look!' one of the tourists said now, standing as he pointed into the distance.

Charity followed his gaze to see dozens of trunks rising from the lake, their brittle remains a contrast to the soft waves of the water below. Some were several feet high, others mere stubs poking out from the water. Bird nests lay in some of their branches, baby birds squawking for food. In the distance, misty mountain ridges sprawled, green shrubs and long grass shrouding the ground in between.

It looked just as it did in Faith's library book.

She'd have loved this, Charity thought.

She *should* be visiting it with Faith just as they'd all agreed all those many years ago. Would she ever stop missing her big sister?

Half an hour later, she was beneath the surface, chirping birds and crickets replaced by the deep sound of her breath and the flap of her fins. The water was misty, the trunks of the trees like black columns in an underwater palace. She watched her white hands float before her, wisps of her black hair shimmering around her mask. It felt like everything was in slow motion here, the water's warmth – such a delicious contrast to diving in Busby-on-Sea – lulling her into a trance-like state as she stared at the trees.

Her dive buddy – a large German man – shot her a thumbs up. She gave him a thumbs up in response then headed towards the tree closest to her. It looked like a sandalwood with its graceful limbs. She pressed her hand against the bark. It amazed her that despite being underwater, it didn't crumble, it stayed true and solid. It was frozen in time, just like she felt she had been, seeming to go back to that fateful night over and over, unable to move on. She thought of Hope, alone in her cottage, writing poems that never seemed to be recognised, as though time had stood still for her too ever since Faith had died. Like these trees, Hope had fossilised into a shadow of what she once was.

Was Charity fossilising too? Together, could they ever move forward?

Charity's snorkel bubbled, reacting to her deep breaths.

Faith wouldn't want them being held back by grief, would she? And look, she was here, wasn't she? Taking the kind of risk Faith would love. She smiled to herself. Yes, Faith would be very proud of her little sister being here. She just wished things were better with Hope.

As Charity looked at the petrified trees spreading out around her, she made a decision: she would return to Busby-on-Sea after this holiday and make a suggestion to Hope. Sell the house. Sell the café. Stop living in the past. They could use the money to go somewhere, anywhere but Busby-on-Sea. Hope could do a proper writing course; Charity could maybe do her masters in psychology. Or they could both do something completely different.

Whatever it was they decided to do, it was time to stop living in the past.

It was time to stop reliving that night, over and over.

That evening, Charity sat in the hotel's restaurant looking out at the lake, sipping a glass of wine. People laughed and chattered around her, waiters and waitresses dressed in traditional Indian outfits weaving between the tables, local dishes filled with spices and colour held aloft.

Charity leant back in her chair and smiled.

Then a whirring engine sounded out from the dark lake. People peered up from their dinners to see a gleam of white rapidly approaching on the lake's surface. As it drew closer, Charity realised it was a speedboat, three people onboard.

'So this is how the rich arrive at the hotel,' a woman on the table next to her murmured to her husband.

As the speedboat drew closer, Charity could hardly believe her eyes.

Chapter Seven

Charity

Kerala, India
April 1987

Dan North was driving the boat, his white shirt billowing out behind him. Niall was standing at the back, camera around his neck, eyes on the lake. And sitting down was Lana, her long hair tied up in a bun.

Charity watched in astonishment. How could this be happening?

The boat pulled up alongside the jetty and Dan moored up before jumping off, putting his hand out to Lana. She took it, giving him a peck on the cheek.

Charity stood up then hurried through the restaurant, head down, shoulders hunched. She'd just have to order room service and hope they were just here for dinner, not staying.

'Charity!'

She froze. Charity heard the click of Lana's shoes on the path and turned to see her jogging towards her, arms out. Beyond her, Dan and Niall looked on, the shock visible on their faces.

'How wonderful to see you here,' Lana said, wrapping her arms around Charity. 'I was hoping we'd find you.'

'Find me? You knew I was here?'

Dan strolled up to them as Niall held back, looking shocked.

'Hello, Charity,' Dan said, kissing her on the cheek. 'You knew she'd be here, darling?' he said to his wife.

'Yes, Sandra in the travel agent's told me,' Lana said with a smile. 'I thought it would be a wonderful surprise for everyone.'

'You followed me?' Charity asked Lana, unable to quite believe it.

'I wouldn't put it quite like that,' Lana said. 'I've been rather taken with these underwater forests ever since we saw the one in Busby-on-Sea. So I asked Niall if I could commission some canvasses for the house. They're going to be huge,' she said, spreading her hands wide. 'They'll take over whole walls, won't they, darling?'

Dan nodded, his brow furrowed slightly as he looked at Charity. Niall finally composed himself and walked over.

'When I discovered you were here and I saw the photos of the lake,' Lana continued. 'Well, it just seemed ideal! And I so love surprising people.'

Charity kept her mouth shut. It was clear to her now that Lana had issues so she just kept quiet while she gathered her thoughts.

'It seemed *ideal*?' Niall asked, the anger evident in his voice.

Lana shrugged. 'Yes, I don't see why it's such a problem, we got on so famously over dinner and during the dive, after all.'

'That was a quite a surprise too, Lana,' Charity said, being careful not to be too accusatory in her tone. 'And now this?'

'My thoughts exactly,' Niall said. 'What are you playing at?'

Lana's navy eyes shimmered with tears. Dan put a protective hand on his wife's back. 'Lana gets a bit over-enthusiastic when it comes to match-making, I'm afraid. Look, I'm so sorry. We can stay somewhere else, there's a villa I wanted to rent on the other side of the lake.'

'You're *staying* here too?' Charity asked, not quite believing this was happening.

86

'Well, I didn't mean to make you all hate me,' Lana said in a sulky voice. She turned away, nibbling at her long nails.

'We don't hate you,' Charity said softly, putting her hand on Lana's arm. 'You're all here now, aren't you? I'm tired anyway and was about to head to bed so please don't leave on my account. Have dinner, you must be hungry.'

'Sorry to disturb your peace, Charity,' Dan said.

'It's fine. Goodnight.' She looked at Niall and smiled sadly. He opened his mouth to say something, then sighed.

She walked away and tears filled her eyes. Everything felt out of sync. She felt manipulated and embarrassed. Most of all her heart ached at how pained Niall had looked. Lana had played a cruel game and while her vulnerability worried Charity, she wanted to shake her and tell her to stop sticking her oar in.

As she headed to her villa, she heard footsteps behind her. She turned to see Niall jogging towards her.

'I couldn't just leave it like that,' he said when he got to her. 'I'm so sorry, Charity, I swear I knew nothing.'

'I believe you.'

'Lana is a mess, honestly. She's not right in the head.'

'Then why did you accept the commission?'

He sighed. 'I need the money. Work's really dried up lately.'

'Sorry to hear that.'

Niall looked out to the lake. The reflection of the moon shimmered on its surface, ripples turned white under its gaze. 'Strange being here together though, isn't it? The lake Faith was so desperate to visit,' he said.

Charity nodded, trying to control her emotions. 'Yes, it is.'

'Have you seen the forest?'

'This morning. It's beautiful, Faith would have loved it. *You'll* love it.'

He peered back at the restaurant. 'I won't see it. I'm going to get out of here as fast as I can.'

Charity thought for a moment. She *could* say nothing, just let him go. But he'd come all this way and something inside yearned for him to stay. So she gave into that something. 'Don't let Lana put you off,' she said. 'You're here now, you must dive it, take photos.'

'Not with that crazy bitch.'

'Niall!'

He sighed. 'Sorry, I just can't believe what she's done.'

'Can't you just dive the forest alone?'

'I can't afford to stay here without Dan funding me.'

'Why should he stop funding you? You can still take the photos they need without them bothering you. I'm sure Dan will understand under the circumstances. He seems nice. *Normal*.'

Niall sighed. 'Maybe you're right. I'll make sure we don't bump into each other, if that's what you want?'

Charity wasn't sure what she wanted. Each time she saw Niall, it reminded her how much she missed him. But she'd only promised herself a few hours ago she'd stop burying herself in the past. Niall was in her past. He *was* her past. 'I think it's best,' she said.

Niall quickly covered the flash of disappointment on his face. 'It's been good seeing you again, Charity. Enjoy the rest of your holiday.'

He walked away.

Niall stuck to his word the next day. Charity didn't see him once as she sunbathed in the small garden outside her villa.

The following morning, as she was getting ready to go out for breakfast, Charity thought of Hope back at home, maybe awake too and scribbling in that book of hers. They'd repair their relationship, wouldn't they? They had to! They were the only family each other had. She thought about phoning her sister.

But then decided against it. Hope needed more time. Back when they were kids, Hope was capable of giving Charity and Faith the silent treatment for days on end if they had one of their arguments – Charity borrowing one of Hope's boho scarves without asking; Faith accidentally spilling milk on her notepad. Charity would always want to drag Hope kicking and screaming out of her moods. But Faith used to tell her, 'Be patient, Charity. She needs time to let it blow over. Let her make the first move.' Faith was always right. A few days later, Hope would suddenly start talking to her sisters, even if it was as simple as asking Charity to pass the salt. Faith would smile at Charity, a small *I told you so*.

Yes, she'd give Hope time. But she could send her a postcard. It wouldn't arrive for a while anyway. As she continued getting ready, there was a knock on her door.

She checked her black hair in the mirror, smoothing it back. It got so frizzy in this heat. She took a deep breath and opened the door and was surprised to see Dan standing there. He was wearing pink shorts, revealing long tanned legs and an immaculate white t-shirt. Beneath the tan though, he looked exhausted.

'I'm so sorry to disturb you yet again,' he said. 'I wouldn't have come if I wasn't desperate.'

'What's wrong?'

'It's Lana. She's a mess. Ever since last night, she's refusing to eat. She even—' He paused, taking in a deep breath, his green eyes swimming with tears. 'She even threatened to commit suicide.'

Charity put her hand on Dan's arm. 'Has she been like this before?'

'Once or twice.'

'Did she see the counsellor I recommended?'

He nodded. 'Twice. But she didn't like him, refused to go again.'

'I think you need to go back to the UK, Dan. Really get her some proper help.'

'But you're here, right here, a qualified therapist.' He looked desperate. 'It doesn't have to be in a professional capacity. Just one chat. She even said herself the only person she'd be willing to talk to is you. I can't tell you how grateful I'd be if you could just spend an hour talking to her. I'll take us on the speedboat to the villa. I'm so worried, Charity.'

Charity would never forgive herself if Lana hurt herself. She had a professional duty to help.

'Okay, I'll come,' she said softly.

Dan surprised her by pulling her into a hug. 'Thank you so much.'

'I can't believe this place,' Charity said as an hour later they walked up to the straw-roofed villa Dan was renting. It lay on the lake's banks and stood on stilts that dipped into the water. In the distance were green mountains and lush trees.

'It's lovely, isn't it?' he said. 'When Lana mentioned the lake, I did some research, found out about this villa. But she insisted we stay at the hotel.' He sighed. 'Obviously, now I know why. She knew you were staying there.' He paused before getting to the door. 'You know,' he said, lowering his voice. 'The more I think about it, the more I think it was less about match-making, more about Lana just needing a friend. I should pay her more attention, work less. You must be very honest with me after you talk to her, I can take it. If *I'm* the one who needs to change, I will. I love Lana very much.' His voice cracked and he tried to cough to hide it. Charity's heart went out to him.

They walked inside and Charity took a moment to breathe in the cool air. Then she looked around. They were standing in an open-plan living room with sprawling white leather sofas, a state-of-the-art kitchen leading out on to the veranda nearby. Rooms led off either end of the living room and kitchen, and there was a small alcove where it looked like Dan had set up an Atari computer and fax machine.

Was he doing work here? Maybe Lana was just very lonely.

'Drink?' Dan asked. 'We have iced tea.'

'Perfect.' She watched him stroll to the large glass-fronted fridge. He seemed relaxed on the surface now but she could sense the stress bubbling beneath.

'Hello, Charity.'

Charity turned to see Lana standing in the doorway to one of the rooms at the back. Dan paused, his face pained as he looked at his wife. She was wearing what looked like one of his light pink shirts, the cuffs hanging over her small hands. Her hair hung in messy strands and there were dark circles under her navy blue eyes. She still managed to look beautiful though.

Charity thought of Faith as she looked at Lana, especially those last couple of weeks she'd been alive, seeming lost in her thoughts, vulnerable. She wished she'd asked Faith what was wrong. She realised in that moment that she was right to come. Lana needed her help.

'Hello, Lana,' she said gently. 'How are you doing?'

Lana's eyes filled with tears and she bit her lip, looking down at her bare feet. 'Not great.'

'I'll leave you both to it,' Dan said, handing Charity her iced tea before placing another one on a glass table for Lana. He gave his wife a quick kiss, looking into her eyes. Then he left the room, his hands in his pockets, head bent.

Lana walked to the sofa, curling her long legs beneath her as she sat down. Though she was tall, she looked tiny against the large sofa. Charity sat on the chair to her side. She preferred to do that with her patients: not too close to invade their personal space, but not directly across from them either otherwise it felt like an interview.

'Dan asked me to come chat to you, Lana,' Charity said, leaning forward and looking her in the eye. 'Is that what you want too?'

'Yes,' Lana said, nodding. 'Definitely.'

'Good. Anything you tell me will be kept between us, okay?'

Lana nodded again.

'You said you're not doing great,' Charity said. 'Do you want to tell me more about that?'

'I just feel like my life is pointless,' Lana said, peering out at the window as she twirled her hair around her finger. 'Dan's Mr Perfect with his perfect business. He's *achieved* something. I just mess things up, like trying to get you and Niall together.'

Charity found it interesting how Lana saw her match-making as a project. It made the boredom theory even more plausible.

'You haven't messed anything up, Lana,' Charity said. 'We all understand the sentiment was there, you wanted to do good. Now, tell me more about this idea you have that your life is pointless. What about that beautiful home you've created? That takes a certain level of talent.'

She pulled a face. 'So what? Home decorating. Wow.'

'Many people make wonderful careers out of interior design.'

'I suppose.'

'Can I ask about your life before you and Dan met, Lana?'

'Not much to say, really. I grew up on a council estate, was rubbish at school. My dad liked to slap my mum around every now and again.'

'And you witnessed that?'

Lana nodded.

'That must have been very hard for you?' Charity asked.

'I wished my mum would grow some backbone and leave the idiot, if that's what you mean.' She laughed. 'And now here *I* am, typical trophy wife, another form of abuse, really.'

Charity waited for her to expand but Lana just sat staring out of the window at Dan.

'What do you mean by abuse?' Charity said.

'It affects my confidence, doesn't it? Knowing I was chosen for my looks.' Lana flickered her hand up to her face then over her body. 'I look good on his arm at parties. I don't overshadow him.'

'And you feel that makes you similar to your mother?'

'In a way. She was really pretty, didn't say much. My dad over-powered her.'

'You use an interesting word there. *Overpowered*. Do you feel powerless?'

Lana nodded vigorously. 'I don't get a say in *anything*.'

'How did you and Dan meet?'

'Modelling assignment fifteen years ago. I was so young then, just eighteen, he was twenty-five. He personally oversaw the casting for an advert for his first shipping business. We got married a year later. A whirlwind romance.' She looked out at Dan. 'Fourteen years we've been married.'

'So you're a model?'

'Was.'

'How did you get into that?'

'A scout noticed me while I was shopping when I was fifteen. I even did a shoot for *Vogue* once.'

Charity smiled. 'Very impressive.'

'It's hardly difficult, is it? Pouting and throwing some poses.'

Charity took a sip of her iced tea. 'I'm sure there's more to it than that, Lana. Did you enjoy it?'

Lana smiled slightly, the first sign of a smile so far. 'I did actually.'

'So you were happy?' Charity asked carefully. 'You didn't have moments like what you've experienced lately?'

'No, that happened when I gave it all up, really.'

'Why *did* you give it all up?'

She shrugged. 'I guess when I married Dan there was no need to make money any more. And I got so busy with renovating the house, I just ran out of time.'

'Have you ever considered going back to modelling?'

'Sometimes.'

'Maybe that's something you should consider.'

Lana nodded. 'You know what, I think I will.'

Charity frowned. It usually wasn't as easy as this.

Her suspicions were confirmed when Lana started laughing. 'God, who am I kidding with this bullshit?' she said. 'Truth is, I'm just telling you what you want to hear, Charity.' Charity looked at her in shock. 'I *hated* modelling,' Lana continued. 'It was full of skinny bores like your sister Hope with the added bonus of a coke addiction.'

Charity blinked, not quite believing she was hearing right. 'I'd rather you didn't mention my family, Lana.'

'Why not, you asked me about mine!'

Charity looked back out of the window at Dan who was staring out at the lake, his hands in his pocket.

'Look, I'm bored out of my fucking mind,' Lana said, leaning back in her chair. 'There's nothing you can do to help me. You need to talk to him,' she said, jutting her chin at Dan. 'He needs to pay me more attention. Or if not that, let me buy the house I want in LA. I *love* that place.'

Charity stared at Lana as she smiled to herself. Was she for real? Or was she trying to cover some deep pain she didn't want Charity to find? She just couldn't figure her out. Either way, she started to feel for Dan.

'Have you been to LA?' Charity asked, trying to bring things back on track.

'On a modelling assignment, and then for mine and Dan's honey-moon.'

'Why do you love it so much?'

'The weather. The people.' She yawned. 'I'm pretty tired actually. Maybe we can continue this chat another time?'

Charity felt a sense of panic. She needed more time with her. What if the last strange few moments were all an act?

'I'd like to talk to you a little longer, if that's okay, Lana?' she said.

'Oh come on, I'm sure you wouldn't. It's like Dan said, you're on holiday.' She jumped up, stretching her arms above her head, her shirt rising above her thighs to reveal a neat triangle of pubic hair. Charity turned away, embarrassed. 'Thanks for coming,' Lana said, leaning down and giving Charity a kiss on her cheek. Then she skipped out of the room.

'I'm here if you need me,' Charity shouted out after her. 'Any time!'

Lana gave no response.

Charity sat where she was a few moments. She'd seen this before, the quick change of subject, the pretending nothing was wrong. Often, it hid something deeper. But she wasn't sure with Lana. Maybe she really *was* simply bored? It would explain her attempted manipulation of Charity and Niall.

Either way, she needed more time. If she missed something and Lana hurt herself, she'd never forgive herself.

She walked out to the beach where Dan was now sitting. He was very tanned, small freckles starting to form on his nose.

'That was quick,' he said.

'She didn't want to talk for long.'

'How is she?'

'I'm not sure. I'd like more time to talk to her.'

'Will she be okay today?' he asked, peering inside, brow furrowed. 'After all her talk of ending it…'

'I think so.'

'You don't seem sure.'

95

'Like you said, we didn't talk for long.'

Dan nodded. 'I understand. Can you stay? Even if it's just for the day? She might want to talk for longer, take it at her own pace.'

Charity squinted up at the sun. She wasn't sure what to do. She could head back to the hotel and do what she'd planned: relax. But with Niall there, it was hard. And knowing Lana was here, possibly on the verge of doing something to hurt herself, it made things even more difficult.

'I'll stay for a couple of hours,' she conceded. 'Maybe if she knows I'm here, she might want to talk again. I don't want her to feel pressured though. If she clearly doesn't, I'll head back.'

Dan nodded, relieved. 'Thank you. Would you like to sit out here? I can get you some shade?'

'That would be nice, thanks, Dan.'

A few minutes later she was sitting on a plush sun lounger with an umbrella above her, another iced tea in her hand, Dan beside her, reading a business report.

She took the time to watch the aqua ripples froth against the soft grass banks of the lake. It felt tranquil, contained, a contrast to the sea she'd grown up beside, which had always seemed wild and vast. Maybe Faith would be disappointed with the lake? She always seemed to enjoy the rough ebb and flow of the English Channel. Would she have been disillusioned visiting this place?

Who knew. That was the problem. If only Charity had had more time with her.

'You seem lost in your thoughts,' Dan said after a while.

'More like lost in the past.'

'Your sister?'

She sighed. 'Yes.'

'I understand. I lost my mother a few years ago. Cancer. Whenever I do manage to sleep, I see her.'

'I'm so sorry to hear that, Dan. You'd think it would get easier over time, wouldn't you?'

Dan shook his head. 'I'm afraid it just gets worse for me.'

'I know the feeling. Each time I leave Busby-on-Sea, I think I can escape the pain. It follows me everywhere though. Then when I return to Busby, it overwhelms me. Everywhere I look, something reminds me of Faith. I'm dreading going back.'

Dan swilled his drink around his glass. 'Interesting how people cope in different ways. I found I wanted to be reminded as much as possible, hence why I wanted to get a house in the area.'

'You grew up in Clayton, didn't you?' Charity asked, referring to the village next to Busby-on-Sea. 'I read it in an article.'

'Yes, funny little town.'

'Aren't they all funny little towns around there?'

They both laughed. Then Dan tilted is head, examining Charity's face. 'Seeing Niall must bring back memories too?'

She sighed. She'd been stupid to think Dan hadn't read the article about Niall's role in her sister's death. 'You must think it's all a bit odd, me and Niall still talking to each other?'

He smiled. 'On the contrary. I think you must truly love each other to have survived such a thing.'

'No, Dan,' she said softly. 'Our love didn't survive it.'

'Are you sure? You must still have feelings for him, I see the way you look at him.' He laughed. 'Sorry, I must sound like Lana. But I'm just saying what I see.'

Charity's face flushed.

'I imagine it's hard for you to admit you still have feelings for the man who was jailed for your sister's death,' Dan continued.

'That's exactly why I don't have feelings for him.'

'He was so young, Charity. From what I read in that article about you both, it *was* just an accident.'

Charity felt herself tense. Should she tell him to mind his own business? But the fact was, she didn't want to. She really felt she could open up to Dan. 'Yes, it was an accident,' Charity said, nodding. 'It really was. But it'll always be there, what happened that night. Plus it wouldn't be fair on Hope. She hates Niall. It's all too much. In the end, the bad outweighs the good when it comes to me and Niall.'

Dan was quiet for a few moments. She wondered if she'd made a mistake opening up like this.

'Do you miss Niall?' he asked eventually.

She thought about it. 'I suppose I do. We were just kids, but we had this connection. And my sisters really did adore him before what happened.'

'So you were all close?'

Charity nodded. 'We used to hang out in the school holidays, five years' worth of them. We grew close. I guess he was like a brother to us. He was such good fun, protective of us too. Seeing him again the past few weeks has brought all that back.' She looked into Dan's kind eyes. 'Can I admit something to you?'

He nodded solemnly. 'Of course.'

'I often wonder what would have become of us if Faith hadn't died.' She shook her head. 'God, that sounds selfish, doesn't it?'

'Of course not! It's perfectly natural.'

She smiled. 'You sound like the counsellor in this conversation.'

He matched her smile, his green eyes sparkling. 'Okay, imagine I am. What should I say to you now?'

'You'd tell me it was time I let go of the past…and the guilt.'

'Guilt?'

'That it was my boyfriend who caused my sister's death. And – and I need to stop judging my feelings for Niall. It was an accident. I loved him. Those feelings were – *are* – valid.'

He nodded. 'Good advice, Charity.'

She leant back in her chair, smiling up at the swaying palm trees as Dan did the same. It was good talking to him.

'This looks cosy.'

Charity looked over her shoulder to see Lana standing by the sliding doors in a bright yellow bikini, a cocktail in her hand.

Dan jumped up. 'Hello, darling, how are you?'

'I'm fine, talking to Charity did me the world of good.' She shot Charity a smile. Charity frowned.

Lana wrapped her arms around Dan's waist, pressing her lips against his cheek. 'You can take Charity back if you want, darling, I'll come with you.' She lifted her leg, wrapping it around Dan's thigh. 'Then we can go to that place we went to yesterday. Remember?' she whispered.

Dan carefully unwrapped Lana's leg. 'Are you sure you're okay, darling?'

Lana sighed. 'I'm fine, honestly. Can we please just stop pretending I'm a mental case? I was drunk when I said I'd top myself.'

Dan looked at Charity, a confused look on his face. Then he sighed. 'Fine. We'll take you back, Charity, thank you for your help.'

'As long as you're sure,' Charity said.

Lana looked Charity in the eye, her navy eyes turning to steel. 'I'm sure.'

After they dropped Charity off, she headed back to her room, her mind buzzing. She just couldn't figure Lana out. But what else could she do? As she was about to open the door to her villa, she noticed Niall walking down the path outside. He had his head down and was fiddling with his camera, his shoulders already deeply tanned. When he saw her, he slowed down to give her time to get into her villa without having to speak to him. But she realised she didn't want him to. After the strange past few hours with the peculiar Norths, she welcomed a familiar *sane* face. Charity smiled to show him she was fine with seeing him.

'You heading out?' she asked him, gesturing to the rucksack on his back.

'Yep, diving the forest.'

'Great. You'll love it.'

'Come with me?'

Charity stared at him, not quite sure what to say.

He laughed. 'Sorry, that just came out without me thinking.'

'Do you know what?' Charity said, thinking of the conversation she'd just had with Dan about her feelings for Niall. 'I think I'd like to go now actually.'

Niall's face lit up. 'Great.'

They both laughed and it was like they were teenagers again.

'It must've been strange seeing the three of us turn up the other night?' Niall said, as they headed out into the lake on Dan's hired boat.

'Very.'

'Lana's an odd one. It looks like Dan's the one with all the power when I think it's actually her.'

Charity sighed. She didn't want to talk about Lana. She gestured to Niall's camera. 'You excited about taking photos?'

'Yep.'

She smiled. 'You used to have that old camera when we were kids but I never thought you wanted to make a career out of it.'

'Faith suggested it to me actually.'

Charity frowned. 'Really?'

'Yeah. I was trying to figure out what to do with my life and she said if I loved diving so much, I ought to look for a career that involved it. She kind of threw the underwater photographer idea in randomly with a few others. I guess it stuck.'

'I like that Faith influenced you like that.' Charity examined Niall's face. His cheeks were red from the sun, the rest of his skin tanned and stubbled. The scar on his chin was puckered and white, his lips slightly dry. His blue eyes stood out, so distinctive and alarming. She couldn't help but feel her body react. 'I don't think I've said how much it meant to me to hear you came back to Busby to find the submerged forest,' she said softly.

'I didn't.'

'What do you mean?'

'I came back for you, Charity.' She swallowed, unable to drag her eyes away from his intense gaze. 'I heard you were back and I couldn't help myself. I needed to see you again, even if it was just one last time.'

Charity's heart thumped against her chest. She thought of their last meeting on that windswept beach the week after Faith died. 'You were the one who said we must never see each other again.'

'For your own good.'

The boat slowed down, the submerged forest coming into view. But Charity and Niall only had eyes for each other. To Charity, it felt as though she'd jumped into the lake already and was swirling in uncontrollable currents as she looked into his eyes.

'We're here,' the captain said.

Niall dragged his eyes away from Charity's. 'Wow,' he said as he looked out at the submerged forest, what remained of the trees darting up from the lake's shimmering surface.

'Impressive, isn't it?' Charity said.

'Very. Shall we get ready?'

Charity nodded, suddenly feeling self-conscious; she'd need to strip down to her navy swimsuit in front of Niall. She pulled her shorts and vest top off with her back to Niall, conscious of her round tummy and dimpled thighs. Out of the corner of her eye she noticed Niall watching her as he pulled his t-shirt off. He held her gaze again and she felt her skin flush. He looked so handsome, blue eyes so vivid. She could hardly breathe.

She reached for her wetsuit, pulling it on. Then Niall helped her shrug her stabiliser jacket on, his warm breath on her cheek making her face flush. She did the same for him and, after popping their masks and fins on, they did a safety check on each other, aware of the tension between them.

'Ready?' Niall said after, smiling to her beneath his mask.

She gave him the thumbs up and they jumped off the side of the boat.

As Charity sunk into the lake, silence descended, visibility was hazy. She noticed Niall's fin turning from yellow to green as the light from the sun above changed the colours around her.

Niall appeared ahead of her. He gestured towards the trees and she nodded, following him towards them. They looked as beautiful as the ones she'd seen a few days before, seeming to sway to some unheard music as the lake rippled. They explored them, carefully touching, Niall taking photos as Charity watched, unable to stop the pride she felt at seeing him do something he was clearly talented at.

After a while, they came to two entangled trees nearby. Faith had told them it was known as 'inosculation'.

'Inoscul-what?' Charity remembered Niall asking when Faith had explained it to them the summer before she started university.

'Inosculation,' Faith repeated, tangling her long fingers together and moving them up and down to demonstrate it. 'The friction caused by two trees rubbing against each other. Over time, it damages the bark, causing them to "self-graft" and grow together. Isn't that cool?'

'Not really. You're a complete dork, Faith,' Niall said as Hope threw a pebble at him and Charity rolled her eyes. But his smile told the sisters he loved her for her dorkiness, just like they did. That night, they'd all been allowed to stay out later, eating fish and chips on the beach, talking and laughing into the night as the sun set. That was the first time Faith had told them she'd got a place at university to study the course she'd so dreamt of. Niall had been so happy for her, he'd high fived her as Charity and Hope laughed.

Niall twisted around so he was lying horizontally, paddling his feet as he took a photo of the surface from below, the conjoined trees darting up above him. His tattoos were bright black beneath the surface, the muscles in his thighs and arms tense as he tried to keep himself steady.

Niall noticed her watching him and swam towards her. He stopped in front of her, paddling his hands to keep upright. A current pushed her closer to him and him to her. Her breath came quick and stuttered, the sound of it loud in her ear. Around them, the water rippled, bits of sea moss lifting eerily in the haze from the trees before them. The sound of bubbles from their snorkels, the feel of the warm water on her arms, made Charity feel so relaxed, she moved towards him again and, before she knew it, she was in his arms.

She leant her chin against his shoulder, knew she'd be crying if she wasn't underwater. All the years wasted, the love lost, spilled out in that embrace.

Then she thought of Hope.

She moved away from Niall, guilt slamming through her. He frowned beneath his mask. She pointed to the surface. She couldn't remain under here with him. She found it impossible to resist him, too many memories from similar moments beneath water drawing them together.

As she swam back up to the top, she turned once, noticing Niall etching into the tree.

'I think I got some great photos,' Niall said, looking down at the camera back at the hotel.

'I *know* you did.'

'I'll send copies, if you want?'

She smiled. 'I'd like that.'

They stood awkwardly in front of each other. 'Well, I guess this is it,' Niall said. 'I'm flying out tomorrow.' He paused, looking behind him at the restaurant. 'Unless you're eating in the restaurant later? Who knows, maybe we'll bump into each other there?'

Charity couldn't help but smile. 'Maybe.'

'Cool,' Niall said casually. 'I'll probably be there around sevenish. Seven's usually a good time for dinner, right?'

Charity nodded, playing along. 'A very good time.'

Niall backed away, glancing at her through his eyelashes. 'Take care.'

'You too!'

But Niall didn't go. Charity was the first to turn away virtually running down the path to her villa and shutting the door behind her, staring up at the ceiling, heart thumping.

Charity spent a while getting ready for dinner that night, comparing her more sombre self to the teenage Charity with her permed black hair and blooming skin, fashionable clothes and bucket loads of confidence.

By the time she got to the restaurant, it was quarter past seven and Niall wasn't there. Maybe he'd left thinking she wasn't coming. She felt a shimmer of disappointment as she sat at the table she'd taken each night. But then she told herself off. It was a good thing.

Just as she was thinking that, Niall appeared. He was wearing grey trousers and a white shirt, his sleeves rolled up to reveal his tattoos. A couple nearby turned to stare at him and Charity wondered what they were thinking. Did they notice his bright blue eyes, so vivid against his olive skin? Or was it the black tattoos twisting up his arms? Maybe it was his shaved head?

Were they intimidated by him? Intrigued?

His face softened when he noticed her. He walked towards her, the bar's lights bouncing off his white shirt. As he sat down, his eyes travelled over her emerald blue dress, the curve of her neck exposed with her dark hair piled high. 'You look lovely,' he said.

'Thank you. You look nice too.'

A waiter came over to take their drink orders. When he left, Charity smiled nervously. 'This feels strange, doesn't it? Sitting here as adults, the very place Faith marked on her map.'

Niall nodded. 'Very strange. But also very right. Does that make sense?'

She laughed. 'Totally.'

'I'm pleased. I was always scared I'd never see you again. Being here with you now…it feels like something more has come from what we had as teenagers. That it didn't abruptly stop.'

Something more?

Charity looked down at the table. What was he expecting of her? 'Niall, I—'

'Sorry, I didn't mean that like it must have sounded. I'm not expecting anything. I mean just us being here, talking like we used to, as *friends*. It feels good.'

Charity smiled. 'It does.'

Niall reached for the menu and raised his eyebrow. 'I have to say though, I think I preferred the price of the fish and chips from the Busby chippie than this stuff,' he said with a low whistle.

'Don't worry, I'll be paying my way,' Charity said.

'You really have changed then.'

They both laughed.

Their waiter brought over their drinks and they ordered their food. Niall leant back in his chair. 'So, I have an idea.'

'Oh yeah?'

'You just mentioned Faith's map. I've decided to photograph all the forests on it.'

'Really?'

He grew serious. 'Yeah, really. You think she'd like that?'

Charity bit her lip, trying not to cry. 'She'd love it. I'll make a copy of the map for you.'

Niall moved his hand towards hers then thought better of it, drawing it away.

'What about you?' he said. 'Any grand plans? Sometimes redundancy makes people re-think their lives. Maybe you can become a dancer after all. Remember you once told me you wanted to be one?'

Charity laughed. 'You're kidding, aren't you? That was yet another pipe dream. You've seen me dance.'

He smiled. He had, once, on the beach on her sixteenth birthday. He'd laid out a midnight picnic for her under the stars near the cave they'd discovered. That was the first night they'd told each other they loved one another…and the night she lost her virginity to him too. Looking at Niall now as the memories flooded between them, she could still remember the wonder of feeling him inside her, the delicate way he'd held her after, how he'd gently wrapped her naked body in the blanket he'd brought with him. She'd been so elated about what they'd done, she'd jumped up, twirling the blanket around as she danced under the moonlight.

She could see those memories in his eyes, hear them in the way his breath grew shallow.

She broke his gaze. 'I want to convince Hope to sell the house, move somewhere new with me. We used to talk about living in Brighton so maybe there.'

'You're very close to Hope now, aren't you?'

'Haven't I always been?'

'I don't know. It always seemed like you and Faith were the close ones, Hope watching from the sidelines.'

Charity felt a pang of pain for Hope.

'It's not your fault,' continued Niall. 'It was clear you and Faith loved her just as much as you loved each other. I guess it's just that Hope was always the quiet one.'

'Maybe. I hope she never felt left out.'

'I'm sure she didn't. I shouldn't have mentioned it.' Charity thought of Hope sitting alone in the house. She was desperate to get back to her, to make amends.

'So, you still into Fleetwood Mac?' Niall asked.

She laughed. 'Of course! And what about you, AC/DC still your thing?'

'A hundred per cent.'

They spent the next hour talking about music, politics and films. By the time dessert arrived, it barely felt as though time had passed.

'We haven't changed, have we?' Charity said. 'Still talking non-stop.'

'Like those times we'd stay up until the sun rose.'

'And I'd rush home so my parents didn't catch me out.'

'I think I even set an alarm on my watch to make sure you got back on time.'

Charity laughed. 'Oh God, yeah. I remember that now.' Charity frowned as a girl walked through the restaurant, blonde hair and long pale limbs, big blue eyes and high cheekbones.

She reminded Charity so much of Faith. Of course, Charity knew that was because she was so present in her mind. But it was enough to make all the excitement drain right out of her. She took a few deep breaths to compose herself, the wine she'd drunk making her head sway.

'You okay?' Niall asked, following her gaze.

'It's nothing. It's just – look, I'm a bit drunk to be honest. But that girl, don't you think she looks just like Faith?'

He followed her gaze, brow furrowing. 'I guess she does. But then sometimes it feels like I see Faith everywhere. Any blonde girl that passes, tall, slim, that way of walking of hers like she was in a hurry to get somewhere.'

Charity didn't say anything, just looked out to the lake.

'I think about that night a lot,' Niall said softly. 'Don't you?'

'I don't want to talk about it, Niall.'

'Same way you haven't asked me what it was like in prison?'

She looked back at him. 'I didn't think you'd want to talk about it.'

'Maybe I do. Maybe I want to talk about that night too. We can't just pretend it never happened.'

Charity pinched the top of her nose. 'Don't do this, please.'

'Don't do what?'

'Ruin things,' she said, wishing she'd never mentioned the girl to him. 'It's in the past. I'm trying to leave it behind. What's there to gain by dredging it up?'

'A counsellor's asking *me* that?' Niall leant forwards. 'There's a lot to gain. Maybe if we talk about it, really talk about it, it'll make things better. It's time to forgive and forget, right?'

Charity's head started to buzz. 'I can't go back there. I just can't think about it.'

'Then what hope do we have?' Niall said, eyes pleading with hers.

She stood up, swaying slightly as she placed some money on the table. 'What hope did we ever have, Niall? What did you think this dinner was about anyway? You're leaving tomorrow. We won't see each other again. It's all been pointless.'

Anger flitted across his face. 'Pointless? Is that what you think?'

'I don't want to argue.'

His face softened. 'Then why are you arguing? Stay, have another drink, we can—'

The Faith lookalike sat down at a table nearby. Charity shook her head. 'Sorry, I need to go, I'm tired. Have a safe journey back, Niall.' She took one last look at him then walked from the restaurant.

As she quickly strode down the path towards her villa, a sob escaped her mouth. She'd been a fool to have dinner with him. Why couldn't she just accept that what they had died with Faith that night? She felt her head swim and sat on a nearby bench, taking a moment to pull herself together.

She really was drunk.

Then she felt a hand on her shoulder. She looked up, surprised to see Dan standing behind her.

'What are you doing here?' she said, trying to keep the slur from her voice.

'Just paying Niall's hotel bill.' He gestured to the empty space next to her. 'May I?'

'Of course.' She shuffled up as he sat next to her.

'I was kind of hoping I'd see you,' he said. 'I didn't feel like sitting alone in that villa tonight.'

'Isn't Lana there?'

He shook his head. 'We argued. She left me a note, she flew back home.'

That sobered her up. 'Is she okay?'

'She's fine.'

'Aren't you worried about her being on her own?'

'She'll be on a plane right now, there's not much she can do. And there's not much *I* can do.' Dan peered closer at her, narrowing his eyes as he examined her face. 'Are you okay, Charity?'

'Fine.'

Dan looked unconvinced. 'Are you sure?'

Charity felt tears slide down her cheeks. 'Oh, Charity.' Dan pulled her into his arms and she sobbed against his shoulder, aware in that drunken way that she was getting mascara all over his expensive-looking blue shirt but enjoying how comforting it was to be held.

After a while, Dan looked down at her. 'Let's get drinks,' he said, getting a crisp napkin from his pocket and gently wiping her mascara streaks away.

Later, as Charity ate another dessert and drank with Dan, she finally felt herself relax. Dan was easy to talk to, so charming and light and happy. He encouraged her to talk about her family and Faith – the good stuff, not the bad stuff – and it somehow didn't hurt. He also kept topping up her glass, the expensive champagne he'd ordered buzzed through her veins, rubbing away the argument she'd had with Niall.

'So, how are you rich enough to afford this ridiculously expensive champagne?' Charity asked, raising the glass she was holding.

Dan smiled sadly. 'My father. He captained small tourist boats, I used to ride with him sometimes. He had a heart attack when I was a teenager.'

'Oh, Dan, I'm so sorry.'

He rubbed the stem of his glass. 'It happened when he was taking a group of school kids out on a day trip. But he somehow managed to steer the boat to safety, despite the pain he must've been in, the fear he must've felt.'

'He was a hero.'

Dan nodded. 'Exactly. But that wasn't enough for the company he worked for. They somehow found a way not to pay us the money he was due.' His grip on his glass tightened, his jaw clenching. 'Not only that, *they* caused his heart attack, I'm sure of it. He was so stressed from the hours they were making him work, all the new rules and regulations. That's why I'm so adamant now to be a good boss and not do that to my employees.'

Charity lifted her glass again, champagne sloshing over the edges. 'Good for you.'

'After seeing his boss being so smug at the inquest into my father's death, I made a promise to myself: one day I'd buy the boat company he owned.'

Charity smiled. 'And that's exactly what you did, isn't it?'

He smiled back at her. 'Exactly. It completely motivated me. I left school at fifteen and got a job at a local docks. I started buying old boats with the money I scraped together and renovated them. It made me enough money to be able to take over the shipping company my father worked for when it fell on hard times.' He smiled. 'The look on the manager's face when I told him who I was. The revenge was *sweet.*'

'Did your mother live to see it happen?'

His face darkened. 'No. She passed away just before. It took the shine off a bit.' He sighed. 'Anyway, enough about me. What about you? Was counselling something you always wanted to get into?'

'Actually, no. I wanted to be a dancer.' Dan raised an eyebrow. 'And an actress and an astronaut,' Charity added, laughing. 'I kept changing my mind, they were just pipe dreams. I used to wish I was more like Faith, so single-minded and focused on her dream of becoming a marine biologist. I guess in the end it was her death that made me want to help people who've been through bad times.'

Dan frowned. 'Your sister went through bad times?'

'Oh no, she was always so happy. Well, she seemed a bit preoccupied the last couple of weeks before the accident. But all-in-all, she was fine.'

'So your sister's death led you to counselling, like my father's death led me to my career?' Charity nodded and Dan sighed. 'Listen to both of us, driven by the past.'

'I know. I love Faith and miss her so desperately, but I wish I could move on.'

'Me too,' Dan said.

They were quiet for a few moments, then Dan suddenly stood up. 'Give me a few moments.'

Five minutes later, he returned, putting his hand out to her.

'Where are we going?' she asked.

'You'll see.'

She took Dan's hand, felt it warm and soft under her grasp. A few minutes later, they were standing in a pretty wooden boat with flowers etched down its side. It was tethered to the hotel's small jetty, bobbing up and down in the dark lake. After a while, the woman Charity recognised as the manager who was sometimes at reception appeared on the deck with a bunch of flowers in her arms, 'Mrs Rangan' written on the label on her sari.

'What's going on?' Charity asked Dan.

He smiled. 'Wait and see.'

Mrs Rangan placed the flowers on the edge of the boat then started plucking off the petals, laying them on the decking one by one until a beautiful circular pattern started to appear under the moonlight.

'Come, help me,' she said, gesturing towards the remaining flowers. Dan and Charity got up, placing petals where she pointed. After ten minutes, the pattern had trebled in size, taking over most of the decking, circles within circles, triangles within squares.

'Wow,' Charity said as they stood back to observe the pattern they'd worked so hard to create. 'It's beautiful.'

'It is, isn't it? It's a mandala,' Mrs Rangan said, leaning under the bench and pulling out two brushes, handing them over to Dan and then Charity.

'What's this for?' Charity asked.

'Now you must sweep the pattern away,' Mrs Rangan explained.

'But it took us such a long time to create.'

'Life is impermanent, like those you have lost,' Mrs Rangan replied. 'You must sweep away the past to move on to the future.'

Charity stared up at the star-speckled sky. 'Faith, my beautiful sister,' she whispered. Then she started sweeping the soft bristles of her brush over the pattern as Dan did the same, watching the petals drift up into the air and over the edge of the boat.

Mrs Rangan let them stay on the boat afterwards. They sat in silence for a while, staring out at the dark lake. It was a comfortable silence and Charity felt at peace for a brief few moments.

'Thank you, Dan. That really helped.' She felt a tear slide down her cheek. Dan leant forward, taking her hand. Under the light, his handsome features were even more accentuated, the small dimple in his chin, his smooth tanned forehead and those eyes, green like the lake in sunlight. For a moment, she wondered what it might be like to have never met Niall but to have been with someone like Dan instead.

Would Faith still be alive?

Dan's eyes dropped to her lips and her heart slammed against her chest, breath deepening.

Laughter rang out from the restaurant.

Charity stood up abruptly. 'I ought to head back,' she said, grabbing on to the side as the boat bobbed up and down.

Dan raked his fingers through his hair, his eyes blinking as though he'd just woken up. 'Yes, of course. I'll walk you back.'

They walked in silence, the tension of what had nearly happened throbbing between them. Charity's mind felt soft with alcohol, the lights lining the path blurring before her. Every now and again, Dan had to help steady her as she swayed. The touch of his hand on her arm sent sparks through her, confusing her. Where had this come from?

When they got to her villa, a figure was waiting for her in the dark. As she drew closer, she realised it was Niall. A frown appeared on his face when he saw Dan. Guilt squirmed inside.

'You've been together?' Niall asked, looking between them.

'Just a few drinks,' Charity said.

'Well, I'll say goodbye now,' Dan said, bowing his head and walking away.

'You're drunk,' Niall said to Charity when Dan left.

'So?'

He shrugged. 'I don't know, I guess I'm surprised you got drunk with Dan North.'

Charity walked past him and put her key in the door. 'Why are you here, Niall?'

'I don't like us arguing.'

She sighed and turned back to him. 'Neither do I.'

'Can we talk?'

She thought of the mandala ceremony earlier, and Mrs Rangan's words of wisdom: *You must sweep away the past to move on to the future.*

'It's late, Niall, and I'm exhausted. Goodnight.'

She let herself in before she could see the look on his face, then leant against the closed door in the darkness for a few moments, trying to steady her hammering heart.

Chapter Eight

Willow

Kerala, India
September 2016

Children peer at me from the doorways of stone buildings the colour of earth, some giggling as they point at my tattoos. Many of the girls are wearing fancy dresses, too fancy for your average day in a southern Indian village. Dogs wander about, sniffing at the ground.

This doesn't feel real. The map of all the submerged forests my mum wanted to visit, which is tucked into my rucksack, doesn't feel real either. I'd called Ajay from the cottage the morning after I found it. When I mentioned the submerged forest he'd grown up next to was on the map I'd found, I hadn't even had to ask if I could visit his home with him. He'd instantly invited me.

I was hanging out with some diving friends in Devon the past few weeks and I started to wonder if I was making a mistake. Was this a pointless homage, as my aunt seemed to suggest? But now I'm here it feels right. Mum would want this. Hopefully she'll be smiling down on me.

'They've dressed especially for you, Willow,' Ajay says as he leads me towards one of three bright blue buildings in the middle of the village. A woman is standing at the doorway with a girl of about seven alongside a boy a couple of years older.

The woman must be Ajay's sister, Satya. She has the same distinctive bone structure as he does, high cheekbones and plump lips, a thick head of dark hair down to her shoulders, a sari made of white material lined with large red flowers draped along her tall body. Next to her, Ajay's niece is wearing a red bejewelled dress and his nephew is clad in a gold shirt over dark blue jeans with gold swirls over them.

I stick out like a sore thumb in my navy blue shorts and black vest top. Even Ajay's wearing some colour, in the form of a bright blue shirt.

'I feel like the Queen,' I say. 'If I'd known, I would have dusted off the only dress I own.'

'You own a *dress*?' Ajay asks in mock shock.

I dig my elbow into his arm and his sister smiles then gives him a big hug, his niece and nephew doing the same. Satya then steps towards me, pressing her palms together and bowing her head in the traditional Indian greeting Ajay told me about. I do the same, and she smiles.

'It is an honour to have you as our guest,' she says in good English, delicately swatting away a fly with her right hand. 'I must apologise for any upheaval, it's Aadrika's *Kadhani Vizha* tomorrow,' she explains, putting her hand on her daughter's shoulder.

'Ear piercing,' Ajay says. 'Big deal for little girls here.'

I put my hand to my own ear, remembering how desperately I'd wanted a piercing when I was ten. My aunt had refused, telling me it was 'common'. I remember screaming at her that Mum would've let me. She'd pursed her lips and turned away, like she always did when I said that.

116

Satya says something in Indian to Ajay and he nods as his niece's eyes light up.

'Satya would like you to come to the ceremony tomorrow,' Ajay says.

'Oh, you don't have to invite me,' I say.

'You're already invited,' Satya says, shooting me a look of steel that says 'subject over'. Maybe the women here aren't so delicate after all? She gestures into her house. 'Come inside, you must be hungry.'

She leads us in into a hallway with faded pink walls and dark tiled floors. A door at the back opens out on to a shaded veranda, the slice of sunlight streaming through it bouncing off the floor and almost blinding me as I step in. Pretty gold-framed pictures line the walls and there's a delicious spicy scent drifting through the house.

After a wonderful dinner, I realise just how exhausted I am, Ajay too, the jetlag finally catching up on us. So Satya shows me to a small room at the front of the house that looks out over land dotted with trees and the huge national park rising in the distance. I open the holdall which contains my life. Clothes all the same colours, blacks, greys and navies, so I don't need to spend vital moments matching colours when I could be diving. It was for this same reason that I chopped my long black hair off when I was twelve, to my aunt's dismay – it was easier to deal with after a swimming session. My playing cards spill from the bag when I pull a top out for tomorrow. I'd developed an obsession with playing patience as a kid and haven't been able to shrug it off. The sticks of chewing gum I've brought with me are another obsession, essential to help me equalise after a deep dive, but Ajay jokes he can follow a trail of gum stuck to walls and under tables if ever he wants to find me.

Next, I pull out the small photo album I carry around with me, a birthday present from my parents when I was five, charting my first years with them from a blinking newborn with a thick patch

117

of black hair curled up against my dad's bare chest, to my first awkward steps, Mum standing over me and holding my hands above my head.

And now the silver bag that was found on the submerged ship joins all these items too.

After changing into an old diving t-shirt and faded blue shorts, I sit cross-legged on the bed and look out at the distant mountains, the full moon above turning the sky a satin grey, the outline of trees in the distance black and jagged. I hold the silver bag close to me. It smells of the sea, of salt and brine. It's a sad smell; makes my heart ache for the fear my mum must have felt in those last moments.

Did the bag's strap slide from Mum's pale shoulders as she ran with Dad to what they thought would be safety? Did she turn, go to reach for it knowing it was a gift from me, watching forlorn as it got trampled under panicked feet?

Or was Mum still holding it as the ship sank? Was it the last thing Dad saw, the silver satin entwined around her as she sunk to the seabed with him? Did they think of me?

Or did she think of the necklace inside, her initials entwined with another man's?

I reach for my small photo album and lie back on the bed, holding it and the bag close to me as the sound of crickets and the rustle of small animals foraging in the plants outside send me to sleep.

We rise with the sun the next day. As I wait for Ajay to shove his diving gear into his brother-in-law's old four-by-four for the car journey to Lake Periyar, I watch the sun rise. It turns the soft clouds a hazy orange, shrouding the trees ahead of us in yellow light. It's calm, peaceful, a contrast to how I'm feeling inside. I'm buzzing, the idea of diving a site my mum was so excited to see fills me with energy, even more so than when I do a normal dive.

'All done,' Ajay says, jumping into the passenger's seat. 'Sure you want to drive? The roads can get dicey around here.'

'I like dicey. You navigate and enjoy the ride.'

He grips on to the edge of his seat and pulls a terrified face as I laugh.

'You have a lovely family,' I say as I start the engine.

He smiles. 'They are very special.'

'I'm envious. I've often wondered what it'd be like to be part of a huge family like yours.'

He frowns slightly. 'It's not all a bed of roses. There's a lot of pressure.'

'To do what?'

'To settle down and get a "real job",' he says, making quotation marks with his fingers. 'It was hard telling my parents I wanted to be a diver after they'd paid for me to study medicine at Oxford.'

'I didn't know you did that.'

He nodded. 'The plan was for me to become a good doctor and meet a good Indian wife.'

'What happened to those plans?'

'I joined the rowing team and remembered how much I loved being on the water.'

I look at him in surprise. 'You rowed for Oxford? God, Ajay, the things I'm learning about you on this trip! Did you help them win?'

He laughed. 'That's the problem. I was better underwater than on top of it. It brought back memories of diving the forest here as a child. So in a moment of madness, I quit and took a diving course.'

'Your parents must have gone spare.'

He sighed. 'Of course. But I have paid them back, three times over. And now they are as proud as they can be of their disappointing son.'

119

The journey takes nearly an hour. The mist hides the surrounding scenery from us for the first thirty minutes, obscuring our view, the long red dusty road and herds of animals we pass our only companions. But soon the sun burns through the mist and it lifts like a veil, revealing stretches of lush green land either side of a road fringed with palm trees. We pass through villages much like Ajay's, watching as people go about their morning chores, filling beautifully coloured pots of all sizes with water from the village tap and getting children dressed in school uniforms made of brown shorts and coral shirts, backpacks snug around their shoulders. They stop and watch us as we pass, not used to seeing a girl with black hair and tattoos driving an Indian man down their roads.

After a while, the foliage around us grows more dense, canals and waterways stretching out in the distance as we enter the heart of the national park.

'We're close,' Ajay says.

My tummy shimmers. How many times had Mum dreamt about making this journey?

Ajay gestures for me to turn right and we bounce over a small dirt track that winds through the forest until we reach a grass clearing.

The lake spreads out before us, clear and shining. And there, darting up from the lake's shimmering depths, the black remains of tree trunks. It makes for a stunning view, the lake glimmering and alive compared to the still dead trunks of these ancient trees.

'Shall we get ready?' Ajay asks.

I take a deep breath. 'Yep.'

It's all business over the next twenty minutes. We shrug our gear on then check each other's equipment. Then we're entering the same water Mum dreamt of diving. It feels like the past is lapping at my shins as my fins tread water.

'Okay?' Ajay asks me.

I nod and continue until the water is up to my shoulders. Ajay gives me the thumbs up and I do the same, then we dive in, kicking our legs to propel ourselves downwards. It's crystal clear underwater, the tree trunks reaching up to the surface in the distance. The warmth of the water surrounds me, the quiet of the deep making me smile around my snorkel.

I glide to the closest tree, a thin one with one branch dipping from the surface into the water. Fish dart away as I approach, and I notice the shadow of birds flocking from the branches above. Amazing to think these ancient trees, long dead, are now home to living creatures.

I gently place my hand against the tree's surface and instantly get a flashback to placing my hand against the cruise ship's walls in Greece a month ago. I see the sunken cruise ship as though it's right there in the distance. It follows me everywhere, my parents' underwater coffin. If I can do this for my mum, live one of her dreams, will her death stop haunting me?

I swim to another tree and then another as Ajay floats around in the distance, his long legs circling above him. I think of his family, so many of them here and some back in the UK, too. How must that feel, to have so many people connected to you, caring about you, their blood running through your veins?

I peer at the trees. There are dozens of them but they look alone, sad, their roots dead beneath the lake's surface. Apart from two trees that stand very close, like sad companions. I thrust myself towards them. As I draw near, I realise they're actually connected, their branches entangled. They lean away from each other as though the entanglement isn't by choice. I think of my aunt and me: forced together, alone despite our blood connection. Is she thinking of me now, out here? Does she think I'm a fool or brave?

Something catches my eye in the bark, a pattern.

Could it be an etching?

121

I urgently kick my legs, gripping a branch to pull myself closer. It's hardly noticeable but I can just about make out the curve of a C tangled around an N…just like the etching in Niall Lane's photos and the necklace. I stare at the letters. They feel alien to me. It ought to be *C&D*. I carefully trace my finger around the curve of Mum's initial. I close my eyes, see her face, the curl of her black hair dipping over her eye as she leans down to pick me up. I smell her perfume, a heady, musky scent. Then I see Dad leaning in to kiss her cheek. My stomach clenches with grief for them both.

I peer up through the lattice of twigs towards the shimmering surface. I usually feel safe beneath the water's surface but it's as though I'm peering through prison bars right now.

Before I know what I'm doing, I start scrubbing at the etching with the knife in my belt, so hard it hurts. But I don't care, it's worth it for the sense of liberation I feel as I watch the bark around the etching fall away, the letters disintegrating until there's nothing left but a hollow.

Chapter Nine

Willow

Kerala, India
September 2016

A couple of hours later, we're sitting in a restaurant where one of Ajay's many cousins works. It's part of a sprawling hotel with fancy-looking accommodation in the form of villas. The restaurant overlooks the lake and is made from dark bamboo, the waiters and waitresses are dressed in colourful outfits. The submerged forest is out of view now and I'm pleased. I don't want to be reminded of that etching…or what I did to that poor tree. I shouldn't have done it, and Ajay's disapproving looks when we emerged from the lake made me feel even worse. Sometimes I just get so full to the brim with feeling, I lash out, throw things, break things. It's stupid, embarrassing.

'You okay?' Ajay asks me now.

I sigh. 'Just feel like a bit of an idiot. I couldn't face seeing Mum's initials with someone else's, you know?'

'Are you even sure it's one of Niall Lane's carvings?'

I reach into my rucksack and dig the print-out of Niall Lane's etching from it, laying it on the table. 'Definitely the same.'

'Have you heard from him?'

I shake my head. 'No reply to my email. I called his agent too, she said she'd pass my message on but nothing. Why invite me to his exhibition if he can't be bothered to get back to me?'

'Ah, I recognise that photo.' We look up to see a plump Indian woman with red hair smiling down at us. She has a manager badge on her sari.

Ajay stands and bows to the woman. 'Hello, Mrs Rangan. My cousin Basheer works here. He says many good things about you.'

'Ah, Basheer, such a wonderful boy.'

Ajay gestures to me. 'This is my friend, Willow.'

'Hello,' I say, not sure whether to bow or not, somehow managing half a bow, half a wave instead.

She smiles. 'We have that picture in our dining room. A couple of guests have been inspired to visit the submerged forest here after seeing Niall Lane's photos. I remember when he stayed here many years ago, he wasn't so famous then. I think people are rather impressed when I tell them I met the elusive Charity his collection is named after.'

Ajay's eyes widen and I find it hard to get my breath for a moment. 'She stayed here?'

She nods. 'Yes, Charity. I always remembered that name, so unusual.'

I dig out the photo of my parents I carry around with me. I'd taken it just the weekend before they left for their cruise. It was lopsided, faded, but it was the first photo I'd ever taken, and the most recent picture of them. They look happy in it, sitting on two garden chairs with cups of tea in their hands, smiles on their faces. I point to my mum. 'Is this her?'

Mrs Rangan leans closer. 'Maybe, I'm not sure. It was a long time ago. Is she a relative of yours?'

'Yes, my mother. Do you remember anything about your meeting with her?'

'I did a closing mandala ceremony for her.'

'What's a mandala ceremony?'

'It's said to cleanse grief,' Ajay explains.

Mrs Rangan nods. 'I think it helped her, she clearly still grieved for her sister.'

I frown. Maybe the woman she met wasn't my mum. 'But her sister's still alive.'

Mrs Rangan smiles sadly. 'Maybe I'm getting confused, it was a long time ago.' She peers behind her towards a queue forming at the front of the restaurant. 'I really must go. But please, these drinks are on us, just tell your waitress Mrs Rangan said so.' She bows down and quickly walks away.

'That was a strange conversation,' I say.

'Maybe Mrs Rangan remembered it wrong. As she said, it was a long time ago.'

'True.' I pull my phone out and connect to the hotel's free wireless access, visiting Niall Lane's website again. He'd named his collection of submerged forest photos after my mum. The other collections have generic labels: a collection of dramatic photos of damaged coral after the Boxing Day tsunami called *Beautiful Disasters*; another of steep underwater sea cliffs called *Into the Abyss*. Only the submerged forests – his most famous collection, it seems – is named after a person. My mum.

I catch sight of a news item that's been recently added to the site. I click on it and zoom in.

New photographs in the works
9 September 2016

To commemorate the 20th anniversary of the launch of Niall's famous Charity Collection, *he is revisiting all the sites of the submerged forests he photographed, starting with Austria this weekend, where he will also be showcasing his work at the Fotogalerie Wien in Vienna on 19th September and the Green Lake hotel in Tragöß in Styria, Austria on 21st September.*

Alongside the news item is a photo of the etching, the C and the N entwined. I click my phone off and look out at the lake. Was my mum here with him?

When we arrive back at Ajay's sister's house, it's a hive of activity in preparation for his niece's ear piercing ceremony. People march back and forth between the house and a larger building in the middle of the village.

I resolve to make my excuses. Last thing I want is to be surrounded by happy people when my mind's a mess. Plus I want to try to call my aunt to sound her out about what Mrs Rangan said. But as we jump out of the car, Ajay's brother-in-law rushes over to us with a huge bowl of rice and hands it to me, his face sweaty and panicked.

'Hello and welcome back! Now, can you take this into the hall, please?' he asks, gesturing towards the large building. 'You,' he says, jabbing his finger at Ajay, 'you help me move tables from house to hall. We didn't get enough.' He puts his hands up to the sky. 'Why does this happen to me?'

I look down at the huge bowl of rice, its sweet scent curling its way up to me, making my tummy rumble. So much for an early night.

As Ajay is dragged off by his brother-in-law, I walk into the hall. There are rows of plastic chairs in red, white and blue. Lining each wall is a long string of red bunting with gold symbols on each triangle. Musicians are setting up on a small stage area. All *this* for a simple ear-piercing?

'Wonderful, the rice.' I turn to see a woman approaching dressed in a beautiful gold sari. Her head is shaved, making her pretty features even more startling. As she draws closer, I realise with shock that it's Ajay's sister, Satya.

'I didn't recognise you,' I say, handing the bowl of rice over.

'We shave our heads for the ceremony, a tribute to our gods.'

'This place looks amazing,' I say, looking around me.

Satya shoots me a stressed smile. 'Thank you so much. But there is much more to be done, and the ceremony starts in less than an hour. The first batch of rice burnt and we didn't have enough tables and chairs so everything is running late.'

'Well, if you need any help…' I say, hoping she doesn't take me up on my offer so I can disappear. But instead, her smile widens and she starts reeling off a list of things I can help with.

'That should leave you with a few minutes to change, I hope that's enough time?' she asks after.

'Change?'

'For the ceremony.'

'I don't have anything appropriate, it's probably best I give it a miss,' I say, backing away.

She smiles. 'Nonsense. I have the perfect outfit!'

Forty minutes later, I'm sitting with Ajay on a bright red seat in a bright pink sari trimmed with silver, his elderly parents in front of us. When they met me, they'd seemed so fixated with the small tattoo of an anchor on my neck, they could barely get their words together.

The hall's packed, women and girls dressed in beautiful saris with colourful flowers in their hair; men and boys in their best shirts and trousers. The sound of chatter and laughter fills the air.

'It suits you,' Ajay says, smiling. He gestures to the sparkly pink sandals his sister lent me. 'And Mad Shoe Lady would approve,' he adds, referring to the homeless woman with her trolley of shoes that I had once told him about.

'Don't get used to it. This'll be a nightmare to get off to go diving,' I add with a smile. I just know he's going to tell all the other divers we know about this.

'Oh, I don't know,' he says. 'I've managed to get some of those saris off very quickly.'

I look at him in surprise. He's always struck me as so straight-laced. In all the time I've known him, he's not had a girlfriend, insisting he's waiting for the 'right one' to come along. When I ask him who that 'right one' is, he shrugs, says he won't know until he meets her. I guess I know what he means, I feel the same.

Who was the right one for my mum? Was it my dad…or Niall Lane? I don't know why this bothers me so much, Mum was bound to have some exes. But to see it all laid bare in his photography collection. I can't help but feel a bit strange about it.

Ajay's niece Aadrika walks in with her proud-looking parents. As the ceremony begins, more family members stand to surround her, babies in the arms of some, and I feel very alone sitting here. I can't even fathom what it must feel like to have such an immense family; to be part of such special rituals.

What exactly was I hoping to achieve with this ridiculous quest of mine? All it's doing is making me feel even lonelier, even more directionless.

I think of Aunt Hope, alone back home.

As Satya pulls her daughter to her after her ear is pierced, I quietly slip out and head to my room, trying to get reception on my mobile phone. Footsteps sound behind me and I turn to see Ajay following me.

'Are you alright?' he asks me.

'I'm fine,' I say, looking at my phone so he can't see my glassy eyes. 'I'd like to call my aunt, thought I'd do it while it's quiet out here. But I can't seem to get reception.'

'Use my sister's telephone,' he says, gesturing towards the house. 'The door's open.'

'Cheers. I'll give her money.'

'You can try but she won't accept it.' He scrutinised my face. 'See you back inside for food?'

'Yep.'

I walk into the house then enter the cluttered living room, making a beeline for the red phone in there and dialling my aunt's number. When she answers, it's hard to hear her, the sounds muffled.

'Aunt Hope?' I say.

'Willow? How's India?'

'Hot.'

She laughs. 'Really? I thought it snowed this time of year.'

'Ha ha.' I pause. How am I going to word this? 'So, Ajay and I went out for lunch…'

'And he proposed?'

I roll my eyes. 'Oh not this again. We're just friends.'

'Good. I think he's gay.'

'Jesus. He's not gay. Anyway, as I was saying. We went to this restaurant where his cousin works and the manager seemed to think Mum stayed there with Niall Lane ages ago.' I pause. 'Niall wasn't just Mum's teenage sweetheart, was he?'

Aunt Hope sighs. 'Oh, I don't know, Willow. You're obsessing too much about this. Just let it go. Really.'

I frown. She seems so adamant for me to forget about Niall Lane. Does this mean there *was* more to them?

'It's not just that. I have a feeling she might be remembering it wrong, but the manager recalls doing some ceremony for Mum and she said Mum had a sister who died. She's got that wrong, right?'

I hear a slight intake of breath.

'Oh God,' I say, putting my hand to my mouth. For a moment, I just stay silent, processing what I've heard. 'Don't tell me it's true?' I ask eventually. 'You have a sister who *died*? Why didn't you *tell* me? Why didn't Mum?'

'There was never any need for you to know,' she says quietly.

'That's ridiculous. She's my aunt. What was her name?'

'Faith.' There's a tremble in my aunt's voice. 'She was the oldest of the three of us.'

'How old was she when she died?' I ask, trying to make my voice softer. She lost her sister. *Two* sisters.

'Nineteen. A hit and run.'

'Oh, Aunt Hope. That's awful.'

She sniffs. Is she crying? Last time I saw her cry was the night we found out Mum died. 'It was a long time ago now,' she says.

'Did it happen in Busby?'

'The main country road leading out of town on that bend. It was in the middle of the night.'

'How did it happen?'

She sighs. 'You don't know how many times I've asked myself that question over the years.'

'What was she like?' I ask, sitting down on the chair and pulling the phone on to my lap. It explains a lot, the intense sadness I've sensed in my aunt over the years. I just wish she'd *tell* me stuff like this.

A pause. Then, 'Faith was wonderful.' I hear a hint of a smile in my aunt's voice. 'Full of life, beautiful, too – she had long blonde hair and loved the sea like you do. We called her our water nymph.'

'Did she dive?' I ask.

'Oh yes,' she replies, the smile evident in her voice. She sounds so different when she's talking about Faith, full of happiness and lightness. 'She used to drag your mother and me out on "undersea adventures", as she used to call them, searching for the submerged forest off Busby-on-Sea. That was before it was discovered, of course. She was obsessed with them, even wanted to become a marine biologist so she could study them.'

'Aunt Hope,' I say, something dawning on me. 'The map I found, the one I'm following now. It wasn't Mum's, was it…? It was Faith's.'

She doesn't say anything for a bit. Then she sighs again. 'Yes.'

My heart sinks. It doesn't feel the same visiting all these forests now. It was the fact I'd be paying homage to my mum that made me want to do this, not someone I've never met.

'Why didn't you tell me? I came out here because I thought it was Mum's dream.'

'We all *wanted* to visit the submerged forests, Willow.' She sighs. 'But we never got the chance.'

'I don't understand why you keep all this stuff from me,' I say. 'I'm not sure how I feel about all of this, not just the fact you had another sister but also that Mum and this photographer were more than teenage sweethearts.'

'Sometimes it hurts too much to say it out loud.'

I don't know what to say to that. Truth is, I understand what she means. Like when people ask me about my parents. Sometimes it's easier to pretend they're still alive.

We sit in silence for a few moments.

'So, what are you going to do now then,' Aunt Hope says suddenly, assuming her usual clipped tones. 'Continue on your little quest, or return home?'

I think of the news item I read on Niall Lane's website. 'Maybe I'll go to Austria,' I say. 'I hear the lake there is awesome. Plus I think Niall Lane might be there at the moment.'

A brief pause. 'He might?'

'Yeah. He's revisiting all the submerged forests he photographed as a commission. I think it's a commemoration of Mum.'

'You might be disappointed with the lake. It isn't so stunning in real life.'

'You've been?' I ask in surprise.

'Many years ago. I went with your mother.'

I shake my head, unable to believe she hasn't mentioned this before either. 'When did you go?'

'Oh, I can't remember, it was a long time ago, I barely remember it.'

'But you remember it enough to say the lake wasn't so stunning in real life. You don't want me to go, do you? Why don't you want me to talk to Niall?'

'You're reading into things. I really must go, Willow. Once you know what you're doing next, let me know, won't you? Take care.'

Then the phone clicks off. I stare at it in disbelief. What's she trying to hide from me?

The next morning I wake to the sound of scratching outside. I reach over and pull the curtain aside to see Ajay's sister Satya sprinkling white powder on the ground outside her front door. She catches me watching her and beckons me to join her. I'm not in the mood really. I've hardly slept, everything I learnt the day before scraping through my mind like a razor.

I sigh and pull on my grey hoodie over my t-shirt and shorts before walking outside, raking my hands through my hair to stop it sticking up.

'Did you sleep well?' Satya asks me. She's wearing a beautiful blue sari.

'Perfect,' I lie. 'What's that?' I ask, gesturing towards the pattern she's making with the powder.

'A mandala. We draw this each morning to bring prosperity.'

'I thought they were used to help with grief?'

'They can be drawn for a variety of reasons.'

'Does it work?'

'You've seen our wonderful children. And the new television,' she adds, laughing. 'Want to try?'

'Yeah, sure.'

She takes hold of my hand and pours what I now realise are fine grains of white rice into my hand. 'Do a circle here,' she says, pointing to the middle of a hexagon she's created. I lean down, carefully pouring the rice so it creates a circle, thinking of my mum doing the same many years ago, thinking of her sister, taken from her too early. 'Good,' Satya says. 'Add a little more to thicken it up.'

I do what she asks and we work in silence for a couple of minutes. Then Satya looks up at me. 'Ajay told me you're visiting submerged forests around the world as a memorial to your mother.'

'Yeah.'

She nods to herself. 'There is a Hindi saying I like.' She murmurs something in Hindi. 'It means "There are only two mistakes one can make along the road to truth; not going all the way, and not starting."' She looks at me, her dark eyes sinking into mine. 'You have started. But will you go all the way?'

I think of the fact that this man who loved my mother is in Austria…and how much my aunt was trying to convince me not to go. I always *did* like doing what she told me not to.

'Maybe I will go all the way,' I say.

Chapter Ten

Charity

Styria, Austria
June 1987

Charity watched her sister take a sip of wine. It was a relief to see her looking better. When Charity had returned from Kerala nearly two months ago, she'd been shocked to learn Hope had been admitted to hospital. She'd gone straight to her, finding Hope pale and thin on her hospital bed. A quiet conversation with her doctor revealed her blood sugar levels were abnormally low, causing her to faint regularly. The reason, as Charity suspected, was that Hope was running herself ragged at the café.

'I'm coming back to help whether you like it or not,' Charity had said when she saw Hope.

Hope had simply shrugged. 'Fine. But you're not baking any cakes,' she added with a trace of a smile. 'We don't want to give the customers food poisoning.'

So the two sisters returned to the cottage together and Charity took on much of the work at the café until Hope seemed better.

Over those few weeks, thoughts of Dan and Niall entered Charity's mind every now and again. She saw Dan pass in his car once or twice. But there was no word from Niall. Despite herself, she'd been half hoping to receive the photo he'd promised of the submerged forest in India. But nothing had arrived.

When Hope's health started to improve after a month, they decided to clear out the cottage and, in the process, found brochures Faith must have stowed away to plan their world tour of submerged forests. One stood out to Charity: Green Lake, the tranquil lake Faith had told them about in Austria.

'Let's go,' Hope said. 'Just you and me.'

So a couple of weeks later, there they were in a traditional Austrian hotel near the lake it was named after, enjoying dinner in its simple restaurant with its varnished birch tables and chairs and clean cream walls.

'More wine?' Hope asked now, picking the bottle up.

'Why not?'

Hope poured some more wine into both their glasses and they clinked them together.

'To Faith,' Hope said.

'To Faith,' Charity replied, smiling sadly.

They were quiet for a few moments, looking out towards the stretch of white-tipped mountains in the distance, the expanse of green that spread out from the hotel.

'So now we've had a few glasses of wine,' Hope said, 'do you want to tell me why the Norths *and* Niall were in India with you?'

Charity sighed. Hope hadn't brought Niall up at all during the past few weeks. Charity had hoped she didn't know Niall had been in India too.

'Dan North's PA told me they flew Niall out there to take photos,' Hope explained. 'Bit of a coincidence that they arrived the same week as you, isn't it?'

'Lana North orchestrated it.'

Hope raised an eyebrow. 'Like she orchestrated the dinner?' Charity nodded as Hope frowned. 'Strange.'

'It is. She seems a little obsessed with Niall and me.' Charity looked into her sisters eyes. 'I hope you now believe I had no intention of having dinner with Niall that evening at the Norths…and I really did bump into him while diving that day.'

Hope took in a deep breath. 'I suppose I do. Lana North is as messed up as I suspected then?'

'I can't figure out if she's damaged in some way, or just a bored and manipulative woman.'

The waiter came over with the dessert menus.

'But why the obsession with you and Niall?' Hope asked, her eyes scanning the menu.

'I don't know, maybe she likes the tragedy of it all.'

'And you?'

Charity frowned. 'Me what?'

'Do you like the tragedy of it all?'

Charity shook her head. 'No. We went out of our way to avoid each other the two days I was in India and, when we did bump into each other, we ended up arguing.'

Hope quirked an eyebrow, eyes intrigued. 'About what?'

'Oh, I can't even remember,' Charity lied.

Hope held Charity's gaze for a few moments, then dropped it, taking a sip of wine. 'What does Dan North say about his wife's little games?'

Dan's handsome face flashed into Charity's mind, the memory of his breath on her lips, the look in his green eyes, like everything could start and end on that boat with him.

'You're blushing,' Hope said. She narrowed her grey eyes. 'Did something happen with Dan North? *Please* tell me it did.' Charity felt her cheeks turn even hotter and Hope's eyes widened. 'Was the argument between you and Niall about *him*?'

'No, not at all!'

'But something did happen between you and Dan North?'

Charity took a large gulp of wine. Maybe she should tell her sister? She'd held it all pent up inside the past few weeks. Her sister might be outspoken and stubborn but she was discreet. Would it help to tell her, to release the tension?

'We nearly kissed,' Charity blurted out.

A smile spread over Hope's face.

'We were *very* drunk,' Charity quickly added.

Hope leant forward, eyes giddy with excitement. 'This is the best news I've heard in a *long* time.'

Charity laughed. It was great to see her sister acting like her old self again. 'Why?'

'Let me see. He's charming, kind and friendly,' Hope said, ticking the attributes off on her thin fingers. 'Plus he's gorgeous and has money, lots of it. Oh, and the best one? He's *not* Niall.'

'You forgot one. He's married.'

'To a manipulative bitch!'

'Oh, Hope, really. You'd make a terrible counsellor.'

Hope tilted her head as she scrutinised Charity's face. 'How do you feel about Dan?'

'I don't know. He confuses me.'

'Well, I'll tell you how I feel. I like him. And I feel *sorry* for him, putting up with that woman. It's your duty to save him from her.'

Charity laughed. 'I'm not sure stealing men from their wives is part of a counsellor's job.'

After the waiter came over to take their dessert order, Hope settled back into her chair, playing with the stem of her wine glass. 'I always thought you'd run away to Paris or something and become a dancer or an actress. You were always so *dramatic.* I was so shocked when you signed up for that psychology course.'

Charity shrugged. 'I guess I've always been fascinated with the human mind, with helping people.'

'Have you?' Hope asked. 'I don't remember that. I think you felt a bit lost after Faith died.'

'I think we both did. You missed that teen literary retreat, remember?'

'I couldn't leave you all at such an awful time.'

'Do you ever think what the retreat could have led to?'

Hope was quiet for a few moments. 'I would have eventually missed out on some opportunity or another to look after Mum and Dad, regardless of Faith.'

'I offered to come back to care for them!'

'You had a job! Anyway, it was always going to be me left at home looking after them, wasn't it? The uglier, least talented sister.'

Charity reached across the table, grabbing her sister's hand. 'Hope! How can you say that?'

'Because it's true. And I don't mind, really,' Hope said, smiling. 'I've never resented you both for it. I adored Faith, and love you completely, you know that. But it's always been clear I'd be the one left on the shelf.'

'What rubbish,' Charity said, shaking her head. 'You're beautiful.'

'No, I'm not,' Hope said quietly.

Charity looked at her sister, her heart aching. 'I wish you weren't so horrid to yourself.'

'I'm not horrid, I'm just honest.'

Charity examined Hope's face. Maybe if Faith had lived Hope wouldn't be so insecure. Faith always had a way of making her sisters feel special. Charity hadn't done enough for Hope. 'I had some time to think while I was in India. Maybe we should move somewhere completely different together?'

Hope contemplated her sister's face. 'You mean move away from Busby-on-Sea?'

'Why not?' Charity leant forward, animated. 'We could sell the café, the house, and use the money to start anew somewhere else. You could do a poetry course, I could – oh, I don't know, join the circus or something.' Hope shot her a look. 'Only kidding. But you know what I mean. Us two, together, starting afresh, not letting the past hold us back.'

'I'm not sure I could do that to Mum and Dad. They wanted one of us to continue with the café, remember?'

'Mum also hoped you'd become a published poet one day! We could go to Brighton. Or Wales, aren't there lots of poetry events in Wales? Or even head north, it's cheaper up there.'

Hope bit her lip, looking out of the window. 'I don't know.'

'But you'll think about it?'

Hope looked back at Charity, a small smile on her face. 'Maybe.'

The waiter arrived with their desserts – two *Germknödels*, white doughy domes sprinkled with powdered sugar, oozing with delicious thick plum preserve. Charity sunk her spoon into hers and lifted the goo out, making Hope do the same. Then they clinked their filled spoons together.

'To a sea change,' she said.

Hope's smile deepened. 'To a sea change.'

The vast Green Lake spread out in front of the sisters the next morning. Tall pine trees lined its borders, the snow-topped Alps standing majestically over it in the distance. Divers stood on its grey gravelled sides preparing their equipment.

'It's as beautiful as the photos Faith showed us,' Charity said.

'Even more so,' Hope said. She picked up the snorkel she'd hired. 'Now, remind me how this diving malarkey works?'

Twenty minutes later, they were both below the surface, gliding over a blanket of grass complete with yellow buttercups that rose still and graceful from the ground. Hope kicked her legs, reaching downwards so her fingers grazed the soft petals. Soon, a submerged bench came into view. Charity and Hope exchanged a look through their masks. Faith had told them about this very bench when she'd told them about submerged forests, she'd even dug out a photo of it. The two sisters swam towards it and both sat on it, eyes smiling at each other under their masks. Charity looked at the empty space next to her and imagined Faith there. Hope looked at her, her eyes swimming with tears, no doubt thinking the same.

A shoal of small pale fish passed over them. Charity pointed up and Hope followed her gaze. They watched the fish pass and Charity reached out for Hope's hand, squeezing it. Everything felt so peaceful right then, like the layers of water around them were keeping all the complicated parts of her life out.

They stayed there a while, just the two of them, quiet, contemplative. Then three divers appeared. So they swam away from the bench, following the long gravelled path that wound its way through the grass.

After a while, Charity noticed a tree standing eerily in the middle of the sunken grass meadow, its branches floating upwards towards the surface as though it were trying to return to dry land. She pointed towards it and Hope nodded. Faith had also shown them a photo of this solitary tree. They swam towards it and both carefully touched its leaves with their fingers.

Then something caught Charity's eye. A looped C entangled with an N. One of Niall's etchings.

She reeled back, water rippling around her. He'd already visited the lake?

Before her sister had a chance to see it, she beckoned Hope towards a large rock, distracting her by showing her some fish scooting in and out of its holes. She didn't want to ruin their holiday with thoughts of Niall.

When they emerged from the lake, they sat on the banks, soaking in the warm sun as they shared a packet of crisps.

'Well, that was quite something,' Hope said, smiling.

'It was, wasn't it?' Charity gazed out at the lake. So many questions were intruding into her mind. When had Niall come? Was he here now? Did he know *she* was here?

Hope smiled. 'I forgot how crazy your hair gets after swimming. Faith always said you had enough hair to supply a whole country. She—' Hope frowned. 'Your hair was wet. Why was your hair wet?'

Charity laughed. 'We've just been in the lake, dork!'

Hope's face paled. 'I mean that night, the night Faith died. Your *hair* was wet. I was too caught up in everything at the time to really take it in, but it was wet, wasn't it?'

The smile disappeared from Charity's face. 'I don't know what you mean.'

'It was raining that night. You were outside, weren't you?' Hope put her hand to her mouth. 'My God, were you with Niall the night he killed Faith?'

Chapter Eleven

Willow

Styria, Austria
September 2016

I should be exhilarated as I stare out at the emerald lake before me. Instead, I feel like a fool.

I came at the wrong time of year.

This is what happens when you make impulsive decisions to fly somewhere without doing your research. It may look pretty here with its white-capped mountains in the background, the lake glittering like a diamond in the midst of it all. But it's too bloody shallow to dive!

At least there's Niall Lane's exhibition tomorrow at the Green Lake hotel I've booked into. It doesn't have to be a wasted trip. I can ask him some questions, try to see if he can fill in the gaps of my mum's past, of her dead sister's past, gaps my aunt Hope refuses to fill.

As I stare out at the lake, I have this moment where I feel tiny and utterly alone in this vast landscape. No fellow divers around me. No Ajay shrugging on his stabiliser jacket. No Aunt Hope writing her poetry from a rock nearby.

I've always been content with my own company, I guess I had to be with Aunt Hope spending so much time writing and disappearing off to poetry events most evenings. Sure, I had some friends from swimming classes, but they were never deep friendships. Just ships passing in the night. I think they sensed something in me, that lone wolf Ajay talks about. I have my 'tribe', all my fellow divers. But they're not always around and that's cool with me.

But right now, being alone bothers me. Maybe it's something about this vigil, about trying to find the missing jigsaw pieces in the puzzle of my life that is making me feel like one very solitary piece. It's not even as though I have a party to go to, like on one of my diving holidays, diving and drinking before tumbling into someone's bed, limbs entangling…just enough to stop the flashes of loneliness I might otherwise get in the dead of the night.

Maybe that's what I need right now. I need to go back to the hotel and grab that Austrian man on reception, all flushed cheeks, blue eyes and cropped blond hair. But the thought makes me feel empty. Just another passing acquaintance. Nothing fixed, nothing substantial.

What if this carries on for the rest of my life? Will I end up like the sad old Mad Shoe Lady in Busby-on-Sea?

Or like Aunt Hope?

'You have to come in June when the snow melts if you want to dive,' a deep Austrian voice says from behind me.

I turn, surprised to see the very receptionist I was just thinking about standing with one foot propped up on a rock, a fishing rod slung over his shoulder. He's wearing a striped blue jumper over jeans that are tucked into big brown boots. At the hotel he looked like a bewildered young man. Here, he looks like a rugged outdoorsy type, as Aunt Hope would say.

'Bugger,' I say. 'I can't believe what an idiot I've been.'

The man smiles slightly.

'You work at the hotel, don't you?' I ask.

'Yes. And you are in room 313,' he says. I raise an eyebrow and he blushes. 'I have a very good memory.'

'Not happened to see an etching on any of these trees, have you?' I ask. 'I'm guessing they'd be underwater in June?'

The man frowns. 'Etching? What is that?'

'A carving made with a knife,' I say, making the carving motion with my hand.

He smiles. 'Ah, yes. So-and-so loves so-and-so.'

'Exactly.'

'There is a carving on one tree still in the lake up there,' he says, pointing into the distance.

I look in the direction he's pointing. There's just more lake and more trees. 'What does it say?'

'There are just two letters. N and C.'

'Can you show me where it is?'

He shrugs. 'Sure. But you'll have to get on my boat. The lake's not deep but it's easier that way. I'm Luki by the way.'

I look him up and down. Does he look like the type to kidnap a tourist stupid enough to try to dive a shallow lake? Maybe. But I reckon I could overpower him.

Ten minutes later, I'm sitting in a small wooden boat in shallow water with Luki the receptionist. It really is very beautiful here. Trees surround us, the autumn sun glints off the lake's surface. Birds chirp in the branches above, the occasional splash in the distance suggesting some animal or another has jumped into what remains of the lake.

'Sail ahoy!' Luki says, grabbing an oar and scooping it into the water. Nope, he's definitely not a mass murderer.

The boat sets off, surprisingly smoothly.

'Aren't you supposed to be hiding behind that reception desk?' I ask him.

'I only work weekend night shifts. Are you from London?'

I laugh. 'Not everyone who lives in England comes from London. I live in a place called Busby-on-Sea.' I'm surprised when I say that. I usually say I'm of no fixed abode when people ask. 'What about you? Do you come from around here?'

'Yes, just ten minutes' walk from here. I come fishing every day for my people.'

'Your people?'

'Yes. My brothers and sisters and mothers and fathers.'

'How can you have more than one mother and father?'

He smiles down at me. 'Why just one mother, one father? Where are the rules that tell us that?'

'Erm, biological fact?'

He smiles. 'Just because it's fact, does not make it right.'

'Okay then,' I say, humouring him.

We sit in silence for a while and I take the chance to admire the park, the changing leaves on the trees, the hints of grass and smooth brown rocks blanketing the lake's edges. A bench appears in the distance. On it is an old white-haired man with a walking stick, a contented smile on his face as he looks out at the green lake.

'That's underwater in the summer,' Luki says, pointing to the bench.

'Yes, I've seen the photos,' I say. 'There's a wooden bridge that gets submerged too, right?'

He nods. We go a little further before he slows the boat down.

'There it is,' he says, pointing to a tree shivering in the lake, branches naked and exposed. As we approach it, I realise the water is just a few feet above the base of the tree. I could just as easily have walked around the edges of the lake then waded in. Maybe Luki is a mass murderer after all.

'So why do you want to see the etching?' Luki asks as he pulls a rope up, leaning his long body across the gap between the boat and tree to tie it around the trunk.

'Oh, just saw it in a photograph,' I say, not wanting to get into it all.

He looks at me sideways, frowning, then pulls the boat closer, the etching coming into view. Moss has grown over it, and it's barely visible – faded by time. But anyone searching for it, like me, can see it's there.

So it seems Niall did this etching in every place he photographed…each submerged forest on my dead aunt's map. Why? Did he know Aunt Faith too? Did he visit the lake with Mum? Why did *she* never tell me?

I don't like that thought.

I guess I'll find out tomorrow.

I stand at the entrance to the temporary exhibition that's been set up in a room to the side of the hotel's reception. I can see glimpses of the submerged trees featured in Niall's photographs, strangely at odds with the wooden panelled walls of the hotel, bone-dry and stiff when the wood featured in Niall Lane's photographs seem to ebb and flow before my eyes.

I stay where I am a moment as people stroll in. I feel awkward in the only suit I own, navy blue, too small, scratchy, especially as people start to float in in jeans and long skirts. Oh well, I'm not here to impress, am I?

I take a deep breath. *Here goes nothing.* I step inside and more photos come into view. They're printed on massive canvasses, just six of them, two on each of the walls facing the entrance. For a moment, I forget why I'm here, I just drink them all in: the lonely majesty of the sunken trees, the misty depths of water, the way he's

147

somehow managed to capture the sensation of time slowing down when beneath the surface.

Then there are the carvings, some barely discernible but all there.

I pick up one of Niall Lane's leaflets, which are lying on the side. The man's talented, I'll give him that.

A woman of about fifty approaches, tall, blonde, graceful. The kind of woman I always think of as the polar opposite of me.

'Welcome,' she says with an Austrian accent. She surveys the photographs, a serene smile on her face. 'Exquisite, aren't they?'

'Quite something,' I reply, hoping I'm not going to be drawn into a discussion about art. I wouldn't have a clue. 'When's Niall Lane arriving?'

'Oh, I'm sorry, he's not coming. Were you hoping to meet him?'

'I was,' I say, trying to hide my disappointment. I didn't really think this through, did I? Just assumed he'd be here. I bet Aunt Hope will be happy when she finds out.

'He was at the Vienna exhibition but not this one. He had another assignment to go to.' She tilts her head, examining my face. 'Do you know Niall?'

'He was a friend of my mum's,' I say.

'Well then, I must insist on showing you around. My name is Viktoria.'

'I'm Willow. So do you know Niall Lane well?'

'I've known Niall many years, I work in tourism for the lake. We use his photos in our promotional materials. Please, come.'

I let her take me around the exhibition, explaining where each photograph was taken. They feature six of the most beautiful submerged forests in the world – Romania, the US, Ghana, Kazakhstan and then Periyar Lake in India, and Green Lake, here in Austria. All of them are on Faith's map…and all have my mum's initials etched into their bark along with Niall Lane's own.

'This is my favourite, apart from his Green Lake photographs, of course,' Viktoria says as we stop in front of one photograph. The small information card below it explains it was taken in Kazakhstan at a lake called Lake Kaindy. The photo is taken from the bottom up, three trees dripping with green leaves looming above in the misty green water. On one is a faint trace of an etching. 'Niall sent me this on a small canvas as a gift when I married,' she said. 'We still have it taking pride of place in our hallway twenty-eight years later.'

'This was taken twenty-eight years ago?'

She looks down at her notes. 'Yes, nineteen eighty-eight. I believe the Charity he named the collection after was with him when he made his carvings. She died less than ten years later. This is why the carvings are so very special to him.'

1988. That was the year before I was born. Mum was with Dad then.

'Niall will be in Kazakhstan next month actually,' she continues.

'And now?'

'I have no idea.' She smiles. 'Niall likes to disappear every now and again. A real nomad.'

I try to muster the enthusiasm to smile back. 'Thanks so much for showing me around, Viktoria.'

'No problem. Shall I tell him you popped by?'

I think about it. 'Yes. Say Charity's daughter said hi.' Then I leave without watching her expression, unable to help the small smile appearing on my face.

I fiddle with the lip of my beer bottle, staring miserably at the leaflet I took from the exhibition.

'Why so miserable?' I swivel around on my bar stool to see Luki the receptionist adjusting the cuffs of his white shirt. He looks weird in his work suit now.

'I think my mum loved someone other than my dad,' I mumble.

He shrugs. 'People can love who they wish, however many people they wish.'

I roll my eyes. 'Let me guess. You don't believe in monogamy.'

He waves his hand about. 'Silly society rules.'

'Everything is silly society rules to you.' I look him up and down. 'Not so keen to break them here, are you?'

'I have to earn money. If we don't, we starve. Anyway,' he says, taking the stool next to me, blue eyes exploring my face, 'I saw you in the exhibition earlier.'

I sigh. 'Yes. My mum is the C in the carving.'

Luki raises an eyebrow. 'Interesting. One of my mothers knows the photographer well.'

I turn to him. 'Really?'

'Yes. He stayed with her when he took the photos.'

'When was that?'

He shrugs. 'Before I was born. Come to dinner tomorrow night. She will talk to you.'

I frown. 'Are you trying to kidnap me?'

He laughs. 'You're very funny. Will you come?'

'Yes. Thank you.'

He gets up and eyes the two empty bottles by my hand. 'Don't get too drunk.'

'That's exactly what I plan to do.'

He smiles. 'Very funny,' he says as he walks away.

I peer back towards the room filled with Niall Lane's photos. The one of Kazakhstan is in view, taunting me. Was my mum out there with Niall Lane? Aunt Hope told me once in a rare moment of openness that Mum and Dad got together a couple of years before I was born. How could she have been in Kazakhstan? Did that mean Mum had an *affair* with Niall Lane?

No. My parents had the perfect relationship. My memories of them together are nothing but smiles, Dad twirling Mum around in the garden as she laughed up at him, Mum bringing Dad cups of tea as he worked in his office, softly kissing his cheek. If they were apart overnight, she'd fling herself into his arms when he returned. Were these the actions of someone who was having an affair with her ex?

But then what do I really know about my parents? I was just seven when they died.

I turn the leaflet over and look at the photo of Niall Lane's face. My blood seems to turn to ice.

He has blue eyes like mine. Dark hair too. He loves diving, taking risks…and he was with Mum a year before I was born.

Could he be my father?

'God, no,' I whisper, putting my hand to my mouth. The beer I've been drinking churns its way up as the world seems to tilt on its axis. I quickly grab my mobile phone and call my aunt, heart clamouring against my chest. When she picks up, there's the clatter of cutlery in the background. I imagine her in that messy old kitchen, phone pressed between her cheek and her thin shoulder as she does a terrible job of washing up.

'So, did you meet Niall Lane then?' she asks.

'No. He isn't here.'

'Good.'

I look at the photo again. Her aversion to my meeting Niall Lane makes even more sense if she thinks he might be my father. And now I think about it, maybe he purposely invited me to his exhibition in Brighton because he knows too.

Maybe, after all these years, he wants to come clean…and Aunt Hope knows it.

'Did Mum go to Kazakhstan with him the year before I was born?' I ask.

She's quiet for a few moments. 'I don't think so.'

'Is there a chance—' I hesitate. This is huge. I almost don't want to know. I see my dad and his sparkling green eyes. I remember the way he used to hold me so close, call me his 'special girl'. I want *him* to be my dad, not this stranger. But I *must* know. 'Could Niall Lane be my father?'

It sounds ridiculous when I say it out loud and I expect Aunt Hope to laugh. But instead she stays quiet.

'Aunt Hope,' I say, aware of the tremble in my voice. 'Please tell me.'

'I don't know,' Aunt Hope says in a resigned voice. 'Your parents had a little falling out back then. Your mother disappeared for a week or so. That's all I know.'

The memory of Dad holding me begins to fade. I feel sick. 'A "little falling out"? What do you mean?'

'You're getting hysterical. Take deep breaths. One, two…'

'Oh my God! Oh my God.' I look up at the ceiling. Is this really happening? 'Why didn't you say?'

'I didn't know myself, Willow. Why rake up old dirt? You loved your father.'

'If he *was* my father.'

I catch a glimpse of my reflection in the mirror behind the bar, I'm sat hunched on my stool, arm wrapped around my tummy, phone to my ear.

'Willow, are you there?' my aunt asks.

'I'm here.' My head swims slightly. I can't tell if it's from the beer or the shock. 'I think I need to lie down, take this all in.'

'Come home,' she says. 'You shouldn't be doing all this alone.'

'I had no choice, did I? If you'd just told me the truth from the start…' I let my voice trail off. What's the point? It feels like we've had this argument a million times lately. 'I'm going to bed.'

'You'll come back to the UK soon?'

'Yes. Soon. I'll call you when I know. Night.' I hang up and lean back in my chair. Then I catch a glimpse of Luki on reception. If his 'mother' can shed some light on Niall Lane, then I need to go there tomorrow.

I drag myself up from the stool, feeling the weight of my mother's secrets on my shoulders.

Luki lives in a huge brown and white chalet with a wooden veranda spread out around it. It looks like it needs some work; some of the wood is rotting, the walls are filthy. It's set on a huge piece of land dotted with animal pens, goats and pigs grazing and snuffling. Neat vegetable gardens stretch across the land, overlooked by those icy mountains.

'How many of you live here?' I ask as we walk towards the house.

'Just twenty-six right now.'

I step over a creepy-looking doll, its smashed eye staring up at me. 'So you're a bit like a commune?'

'We don't define ourselves.'

I smile. 'No, I thought you wouldn't.'

We walk around the back of the house. A few people are strolling around in the late afternoon light, hugging each other in greeting, tending to the vegetables or animals. All of them have buzz cuts like Luki...even the women. I put my hand to my hair. A few inches shorter and I'd fit right in. They're dressed pretty normally though, no hippy skirts or bare feet. A woman in her forties with startling green eyes spots Luki and runs towards him, pressing her lips against his. Then she skips off again.

'One of my mothers,' he explains.

'Interesting way to kiss your mother.'

He rolls his eyes. 'See? Silly society rules. It's just lips.'

'If you say so. How many *mothers* have you got?'

'Seven.'

'And your real mother, as in the one who gave birth to you?'

'Judy gave birth to me,' Luki says.

We step on to the veranda. In the corner is a woman breastfeeding a chubby baby, a thick fur blanket slung around them. She looks up at me and smiles. I wonder if she's the baby's biological mother.

'Do you have lots of fathers too?' I ask him.

He nods. 'Children born here don't know who their biological fathers are.'

I raise an eyebrow. But then, who am I to judge? Turns out I might not either. And haven't I had more than one woman caring for me? First the mother who gave birth to me, then my aunt.

I rub my temples. This is all giving me a headache. I hope they have beer.

We step into the house. It looks like all the walls have been knocked down to create just one huge area with a fire pit in the middle, orange flames sparking off each other. A long table lines its centre and beyond, cushions are scattered all over a red felt floor, and there are some wooden benches too. On one of those benches sits a woman in her fifties with very pale skin and eyelashes. She's dressed in jeans and a red turtleneck jumper...and, of course, the obligatory crew cut.

'Darling Luki,' the woman says in a British accent as she kisses Luki.

'This is Willow,' Luki says, introducing us.

She smiles. I stay where I am for a moment, worried she might kiss me on the lips too. But instead, she gestures to the bright blue cushion. 'Please sit, Willow,' she says. 'We're happy to welcome you. I'll make you a warm drink.' She heads over to what looks like a cauldron and uses a ladle to pour a dark liquid into two chunky stone mugs. When she brings them over the strong scent of chocolate, cinnamon and spices make my mouth water. I take a sip and it tastes like a small slice of heaven.

154

'My own recipe for *heisse schokolade*,' she says. 'Chocolate, cinnamon, vanilla and cayenne peppers with just a little hint of rum,' she adds, pinching her fingers together to show a small measurement before letting her fingers move apart as Luki laughs.

'This is just what I needed, thank you,' I say, taking another sip.

'Where do you live?' she asks me.

'Everywhere and nowhere,' I say. 'I don't really have a base.'

'A nomad.'

'I suppose.' Isn't that how Viktoria described Niall? I squirm in my seat. I don't know whether Niall and I really are so similar, or if I'm just reading into it.

'Has Luki explained how we live?' she asks.

'A little.'

'Did he tell you about Otto?'

I shake my head.

'Good,' she says, nodding. 'It means you will come to this with an open mind.'

'Why do I need an open mind?' I ask.

'The artist Otto Muehl ran a commune just outside Vienna,' Luki explains. 'There were many good things about it.' His face darkens. 'But many more bad things too.'

'We don't have to talk about that,' Judy says, waving her hand around. 'That's in the past. All that matters is that Jens, the first man who came here, was once a member of that community.'

'So is that where your unique approach to family comes from?'

She nods. 'We believe everything should be shared, possessions, love, everything. No one person has the right to own the title of, say, "mother" or "son" or "nephew". We are all responsible, we are *all* family.'

I think of Aunt Hope. She always made it clear to me that she wasn't my mother, she was my *aunt*. It confused me to begin with. Everyone else had a mummy, why couldn't Aunt Hope be mine? I lived with her, she tucked me into bed, read to me like the other mummies did. But as I grew older, it suited me not to call her my mum. In my mind, it was clear: Aunt Hope didn't give birth to me so she wasn't my mother, never would be. But now I wonder if that was just a security blanket for me, a way to deal with the hurt and confusion of not being allowed to see her as a mother. One of my friends was adopted. There was absolutely no confusion for her: her parents were her parents, full stop. The woman who gave birth to her, the man who was her biological father? Yes, there was a blood connection but beyond that, it was nothing compared to what she had with her parents. So why couldn't it have been that way with Aunt Hope?

'Anyway, we talk too much about ourselves,' Judy says. 'What's brought you here?'

'She knows Niall,' Luki explains. 'The C from the tree is her mother.'

Judy nods, a small smile on her lips. 'I see.'

'How did you know Niall?' I ask.

'He stayed here many years ago.'

'Did he say anything about my mum?'

Her smile deepens. 'She was his great love.'

I look down into my hot chocolate, trying to control my breathing. 'Was she here with him?' I ask, not really wanting to know the answer. 'No.'

I let out a breath of relief. 'Did he say anything else about my mum, about their relationship?'

'Yes, many things, I'm sure.' She leans across and puts her hand on my arm, looking into my eyes, pity in her own. 'But it was many years ago, Willow, and I can't remember. All I do remember is that they lived together near where I was born in Norfolk at some point.'

Norfolk. The location of yet another submerged forest.

'They *lived* together?' She nods and I feel my cheeks flush. Aunt Hope hadn't mentioned they'd lived together. But then she hadn't mentioned much else either. 'Anything else you can remember? Did he say anything about Kazakhstan?'

'He was there with your mother.'

Laughter and chatter fills the room as people enter, plates of food in their hands.

'You must stay for dinner,' Judy says.

'I really ought to get back,' I say, needing to be alone to process everything.

'What for?' Luki says. 'We have good food and even better wine. Please?'

I watch people take their seats, the children running over and grabbing bread rolls. Some peer up and wave at me. Maybe I should stay. Luki's right, what have I got to go back to, another lonely night in a hotel room?

I shrug. 'Why not?'

Luki keeps an eye on me throughout dinner, introducing me to everyone, drawing me into conversations, keeping my glass filled with delicious sweet wine. And Judy watches me often, smiling whenever I catch her eye. At first, it makes me feel a little uncomfortable. But the more wine I drink, the more I like it, as though someone's watching out for me.

When I'm not being drawn into a conversation, I find myself trying to figure out which kid belongs to whom. But I really can't tell. All the kids seem comfortable with all the adults, running around for cuddles and attention from each one. If one goes too far – like a little boy who decides to jump on to the table and try to walk down its centre – they're punished with a quick smack to the bum by whichever adult is closest.

I also watch the couples in the crowd. Do they swap around? Luki seemed to suggest that. Maybe Mum and Dad had an open relationship. No, that feels wrong. But whatever it was they had, it's clear Mum loved Niall too at some point if she lived with him, travelled with him.

157

After dinner, we all sit down on the cushions and that's when the entertainment starts. One by one, people are encouraged by Jens, the man who started everything and who seems to be in charge, to perform, whether that be singing, playing some instrument, dancing, even reading poetry, which makes me think of Aunt Hope. Even Luki gets up to sing some traditional Austrian song in an off-key voice, though you wouldn't guess it the way everyone cheers and claps. It takes all my strength to stop myself from bursting out laughing.

'I've never had such a surreal dinner in my life,' I say, a couple of hours later as I sit outside with Luki, staring up at the stars. We're sitting on the back of a truck, a thick blanket wrapped around us as we share a bottle of red wine. I ought to be cold, it's autumn after all, but the wine and Luki's proximity keep me warm.

'Why surreal?' he asks, taking a sip of the drink before passing the bottle to me. His lips are red from the wine, the hints of blond hair on his shorn head turned white under the glare of the moon. He looks like a boy.

'Oh, I don't know,' I say, smiling to myself. 'I don't mean it in a bad way, just different from what I'm used to.'

'Well, it's very normal for me. I would probably find your family life strange.'

'Family? I don't really have a family.'

'What about your aunt?'

I take a slug of wine. 'We don't see much of each other nowadays.'

'She took you in though, cared for you, gave you a home.'

'I know. But—' I glance towards the tent, see the spark of orange light coming from it, the laughter and the music. 'My childhood wasn't loud and warm like it is here. When I look back on it, it all feels very cold and very quiet. I get scared sometimes. When my aunt Hope dies, I'll have no family and I'll just end up like Mad Shoe Lady.'

'Mad Shoe Lady?'

I explain about the homeless woman in Busby-on-Sea.

'You will never be a Mad Shoe Lady, you clearly have terrible taste in shoes,' he says, gesturing towards my dusty walking boots.

I can't help but laugh. 'I bet you had a wonderful childhood.'

Luki looks thoughtful for a few moments. 'It wasn't so wonderful,' he says after a while. 'I'd have liked to have known my father.'

'I thought you said you have many fathers?'

He looks up at me, blue eyes sad. 'I know who my father is, Willow. My biological father, as you say. I pretend it doesn't matter but it does.'

I think of the men I saw earlier. 'Does he live here?'

He shakes his head. 'He lives everywhere and nowhere.'

I go very still.

'That is why I go to the lake,' he says. 'I like to visit the etching. It's all I know of him.'

'Niall Lane's your father?'

He nods.

I examine his face.

Everything is different now. Luki could be my *brother*.

'How do you know?' I ask, my voice trembling.

'My mother told me.'

'Does Niall know?'

'Yes, he sends me his photos.'

'Just photos? So you've never met him?'

He shakes his head.

I look at him in disbelief. Is this what Niall Lane does, sow his seed then disappear?

'What's wrong, Willow? You look very shocked.'

'I am. And—' I pause. How can I say this? 'There's a small chance – okay, *more* than a small chance – he might be my father too.'

His eyes widen. Then his face breaks out into a huge smile. 'I have a sister?'

159

'Don't get carried away!' I say, unable to stop myself smiling with him. 'He totally might not be my dad. It's just a possibility.'

'Why do you think this, Willow?' he asks, breathless with excitement.

I explain what I've learnt about their time in Kazakhstan. His smile widens, if that's at all possible. 'Willow, this is wonderful. You will not be Mad Shoe Lady!'

I laugh. His excitement is contagious. Then I impulsively hug him, hold him so tight I think I might have hurt him a little. But I'm worried that if he moved away now, he'll see the tears of happiness in my eyes. I eventually let him go and he jumps up.

'You will need to stay now,' he says. 'It's too late for you to go back. I will not have any sister of mine being in danger. We can sleep in the room where the children like to sleep, you can see the stars from there.'

He puts his hand out to me. I look up at him, try to find my features in his. Could he really be my brother? The idea makes me shiver with excitement. I've always wanted a brother or sister.

But then that means the dad I knew and loved isn't my actual dad. My stomach crinkles as I think of Dad's handsome face, the dad I knew for seven years. I *want* him to be my real dad, the kind, funny man who'd whirl me around and take me out for ice creams and help me paddle my feet in the frothy sea near our house. The man who made people's faces light up when he walked into the room; who I'd watch in his office, his legs propped up on the table, head thrown back as he laughed.

But he's gone. What's better, a father who's dead or one who's alive? I feel guilty.

Either way, I need to find out. I can't live my life not knowing who my father is. Maybe Norfolk holds the key? If I can find out where my mum and Niall lived together.

But for now, I can at least pretend I have a brother, can't I?

I take Luki's hand, letting him lead me back into the noisy house.

Chapter Twelve

Charity

Norfolk, UK
October 1987

Wizened old tree stumps littered the patch of windswept beach Charity was standing on, looking eerie and forlorn under heavy grey skies. She wrapped her raincoat around herself, specks of rain falling on her head.

This wasn't quite like the ethereal underwater forests she'd seen in Busby-on-Sea and in India. Faith would probably still like it though. Hope would *love* it. So moody and dramatic, perfect fodder for her poems.

Charity sighed just as she always did each time she thought of her sister. They hadn't talked once since Charity moved to Norfolk three months ago to cover someone's maternity leave. In fact, they'd barely talked at all since that night in Austria when Charity confirmed Hope's suspicions.

'What happened?' Hope had asked with a trembling voice. 'I want to know *exactly* what happened.'

Charity stared at her sister, trying to find the words. She hadn't been able to find them for the past ten years. She'd been a coward. But she had been so young and secrets can grow like a weed.

'I snuck out to meet Niall,' Charity began, trying to stop herself from crying. She knew Hope would resent her tears. 'We'd decided to sleep the night on the beach near Seaford. We just wanted to spend a whole night together, and I knew no one would notice as long as I was back in the early hours. He drove me back in his new car. It was raining, the car skidded slightly as it went around the bend. You know how notorious that bend is, even before Faith died. And—' She shuddered at the memory. 'We – we felt a bump but it didn't feel like a—' Charity swallowed. 'A person,' she finally managed.

Hope grimaced, turning away.

'Niall stopped. He did stop, Hope,' Charity said, reaching her hand out to take her sister's. But Hope just shoved her away. 'We both got out to look,' Charity continued. 'But it was so dark and the rain…'

She took a deep shuddery breath, the night coming back to her, the sheer force of the rain, the feel of it drenching her skin, the sight of Niall's headlights on the shiny road.

'We couldn't see anything,' she said. 'The police said Niall would have known, but we really didn't, Hope! How were we to know she fell down the slope? I was so young, so *scared*. Niall convinced me not to say anything, told me it would just make things worse. And I didn't want to make things worse, Hope, it was already so horrible.'

'And when the police came? You knew then that what you felt when the car bumped into something was her, didn't you? That's why you ran into your room and hid your face when Mum and Dad told us, you knew I would see it in your eyes.'

'I think deep down I knew. But I'd only just snuck back when the doorbell went and I was in shock. I didn't want to say anything unless I was sure. If I could go back,' Charity said, looking into her sister's eyes, 'I would have told you. But I was so so scared. And... Niall convinced me when I saw him next that it wasn't a good idea.'

'And all these years, this secret...'

'It grew so big, I just couldn't get a grip on it.'

Hope laughed bitterly.

Charity put her head in her hands, the guilt overwhelming. 'I'm so sorry.'

When she looked up, her sister was walking away from her. She tried to follow, but Hope shoved her away. So she left her, remembering what Faith always said to her about Hope: she needed time.

Four months later, Hope still wasn't ready, despite Charity leaving her contact details before she left for Norfolk. She thought of Faith. Would she be sad to know she and Hope weren't speaking? Would she try to get them to reconcile?

Or would she be just as angry with Charity?

Charity looked up as she heard the roar of a motorbike.

Niall was here, right on time.

She smiled to herself. A couple of months ago, Niall had finally sent her the photos he'd taken of the submerged forest in India. Before she'd left for Norfolk, she'd impulsively passed her new address on to his agency just in case he needed to get in touch. With the photos was a letter:

Dear Charity,

Thanks for sending on your new address. Norfolk, hey? You know there's a submerged forest there, don't you?

I hope you're good and you're enjoying your new job. It feels weird writing this. I've never been one for writing. I guess that's why I never replied to your letters when I was inside. Who am I kidding? Truth is, I wanted you to get on with your life.

Just like I do now.

I miss you though. I can't deny it. So if you want to write back, I've included the address of a PO Box I've set up. Maybe I can make up for all those unanswered letters?

I hope you like the photos. Maybe if you take some pictures of the submerged forest in Norfolk, you can send them to me. I promise I won't critique them…

Take care,
Niall

She'd found herself writing a letter straight back to Niall and before she knew it, she'd written several pages about her new job, the quirky little beach hut she was staying in…nothing serious. It just felt good to share it with someone, especially Niall. Over the next couple of months, they exchanged more letters, Niall writing about an assignment he'd recently returned from in Australia, Charity about the quirks of the local community where she was living. They also wrote about the past, the drives down the coast during their last summer together, and life in Busby-on-Sea. Each time a letter arrived, Charity's stomach would tilt, face flushing with excitement.

When Niall brought up the possibility of him visiting to take photos of the submerged forest Charity had hesitated. The truth was, the idea made her happy. His letters were the highlight of her week. But she was also apprehensive. But before she could stop herself, she suggested they meet if he did decide to visit.

So here she was. She watched Niall jump off his bike, removing his helmet and approaching her with a huge smile on his face. He was more tanned than she'd ever seen him and the beginning of a dark beard was growing over his cheeks and chin, making his blue eyes even more vivid.

'What time do you call this?' she shouted above the bluster.

He laughed. 'Sorry, bad traffic.' He gave her a quick peck on her cheek. 'It's great to see you, Charity.'

'Looks like a storm's coming,' Charity shouted above the wind. She looked at the camera Niall had slung around his neck. 'Better get on with it soon if you want to take some photos. Then we can get some fish and chips down the road.'

His face lit up. 'Sounds perfect.'

As Niall took photos, Charity took the chance to observe the forest. It was a complete contrast to the submerged forest in India. The tree stumps were on land here, the ground beneath the soles of her wellies sludgy with brown peat. It was more of a ghostlike wasteland than an ethereal underwater world.

After a while, Niall pulled his small knife out. 'Want to do the honours?'

'You mean an etching?' He nodded. Charity shook her head. 'No, I feel bad doing it myself. Go ahead if you want to.'

'Oh come on, it's art.' He lay on his belly in the sand, carving their initials into what remained of the tree. Then he pressed his camera close to his face to take a photo. Watching him like that made Charity's insides clench.

'I saw your etching in Austria,' Charity said. 'When were you there?'

'I went there straight from India. I ended up getting a commission from the tourist board – they want me to go back and take photos for their brochures. The lake's out of this world, isn't it?'

'Yes, Hope and I—' Charity paused. It still hurt to think about what had happened in Austria between them.

'I know what happened out there,' Niall said softy. 'Hope told me.'

'When?'

'Just before I wrote that letter suggesting I visit. I had to go back to Busby to take a couple more photos of the submerged forest there for a commission. Hope saw me when I was in town briefly. She was annoyed, had a go at me like I purposely dragged you out that night with the sole intention of killing Faith.' Charity flinched and Niall shook his head. 'Sorry.'

Charity took in a deep breath. 'It's fine. I should have told them all those years ago.'

'You were right not to.'

'I'm not so sure.'

'I think Hope's being unfair.'

'Is she?' Charity said, feeling angry all of a sudden. 'Would it really have been so terrible if I'd just told my parents and Hope I was there?'

'Yes!' Niall said. 'Look at how Hope has reacted. Your family was everything to you. It would have destroyed you if it changed the way they saw you back then, *and* it would have destroyed them.'

'No,' she said, shaking her head. 'We made a mistake not saying anything, Niall. It's haunted me ever since.'

Charity let out a sob and Niall pulled her into his arms.

'It's okay,' Niall whispered into her ear. 'I know how hard this must be for you.'

She looked up at him. 'How did Hope seem when you saw her?'

'Hope is fine, you know how she is.'

'But it's been months and she hasn't been in touch.'

'This isn't an argument about you borrowing one of her scarves, Charity.'

She stepped away from him, wiping her eyes. 'I know.'

Niall peered up at the blackening skies. 'I think the heavens are about to open. Time for fish and chips?'

Ten minutes later they were sitting in the tiny fish and chip café overlooking blustery seas.

166

'I forgot how much you liked your ketchip sarnies,' Charity said as she watched Niall place some chips into his slice of bread and slather it in tomato ketchup.

'Ketchip! I forgot we called them that.' He looked at Charity's plate. 'And *I* forgot how much you loved your mushy peas. Is that a double helping?'

'I'm trying to be healthy. They're vegetables, aren't they?' She scooped up some of her peas and slathered them over Niall's sandwich. 'There, now you can be healthy too.'

He frowned as he looked at it. Then he smiled. 'A ketchipea sarnie.'

They both burst out laughing, people in the café turned to look at them. They continued talking, ordering puddings then tea to avoid having to leave and go their separate ways. When they eventually ran out of things to order, they huddled under the café's doorway against the rain.

'It's been good seeing you,' Niall said.

'Yeah, I've enjoyed it.'

'Maybe we can do lunch tomorrow? I'm here until Sunday.'

Charity smiled. 'I'd like that. I know a good place near my hut. You've got my address, why don't you come by at twelvish?' She glanced up at the rain. 'I better head back before this gets worse. My landlady promises me the hut doesn't flood but I'm not sure it'll be able to handle anything more than this.'

Niall frowned. 'Call if it does flood. Don't feel like you have to deal with it alone.'

She smiled. 'Oh, Niall, I'm not a helpless girl any more.'

Niall didn't say anything, just watched her. She felt her cheeks flush.

'Bye then, Niall,' she said, stepping away from the doorway. 'Take care.'

'You too, Charity,' Niall replied.

She put her head down and walked away.

That night, Charity was woken by a howling noise from outside. She got up and peered out of her window to see trees arched by intense winds, the sea so violent, waves were nearly reaching her door. In the distance the little white lighthouse seemed to tremble at the violence of the sea. Nearby, several people were battling against the winds to place sandbags along the beach, including Charity's landlady and her sullen looking daughter.

Charity pulled her jeans and jumper on, grabbing her raincoat and wellies. When she got outside, her door nearly flew off its hinges. The roar of the wind and the sea were so loud it deafened her. But she battled against it, going to the group and helping them to lay sandbags across the lane in front of her hut as her landlady smiled a thanks at her.

As she was reaching for another sandbag, she heard a creaking sound and looked up to see a tree bending towards her. Before she had a chance to jump out of the way, someone pulled her from its path as it crashed on to the lane.

She turned to see it was Niall, face wet from the rain, the hood of his coat blowing up around him. She struggled to take a breath at the sight of him.

'Are you okay?' he shouted to her over the storm. 'I woke to the storm and was worried.'

'I'm fine.' He was still holding her. She looked into his eyes, trying to compose herself.

'Don't just stand there!' the landlady said to Niall. 'You look strong. Come and help.'

They both jogged over, helping with the sandbags, the storm around them seeming to stir all sorts of feelings. When Niall handed a sandbag to Charity, their fingertips touched, sparking something. He held her gaze and she tried to control her breathing.

'We should get inside,' her landlady shouted to them. 'We've done what we can. The storm's getting worse, it's dangerous out here.'

'Come to the hut,' Charity said to Niall. 'I'll make us tea and we can wait the storm out.'

They both jogged towards her hut, Niall shielding Charity from the rain with his coat, and she let them in, slamming the door shut against the storm. They stood looking at each other in the semi darkness, rain dripping off their hair and skin.

'God, you're beautiful,' Niall said.

He pulled her towards him, his lips finding hers, his fingertips digging into her wet hair. The familiar feel of Niall's lips sent Charity plunging back into the past; into other nights like this, stolen kisses in the darkness, whispers of love, the way she was feeling inside matching the storm raging outside.

He kissed her neck, then her collarbone, her feelings mounting as he yanked her coat off, she his, both hungry for each other after all these years.

When Niall moved his hand beneath the waistband of her jeans, the sweet ache she remembered as a teenager hummed through her as he slipped his fingers inside her. She leant her head back and let out a moan as he buried his lips in her hot neck.

They stumbled into the living room, finding the sofa in the darkness. Niall tugged her jeans off then her knickers as she frantically undid his jeans, feeling the same thrill she used to feel at the soft sound of his zip in contrast to the feel of him, hard against her palm.

'God, I've missed you,' he murmured into her ear.

The storm lashed outside, the noise filling her ears, blocking her senses and thoughts of anything but the way Niall was making her feel when he touched her.

169

As he plunged into her, the storm seemed to reach its peak, roaring in her ears as she cried out.

When Charity woke the next morning, she watched Niall sleeping for a few moments. She'd never seen him sleep. He didn't look peaceful. He seemed troubled, brow furrowed, breath deep and low. It was exactly how she imagined he would sleep, dreams in turmoil.

She looked down at his naked body, tanned and muscular. Had they really done what they had done? She ought to feel guilty, regretful. But instead, it felt *right*.

She shrugged the blanket they'd thrown over each other off and knelt up to look out of the window. The beach looked ravaged, rubbish and fallen trees strewn all over, water pooling on the path as sirens sounded in the distance. But it was calmer. Charity felt the same, a mixture of tender aching, but calm too.

She felt Niall's hands slide up her body and grasp her breasts. Then he pulled her on top of him.

She looked into his eyes. 'This is right, isn't it?'

He frowned. 'Why wouldn't it be?'

She thought of her sister and how angry she'd be. 'Hope.'

Niall sighed. 'You can't keep basing your actions on what your sister might think.'

'But she's all the family I have.'

'And you're all the family she has. She needs to give you a break. Look, I love you, Charity. Always have, simple as that. That's all that matters. There's been no one like you since.'

'Like me?' she said, sliding off him and leaning on her hand as she looked at him. 'So there have been others?'

'Are we doing the ex talk?' he asked, smiling.

'We certainly are. So?'

He laughed. 'There have been others. But just casual, nothing special.'

'Same for me. Well, there was Ashton the firefighter.'

Niall quirked an eyebrow. 'You never said anything about a firefighter.'

'It lasted six months. There are only so many jokes about climbing poles a woman can take.'

He wrapped his arms around her. 'I don't want you thinking about fireman poles right now. All I want you thinking about is me.'

'That's easy,' she said, growing serious. 'You're all I've ever thought about for the past ten years.'

She'd just been thirteen when she'd started falling for him. But every relationship since – if you could call them that – had been dominated by thoughts and comparisons to Niall. Now he was here, right in front of her, in her bed…naked. She felt the thrill of that fact shimmer through her and she pressed her body against his. 'You're right. *This* is all that matters.'

As they sunk back down on to the bed together, Niall's lips exploring her body, she got a brief flash of Faith's beautiful face in her mind. She quickly buried it away.

Niall stayed after that. It was just the way it was. He had nowhere else to be, and she wanted him there, with her.

Her favourite times were at night when she got back from work to find Niall sitting at the small table, photos sprawled out over its surface as he got his portfolio together to send out to agencies. After dinner, she and Niall would curl up together, watching a film or just talking. It felt like they were teenagers again, when they used to huddle together at night in their cave, keeping each other warm and talking into the night about their future together. The only difference now was that they talked about the past, the *good* past, before Faith died. The future seemed to slip and slide out of Charity's grasp when she tried to fathom it, and she could tell Niall felt the same. Their future together had been snatched away from them when they were teenagers, so they weren't sure what to do with it now they had it back. Charity's contract would run out in April, that's all that was certain.

Over two months after their first night together, they celebrated their first Christmas together. Charity cooked them a turkey dinner and, as they said cheers, it almost felt like this was the way Christmas was meant to be, apart from the thoughts of Hope that niggled at the back of Charity's mind. She'd sent her sister a card and a present – a small scarf she'd found in a local market with lines from famous poems scribbled all over it. She'd also included yet another letter, asking Hope for forgiveness, telling her how much she missed her. But she had received nothing back. When she tried to call Hope on Christmas morning, there was no answer. So she left a message on their ancient answering machine, asking her to at least call or write to let Charity know she was okay.

'Let's go out,' Niall said as he watched Charity nibble at her nails, worrying about Hope.

'Where?'

'You'll see.'

After a short drive, they reached a stretch of beach, a shipwreck visible in the distance. The wreck looked lonely on the vast beach that spread out around it.

'It's called the SS *Vina*,' Niall explained as they walked towards it under bright blue skies. Charity zipped her coat up and dug her gloves out. It might be bright and beautiful, but it was cold too. 'It was used as a naval vessel in the Second World War,' Niall continued. 'Then the RAF used it for target practice. We're lucky, you can't always walk to it if the tide is in.'

As they drew closer to the wreck, all of it came into view. There were three main parts to rusting ship, with other items scattered all around, including several pieces of long metal that jutted up from the water, reminding Charity of the submerged forest in India. The front of the wreck was the largest part, black, mossy and littered with sea snails. Most of the wreck was so overtaken with moss and sea snails that she could barely see it was a ship any more.

Niall pulled his camera out of his rucksack and started taking photos.

'Oh, I see, you brought me here for selfish purposes,' Charity said as she watched him.

Niall smiled. 'No, I'll show you why I brought you here.' He took her hand and led her to a small archway that may have once been a door. 'There are no caves around here. So I thought this would be the closest thing we'd get.'

He pulled a picnic blanket out of his bag and lay it on the wet sand. Then he got out some candles and matches, a small turquoise cushion and another blanket. Charity smiled. He was trying to recreate the cave hideaway they spent hours in during their teenage years. He sat down on the picnic blanket and patted the space next to him. 'Come on.'

She sat beside him, teeth chattering from the freezing cold. He lay a blanket over their legs and she smiled.

'What's in there?' she asked, pointing to the plastic box.

He opened it to reveal a small Christmas pudding. She laughed. 'I love it.'

'Happy Christmas.'

'Happy Christmas to you.'

They kissed then looked out at the calm sea, eating Christmas pudding as they huddled together, the flames from the candle flickering in the dark archway.

Chapter Thirteen

Charity

Norfolk, UK
January 1988

Charity watched Niall preparing his diving equipment, a look of concentration on his face, his broad shoulders hunched as he examined his camera. Her eyes travelled over the nape of his neck and the dark bristles of his hair, and she had to stop herself marching out there and dragging him back into the hut to make love again. She smiled to herself. It was like she was a teenager again. She felt the same as she had in those heady days, carefree and happy.

She was about to get up and make some tea when Niall let out a yell of frustration and threw his camera against a nearby wall.

She ran outside, wrapping her cardigan around herself, picking up the pieces of his camera as Niall paced up and down in frustration. 'Why did you do that?'

'It's busted.'

'Are you sure?'

'Yeah. I had a feeling this might happen, I've had it years. This is a fucking nightmare.'

'Can't you get another one?'

He laughed bitterly. 'With what money? It's run out, Charity. Haven't you been wondering why I haven't offered to contribute towards the rent?'

'I didn't realise your money situation was that bad,' she said.

Niall sighed. 'Well, it is. I was hoping I'd get an assignment from the portfolios I sent out, but nothing. Maybe people are starting to realise I'm no good.'

Charity put the camera pieces down and ran up to him, wrapping her arms around him. 'Don't be ridiculous. You're talented, Niall.'

'Nothing I can do about it now though, is there?' he said, looking towards the broken camera.

'I have a bit of money.'

He shook his head, face vehement. 'No. Your contract's up in April. You'll need that to tide you over to your next job.'

'Honestly, Niall, I don't mind.'

'But I do.' He stepped away from her, looking out to sea. 'Don't worry, I'll figure something out.'

Two weeks later, Niall came home with a brand new, very expensive-looking camera.

'How'd you get this?' she asked him.

'Advance from a new assignment.'

'That's wonderful, Niall! What sort of assignment is it?'

'I'm taking photos of submerged forests around the UK for some adverts.'

'They must have really liked the photos you took in Busby and India.'

Niall nodded. 'I'll be heading up north to the Wirral next week to take some photos of the forest there. I'll be able to give you some rent after.'

'How long will you be gone for?'

'Just a week.' He smiled, leaning over to kiss her on the lips. 'We better make the most of the days we have left.'

Over the next couple of months Niall visited different submerged forests around the UK's coastline. He'd return and they would carry on as normal, but Charity noticed that he seemed preoccupied. When he returned from a visit to Dartmouth, he seemed in better spirits, grabbing her into a hug and twirling her around when she got back from work.

'You seem happy,' she said, laughing.

'They're going to exhibit my work!'

'Who are?'

'A gallery in King's Lynn. I just got the call while you were at work. The owner heard about the work I do and he wants to dedicate an entire space to my photographs.'

'That's brilliant, Niall!'

'I feel like things are really happening,' Niall said, blue eyes sparking with excitement. 'People are starting to take notice.'

'And so they should.'

'They're even having a drinks reception.' He quirked an eyebrow. 'I might need to buy a suit…and a dress for you. I'm going to treat you to one with the money I've earned.'

She smiled. 'I better make sure I'm not on call that night. When is it?'

'Twenty-first of March.' He closed his eyes. 'Shit, Charity, I'm so sorry. The anniversary of Faith's death. I'll get it changed.'

'No,' Charity said, shaking her head. 'I think it's a good thing.'

'You sure?'

She nodded. 'I'm sure.'

The reflection of the flame in the window seemed to dance over King's Lynn's cobbled streets outside. Charity took Niall's hand.

They were standing in the small gallery surrounded by Niall's photos, taking a few moments before people started arriving for his event to look at the candle Niall had lit for Faith.

They were quiet for a few moments and then Niall looked at Charity. 'Do you ever wonder why Faith was walking on the road in the middle of the night?'

Charity continued staring at the flame. 'Everyone did: my parents, the police. But we never found out. It's in the past.'

'She'd seemed different when I saw her a couple of weeks before. Preoccupied.'

'She was busy with her studies.'

Niall frowned. 'I don't know, I think it was more than that.'

Charity sighed. 'We'll never know, will we? Why bring it up now, Niall?'

'It's something I always think about on the anniversary. Not just what happened but why Faith was there, on that road.'

'Look, this is your night,' Charity said, squeezing his hand. 'Let's not ruin it.'

'You're right.' He reached into his pocket, pulling a box out. 'I have something for you.'

She opened it to find a delicate necklace inside, their two initials entwined in a pendant, just like the etchings.

'It's beautiful, Niall,' she said as he helped her put it on.

'All ready?' They turned to see the gallery owner, a short thin man with a bald head, smiling at them.

'As ready as I'll ever be,' Niall said, taking a deep breath as he looked around him at the photos he'd taken from his recent visits to the UK's submerged forests. Most of them were on land, eerie tree stumps spreading out over vast wastelands.

'It looks amazing,' Charity said, adjusting his tie. 'Now just enjoy yourself.'

Thirty minutes later, the tiny gallery was filled with people drinking wine and admiring the photos. Niall had been dragged away to talk to a local journalist and Charity stayed by the candle, watching him with pride. It almost felt as though Faith was by her side. She imagined her dressed in a beautiful pale blue dress, long blonde hair down her back, watching proudly too. But then the mirage of Faith seemed to change before Charity's eyes, hair dripping with rainwater, face bloody, a puddle around her bare feet.

Why *had* Faith been walking along the road alone that night?

Charity quickly drank some of her sparkling wine, willing the image away.

'You okay?' Niall asked, walking over to her.

'Fine. How's it going?'

His face lit up. 'Four photographs sold.'

'Already? Wow!'

'Charity! Niall!' a familiar voice exclaimed from nearby.

They both turned to see Lana North heading towards them, the hem of her sleek black dress swishing around her ankles. Dan was behind her, a glass of champagne in his hand, a small smile on his face. He was wearing light blue chinos and a casual white shirt, his handsome face was deeply tanned. His hair was a little longer, his blond fringe sweeping over the top of his green eyes.

Charity felt her stomach flip, remembering his green eyes burning into hers as he leant close to her on that boat.

She gripped Niall's hand tighter as though it was an anchor. He stared at Dan, his neck flushing.

'It's so great to see you both,' Lana said, leaning down to kiss Charity on the cheek. Charity smelt the strong scent of alcohol. 'We were so excited when we read about Niall's exhibition, we knew we had to come, didn't we, Dan? Especially seeing as we bought Niall the camera that took all these exquisite photos.'

Charity looked at Niall, confused. 'I don't understand.'

Niall's face flushed.

'You didn't tell Charity?' Lana asked. 'How strange.'

'Why would he, darling?' Dan said. He shook Niall's hand then gave Charity a quick kiss on the cheek. 'It was just a loan, wasn't it, Niall? Most of it's paid off now.'

Niall looked at Charity. 'I was going to mention it. But it's like Dan said, I've nearly paid it off.'

Charity stared at him, trying to control her emotions.

'These are wonderful, Niall,' Dan said, looking around him. 'You really are a true talent.'

Niall smiled tightly. 'Thank you, Dan. I wish we could stay and talk. But I hope you understand, there's a bunch of people I need to talk to. Thanks for coming.'

'Of course,' Dan said as Lana looked disappointed. 'Go mingle.'

'Why didn't you tell me you contacted Dan when you broke your camera?' Charity asked as they walked away.

'I was desperate, Charity,' Niall said under his breath. 'It was just a loan.'

'That's not the issue. It's the fact you didn't tell me.'

He sighed. 'Look, I was embarrassed, alright? All my talk of Dan being bourgeois and I go running to him for help.'

'There's nothing wrong with that, Niall. You shouldn't be ashamed. You know I'd never judge you.'

His face softened. 'I know. I should have told you. I'm sorry.'

'It's fine,' Charity said, stroking his cheek.

Niall peered towards Dan and Lana, grimacing. 'I wish they hadn't come, especially Lana. She's clearly drunk.'

'She's not that bad. And isn't it worth it? Without Dan's help you wouldn't have been able to take all those photos.'

His eyes remained on Lana, brow creased. 'I guess.'

An elderly couple approached Niall and started asking him questions. Charity excused herself and went to get a drink.

'Here, let me.' She turned to see Dan standing beside her, bottle in hand. He smiled, looking her up and down. 'I have to say, you look rather stunning tonight, Charity.'

Charity blushed. 'Thank you. That's quite a compliment coming from a man whose wife used to be a model.'

He looked down into his glass, frowning.

'Is everything okay?' Charity asked.

'Lana's still not great.'

'I'm sorry. So she didn't see any other counsellors after we spoke?'

'A few. Same old story, she grows bored of them. She's drinking a lot now too.'

'I noticed.'

'Sometimes I wonder…' He sighed, shaking his head. 'No, I'm being silly.'

'Tell me.'

He looked at her, his green eyes sinking into hers. 'Sometimes I wonder how different my life would be if I'd met someone like you instead of Lana.'

Charity looked at him in shock. 'Dan…'

He stepped towards her, his handsome face pained. 'That night on the boat. I think of it often, Charity. Don't you?'

'What night?' They both turned to see Lana standing behind him, a look of horror on her face.

'It was nothing, darling,' Dan said quickly.

Lana ignored him, just stared at Charity. 'Charity?' she asked, her voice trembling.

Charity tried to find the words. She looked up at Dan quickly, then away.

Lana's eyes filled with tears. 'God, look at the two of you, you can't keep your eyes off each other! Why am I surprised?'

She had raised her voice, and people around the room were glancing over. Charity's eyes searched the crowd, trying to find Niall.

'Oh well, I'm one to talk, aren't I, Dan?' Lana said, face hardening.

A fleeting look of panic crossed Dan's face. He tried to steer Lana away. 'Lana, darling, I think it's time we left, don't you?'

But Lana shrugged his arm off. 'We might as well just tell her,' Lana said. 'Then it'll *all* be out in the open.'

'Tell me what?' Charity asked. 'I don't understand.'

'Niall and I slept together in India,' Lana said, crossing her arms and shooting Charity a triumphant look.

Charity's stomach plummeted as she looked at Lana. 'What?'

Dan sighed. 'Oh, Lana.'

'You knew?' Charity asked him.

'Lana told me a few months ago.'

'When did it happen?' Charity asked, trying to keep the tremble from her voice.

'Dan and I argued,' Lana said, sounding bored. 'I came to the hotel to find him. I'd pretended I'd left but I hadn't. I didn't expect him to go running to you. I ended up finding a very depressed and drunk Niall instead and one thing led to another…' Her voice trailed off as she shrugged. 'These things happen.'

Charity thought back to that night when she found him waiting outside her villa. Had he been with Lana just before that?

But what about her and Dan? Hadn't they nearly kissed too?

What a mess.

Niall appeared from the crowds, a smile on his face when he noticed Charity. She looked at him, unable to comprehend what Lana had said. She shoved past Lana and went to him.

'Is it true?' she asked. 'You and Lana in India. Is it true?'

He closed his eyes briefly. Then he reached for Charity's hand, his face desperate. 'I was drunk. Very drunk.'

'I can't believe this.'

'You and I weren't together then, Charity.'

'But we'd shared those moments. Then you go and *sleep* with Lana?'

'We argued, remember? I had a few drinks, I hardly remember it,' Niall said. 'I don't care about all this, all I care about is you. Let's just go back to our hotel and—'

'And what? No, I need to be alone.'

She shrugged his hand off and strode from the gallery, jumping into her car. As she drove back to the hut, she tried to block out the thought of Niall with Lana. When she drew up outside the hut forty-five minutes later, she was shocked to see Hope sitting on the bench outside, a suitcase by her feet. Charity jumped out of her car and ran to her, grabbing her into a hug. 'You don't know how happy I am to see you right now.'

'Clearly!' Hope pulled away from her, looking Charity up and down. 'Where have you just come from, a school prom?'

Charity looked down at her dress. 'Just a party. What are you doing here?'

'I said I'd contact you when I was ready, didn't I? I didn't expect to have to wait in the freezing cold for three hours though.' She pulled her long purple suede coat around her small frame and shivered.

'You've been here three hours? You should have called first!'

'I didn't know I was going to forgive you. I just woke this morning and realised I had.'

Charity couldn't help but smile. 'So I'm forgiven?'

'You were a kid, foolish and in love. I just wish you'd told me you were in the car when it happened.'

Charity squeezed her sister's hand. 'I'm sorry. Truly.'

Hope examined Charity's face under the lamplight. 'Have you been crying?'

Charity nodded.

'What happened?' Hope asked.

'Long story. Let's get you inside.'

'Is it Niall?' Hope asked.

'How did you know?'

Hope jutted her chin towards Niall's motorbike that was parked down the side of the hut.

'Oh.'

Hope looked up at the dark sky in frustration. 'How could you go running back to him, Charity?'

Charity didn't say anything, just looked out to sea.

'Tell me what happened?' said Hope.

After Charity told her sister, Hope wrinkled her nose. 'Really? Niall and Lana North?' She shrugged. 'Maybe they suit each other. And didn't you and Dan nearly kiss? I think this speaks volumes about you and Niall.'

'What do you mean?'

'What you have is shallow. You *think* you love Niall. But what you love is the memory of those exciting months *before* Faith was snatched away from us – before he took her away.' Hope shifted around on the bench so she was facing Charity, strands of her long red hair lifting in the wind. 'Don't you see, it was your golden age, exhilarating trysts with a rebellious young man, stolen kisses on the beach. It's everything a teenage girl dreams of. Well, I dreamt about what book I was going to read next but that's by the by.' She took Charity's hand, looking into her eyes. 'The point is, after Faith died, everything turned grey. You've been hoping to get back those days when Faith was alive by rekindling your romance with Niall. That's why you don't blame Niall for what happened that

184

night. If you did, you'd lose him…and therefore everything that happened before. To move on, Charity, you need to move on from Niall. But it scares you because it's the unknown.'

Charity let out a slow breath.

'Charity?'

They both looked up to see Niall approaching them in the darkness.

'The question now is,' Hope said quietly as she watched him walk towards them, 'are you ready to move on from the past?' She turned to Charity. 'Are *we*?'

'What do you mean, we?'

Hope smiled. 'I've put the café up for sale. Fancy running away somewhere?'

Charity looked between Niall and Hope.

Time to choose.

Chapter Fourteen

Willow

Norfolk, UK
October 2016

I take in the rotting tree stumps littered around the beach then peer up at the grey skies, letting the fine mist of drizzle wet my face. I need the cool rain to calm me down. Ever since I left Austria two weeks ago, I've felt something buzzing inside: a hunger to know more about my family's past…and its future. If Niall Lane is my father and Luki is my brother, that changes everything.

I pull Niall Lane's photograph of this forest out of my rucksack. He's a gifted photographer, somehow making what's a dull wedge of a place into something right out of some gothic novel. Maybe it's the angle he chose, down low so the camera lens is looking right up at a tree stump, dozens of stumps spreading out in the background. Even the brown seaweed that slimes over the tree stumps looks arty, the stumps' roots reaching out like rotting innards.

As I look at the photograph, I think of the fact Mum might have been here when Niall Lane took it. They'd lived here together after all. I shrug my rucksack over my shoulder and take a deep weary breath. I'm not entirely sure what I'm hoping to achieve by being here. Aunt Hope seemed to have developed yet another case of amnesia when I asked her where Mum and Niall lived. So it's not like I can visit their place. But I felt drawn here, like I needed to come to the place Mum once lived.

I walk around the submerged remains of the trees trying to see if I can find another etching, squatting down to get a look at each stump. After a while my knees begin to ache. It's easier doing this underwater. Finally, I find it, a hint of a looping 'C' under some seaweed. I pull the seaweed away and settle back on my heels, ignoring the pain in my knees as I stare at the etching.

'So,' I say to myself, 'here it is.' I take a photo with my phone, might as well keep a memento of my own. I think of the way I obliterated the etching I found in India. I won't be so childish this time. Instead I trace my finger across Mum's initial. Maybe she touched it too? Thinking about that gets me all choked up.

I stand, wiping the tears from my cheeks as I pull my grey woollen coat around myself. It's getting windy, and bloody freezing. Time for a bath, maybe some Irish coffee. Then I can figure out how to find out where Mum and Niall lived.

As I head back to my hotel in my hired car a few minutes later, I'm relieved to be leaving the forlorn landscape behind, the view outside my car window replaced by wispy green marshes, even a hint of blue sky. It's like the clouds gathered just for my visit to the submerged forest. Now I'm gone, they've scattered.

After a while, I realise I'm driving through a village I don't recognise. White cottages topped with thatched roofs line the road, the spire of a church rising ahead of me.

'Bugger, I'm lost,' I murmur to myself.

I stop outside a small newsagent's and try to get the sat nav up on my phone. But there's no reception. I jump out of the car and stride into the shop. It's tiny, so tiny I knock a row of crisps off a shelf as I squeeze down the narrow aisle. I grab some supplies – an energy drink, some cereal bars and, what the hell, a few bottles of beer. As I pay, I ask the bored teenager behind the counter if he knows where my hotel is. He mumbles some directions and I head back out, carrier bag swinging.

That's when I notice the lighthouse in the distance. It looks just like the lighthouse from a photo that was packed away with a bunch of others from Mum's study after she died. I'd scoured them for hours, picking out all the tiny details.

It can't be a coincidence.

I head towards it. When I get there, marshes spread out before me, the sea soft and calm beyond. I'm on a small lane looking out on to the sea, a weather-beaten old bench perched on the marshes to my left, something else I recognise from the photo. I look around the corner and see a row of beach huts lining the lane. They're all the same army-green colour, the paint peeling.

The photo must have been taken from outside one of those huts, judging by the angle.

Did Mum stay here with Niall Lane? Did *he* take the photo?

I go to the first hut. Like the others, it has a small veranda at its front. It seems empty so I'm not surprised when there's no answer to my knock. Bright blue curtains hang from the window in the hut next to it, a gold wind chime tinkling in the breeze. There's a TV on inside. I take a deep breath and knock on the door. The TV goes silent then I hear floorboards creaking before the door swings open to reveal a woman in her mid forties with white hair and sparkling blue eyes.

'How can I help?' she asks in a brisk voice.

'I think my mum may have stayed in one of these huts years ago,' I reply. 'She passed away when I was a kid so I'm visiting all the places she stayed.'

Her face softens. 'Oh, I'm sorry to hear that. There's a chance she may have rented the place. My mother used to rent it out back in the day. No records mind, my mother was scatty as anything.' My heart sinks. 'But we've got a box of items people left behind over the years just in case they come back for them. You could have a look through, see if there's anything you recognise?' She opens the door wide. 'I'm Jean. Come in, have a cuppa while you're looking through it all.'

'Are you sure?'

'Sure I'm sure.'

I might as well give it a go. What else have I got to do? Gorge myself on energy drinks, chocolate and beer all alone in my hotel room?

'Thanks,' I say as I walk inside. 'I'm Willow, by the way.'

'Lovely name.'

I welcome the warmth as I walk in. It's brightly decorated inside with sapphire blue walls and framed paintings of lions and tigers on the walls. Expensive-looking teddy bears of different colours line the top of the cream sofas and I almost miss the tabby who's licking its paws next to one of them.

'When did your mum pass away, Willow?' Jean asks.

'When I was seven.'

She sighs. 'That must have been difficult for you.'

I make my face a mask like I always do when people get like this. 'I was too young to understand really,' I lie.

'Make yourself at home, I'll go put the kettle on.' As she walks from the room I sit down on one of the sofas and place my hand on its seat. Did Mum sit here once? The sofa doesn't look old enough to have been here nearly thirty years.

I look around the room. There's a long mahogany bureau that lines the wall across from me with several framed photos of smiling families behind the glass doors. Aunt Hope only has one photo on display in the house, an old one of her with the poet Ted Hughes from an event she attended. None of Mum, or of my grandparents. None of me neither…nor my Aunt Faith. Maybe it's for the same reason she doesn't tell me much, it hurts.

Jean comes out with a tray of tea and biscuits, placing it on the scratched mahogany coffee table in the middle of the room. Then she strides back into the kitchen before bringing out a large cardboard box.

'Let me help,' I say, jumping up.

'No, no, it's fine, really. I'm stronger than I look thanks to all the gardening I do.' She gestures towards patio doors that look out on to a small well-kept garden.

'Very nice,' I say.

'Thank you. Keeps me busy…and fit.'

She places the box on a pine table in the corner of the room then settles into the seat across from me.

'Sugar?' she asks as she pours me tea.

'Three please.'

She laughs. 'Good for you. Too many girls your age obsess about dieting. I bet you're like me, as long as you're fit and active, you keep the pounds off.'

I smile. 'I think I am.'

'So, do you know when your mother stayed here?'

'I'm not sure. There's a photo my mum had of the area just outside this place. There was a banner across one of the gift shops in the distance saying something about the village's two hundred year centenary?'

'That'd be 1987. She may have been here when the Great Storm hit.'

'Storm?'

She smiles sadly. 'It barely appears on the radar for you youngsters. It affected most of the UK, eighteen people died, one of them

191

from Norfolk. I had to muck in that night with my mum,' she says, peering towards a photo of what I presume is a teenage Jean standing next to a woman with short blonde hair, the lighthouse in the background.

I ache for photos like that of a teenage me with Mum. I don't even think I have any of me with Aunt Hope, she was never one for cameras. The only photos from my teen years are ones taken at school.

Jean hands me my tea in a 'World's Greatest Grandma' mug and I take a sip.

I look towards an old photo she has of her with an elderly lady who I presume is her mum, their arms around each other. 'You're lucky to have had such a special relationship with your mum,' I say.

'Oh, it wasn't always like that. We used to argue like crazy, I always thought she was a battle-axe and she thought I was a spoilt brat.' She offers me more biscuits. 'You look disappointed to hear that.'

'Do I? I guess I had this vision of you two being some mother-daughter superhero act.'

She chuckles. 'Mum would like that description! No, on the contrary, she had to force me to help her with the storm. But you know what? Now I have my daughters, I realise it's a rite of passage, hating your mother for a bit.' She puts her hand to her mouth. 'Oh, Willow, I'm sorry. Here's me going on about mother and daughter relationships and your mum passed away before you had a chance to know any of this.'

'Don't apologise, it's fine, really.'

'Did you grow up with your dad?'

'My dad passed away too. Remember the cruise ship that sank in Greece, the MS *Haven*? They were on it.' I feel sick, the orange jelly of the Jaffa Cake squirming over my tongue.

Jean shakes her head. 'Oh good Lord, how terrible. Did family take you in?'

'My aunt.'

'How wonderful of her. Do you get on?'

I hesitate.

'Ah, so you *did* experience a mother-daughter relationship,' she says.

'I wouldn't quite say that. We really clashed, still do.'

'Maybe it's because you're so similar, that's why my mum and I clashed.'

I shake my head. 'No, we're not at all alike.' I look at the box. 'Okay if I look through?' I ask, wiping the crumbs from my hands.

'Of course,' she says, standing up. 'I'll give you some space. Shout if you need anything.'

When she leaves the room, I approach the box. Written across it in faded black is 'Lost Property'. I open it up, dust bursting out at me. I wave my hands about, coughing. It's clearly been a while since anyone's opened it. There are the usual suspects in there, scarves and partner-less gloves; battered old books and lipsticks. As I delve further, I find some more unusual items, like a bright blue wig, a long sharp animal tooth and even a pair of false teeth which I try not to touch.

I flick through the books, try to find any writing inside and search a notepad too. But all it contains are passages from the Bible. There are a couple of newspaper cuttings, one about a baby winning a child model contest – the baby looks like Winston Churchill to me, but then they all do. And then some letters, mainly gas bills.

Then as I get to the bottom of the pile I notice a blurry photo of four teenagers – three girls, one boy – on a beach.

And behind them, Aunt Hope's house, the one I grew up in.

This clearly belonged to Mum.

The sea is grey behind them, the skies above thick with white cloud. I recognise my mum instantly with her distinctive cloud of black hair and beautiful face, her head thrown back in laughter, shapely legs darting out from cut-off denim shorts as she sits on the pebbles. She must be about fifteen or sixteen in this photo. I recognise Aunt Hope too, how can you not with that long red hair, her skinny pale arms? She's sitting on a rock, knees drawn up to her chest with her chin resting on her knees as she watches another girl.

My Aunt Faith?

I peer closer. She really is beautiful, long blonde hair to her waist, round cheeks and blue eyes. She's wearing a simple white dress, long legs crossed beneath her, a concentrated look on her face as she cleans her diving mask.

And then next to her, a boy about Mum's age with dark skin and hair, his blue eyes on Mum.

Niall Lane.

It's clear from this photo that he knew all three sisters, not just Mum. Plus he dived with them.

'Find something?' Jean asks, coming back into the room.

'Yes, a photo,' I say. 'Okay if I take it?'

'Of course,' she says.

I look at her family photos in the bureau again and feel unbearably lonely.

I quickly gulp down the tea she made, scorching my tongue. 'I better head back,' I say. 'Thanks for the tea.'

'Not a problem. You take care alright?'

I smile. 'I will.'

When I get back to my room, I open my beer and sit by the window, feet up as I stare out at the sea. It looks infinite. The clouds have completely disappeared now, the sun streaming in, warming my skin. I lean back, taking a sip of beer as I imagine all the summer holidays Mum, Hope and Faith must have spent together by the beach. Was Niall with them during all those summers too?

I reach for my rucksack and pull the map of submerged forests out. Why has Niall Lane spent most of his life taking photos of submerged forests? Did it start as an homage to Faith? Or was he the one who inspired Faith to do this map?

Something catches my eye under the glare of sunlight. I peer closer. It's an imprint of writing, like someone has leant on the map to write a letter.

I sit up, manoeuvring the map around, trying to make out what it says.

…just not sure I can do it. The past few weeks have been
the unhappiest of my life. I'm so confused but most of all
I'm scared.
  I just wish you'd understand what I'm going through.

Faith. x

I look at the photo of Faith. She was scared? I reach for my phone and call Aunt Hope.

'Hello?' she asks when she answers. She sounds tired.

'It's Willow.'

'Are you back?'

'Yes, I got back yesterday.'

'Where are you then?'

'Norfolk. I found the place Mum lived with Niall Lane.'

'I see.'

'I found a photo of you with Mum, Faith and Niall too. Were you all friends?'

'I wouldn't call Niall a *friend* as such. He just turned up one day and we couldn't quite get rid of him.' She sighs. 'Willow, I hope you're not trying to find him. I'm certain he isn't your father.'

'Wouldn't you want to know who your father was if there was a chance the one you grew up with wasn't?'

'I suppose,' she says begrudgingly. 'But Dan was a good man, Willow. Niall…well, put it this way, you're better off not having someone like him as your father.'

'What's that supposed to mean?'

There's a pause. 'Niall Lane killed my sister Faith.'

I sit up in my chair, nearly dropping my beer. 'What?'

'He was driving the car that hit her.'

'Jesus. Why didn't you tell me?'

'I've told you already, I don't see any sense dredging up the past.'

'I Googled him though, it didn't come up in any searches.'

'He was young and it was before the internet was used the way it is today.'

I look at Niall's sullen young face in the photo, then at Faith's beautiful one. Then I think of what I've just read on the map. 'Did he mean to do it?' I ask Aunt Hope.

'No. Why would you ask that?'

I explain what I've just read.

'Scared?' Aunt Hope says after, voice trembling. 'I don't understand. I want to see her writing.'

'I don't understand either. But you're saying Niall Lane was responsible for her death.'

'It was an accident. I hate him for it but it was an accident. He wouldn't have done it on purpose. He adored Faith, just like we all did.'

Aunt Hope is quiet for a moment. Then I hear the quiet sound of her sobbing.

'Oh, Aunt Hope,' I say, my heart going out to her.

'It's just bringing it all back, that's all,' she says, sniffing. 'Faith didn't seem herself before she died. But she had just started university. Oh, I don't know. Clearly something was upsetting her. But to be frightened? That makes no sense.'

I continue staring at the photograph of Niall. 'I need to meet Niall Lane, ask him about all this.'

'He doesn't know any more than we do.'

'How will we know until I ask him? It's not just Faith,' I say. 'I need to do it for me, too. I need to look him in the face and ask him if he's my father.'

'You won't be able to find him. He's here, there and everywhere.'

'Actually,' I say, looking at the outline of Kazakhstan on the map and thinking of what the woman at the gallery in Austria had told me, 'I think I know where he'll be.'

Chapter Fifteen

Charity

Busby-on-Sea, UK
May 1988

Charity swept her cloth across the table then paused, looking out at the grey sea. Hard to believe she was here, summer chasing her tail again. At least it was different this time. She'd be leaving soon.

She peered at her sister who looked thoroughly bored as some tourists tried to make conversation with her. She just wished Hope was coming with her. The sale of the café had fallen through after the survey revealed some problems, and no other buyers had come forward since. In the meantime, another opportunity had come up for Charity, this time a permanent job as a student counsellor at Southampton University – the university Faith had attended. She even got reduced rate accommodation, meaning she wouldn't have to travel there and back. She and Hope agreed she'd do it for six months, giving them enough money to help sort some of the problems with the café and finally get it sold. But the fact it was a permanent contract felt strange to Charity, like maybe she'd never be back.

If she didn't return, did that mean she'd never see Niall again? She thought back to the last time she'd seen him, the night of his gallery opening when he'd turned up outside the beach hut.

'I feel like I don't really know you,' Charity had said to him.

'I'm still the same man. You know me better than anyone!'

'Do I? Maybe I'm just in love with the past, the *good* past, before Faith died,' Charity said, repeating what Hope had said to her.

Niall's face had dropped. 'So what are you saying? You're not in love with me?'

'I – I don't know. We've been living in a bubble for the past few months. Now reality has hit and I'm not sure I know what's real and what's just based on what I remember.'

He shook his head. 'I don't believe you. You're just upset about Lana.'

'It's not just about Lana, Niall. Dan and I nearly kissed too.'

Niall looked at her in disbelief. 'When?'

'In India, after we argued. Doesn't that speak volumes?'

His blue eyes flashed with anger. 'It tells me you're a hypocrite. How can you be annoyed about what happened with Lana when you and Dan did what you did?'

'But the difference is we didn't actually do anything! Look,' Charity said, putting her head in her hands. 'I just need time away from the bubble. I need to figure out if what we have is real or if it's just based on the past.'

'You take your time, Charity,' Niall said, standing. 'But don't take too long. The longer you take, the more I'll start to believe you really don't love me.'

Then he'd walked away.

Charity looked out at the sea now, wondering where Niall was. She hadn't heard from him since that night. That was a good thing; she *did* need time to think. But what if she couldn't get hold of him when she needed to? Truth was, her heart ached for him, her body missed his touch. But each time she thought of him, she also thought of Lana…and what Hope had said about Charity being in love with the past.

'Hello, love!' a man called from a table nearby. 'Can we order some food, please?'

'Of course, sorry! Was in my own little world there!' She rushed over and took an order from the couple. As she walked away, something caught her eye in the distance: a man standing at the end of the promenade in a long grey wool coat, shoulders hunched as he huddled against the cold. Something about the blond of his hair and the tanned curve of his neck sparked a flicker of recognition. He turned as though sensing her eyes on him.

Dan.

Even from where she was standing, Charity could tell he looked terrible. His blond hair was longer, messy, his face specked with stubble. There were circles under his eyes, a pained expression on his face.

She'd heard he had gone to the States on business since she'd seen him in Norfolk. She reached her hand up to wave at him. He did the same and stepped forward, then paused, brow creasing. Maybe he felt awkward? She beckoned him over, not wanting him to feel like that around her. It wasn't his fault what had happened between Niall and Lana, was it?

He seemed to relax and strolled towards her. When he got to her, she quickly leant in, pressing her lips against his cheek in greeting. His skin felt stubbled beneath her lips, a soft hint of citrus rising from his neck. She breathed it in, felt her heart begin to race. She quickly moved away from him and they stood looking at each other, awkwardness swelling around them.

She opened her mouth. 'So how—'

'When did you—' Dan said at the same time.

They both laughed.

'I was going to ask,' Dan said, 'when did you return to Busby?'

'Over a month ago. But I'll be leaving again soon. I'm moving to Southampton.'

His face flickered. 'My office is based there.'

Charity smiled. 'I had no idea. We could meet up!'

'I'm afraid I'm selling the mansion then moving to the States.'

'The States?'

He nodded. 'I'm interested in learning more about the world of cruise ships. They seem to know how to do it out there.'

'And they don't know it in Southampton?'

'Not at the grand scale I'm aiming for.'

Her heart sank. 'That sounds exciting.'

'So does your new job, Charity. You'll be wonderful there.' He paused a moment. 'You're going alone?' he asked carefully.

'Yes. Niall and I are taking a break.' That felt strange to say out loud.

Dan sighed. 'Snap. Lana and I are having a break too.'

'I'm sorry to hear that.' The bin nearby shuddered as a large seagull landed on it, pecking at a half-eaten sandwich. 'I won't miss those things,' Charity said, shooing it away. Dan watched her, eyes hooded. 'Are you coming in for a cuppa? It's quiet. I might even be able to grab a drink with you, I'm due a break.'

He shook his head, his blond hair falling into his tired eyes. 'No, sorry, I need to head back. I'm meeting with an estate agent.'

'Maybe before we both disappear, we can grab a coffee? I'm working here every day until I leave.'

Hesitation registered in his eyes. 'I'll try. It's pretty hectic at the moment. Take care, Charity.' He looked into her eyes, the emotion that she saw in his almost took her breath away. Then he turned and strode down the promenade, the wind whipping up the tails of his coat.

Charity put her hand to her beating heart. Why was she reacting like this?

She turned around and caught her sister watching her with a smile on her face. She shushed her away, hurrying into the café.

When Dan didn't turn up at the café the next day, Charity impulsively decided to drive to his house. As she turned into his drive, she was surprised to see the once immaculate lawns were now messy with weeds, the hedges misshapen and overgrown. Surely with Dan's money he had gardeners to keep the place tidy when he was away? Even the ruby gates were open, the marble stairs leading to the front door filthy with mud and leaves.

When she rang the doorbell, nobody answered. But just as she went to walk away, the door swung open and Dan appeared. He was wearing jeans and a loose black jumper, his face creased as though he'd been sleeping.

He frowned. 'Charity?'

'I wanted to say goodbye. I was at work yesterday so couldn't talk properly, and it just doesn't feel right, that being the last time we might ever speak.' She realised she was talking in a garble. 'Bit of an impulsive decision really. Just as well you're in,' she joked.

He didn't invite her in, just stood staring at her, blinking. She thrust her hands into the pockets of her coat.

'Sorry, where are my manners,' he said, seeming to suddenly wake up. 'Please, do come in.'

She stepped inside. There were cardboard boxes strewn all over the huge hallway and the tropical heat that had greeted her the first time she'd been there was replaced by a draught.

Dan closed the door then smoothed his messy hair down. He still hadn't shaved. 'Come through,' he said, leading Charity past the dining room they'd had dinner in over a year ago. Charity glanced inside, noticing the explicit murals had been scraped off the wall. Had Dan done that, or Lana? She'd seen patients do this in the past too, strip away the wallpaper they'd carefully put up with their ex-partner; taking new sofas they'd bought together to the dump. She didn't have much of Niall's to throw away.

They entered a large all-white kitchen at the back of the house.

'Sorry for the mess,' Dan said as he pulled some newspapers off a stool so Charity could sit down at the marble bar table. 'Been pretty busy sorting out my move over to the States. Cup of tea?'

'Yes, thanks.'

Dan made the tea then handed her a mug, taking the stool next to her, brow creased as he looked into his tea.

'Are you okay, Dan?' she asked him.

He peered up, his tired eyes looking into hers. 'I'm fine.' She raised an eyebrow at him and he smiled. 'I suppose you're not a qualified counsellor for nothing. Okay, here's the truth. The reason I'm such a mess is I'm lonely and it scares the hell out of me.'

'I understand, trust me.'

'Hold on with the sympathy for a moment. It's not Lana herself I miss, but the knowledge that someone's always here when I get home. It really hit me after coming home from the States to this ridiculously huge house,' he said, looking around him. 'It feels impossibly empty with just me here. Is that selfish of me, not to miss Lana but the fact the house seemed less empty with her in it?'

Charity took a sip of her tea. 'Of course not.'

Over the next couple of hours they drank more tea and Dan talked about how difficult things were with Lana and how devastated he'd been when she'd confessed that she'd slept with Niall. Soon darkness fell outside, the rain providing a soft rhythmic thrum against the kitchen's vast windows. Charity knew she ought to head back home but she didn't want to. She wanted to stay and listen to Dan's low voice, watch the way his black lashes cast shadows across his tanned cheeks. If she left now, there'd only be one day left before she'd be miles away and there was every chance she might never see him again.

She didn't like that feeling. She wasn't quite sure what she could do about it but she knew she didn't want to leave right now.

'Are you hungry?' Dan asked.

'I am actually.'

'We can order something in,' he said, gesturing towards a pile of takeaway leaflets on the table.

'I can cook something.'

He peered at the fridge. 'Nothing here to cook.'

'Then come to my house,' Charity said impulsively. 'Hope will be at one of her readings. I make a mean lasagne.'

Dan hesitated a moment then he took in a deep breath. 'Alright. What the hell?'

Fifteen minutes later Charity was letting Dan into her family's home. As she walked down the hallway towards the living room she was praying her sister had collected the bras they'd both been drying on the radiators and put them upstairs. As she turned the lights on, she saw that she hadn't.

'Sorry, bit of a mess,' she said, grabbing the bras and shoving them into a drawer as Dan raised an eyebrow.

Dan glided his fingers over a cat ornament sitting on one of the tables in the narrow hallway. 'Don't worry. It's nice to see somewhere that looks lived in.'

'It's lived in alright. Come through to the kitchen.' She led him through to their kitchen with its huge pine table and old-fashioned units.

'Take a seat, I'll get you a glass of wine,' Charity said, gesturing towards one of the chairs around the table. 'You can have one glass of wine, right?'

205

'Sure. But let me help cook.'

'No, really.'

'Please,' Dan said, rolling up the sleeves of his jumper. 'I insist.'

'Fine then, you can chop the veg.'

Over the next few minutes, they worked together to make dinner, falling into a natural rhythm.

'How do you feel about leaving the town behind again?' Dan asked.

Charity stared out of the window at the scene she'd woken up to every morning as a child, the long wisps of grass fringing a stretch of pebbly beach; the grey turbulent sea beyond. 'It's strange, I've always been so desperate to leave Busby-on-Sea and my memories behind that I sometimes forget the good memories.'

'But being away from here will help ease the grief, like you said it did when you went to London.'

'*Ease* it,' Charity said, turning the gas hob on. 'But it'll still be there.' She peered behind her at Dan. 'Is that why you're going to the States, to leave the memories of your parents behind? And Lana?'

He smiled. 'I thought I'd give it a go. It worked for you when you went to London years ago, didn't it?'

'Maybe. Maybe not.'

'So tell me about your new job.'

'I'll be counselling students. I imagine a lot of what I'll be dealing with will be exam-related stress. But there will also be new students struggling with being away from home and students who will come to me with historic problems. It'll make a change from the stuff I've done in the past.'

'You seem excited.'

She smiled. 'I am.'

'What would you say is the most important skill for a counsellor to have?'

Charity thought about it for a moment. 'Sounds obvious really, but listening. My sister Faith used to tell me I talked too much and didn't listen enough. She used to quote Winston Churchill: "Courage is what it takes to stand up and speak; courage is also what it takes to sit down and listen."'

Dan smiled. 'I like that.'

Charity threw some mince into a saucepan and watched it sizzle as she stirred it around. Dan carried the vegetables over, scraping them in with the meat as Charity poured chopped tomatoes and stock over the mixture. Once the dish was in the oven, cheese gratings and vegetable skins all over the floor, they both collapsed on to the old brown sofa with their half-empty glasses of wine.

'Smells good,' Dan said, twisting around to face Charity, his arm resting against hers. 'Haven't had a home-cooked meal in God knows how long.'

'Hope and I cook together every night. I guess it's a habit.' Dan looked towards the book Hope was always scribbling in, open flat down on the table, its spine battered and creased. It was made from dark brown leather, an intricate floral pattern all over it. Faith had got it for her when she was just ten. 'Has your sister ever been in love?' Dan asked.

'I don't think she has. I mean, she reads and writes about all these romantic liaisons, but doesn't seem to have had any herself. You know, she was accepted on to a really great writing course in East Anglia before Faith died. She turned it down so she could stay and be there for us all.'

'I didn't know that.'

'Hope's made a lot of sacrifices for our family.' Charity felt her eyes fill with tears. 'I feel a bit selfish actually. What have I ever done for her?'

Dan put his hand on Charity's arm. 'You've worked at the café, looked after her when she was ill, been there for her as she has been for you. You mustn't always feel so guilty, Charity. You're a special woman.'

Charity thought of what he'd said in Norfolk about wondering how his life would have been if he'd met her instead of Lana. How would *her* life have been if Dan had been that boy they'd met on the beach all those years ago?

Would Faith still be alive?

They both fell silent and the atmosphere suddenly felt charged, the space between them electric.

'Charity,' Dan said, eyes searching hers, 'am I imagining what's happening between us?'

'No.'

The front door opened and they both went quiet as Hope appeared in the hallway, her whole body drenched, her red hair loose to her waist, rain dripping on to the floor from its ends. She blinked in the semi-darkness at Charity and Dan, a haunted look in her eyes.

'Hope, are you okay?' Charity asked, jumping up and striding towards her sister.

Hope scrabbled around in her bag, avoiding Charity's gaze. 'Fine, all fine.' Her voice was trembling.

'You're not fine, what happened?'

'I saw the police officer, if you must know,' Hope said, eyes still on her bag.

'Police officer?' Charity said. 'I don't understand.'

Hope looked up at her sister, her grey eyes slightly wild. 'The one who was in charge of the investigation into Faith's death.'

Charity went very still as Dan hovered in the kitchen, brow puckered as he watched the two sisters.

'He was in the pub where they were holding the poetry reading,' Hope continued. 'I recognised him straight away. He was older but – but it was definitely him. Funny how some faces scorch themselves on to your soul, isn't it?' She let out a muffled sob, slamming her hand over her mouth.

Charity put her arm around her sister's thin shoulders and steered her to the bench in the hallway to put some space between the two of them and Dan. Hope slumped down on to it, clutching the wooden seat with her fingers as she stared at the wall.

'Why are you soaked through?' Charity asked.

'I was supposed to be getting a lift with Angela but she was faffing about. I had to get out of there.' She stopped talking, peering into the kitchen at Dan. Her gaze dropped away from him. 'Anyway, I couldn't wait for her, so I just walked home.'

'In the rain?' Charity asked. 'That pub's ages away.'

'I had to get out of there.'

The aroma of garlic and roasting tomatoes wafted around them, reminding Charity of the lasagne in the oven. Wind lashed against the window and it seemed to force Dan out of his reverie. He grabbed his coat and strode down the hallway. 'I'll leave you both to it.'

Charity stood. 'Dan, you don't have to—'

He looked into her eyes. 'You have to be here for your sister.' He quickly kissed her on the cheek, the heat of his lips a shock on her cold skin. 'Good luck with the new job, Charity.' Then he let himself out into the rain. Charity closed the door and turned to her sister.

'Hope, what's wrong?' she asked her.

Hope shook her head, tears streaming down her pale cheeks. 'Our poor darling sister was pregnant when she died, Charity. That bastard didn't just kill our Faith, he killed our niece or nephew too.'

Charity tried to focus on scrubbing a particularly stubborn stain from one of the café's tables the next morning. But all she could see was Faith, her poor vulnerable *pregnant* sister. She quickly wiped away a tear as a couple nearby watched her with knitted brows. Surely her parents would have known, they'd have been told about the autopsy results. What a shock it must have been for them. And thank God they hadn't passed the information on to her and Hope; Charity wasn't sure she'd have been able to cope.

Could she cope now?

Dark emotions swelled inside her chest. She thought of that night, the car's headlights bouncing all over the dark road as the car slid down it in the rain, knocking her sister off the road.

Her sister and her baby.

'Oh, Jesus,' Charity whispered, putting her hand to her mouth

'Are you okay, Charity?' asked a woman with a small baby.

'Yep,' Charity said, forcing herself to speak, trying desperately not to look at the baby and think of Faith's baby. 'Must've been something I ate last night.' She quickly strode out of the café to the railings protecting the promenade from the sea and clutched at them, the cloth she'd been holding lifting in the wind and tumbling into the lashing waves below. She wanted to be under those waves right at that moment, sickening memories muffled by torrid waves, pulling her deeper and deeper.

She felt a hand on her shoulder and turned to see her sister watching her, face twisted with sadness.

'Can I have a break?' Charity said. 'Just a few minutes, I just need to walk. I just—' She swallowed, mouth feeling incredibly dry. 'Just a few minutes.'

'Shall I come with you, I could close the café for a bit?'

Charity shook her head. She needed to be alone. She'd just feel even worse with Hope's sad eyes watching her. Hope was lucky; she hadn't been there that night. She didn't have this terrible guilt to contend with. Charity quickly grabbed her sister's hand, giving it a squeeze before letting it go and hurrying down the promenade.

Thank God she was leaving Busby-on-Sea soon. She couldn't have stayed here with all these memories, even more so now.

Listen to yourself! she thought. Selfish, selfish, selfish. Maybe she *should* stay and punish herself. Why should she be given the chance of a decent life when Faith had had that snatched away? She should call her new boss, tell her she couldn't take the job, carry on working at the café all her life and all the sad memories Busby-on-Sea represented until the day she died. That's what she deserved for being there that night, for not making Niall turn back.

The thought made her shudder. Every instinct made her want to run away. She'd die if she stayed, throw herself into the sea because how else would she be able to deal with things?

Worried she'd do just that, she walked away from the sea, eyes on the ground, fists dug deep into her pockets as tears streamed down her face.

Had Faith been planning to keep the baby? She was only nineteen but she'd always been so gentle, always wanting every creature to live. Charity wasn't sure Faith would have been able to face having an abortion. No wonder she was so unhappy those last few weeks.

Oh God, *two* lives snatched away in a few reckless seconds on a foggy road. It was unbearable! What would Niall say if he ever found out?

The sound of cars beeping dragged her from her thoughts. She was in the middle of the road.

Someone grabbed her arm, pulling her back to the promenade. Dan.

She let out a sob and he pulled her into his arms, the citrus smell of him wrapping itself around her. She felt cocooned, protected from the force of the wind, the memories and the terrible guilt. He let her sob against him, stroking her hair, whispering that everything would be okay.

'But it won't,' she mumbled into his coat. 'Nothing will ever be okay.'

Dan put his finger gently under her chin and tilted her face up. 'Is this because of what your sister was so upset about last night?'

She swallowed, unable to get the words out at first. But the way he was looking at her, face heavy with emotion, fingers soft, made her want to tell him everything. 'Faith was pregnant,' she whispered. '*Pregnant*,' she said again, the word fierce on her lips.

Dan took in a deep breath. 'I'm so sorry, Charity.'

Charity shook her head, the pain of the memories was excruciating. Dan placed his hands either side of her face and made her look at him again, his green eyes desperate. 'Stop tearing yourself apart over the past, I can't bear watching it.'

'I deserve it, can't you see that?' she said, so tempted to tell him she'd been in the car that night but unable to bring herself to.

'No. All I can see is a woman who's had her life monopolised by the actions of a boy she was once besotted with. You have to move on. Niall has. Why can't you?'

His eyes explored hers. Their faces were so close, his hands warm on her cold skin. When she looked into his eyes, it was like she was swimming under warm seas, sheltered, safe. She imagined what it must feel like to kiss him, to feel his lips against hers, soft and sealing a promise of something new, something good. It was irrational, inappropriate, but she wanted to know how that felt, to be kissed by someone who could help her forget.

A cloud moved over the hazy May sun above and shadows crept across the promenade. Dan sighed as though he was giving in and it set something in motion inside her. Before she even knew how she'd got there, she was pressing her lips against his, softly at first. Then their kiss grew more urgent and Charity clung on to him, scared she might fall if she let go. Her whole body weakened, softened, a contrast to when she kissed Niall, when all her nerves, all her fibres and her core buzzed with feeling.

Eventually, she had to pull away from Dan, scared she'd dissolve all together. They were both out of breath, eyes searching each other's face, hands entwined.

'When are you leaving for Southampton?' he asked her.

'Tomorrow morning.'

'I'm coming with you.'

'Yes,' she said, knowing it was the only right answer.

Chapter Sixteen

Charity

Busby-on-Sea, UK
May 1988

Charity lay in bed that night staring up at the ceiling, unable to stop herself from smiling. She thought of Dan's lips soft against hers, his green eyes heavy with emotion, and her cheeks grew hot. She turned on her side, scrunched her pillow to her belly. It just felt so right! She'd not wanted to leave his arms after that kiss. She'd felt so safe and protected from everything. But she had to get back to the café so they'd reluctantly parted, Dan telling her he'd be at the house the next morning at eight. He somehow understood she needed the night with her sister, their last together before Charity left.

But as she ate dinner silently with Hope that night, she wished she'd just gone to Dan's and continued what that kiss had started. There was too much sadness here, too many memories. She wanted to escape. Whenever Hope caught her eye, all she could think about was Faith and the child she'd been holding.

'Are you nervous?' Hope asked her as she took her plate.

'No, not really.'

'You seem nervous. Or preoccupied. *Something*. I can't put my finger on it.'

Her sister knew her so well.

'Dan and I kissed,' Charity admitted.

Hope shoved the plates in the sink and took her seat again, leaning forward to look Charity in the eye. 'When?'

'Earlier today, when I went for that walk.'

'When you were upset?'

Charity nodded. 'He comforted me. I feel—' She paused. 'I feel safe when I'm with him. Hopeful.'

'That's because all you're used to is Niall, who's anything but safe and hopeful.'

Charity didn't say anything.

'I'm pleased,' Hope said, a small smile on her face. 'I like Dan. Mainly because he's not Niall Lane. But also because he seems like a good person.'

'He's moving to the States.'

Hope's face fell. 'Oh, that's a shame.'

'He's giving me a lift to Southampton though.'

Hope raised an eyebrow. 'He *is* keen.'

'I guess. It feels a bit crazy.'

'The good kind of crazy?'

Charity nodded. 'The good kind. I'm not sure I could cope with any more of the bad kind of crazy.'

'Me neither. In fact, I have some news myself of the good kind of crazy.'

Charity smiled. 'You do?'

'I sent those poems I wrote in Austria off to a small publishing house and guess who called me today?'

'An editor?'

Hope nodded, the excitement in her eyes making Charity yelp with happiness. She jumped up and ran around the table, hugging her sister from behind. 'That's amazing, Hope!'

'He thinks they would make a wonderful book of poetry,' Hope said, peering up at Charity. 'I just need a few more poems to send to him then he wants us to meet up in Oxford. So I've done something spontaneous. I've booked a holiday to Kazakhstan to see the forest Faith loved the most.'

Charity's mouth dropped open. 'Wow, when?'

'July. Remember, Faith told us the forest was flooded after an earthquake in 1911 which caused a landslide? One of the survivors is turning a hundred and there's going to be a special vigil for him by the lake. The editor who's interested in my work thinks it will be really inspiring to go.'

'Sounds it. You're going alone?'

'Didn't you go to India alone? I'll have diving buddies.'

'That's brilliant, Hope, bloody brilliant.'

'I know. I'm so excited.' Hope grabbed Charity's hands and squeezed them, her grey eyes filling with tears. 'I know it's not far but I'll miss you. We *are* going to sell the café, you know.'

Charity felt tears spring to her own eyes. She loved her sister so much. 'We will. And anyway, it's just a six-month contract. I'll come back for your birthday and then there's that festival we said we'd go to together.'

Hope nodded resolutely. 'We will.'

The next morning, just as she had the first time she'd left home, Charity stood in the middle of the living room with her large red suitcase, looking around and breathing in the memories: a teenage Hope leaning down to pull a book out from one of the piles around the room, red hair trailing the floor. Faith curled up on the patchwork red and black armchair as she flicked through photos of underwater plants, a look of concentration on her pretty face. And then their parents, watching some documentary or another, her father's legs stretched out on his old leg-rest, her mother's curled under her, like Faith's. And there, a teenage Charity sitting on the window seat, seeing if she could see any sign of Niall in the distance.

Charity's stomach sank. Niall. He'd be devastated if he found out about her and Dan. But he'd made his bed, hadn't he?

An engine rumbled outside. She looked up to see one of Dan's plush cars pull up outside, a sleek green Jaguar. She smiled.

'Not a bad chariot,' Hope said from the doorway, a cup of herbal tea in her hands. She put it down and walked to the window, the two sisters watched as Dan stepped out of the car. He looked unbearably handsome, his blond hair shining under the sunshine. He adjusted the collar of his blue polo shirt then squinted up at the sun.

'He's rather gorgeous, isn't he?' Hope said.

Charity smiled. 'Not bad.'

'Don't get chocolate on those expensive car seats.'

'I'll try not to.'

'And remember to say *loo*, not toilet. Posh people don't like the word toilet.'

'His father ran tourist boats, Hope. He isn't the Prince of Wales.'

Hope smiled. 'Shame. I've always wanted to meet Princess Di. Do you think we look a bit weird just standing here watching him?'

'Completely.'

Dan looked up and Charity waved at him then turned to her sister. 'Obviously, this isn't goodbye.'

'Obviously. Just a brief interlude in the drama of Hope and Charity.'

'Very brief. There's the festival…'

'…and my birthday.'

Charity's face collapsed and she turned away. It felt like she was leaving for good, which ought to make her happy but she knew she'd miss her sister.

'Oh come on,' Hope said, pulling Charity into her arms, her own voice filled with tears. 'It's just Southampton, not Timbuktu. And you'll only be gone six months.'

'I know, but I'll miss you.'

'I'll miss you too,' Hope said, her voice sounding very small for a moment.

Charity put her hands either side of her sister's thin face. 'Remember to be nice to the customers.'

'I'm always nice to the customers!'

'And stop feeding the seagulls leftovers. You think I don't notice but I do.'

Hope sighed. 'If I must.' She picked up Charity's box and opened the door, Charity following with her suitcase. Dan was standing on the pathway, his hands in the pockets of his jeans. Charity held her breath for a moment as he looked into her eyes, her head swimming slightly.

'Drive carefully,' Hope said to him. 'Precious cargo on board.'

'I will,' Dan said, his eyes still on Charity.

'And don't let her feed any seagulls,' Hope added.

Charity laughed. 'Oh, Hope, I really will miss you.' They gave each other a hug and, as they pulled away, Charity noticed tears fill Hope eyes. 'I love you,' she said quickly. She didn't often say that to her sister but she'd so wished she'd said it to Faith before they lost her.

Hope smiled. 'You too, Charity.'

Dan took Charity's suitcase and Charity gave Hope's hand a quick squeeze then she followed Dan down the path, away from the home that she'd grown up in, and which held such wonderful and terrible memories.

During the journey they talked as though the kiss hadn't happened. But the tension in the car was there, slight glances, the way Dan watched her lips when she talked, her desperate desire to slide her hand over his each time he changed gear.

Halfway there, Dan pulled over on to the hard shoulder and pulled her into his arms, kissing her as cars whizzed by, making the car rock gently each time. Charity reached up, smoothing her fingertips through his hair, moving closer to him, her chest now against his, feeling the thump of his heart.

After a while they both looked up at each other.

'Sorry, I had to do that before I crashed the car,' he said.

She searched his face, saw the fine lines around his green eyes, those long black lashes, the straight line of his tanned nose. She couldn't help herself as she reached up, her fingers tracing a line down his cheek.

He put his hand over hers and leant down, pressing his lips softly against hers again. She sighed and folded into him.

'I suppose we better carry on driving if we want to get there by lunch,' Dan said reluctantly.

'I suppose.'

He started the car up again and it wasn't long before they arrived in Southampton. Her flat was housed in a tall brown brick house with large white sash windows. She hadn't actually visited it yet, just agreed to rent it after seeing photos that were sent to her in the post. But it was perfect, just a few minutes' walk from the university with a large sitting room and bedroom, and lovely period features such as ornate cladding on the ceilings and marble fireplace.

When they got into the flat, she looked out of the window imagining Faith jogging along the streets below to get to a lecture,

'Gorgeous view,' she said.

Dan didn't respond so she turned around. He was watching her intently, his chest rising and falling, and, before she knew it, they were walking towards each other. Dan wrapped his arms around her and pressed his lips gently against hers. She felt that softening she'd felt the day before during their first kiss, right in the very core of her, making her relax against him.

As their kisses grew deeper, Dan carefully pulled her jumper over her head, both of them laughing as Charity's dark hair grew static, standing on end. As she unbuttoned his shirt and pressed her hands against his warm tanned chest, they smiled at each other. With his eyes still on hers, Dan undid each button of her jeans and pulled them off for her, kissing her bare feet as he did so. She unbuttoned his jeans, gliding her fingers over the gold hair on his calves, feeling the muscles and soft skin.

They touched each other gently, carefully, Dan's face intense as his fingers, lips and tongue explored every part of her, savouring her until she couldn't bear it any more. She wrapped her legs around him, pressing herself against him, making him enter her with a gasp, and she saw a brief moment of vulnerability in his eyes.

It was so different from being with Niall. He'd been fast, passionate, lifting her into positions, nipping at her ear, moaning and rocking. Being with Dan was like soft ripples building in intensity instead of violent storms.

Charity woke later not even aware she'd fallen asleep. Dan was in the small kitchen in just his pale blue boxer shorts, blond hair in his eyes as he beat an egg in a bowl.

'I didn't know I'd brought eggs with me,' Charity said, wrapping the sheet around herself and padding into the kitchen.

He glanced up, smiling. 'I did.'

'You're so organised.'

He put the whisk down and reached for her hand, pulling her into his arms. 'You smell divine,' he murmured into her ear. 'Just you, no perfume. Natural. I like it.'

'I *do* wear deodorant.'

He laughed. 'I know.' His face grew serious as he gently moved her sheet away. 'Let me look at you.' She shook her head shyly, burying her face into his neck. 'After what we've just done together, I can't believe you're so shy,' he said.

'I can't help it.'

He slipped a hand beneath the sheet, smoothing it over her curves. 'I can't stop touching you,' he said. 'I feel like Christopher Columbus discovering new lands.'

'Now I know how you win over models, it's those cheesy lines.'

'It's true though. I'm used to straight lines, you're all curves.'

Charity frowned. 'I'm not sure that's a good thing.'

'It's wonderful.' He looked into her eyes. 'You're wonderful.'

'I can't believe you're here with me.'

He shook his head, incredulous. 'Me neither. It's a bit crazy, isn't it?'

'A good kind of crazy,' Charity said, thinking of the conversation she'd had with Hope. 'When do you need to go to the States?'

'Need? You forget I'm my own boss. I choose when to go. You start your job in a week, right?' Charity nodded. 'Okay, let's enjoy this week together. How's that sound?'

Charity smiled. 'Perfect.'

When Charity woke each morning over the next week to find Dan there, she was amazed. She watched him sleep, cheeks flushed, blond hair hanging over his closed eyes, and her heart throbbed. She'd wondered how he would cope in her little flat considering he was used to space and luxury. But he seemed at home, in fact, they hardly left the flat, both of them discovering they were too desperate to get back into the flat's small bed to waste time going out for dinner. When Charity did leave to do some shopping, she loved returning to find Dan's long body draped across the blue sofa, a book in his hand, designer glasses perched on his nose. Or a phone pressed between his ear and shoulder as he whisked a stir fry up in the kitchen, one hand stirring the food, the other flicking through paperwork, somehow managing to continue running his company despite being in the middle of Southampton in a tiny flat.

When they made love, she loved how Dan's gentle way of touching could make her feel so frantic with feeling. It didn't surprise her that he seemed to know just how to make her react: a touch here, a kiss there and she was arching her back, moaning, melting into him and wanting more. She imagined he was like that in every part of his life, careful, measured, aiming for the best possible result. Perhaps it ought to feel cold, but it didn't. The way he looked at her, like she was the most remarkable thing he'd ever seen, filled her with warmth.

At night he woke instantly when she had nightmares about Faith. And the images would quickly disappear as Dan whispered in her ear to calm her. Niall had been a deep sleeper, barely noticing when she cried out.

The night before her first day at work, he made her dinner and the small flat was abuzz with tension. She was nervous, not just because it was a new job but also because she'd be based on the very campus her sister had been based on. She also couldn't bear the idea of Dan leaving. He seemed to feel the same, brow creased as he ate.

After a while, he sighed, putting his fork down. 'It's no good. I can't leave you.'

Charity let out a breath of relief. 'Thank God.'

He laughed. 'I know, right? It's just too awful to think about.'

223

'But what about the States?'

'I've been thinking, why go to the States when my office is already based in the centre of the UK's cruise world?'

'You're actually going to build a cruise ship?'

Dan's eyes sparked with excitement. 'Why not? I've always dreamt of doing it. I've seen an apartment in town I can rent, too.'

Charity bit her lip. 'I'm only really planning to stay for six months. Hope and I had plans…'

'I know. Look, I'm not just doing this for you, Charity.' He sighed. 'Truth is, I was running away by choosing the States. But being with you makes me want to stay in the UK, whatever transpires between us.'

Charity explored his face. 'What *is* going to transpire between us?'

He leant over, stroking her cheek. 'I don't know. But it seems pretty promising so far, doesn't it?'

She smiled. 'It does.'

The next morning, she woke to find Dan had made her breakfast in bed. As she dressed, butterflies in her stomach at the prospect of starting her new job, Dan watched her with a small smile on his face.

'What's so funny?' she asked.

'It's just great watching you get ready for work. It's great being with someone who cares as much for their job as I do.'

'Is this alright?' she asked, looking down at her black skirt and patterned blouse.

'Gorgeous.'

'I wasn't sure if—'

'Gorgeous,' Dan repeated, coming up behind her and putting his arms around her as he kissed her neck. She watched them in the mirror. They were a contrast, his blond hair against her dark hair, his tanned skin against her pale skin. While she was all soft curves, he was long and wiry.

'We fit perfectly, don't we?' he said as he examined them.

She smiled. 'Yes.'

He reached into his pocket, pulling out a long rectangular box. 'I hope this fits perfectly too.'

'What's this?' she asked, taking it.

'Just a good-luck present.'

She opened it, not believing her eyes when she saw a delicate gold watch with a pearlescent clock face inside. 'Oh, Dan, you shouldn't have.'

'Try it on.'

She carefully took it out of the box, noticing an engraving on the back simply saying 'Courage'. Then written on a note inside:

> 'Courage is what it takes to stand up and speak; courage is also what it takes to sit down and listen.' Winston Churchill.
>
> Dan x

Her eyes filled with tears. 'Faith's quote. How wonderful. It's perfect, thank you.'

'You'll be brilliant,' Dan said as he lifted the watch out, clasping it around her wrist.

She took a deep breath. 'Right, I better go then.'

Over the next few weeks, Charity settled into her new job, pleasantly surprised by the variety of different cases she was dealing with. Some of the foundation-year girls she treated reminded her of her sister, that same contradiction of excitement and fear of living away from home for the first time. She and Dan also met up most nights for dinner, either out or at the stunning penthouse apartment Dan was renting.

A month after Charity started her job, they enjoyed a long leisurely pub lunch with Hope for her birthday, in a beautiful village just outside Busby-on-Sea. Charity loved how much Hope and Dan seemed to get on. After they dropped Hope off at home, they discovered an elderly couple with a broken-down car on the side of the road, so Dan pulled over to offer them a lift. Their large white cottage was beautiful, set overlooking the sea with a black slate roof. There was a pretty sign at its red door – *Poppy Acres* – and it was divided into sections, one larger section with six white windows looking out over the sea, then a smaller one with one window. There were no other buildings for miles, just the sea and the long sandy banks and the sky for company.

It was Charity's idea of heaven.

When the couple invited them in for a cup of tea and a cake, Charity could see the house was just as perfect inside. It needed a lot of work, but the traditional dark slate floors, white walls and high beams were charming.

As Charity and the couple talked, Dan grew quiet, eyes on the sea outside. When it was time to go, the lady gave them a Victoria Sponge to take away and they walked towards Dan's car.

'Look at the view,' Charity said, looking out at the sea, the waves satin grey below them, the moon a bright spark above. 'Isn't it just gorgeous?'

'You really like it here, don't you?' Dan asked her.

'It's perfect.'

'Let's stay for a few moments. No need to hurry away.' He took her hand and led her to a bench at the edge of the small stretch of sandy beach in front of the cottage.

'They're a lovely couple, aren't they?' Charity said, leaning her head on Dan's shoulder. 'I think my mum and dad would have been a bit like them if they were still around.'

Dan looked down at her, smoothing a stray hair behind her ear. 'What were your parents like?'

'Perfect in their imperfections, that's how Hope always described them,' Charity replied, smiling. 'The house was always a mess, they let us stay up late and eat ice cream, Mum forgot to pick us all up from school once when it snowed so one of our teachers had to take us home.' Charity laughed at the memory. 'But they absolutely adored us, were always hugging us and telling us they loved us. And they adored each other too.'

Dan looked down at the ground, a frown appearing on his face.

'Are you thinking about your own parents?' Charity asked softly.

He nodded. 'I wish they were as perfect as yours. My father was having an affair when he died, you know.'

Charity frowned. 'I'm so sorry, Dan.'

'My mother knew but she stayed with him. She was completely besotted. When someone feels that kind of overwhelming obsessive love, it can block everything else out.' He clenched his jaw. 'My father's name was the last thing she said when she died, even though I was there with her, had nursed her through her illness. She just looked at me blankly then said his name, "Mark", and then she was gone. I sometimes wonder if she even loved me.'

Charity squeezed his hand. 'Of course she loved you, she was your mother.'

'You can't know that.'

'I can,' she said softly. 'I know how easy it is to love you.' She watched Dan's face. This was the first time she'd told him she loved him. It was the first time she'd admitted it to herself.

As she watched Dan, though, he didn't react.

Instead, he carried on talking. 'Is it easy to love me? Maybe you see me with rose-tinted glasses. We barely know each other after all.'

Charity tried to hide her disappointment. What was she expecting, some flamboyant declaration of love in response? '*I* feel like we know each other,' she said.

He sighed, raking his fingers through his blond hair. 'Sorry, I'm being glum. I always get like this when I talk about my parents.'

He looked at her. 'I just worry you're putting me on a pedestal. I haven't got this far in my business without stepping on a few heads.'

'How do you mean?'

'I'm not perfect, that's all I'm saying.'

'Nobody is, Dan. God knows I'm not. But you're a good man.'

His face softened. 'This is what I like about you, seeing myself through your eyes.'

Like but not *love*.

She looked down at their joined hands. Maybe she was getting this all wrong? Maybe this was a fling, a crazy extended rendezvous before Dan started his new life in the States. They hadn't discussed any kind of future, they'd just lived huddled up in their own world the past few weeks, making love and talking about everything but what they really meant to each other. It had always been so over the top with Niall, declarations of love within a week of first kissing each other. Yes, things had moved quickly with Dan physically, but what about emotionally?

'Charity, what's wrong?' Dan asked, frowning.

'I don't know. I guess – I guess I'm just curious about how you see us.' She smiled quickly. She didn't want to appear desperate.

He shook his head incredulously. 'How can you not know?'

'Know what?'

'That I love you, completely and utterly. It's obvious, isn't it?' He pulled her close, looking down at her with his sparkling green eyes, the moon a bright orb above his head. 'I just don't want to disappoint you, that's all.'

'You won't.'

The next morning, Charity and Hope shared one of their regular Saturday morning phone calls.

'How's the job?' Hope asked.

'Great, actually. My boss is lovely and the students are wonderful.'

'Surely students being *wonderful* means you don't have much of a job to do?'

Charity smiled to herself. 'People who see counsellors can be wonderful too, Hope.'

'Like Lana North? Speaking of whom, how's Don Johnson?'

'What are you talking about?'

'Don Johnson from *Miami Vice*, don't you think Dan looks a bit like him?'

'I thought you hated TV.'

'My new girl Suzanne loves him. She tried to make me stick a poster up in the café, said it was *art*, can you believe it?'

Charity laughed. She loved talking to her sister.

'I told her if I saw it anywhere in the café,' Hope continued, 'she'd have no chance of becoming the café's manager in a few years if I have my way.'

'Well, you won't because you'll be long gone by then.'

Hope went quiet. 'Maybe not.'

'What do you mean?'

She sighed. 'There's just too much work to do to make it saleable, Charity. And that's just the café. I had that surveyor out to value the house the other day. He said the market's a mess and it could take us years to sell it considering how much updating it needs.'

'Then we update it.'

'With what money?'

'The money I'm earning here!'

'But you need to pay your rent there, you need to eat and live. Let's just face it, it's not going to happen.'

Charity slumped down on to her sofa. 'Is it really that bad?' she asked.

'Really. But you know what? I don't mind. You know how much I love this place. Maybe it was just a pipe dream. I've got these poems to write for that editor, that's keeping me busy.'

'But you're on your own there.'

'You know me, Charity. It suits me. The truth is I've never heard you sound as happy as you are right now. It's either the air out there or it's a certain blond businessman called Dan North. I don't want you to give that up. Southampton is closer than London was. You can pop back to Busby-on-Sea with Dan and give Suzanne a heart attack when a Don Johnson lookalike walks into the café.'

'I *am* happy. But are you?'

'Yes. This is where my life is, I think the universe was trying to tell me that by making the café and house unsaleable. Now, tell me more about Don Johnson.'

As they talked over the next half an hour, Charity felt tears prick her eyelashes. When she could finally put the phone down, she burst into tears.

'Oh, Hope,' she whispered.

Her doorbell sounded. She opened the door to find Dan the other side.

He frowned. 'Charity, what on earth's the matter?'

'Hope can't sell the café or the house. She's insisting I stay here.'

He pulled her into his arms. 'Is that such a bad thing?'

'I'll miss her.'

'But you're happy to stay despite this, aren't you?'

She looked up at him. 'Hope said I'm the happiest she's ever seen me. And you know what? I am.'

His face lit up. 'You don't know how that makes me feel to hear you say that. Does this really mean you're staying here in Southampton?'

'My boss did mention there might be an opportunity to extend my contract.'

He smiled. 'Then that's settled. You're staying. Looks like we have some celebrating to do.'

Over the next few weeks, the concerns Charity had about Hope dissipated. She seemed genuinely happy when they talked on the phone and when they met for the occasional lunch at a pub between their two places.

When they were out at dinner one evening, Dan presented Charity with a box.

'Not another gift,' she said, opening it. 'I feel bad, I only got you that new tie.'

'And I love it,' he said, looking down at the aqua tie she'd got him. 'Let me spoil you, darling. I work hard and this makes me happy.'

She smiled. 'If you insist.'

When she opened it, she was surprised to see a key inside along with a beautiful red poppy brooch encrusted with diamonds. She frowned. 'It's beautiful, Dan. But what's the key for?'

'Our house.'

She looked up at him. '*Our* house?'

'Poppy Acres. I bought the cottage by the sea you so loved.'

'But the elderly couple who lived there…?'

'It became too much for them. They've been meaning to move into a bungalow on a complex for the elderly and were thinking about putting the house up for sale when I dropped in a few weeks ago.'

'You visited them again?'

Dan nodded, clasping her hands in his own, his eyes excited. 'I just kept thinking about the house and couldn't resist visiting it again. When they told me they wanted to sell it, I knew I'd be a fool not to put an offer in. You adored it, plus it's closer to Busby-on-Sea for visiting Hope, but still an easy commute to Southampton for us.'

Charity shook her head. 'I can't believe you bought it for us.'

Dan's smile faltered. 'Was I wrong to?'

'No, I just—' Charity smiled. 'Sorry, I sound so ungrateful. It's a beautiful house, exactly the sort of place I imagine myself living. *Us* living.'

'Am I rushing things? I didn't mean for us to move in straight away, I was waiting until the time was right. But I couldn't miss the opportunity.'

'No, no, I'd love to live with you,' Charity said, realising she really would. 'I hate the nights we're apart. I guess I'm just not used to people buying houses for me. Can I put some money towards it? I need to feel like this is *our* house, do you understand?'

Dan smiled. 'Of course, if that's what you want.'

Charity nodded, finally letting herself feel excited. 'Oh, Dan, is this really happening?'

He laughed. 'Yes, it really is.' He gestured to the waiter, who came rushing over. 'A bottle of your best champagne,' he said. 'We're celebrating.'

A few weeks later, Charity walked across the forecourt towards her office. It was housed in an impressive new building. The faces around her seemed happy at the prospect of summer in full bloom, the day warm, the skies above blue. Charity was happy too. She'd been working hard on the house all weekend with Dan, painting the walls, moving furniture around. They'd moved in a month ago and it already felt like home, despite the work that needed to be done on it, which was mainly cosmetic but still kept her busy. She loved being hands-on, watching the house transform before her eyes into her dream home. And she'd surprised herself by really enjoying bossing around the plasterers and decorators that Dan had hired while he was away on business the other weekend.

Charity walked into the building where her office was. On the way, she saw a couple of students she'd been treating, a girl who was struggling after telling her parents she was a lesbian and a boy who was still getting to grips with the pressure of his studies. They were the same age Faith was when she passed away. Charity couldn't help Faith, but she could help these students. It felt good.

She smiled to herself. Things felt hopeful, like finally she was moving on with her life.

The only small glitch was Hope. Charity hadn't told her she'd bought a house with Dan. She knew her sister would tell her it was all too soon.

Tomorrow, she kept telling herself. *I'll call Hope and tell her tomorrow.*

As she stepped inside the office, her boss, Amanda, was talking in hushed tones to a tall woman Charity recognised from the deanery administration team. They went quiet as Charity walked in. The tall woman said her goodbyes then strolled out, smiling vaguely at Charity.

'Something I said?' Charity asked, slinging her bag under her desk.

'No, poor Di's struggling because her parents are staying with her. Their house was declared a severe flood risk so they had to move out with hardly any notice.'

'Oh, don't say that, I live right by the sea.'

Amanda laughed. 'Don't worry, it would have come up in your searches. They probably didn't live too far from where you've just moved actually. Poppy Acres?'

Charity's blood turned to ice.

Amanda's phone went and she rolled her eyes. 'Can't they at least give me five minutes to get a cuppa?'

As she answered the call, Charity sat at her desk, staring into the distance. Dan hadn't mentioned anything about a flood risk, just that the couple wanted to move into a bungalow.

233

As soon as she was alone she called Dan's office. But his PA, a woman in her fifties called Penny, told Charity he was in a meeting.

'You liaised with our estate agent about the cottage, didn't you, Penny?' Charity asked her.

'Yes, just a few bits and pieces,' Penny replied.

'Did anything ever come up about it being a flood risk?'

'Yes. But Dan's getting those defences sorted. I thought you knew?'

'Maybe he mentioned it,' Charity lied. 'It probably slipped my mind. Do you know what happened to the old couple who lived there?'

'No,' Penny said slowly, the worry evident in her voice as it dawned on her she shouldn't be disclosing this information. 'Shall I ask Dan to call you?'

'No, it's fine, I'll chat to him when I get home. Thanks, Penny.'

Charity put the phone down and leant back in her chair. Why had Dan kept it from her? Maybe he just didn't want to worry her. But she didn't need protecting. She preferred to know the truth.

'Hello, beautiful,' Dan said when he got in that evening, leaning down to kiss her on the lips as she put the decorating book she was reading down.

'Did Penny mention I called?' Charity asked him.

'She did indeed,' Dan said, loosening his tie as he sank down on to the sofa next to her. 'I'm intrigued why you're suddenly taking an interest in the sale.'

'I've always been interested in the house. You just took it all out of my hands.'

He frowned. 'Is that a problem?'

'No, but you should have mentioned the flood risk.'

'It's minor, honestly, darling. I'm taking measures to deal with it.'

Charity propped her reading glasses on to the top of her head. 'But what about the old couple who used to live here?'

'What about them?'

She told him what Amanda had said. 'If the risk was bad enough for them to have to move out that quickly, why didn't it stop us moving *in*?'

Dan took her hand. 'I would never have you living here if there was any risk of you getting hurt. As for the previous owners, they told me they wanted to move anyway.' He kissed her neck. 'Stop worrying,' he murmured. 'This house is perfect, *you're* perfect.'

She pulled away from him, looking him in the eyes. 'Don't keep things from me, Dan. I'm a grown-up and we're a partnership, right?'

He nodded, face serious. 'I've learnt my lesson. I'm sorry, darling.'

Charity ducked under her umbrella as rain pelted down on her. She had twenty minutes left of her lunch break to find something to wear to a dinner with some business associates of Dan's. She entered a small boutique shop, shaking her umbrella out. As she looked up she noticed Dan's PA Penny standing by the jewellery counter, miserably trying on rings.

'Penny!' Charity called out.

Penny didn't respond, instead turned away. Maybe she hadn't heard Charity? Charity strode towards her, tapping her on the shoulder. 'Penny?'

Penny turned around, eyes filling with tears.

'What's wrong?' Charity asked.

'He hasn't told you, has he?'

'Told me what?'

'Mr North fired me. He didn't even give me a warning. '

Charity stared at her in shock. 'I'm sorry, Penny. I had no idea.'

Her face filled with anger. 'I did so much for him, even missed my sister's fortieth birthday to call around all those advertising agencies to do his dirty work.'

'What do you mean?'

Penny paused and bit her lip but then clearly resolved to hold nothing back. 'There was a photographer,' she said. 'An arty type. Mr North had me call around various advertising agencies to report that he'd over-charged him for some photographs and had got drunk during an assignment. Thing is, the photographer did nothing like that according to records we've kept. But Mr North has clout and when he says something, people listen.'

'Photographer?' Charity asked, a churning feeling in her belly. 'What was his name?'

'Oh, gosh. Neil? Nathan?'

'Was it Niall Lane?'

'Yes! That's him.'

Charity thought back to when Niall had told her all his work had suddenly dried up. 'Jesus,' Charity whispered to herself.

Penny crossed her arms, looking pleased with herself for putting Dan in it.

Charity looked at her watch. She only had a few minutes left to get back to campus. Work would have to wait. She needed to speak to Dan *right now*.

Dan's office was a large three-storey building overlooking the sea. When the taxi drew up upside, she shoved money into the driver's hand and then ran inside, smiling tightly at the receptionist. Behind the glossy black reception desk was an artist's impression of the cruise ship, white and sparkling, MS *Haven* emblazoned down its side.

'Hi, Vicky,' Charity said, smiling at the receptionist. She wondered how Vicky felt about Penny being fired. 'Is Dan in?' she asked her.

'Yes, he's in his office.'

'Great, thanks.' She strolled down the hallway through some glass doors, past several offices, people busy working. She found Dan walking out of his office at the end of the corridor, a confused look appearing on his face when he saw her.

'Everything okay, darling?' he asked, reaching for her to give her a kiss.

She stepped away from him. 'I just bumped into your old PA, Penny. She told me you fired her. Was it because she told me about the flood risk? Why were you so desperate to hide it from me?'

He took her hand. 'Come into my office,' he said softly, glancing behind her as one of his employees walked down the hallway.

She followed him into his large office, the heels of her shoes digging into the thick patterned carpet. A large window sat behind his chrome desk offering views of the sea. To either side were white leather sofas, a drinks cabinet and surround sound speakers above.

'So?' Charity asked as he closed the door.

'I used your phone conversation with Penny as an excuse, Charity,' Dan said, sitting on the edge of his desk and folding his arms. 'Truth is her work's been slipping lately.'

'But she was your PA for seven years!'

'I gave her lots of chances.'

'What about the flood risk? Did you exaggerate it so the old couple would move out and we could move in?' His jaw tensed slightly and he didn't say anything. '*Dan*?'

He sighed. 'I didn't exaggerate it. I told them the truth, that's all. Their house *was* at risk of flooding.' He strolled over to her and put his hands on her arms. 'It's your dream house, Charity.'

'I don't care,' Charity said, shrugging his hands away. 'We made an old couple homeless.'

'They're not homeless, they have their daughter!'

'There's that too. You told me they'd moved into a bungalow!' She took in a deep breath. 'And Penny told me you asked her to badmouth Niall to the advertising agencies he worked for. Why would you do that?'

Dan's voice was calm, measured, his face unreadable. 'It's the truth, isn't it?'

Then he sighed. 'Look, let's go for lunch. We can talk and—'

She looked up at the clock. 'No. I have a session in half an hour.'

'Cancel it. This is more important.'

'No. I'm so disappointed in you, Dan.' Then she turned on her heel and walked out.

Charity tried her best to focus on her sessions that afternoon but she couldn't help going over and over what Dan had said. Maybe being a bit over-zealous about getting their dream house was expected of a man like him, used to getting everything he wanted. But what on earth had he been thinking causing all that trouble for Niall?

As Charity stepped out into the early evening sunshine later, she didn't feel the same optimism she'd felt earlier that week. Did she really know Dan?

As she walked to the car park, something caught her eye: a poster featuring an eerie underwater scene of a submerged tree against the backdrop of coral.

Fri 15th July to 1st August
Southampton City Art Gallery
The Layers of Me
A celebration of the work of local Underwater Photography
Grand Prix winner Niall Lane.

She shouldn't be surprised, he was born in the area after all. But she presumed he'd be travelling. She quickly turned away, continuing towards the car park.

Just because his work was being exhibited here didn't mean he was in town. And even if he was, she probably wouldn't bump into him, Southampton was a large town after all. But it still felt strange knowing his work was being shown here.

'Charity?' She looked up to see Dan across the forecourt, leaning against his car with folded arms, not caring a jot that he was parked on double yellow lines. He was wearing sunglasses and a white shirt, blue jeans, his handsome face making her insides ache with want despite herself.

'What are you doing here?' she asked.

'I'd like to take you somewhere,' he said softly.

'Can't we just go home?'

'Please. We need to talk. We can pick your car up after.'

She frowned. 'Alright.'

She sat in silence as Dan drove them along the coast. Seagulls swooped through blue skies, people laughed and talked as they walked through the sunshine to get home from work or lectures.

After a while, Dan drove into a small seaside town not unlike Busby-on-Sea. They turned in to a car park, white cliffs to their left, the sea in front of them.

'Seaford,' Dan said when he came to a stop, peering up at the cliffs. 'This is where I grew up. I used to go for walks along the cliffs to clear my head. I keep meaning to bring you out here but never get around to it. Shall we got for a walk?'

'That'll be nice.' She stepped out of the car as Dan opened her door for her. They walked in silence up a pathway on to the lush green cliff tops, the shriek of seagulls and the soft putting sounds of the golf course for company.

When they got to the top, they paused for a moment to take in the view of the lashing sea below. The wind swirled around them both, whistling in Charity's ears. It *was* very pretty up here. In the distance, a cruise ship passed, a spark of white on the horizon.

Dan smiled. 'I used to come here and watch ships pass, dreaming I'd own one one day.'

'Now you will.'

He took Charity's hand. 'Let's go a little further, shall we?'

They carried on walking. After a few minutes, Charity noticed something ahead of them – a brown leather sofa in the middle of the grass, a small round table with a bottle of wine in a bucket of ice and a huge cold buffet of meat cuts, cheese and bread.

'What is all this?' she asked as Dan led her towards it.

'I had it all brought up here. Thought it'd be nice to enjoy the view this way.'

Charity couldn't help but smile as she sat on the sofa. 'So typical of you to have a sofa carted all the way up here.'

Dan poured some wine for them both. She took a sip of hers and leant back against the soft sofa, taking in the stunning view of the sea, the low sun casting a sweet yellow hue against it.

'I don't want you to think badly of me, Charity,' Dan said, turning towards her. 'I only wanted us to have the perfect house. I should have been more transparent with you. I just get so wrapped up in the excitement of it all, I don't realise when I might be overstepping the mark.'

Charity frowned down into her wine. 'What about badmouthing Niall?' she asked.

His jaw tightened. 'It was childish of me. I'd just found out about him and Lana.'

Charity looked up, noticing how pained Dan looked. 'I didn't take you as the type who'd do something like that, Dan, even considering the circumstances.'

Dan sighed. 'I'm not. I wasn't thinking straight. I regretted it after.' Dan looked into her eyes. 'We can't all be as good as you, Charity.'

Charity thought of the night Faith died, the bump felt on the side of Niall's car. She'd had her own secrets too, hadn't she? She hadn't told Dan about that yet...or that Niall's work was being exhibited in Southampton. Maybe he knew already? But still, why *hadn't* she mentioned it? 'I'm not that good, Dan.'

'Yes, you are. You make me want to be good too.' He laced his fingers through hers. 'I promise I won't do anything like that again.'

She looked into his green eyes and felt herself melting. 'You better not.'

Over the next couple of hours, they ate and drank. Then Dan pulled her close, his lips brushing against hers, sending waves of sensation through her. She pressed her fingers against the nape of his neck, pulling him even closer, their kiss growing deeper.

In the background, the sun dipped beneath the sea, darkness crawling over the hill towards them as Dan's hand slipped under the neckline of her jumper. She heard the distant crash of a wave and Niall flashed through her mind. She pushed the thought away, guilt squirming in her stomach.

Things returned to normal after that, with romantic dinners and long beach walks, even a weekend away in Paris. While shopping in Southampton one Saturday when Dan was at work, she found herself walking towards the gallery where Niall's work was being exhibited. When she entered the space, she froze, unable to believe what she was seeing. Each wall was dominated by large exquisite canvasses featuring Niall's photographs of submerged trees, and in each one was an engraving: the C and N intertwined.

It was haunting, eerie, utterly beautiful.

Charity put her hand to her chest, emotion building inside.

'Charity?' She knew before she turned that it was him.

Her heart thumped as she turned around. He was wearing a pair of smart dark jeans and a white shirt. His dark hair was longer now and he wasn't as tanned. But he looked healthy, blue eyes as vivid as ever.

'You're here,' she said.

He smiled. 'Well, they are exhibiting my work. You here to do some shopping?' he asked, looking at her bags.

'I live here now. I got a job as a student counsellor.'

'That's great news!' He looked around him. 'Do you like it?'

'It's beautiful.' She walked to the photo closest to her. It was one of the photographs he'd sent her of the forest in India, the branches feathering above in the misty lake, ethereal, astounding. 'I heard you won an award?'

Niall shrugged. 'No big deal.'

He smiled and her tummy tilted. It always had that effect on her, his smile. 'It's all working out for us, isn't it, Charity?'

She smiled back at him. 'Yes, I suppose it is.'

He searched her face with his eyes. 'I've missed you, Charity.'

She sighed. They couldn't get into this. 'Niall…'

He stepped towards her, taking her hand. 'I never really got the chance to—' He frowned as he looked over her shoulder. She followed his gaze to see Dan standing at the entrance to the exhibition, eyes wide as he looked at the photos. Then his gaze landed on Charity, focusing on her and Niall's conjoined hands.

Charity pulled her hand away from Niall's but it was too late, Dan was striding out. She ran after him but he'd disappeared into a crowd coming out of the cinema. She called out his name, tried to search for his blond hair among the sea of people. But he was nowhere.

'What's Dan doing here?' She turned and saw Niall standing behind her, a confused expression on his face.

She took a few moments to compose herself. How was she going to tell him? 'We live together here,' she said.

She watched as his expression changed from confusion to incredulity. 'You and Dan? *Together*?'

'Yes.'

He shook his head, still incredulous. 'I always knew he liked you. But *you* liking him? How long have you been together?'

'Just three months.'

'Is it serious?'

She paused. 'We have a place together.'

'Already? Jesus, he moves fast.'

She looked back out at the crowds. 'I need to find him. Sorry, Niall.' Then she jogged away.

When Charity got home, the house was empty. She sank down on to the sofa, trying to process her feelings. She stayed like that for a very long time, darkness falling on the house, a chill seeping in. Finally there was the roar of an engine outside. She slowly stood up and looked out of the window just as Dan stepped out of his car. He looked exhausted under the moonlight, his eyes pained.

Charity walked to the front door, heart thumping painfully against her chest.

'Where have you been?' she asked Dan when he walked in, the cool night air sweeping in through the open door and encircling her bare legs.

'Just driving.'

'Nothing's going on between Niall and me, you know. I didn't even know he was exhibiting here until a few weeks ago.'

He walked into the hallway and shut the door behind him. 'But you did know a few weeks ago, and yet you didn't say a word about it?'

'I didn't see the point.'

243

'You were holding his hand, Charity.' He flinched as he said that.

'He was upset. It was nothing. Dan. I love *you*.'

He looked at Charity, his green eyes intense. 'I love you too, so much. Let's just forget about Niall, shall we?'

As Dan pulled her into his arms, Niall's face popped into Charity's mind again. Again she squeezed the image away.

'Oh go on, tell us the juicy stuff about your patients,' the woman sitting next to Charity said. She and Dan were in a beautiful Italian restaurant in the heart of Southampton having dinner with one of his business associates – a large man with red cheeks and a mop of black hair who owned a cruise line. Dan was trying to court him with a view to possibly selling him the ship. Charity had only been on two such dinners since she'd been with Dan, and had been surprised how much she'd enjoyed them. She'd always had this impression the wives would be vacant, the men chauvinists. Maybe it was a stereotype she had caught from TV programmes and films. But the truth was they were usually rather fascinating: one wife she met the month before was an A&E doctor and Caroline, the woman sitting next to Charity now, was a TV producer.

'Certainly not,' Charity said, taking a sip of her wine. 'Otherwise Dan and I will be settling down to watch one of the wonderful dramas you've produced and I'll see one of my patient's stories on there.'

Everyone laughed and Dan squeezed her leg under the table, smiling at her.

'So Caroline, how—' Charity paused. Niall had just walked in on the other side of the restaurant. He was wearing a smart pair of jeans and a dark blue shirt, and was with two women and an older man.

Dan followed her gaze, his face tensing.

'Charity?' Caroline asked.

She dragged her eyes away and looked at Caroline. 'I was just wondering how long you've worked at the BBC?'

'Ten years, feels more like fifty.' As she talked about how she got her job, Charity couldn't help but look back at Niall again. A waiter was leading him and his companions over to the table next to them.

'Well well well,' Caroline's husband Miles said quietly as the group sat down. 'There's our local politician. You really have brought us to the best restaurant in Southampton, Dan.'

'Oh, that's the photographer Niall Lane with him too,' Caroline said. 'I saw his exhibition the other week, such a talented man. Real rising star.'

Dan watched Niall with narrowed eyes.

'So, Dan,' Miles said. 'When will work start on the building of your wonderful ship?'

'Next spring, I hope,' Dan replied. 'I have a brilliant naval architect on board. Now *he's* a rising star. You should see the plans he's drawn up, they're astounding.'

Niall looked up at the sound of Dan's voice. He noticed Charity, his eyes widening.

'So when will I see the plans?' the man asked, leaning back in his chair as he nursed his brandy.

Dan shot him a big smile. 'Well, never of course.'

Niall frowned, clearly hearing the conversation thanks to Dan's raised voice.

The man frowned as well. 'But I'll need to see them if I want to get the ball rolling on our purchase.'

Dan shrugged. 'You won't be purchasing it.'

Charity and Caroline exchanged confused looks. Wasn't that what this meal was all about?

The man examined Dan's handsome face. 'You're joking with me, aren't you?'

'Not at all,' Dan said, casually flecking some fluff off his pink tie. 'North Cruises will own the ship.'

Miles's cheeks went even redder as his wife raised her eyebrow. '*You're* launching a cruise line?' Miles asked.

Dan nodded his head, clearly enjoying the man's confusion. 'Yes, that's exactly what I'm doing.'

Charity looked at Dan, surprised. He hadn't mentioned anything to her. It had always been about building the best cruise ship he could and then selling it to the highest bidder…not running a whole cruise line himself.

'Then what was this dinner all about?' the man said, his voice raised. Other diners turned to look, including Niall.

'No harm assessing the competition, is there?' Dan said. 'I've learnt a few trade secrets in the past three hours that will help me.'

Niall watched Dan, eyes hard.

Miles pushed his chair away and stood up as his wife looked on, bemused. 'You won't get anywhere in this business playing dirty. We're going.'

Caroline placed her napkin on the table and turned to Charity. 'Well, despite this nonsense, it's been a real pleasure meeting you, Charity.'

'You too, Caroline.'

'Watch this one, though,' Caroline said as she stood up, tipping her chin at Dan. She smiled. 'Good luck, Dan.' Then they both walked from the restaurant.

Niall looked at Charity, frowning. Did he feel sorry for her?

She turned to Dan. 'Why didn't you tell me about your plans? I looked like a clueless bimbo just now.'

'I hadn't quite made my mind up until now.'

'But it's a massive decision. You can't just make it over dinner.'

'Darling,' Dan said, placing his hand over hers. 'It's been in the pipeline for months. I just needed a few more details in order to make my decision, Miles provided them. Amazing what a bottle of champagne can do to a man like him.'

'I thought it was rather cruel.'

Dan tensed. 'Really? You do know how much this meal will cost, don't you? The champagne alone was over a hundred pounds a bottle. I think I paid rather handsomely for his time.'

Charity shook her head.

'Oh, Charity,' Dan said. 'This is the way business works. We're all pieces on a chessboard.'

'What does that make me then? The pawn, brought here to look pretty and lull him into a false sense of security?'

Dan's face grew serious. 'You're more than just pretty, Charity, and you know it.'

'We should get the bill,' she said, feeling people's eyes on them, including Niall's.

'But we said we'd stay on after, get a few more drinks. '

'No, Dan. I want to go home.'

Dan grabbed her arm, leaning towards her. 'It's because of Niall, isn't it? You can't handle being in the same room as him.'

Niall stood up and walked over to the table, his eyes on Dan's hand. 'Everything okay, Charity?'

Dan released his grip and stood up, shaking Niall's hand. 'Niall, how are you?'

Niall ignored him, still looking down at Charity. 'Charity?'

'I'm fine,' Charity said. 'We were about to leave. Shall we get the bill?'

'You don't look fine.'

Dan glared at Niall. 'She said she's fine.'

Niall's blue eyes slid over to Dan. 'I heard what just happened now with that cruise line owner. That's the problem with people like you, you'll do anything to anyone to get to the top.'

Dan laughed. 'Says the man having dinner with the politician.'

247

'He's a good man, done more for this community than you ever will.'

'Really? He's paid towards the opening of a new community centre, has he? I think I've achieved more here in the past three months than that man has. Action, Niall, not talk talk talk.'

Charity stood up. 'Oh God, you two, will you both just shut up?' She walked out from behind the table. 'Sort the bill out, Dan, I'll get us a taxi.'

Dan reached for her. 'Charity, don't—'

'Dan North?' a man said, walking up to the table. 'Gareth Jones, we met two months ago. I was meaning to talk to you actually, I might just be able to help you with that problem you were having with steel supplies.'

'Ah, Gareth,' Dan said, fixing a smile on to his face, half an eye on Charity as she walked out of the restaurant, Niall following.

'Don't follow me, Niall,' Charity said as she shrugged her coat on and opened the door, stepping outside.

'I don't like the idea of you being with someone like him.' He strode alongside her as she walked down the road towards the taxi rank. 'Are you sure you trust him?'

'What does that mean?'

'Lana told me Dan manipulated her into making a pass at me in India.'

Charity raised an eyebrow. 'And you believe her?'

He sighed, running his hand over his stubbled face as though exhausted. 'I think I do, actually. After the exhibition in Norfolk, we talked. She thinks Dan wanted something to happen between me and her. On the way to India, he kept talking to her about how needy she was; how he wished she could appear more unavailable to him.'

Charity shook her head. 'I can't see Dan saying something like that to someone as vulnerable as Lana.'

248

'She seemed sincere. She told me he actually said to her that if she showed him other men could find her attractive, he might find her appealing too. He mentioned me specifically. She said he pretty much bet her she couldn't seduce me, that I probably found her too needy too. That's a form of psychological manipulation, right?'

Charity tried to wrap her head around the notion. 'That's ridiculous. Lana might be vulnerable but she wouldn't just sleep with someone at Dan's command.'

'Really? He's clever, Charity, manipulative. He knew what he was doing.' She thought of all she'd learnt about Dan the past couple of weeks: the underhand way he'd got the cottage; the lengths he'd gone to to discredit Niall. But what about the kind, caring Dan she knew? Could she really let a couple of incidences reported by people who clearly had a reason to be negative discredit everything she knew about him? And her own discussions with Lana had shown her just how manipulative she could be.

'I think he did it to get me out of the picture too,' Niall continued. 'I think that's been his game plan from the start, to get you.' He laughed bitterly. 'And well done to him as it looks like he has, hook, line and sinker.'

'I'm not a fish that can just be caught, Niall,' Charity said, feeling anger build inside. 'I choose who to love. I don't need your protection, Niall.'

'Are you sure? Isn't that what I've always done, protected you ever since the night Faith died? Now you need my protection more than ever. Seeing you here with Dan makes me—'

'Makes you what?' a voice said from behind them. They both turned to see Dan standing there. 'What does seeing Charity here with me make you want to do? Does it makes you jealous because you can see how much she loves me, and I love her?'

Niall laughed. 'Yeah, sure, lots of love there.'

Dan took a step towards Niall but Charity stood between them, her back to Dan. 'I love Dan,' she said, looking into Niall's eyes. He flinched and she felt terrible. 'I can look after myself. I'll be *okay*. Now go back to your dinner, get on with your life.'

Niall held her gaze and she felt Dan's breath on her ear. Then Niall sighed, his face softening. 'If ever you're not okay, I'm here for you.' Then he walked away.

Charity closed her eyes for a few moments, composing herself. Then she turned to Dan.

'What did he mean about protecting you since the night Faith died?' Dan asked. 'Is there something you're not telling me? We said no more lies, remember.'

Tears filled her eyes. She took a breath. 'I was in the car with Niall that night.'

Dan's eyes widened. 'When he knocked over your sister?'

'Yes. We had no idea, I swear. There – there was a small bump, so we got out to look but there was no sign of her. The impact must have made her tumble down the slope.'

'Why didn't you tell me?'

'But it has nothing to do with you, Dan,' she said softly. 'There was no need for you to know.'

'It has *everything* to do with me because it's a major part of your life! You've been lying to me, Charity, and yet you lambast me for lying to you. Do you realise what a hypocrite that makes you?' He shook his head. 'Unbelievable. Maybe Niall's right. Maybe we're not right for each other.'

'Don't say that.'

His face softened. 'We're so different, Charity. Seeing you and Niall together…it's hard, really hard, because the truth is, I see it. I see why you love each other.'

'*Loved* not love. He's my past.'

Dan looked out towards the sea, his hands in his pockets.

'Let's just get home,' Charity said, putting her hand on his arm. 'It's been a crazy night.'

Dan nodded and they walked to the taxi rank in silence. This was exactly what she'd feared. Dan could hardly look at her.

They spent the car journey back in silence and when they got home Dan said he had a headache from all the champagne he'd drunk and needed to go to bed. Charity hardly slept, watching his rigid back. When she finally did sleep, she woke in the early hours to find him gone from his side of the bed. She quickly grabbed her dressing gown and jogged downstairs, finding him in the kitchen, drinking coffee and already dressed.

'It's only four,' she said. 'Why are you dressed?'

He looked up at her, eyes unreadable. 'Maybe it was a mistake we moved in together so quickly.'

She looked at him in shock. 'What?'

'We didn't spend enough time getting to know one another. Niall's right, you don't know me.'

She walked towards him, taking his hand and looking into his eyes. 'Dan, what's this really about?

He sighed. 'Seeing you and Niall together, it made me realise how unsuited *we* are. I told you I had to do certain things to get to where I am. But you clearly didn't take it on board and now you're panicking because you've started to see me for what I am: a businessman, someone who will go to certain lengths to get what he wants. You're clearly not comfortable with that. You're more comfortable with a bleeding heart liberal like Niall.'

'That's ridiculous, Dan.' She tried to put her arms around him but he coolly stepped away.

'Look,' he said, 'I know when an investment has no chance of success, I have a gut instinct for these things.'

251

Anger overtook the panic. '*Investment*? You see our relationship as an investment?'

'Isn't everything in life?' he said coldly. 'We invest our feelings, our time, our bodies and minds. You need to weigh up whether it's worth it in the end.'

'My God, listen to yourself.'

'I am! This is me, Charity. This is the point I'm trying to make. Now you know the real me, it horrifies you. So what's the point?' His eyes were lifeless, dispassionate.

She felt tears well up in her own eyes. 'Why are you talking like this? Why are you trying to push me away?'

He shook his head and strode towards the door.

'Where are you going?' she asked.

'A drive.'

'The alcohol might not be out of your system, you should wait a bit before driving.'

'Why, are you worried I'll run a young girl over and leave her for dead?' he shouted over his shoulder.

Charity felt like she'd been punched in the stomach. She watched him let himself out, flinching when he slammed the door.

Charity spent the rest of the day waiting for Dan to return, unable to eat or focus on anything but him. She paced the house, peering out of the windows and waiting for any sign he was there.

But nothing.

When midnight struck, she was beside herself with worry. What if he'd hurt himself? She called some local hospitals but there had been no men of his description admitted. When two more hours passed, she got into her own car and drove around the quiet dark roads for any sign of him, thinking of Faith and the way her life had been taken.

She returned home in the early hours, exhausted, still no sign of Dan. When the clock struck eight am, she called his office.

'Hello, Charity,' his new PA Maxine said.

'Is Dan in?'

'No, didn't he tell you?'

'Tell me what?'

'He decided to fly out to Germany to meet with his naval architect.'

'He flew out yesterday?'

'Yes, in the morning.'

She sank into the sofa. 'Did he say how long he'd be there?'

'A couple of weeks.'

'Right. Thank you.'

She put the phone down, struggling to contain her anger. How could he just fly out like that without telling her? And for two weeks. Was that a signal to Charity, it really was over between them? How could he just finish things like that?

Maybe Niall was right. Maybe *Dan* was right. She didn't really know him. If he could leave at the drop of a hat, turn off a relationship like a tap, deceive business associates, force an elderly couple out of their home…did she really know him? Did she *want* to know him?

When early evening came, she couldn't face staying in the empty cottage, so she walked down to the beach as the sun started to set. Ripples of sand spread out before her, pools of water turned to pink satin under the setting sun.

She looked out to the sea and imagined a submerged forest beneath it. Hope would be flying out to Kazakhstan soon to dive the forest there. She smiled to herself. At least things were going well for her sister.

That's when it struck her. She'd go to see Hope in Kazakhstan.

Chapter Seventeen

Willow

Kazakhstan
October 2016

Ajay throws my bag into the backseat of the four-by-four we've hired. Cars sweep past, some tooting. He's grown a short beard and moustache in the month or so since we last saw each other. He looks slightly ridiculous but somehow I like it. Behind us the curved white roof of Almaty International Airport gleams in the sun. My first glimpses of Kazakhstan have completely surprised me. No goats and dusty roads here, instead there are new buildings and smart-looking people in the country's biggest city. It'll probably change once we get on the road. I hope so anyway. I've never felt comfortable in places like this, all sparkly new and open. Probably because I spent my childhood in a small seaside village.

I guess that's why I asked Ajay if he wanted to come with me. The first thing I did after putting the phone down on Aunt Hope was call Ajay to ask him if he fancied a trip to Lake Kaindy in Kazakhstan. He jumped at the chance.

As Ajay drives us away from the airport, I look down at the map I've printed out. It's quite a trek to Lake Kaindy, six hours. All this to try to track down Niall Lane and get some answers when there's a chance he won't be there. According to the woman I met at the gallery in Austria and some dates on his website, he is in Kazakhstan this week and will be photographing the lake. But I have no idea exactly when. My emails to him remained unanswered.

After a while the modern roads give away to dirt tracks, barren hills and green shrubs. Dust poufs up from our wheels in the rear-view mirror, car jiggling about over the uneven ground.

'Have you thought about what you'll say to Niall Lane if we find him?' Ajay asks.

'Yeah, who's my real dad and what the hell happened to my dead aunt?'

He laughs. 'Straight to the point, I guess. What did your aunt tell you about the accident?'

'The bare facts. She doesn't know why she was walking on that road all alone that night. Maybe Niall has some ideas?'

'Maybe.' Ajay grows serious. 'How will you feel if he is your father?'

I shrug. 'I don't know. It would mean I have a brother and a father who's alive, I guess.'

'A semblance of a family.'

'Yep. But then maybe it would make me feel even less like I was ever part of a family, all my childhood memories would be fake.'

We're both quiet as we contemplate that possibility. I've thought about it a lot the past couple of weeks. I stayed on in Austria with Luki, taking part in the daily routine at the commune. For the first time, I felt like I was part of something.

'So what's next for you after this, any jobs on the horizon?' Ajay asks.

'Nothing yet.' I play with the zipper on my grey hoodie. 'But Luki and Judy asked me to consider staying with them in Austria.'

He raises an eyebrow. 'I can't see you living in a commune, Willow.'

'Maybe I'll surprise you.'

'You're seriously considering it?'

'I guess.'

'Because of Luki? What if it turns out Niall isn't your father?'

'It's not just that. I really like being there.'

'You don't need to move to a commune to feel part of something. You're only young. Don't feel in a rush to figure everything out right away.'

'Alright, Granddad.'

Ajay laughs.

'We keep talking about me,' I say. 'What about you?'

'Want the truth?' he says. I nod. 'I'm thinking about opening a dive centre somewhere in the UK.'

I look at him in surprise. 'Really?'

'Why? You know I love training divers. I feel I've left that behind lately.' He shrugs. 'It's just an idea.'

I smile. 'It sounds cool. I can imagine you sitting on a deck chair, legs up while you watch the sea outside your centre.'

He smiles with me. 'I can imagine it too.'

I switch on the radio, finding a station that plays dodgy Kazakhstani pop music. Over the next couple of hours Ajay and I occupy ourselves making up new lyrics to the songs we hear as we take in the scenery and talk about our childhoods.

After a while, even taller mountains appear and we go properly off-road, bouncing over the ground as we head towards the peaks. In the distance, we see a group of people gathered around the skeletons of two round structures. Nearby, a herd of sheep, yaks and goats graze happily.

'We need a break,' Ajay says as he slows down. 'Fancy chatting to some locals?'

257

'Sure.'

As we approach, they all stop what they're doing and peer at us. There are about thirty people, a mix of men, women and children. They're dressed in colourful clothes with hints of bright pinks and sparkling turquoises, their faces dusty and curious. Ajay steers the car to a stop a few metres away from them, and we jump out. An older man approaches, saying something in Kazakh.

'Just stopping for a drink,' Ajay says, holding up a can of Coke. 'Thought we'd say hello.'

I laugh. 'He doesn't speak English, dufus.'

Ajay shrugs. 'Coca-Cola's an international language.'

'English?' a young woman says. She's in her early twenties and has an interesting-looking green and red hat on her head, a bright pink cardigan and green skirt.

'Yes, we're English,' I say.

She wipes her hands on her skirt and nods enthusiastically. 'My aunt taught me,' she says, gesturing towards an old woman with a wizened face and long grey hair who's sitting with some other woman. The girl takes my hand, shaking it vigorously, doing the same with Ajay after. 'I'm Gulsara,' she says, putting her hand to her chest. Ajay and I introduce ourselves too.

'We're coming to see Lake Kaindy,' I explain.

'Ah, yes,' Gulsara says, smiling. 'Pretty.'

I smile back at her. 'So we've heard.'

Ajay points to the structures. 'What are those?'

'Our yurts. We follow the herd, so they're easy to put up, easy to take down. Hungry?' Gulsara asks. 'You must eat with us.'

'Are you sure?' Ajay asks.

'Of course. We will stop and eat when the roof is done.'

'We'll help you then,' I say. 'We have time right?' I ask Ajay.

'Yep.'

Gulsara leads us past two elderly women who are rolling large powdery white balls, placing them in neat rows on a mat. They look up and smile as we pass. When we get to the structures, I see they're round with pointy roofs, made from long lengths of crisscrossed wood. Several men of different ages are gathered around them, kneeling down or reaching up to secure the wood in place. Another two approach with a huge roll of bamboo sheet. Ajay jogs over, helping them to unroll it and place it against the wood. Gulsara leads me to where her aunt is sitting with two other women, one yanking at the end of half-formed rope, another woman binding its other end together from wild-looking animal hair. 'Yak hair,' Gulsara explains. 'You can help us.'

I look towards the half-made yurts. I'm strong enough to help the men. But I ought to be polite. So I sit cross-legged with the women, letting them show me how to twist and bind the yak's hair. In the end, I find it quite impressive, the way it eventually creates a strong piece of rope.

'You have come to swim in the lake?' Gulsara's aunt asks in good English. She has a turquoise hat on her head – a bit like a beanie – with silver thread etchings. There's a red scarf wrapped around her neck and she's wearing a green felt outfit.

'We're diving,' I explain.

She smiles, revealing two missing teeth. 'Hide.'

'Excuse me?'

'You like to hide under the water,' she says. 'I did the same as a child. Put my head beneath the lake, and hide.'

Is that why I dive now? To hide from a world where I feel like I have nothing? I look down at the end of the rope I'm working on and shrug. 'I suppose you're right.'

None of us says anything over the next half an hour. It feels peaceful, sitting here in the middle of this vast field, mountains peering over us as I rhythmically bind the rope together. Maybe I could live like this, moving from one place to the next. Niall's website stated he was a nomad, preferring his own company. We're so alike in that respect. Does that mean he's actually my father? Dad – *Dan* – he was always so social, holding parties, visiting friends and colleagues. Mum too in her way. So where have I got these qualities from?

I feel tears sting at my eyes. One of the women looks at me and gently puts her hand on my arm. It makes me want to cry even more. God, what's wrong with me?

'Dust,' I say, gesturing towards my eyes.

She smiles and nods. I know she doesn't believe me but that's fine.

When we've finished making the rope, we carry it over to the men, who use it to bind the bamboo sheets to the structure. Then we help bring across heavy fabric, throwing it over the bamboo and tying that down too. Finally, it's time to create the roof, draping a white canvas sheet over the top of each yurt followed by a huge black waterproof sheet and then some more colourful sheets, securing everything with rope.

Ajay strolls over and we help bring colourful rugs into each yurt, fixing them on to the walls inside and draping them over the dusty ground.

'That was fun,' Ajay says after, wiping his brow.

A huge pot is carried past us, filled with a delicious smelling stew, and we sit down at a low-lying table of sorts, a thick rug beneath our shins. On the table is an array of food, from a huge bowl of what looks like spaghetti to smaller bowls filled with different meat and vegetable dishes. The floury balls I'd seen being prepared earlier are actually huge cheese curd balls, absolutely delicious as they melt in my mouth.

As we eat, Gulsara's aunt stands and starts talking in a deep, rhythmic voice.

'She is telling stories of our founding clans,' Gulsara explains in a low voice. 'We must know these stories from many generations back, it is our *şejire*.'

'Isn't that Arabic for "tree"?' Ajay asks.

Gulsara nods. 'What you might call a family tree.'

I think of the drowned trees around the world where my mum's name has been etched with another man's. Is that my true family tree, my legacy? Are those etchings where it all starts for me...and ends?

I've never heard stories from past generations, only Aunt Hope's occasional mentions of when the café was first opened by my grand-parents and what it was like growing up in their messy house. But that's it, no *şejire* for me.

What about Faith? What's her story?

'Are your parents here?' Ajay asks Gulsara.

'No. They died when I was very young.' She looks at her aunt, smiling affectionately. 'My aunt is my mother now.'

'Same as Willow,' Ajay says. 'Your aunt brought you up, didn't she?' he asks me.

Gulsara looks at me. 'You too?'

'Well, I wouldn't call her my mother.'

'But she loved you and cared for you?' she asks.

I shrug. 'I guess.'

'Then she is your mother,' she says.

A group of children burst into giggles nearby. I notice they're looking at some Polaroid photos. From here I can see one quite clearly, an image of them all standing proudly around a tall tanned man with a grey beard. Ajay frowns. 'Isn't that—'

'Niall,' I finish, heart thumping. 'May I look?' I ask the little boy who's holding the photo.

He grasps my meaning and nods shyly as he hands it over. I look at the man in it. Those blue eyes are unmistakable, as are the black tattoos weaving their way up his arms. He looks older than the photo on his website, but happy, a big smile on his face. In the background I recognise the same hills that are overlooking the yurts right now.

'Was this taken recently?' I ask, showing it to Gulsara.

She nods. 'This morning.'

I exchange a look with Ajay. 'Where did the man go?' he asks

'The lake,' Gulsara says, peering outside. 'He tell me he go underwater with big camera, take special photos.'

Ajay and I look at each other as I try to contain my emotions. 'Let's go,' I say.

We stand at the edge of the lake. It's beautiful, glittering blue, surreal-looking. The branchless spruces that are spread out in rows across the lake's surface look frozen in time.

But I barely notice the lake's beauty. Instead, my eyes are scouring its banks for a lone figure, a tattooed man with a grey beard, a camera slung over his shoulder.

But there's just Ajay and me.

'Maybe he's under the surface,' Ajay says.

'His things would be on the side.'

I stare at the glimmering water, wanting to dive in and hide beneath its depths, just like Gulsara's aunt said. 'Shall we dive?' I say, already shrugging my hoodie off, desperate to get in and away from the glare of the sun.

Ajay smiles as he surveys the lake. 'Please.'

The water is crystal clear as we splash into it half an hour later. Freezing cold despite the warm air above. The trees transform as we delve below, each one heavy with branches weighed down by pines, a contrast to their bare branches above, the trees kept alive by the freezing temperatures down here. The effect is quite something, making our underwater world feel ethereal. Ajay's smiling from ear to ear as he swims around the trees, taking it all in.

I stay above for a moment, waiting for the bubbles from his snorkel to create a mushroom-shaped fizz below me. I do this sometimes, wait above, watch for the 'mushroom bubble', hoping it's clear enough to see my reflection in it. This time it is and I see myself floating in it, my short black hair spiking above my head, my blue eyes staring back at me through my mask. I look like a little girl. Maybe I still am, stuck in that time before my parents passed away. How can I move on?

I need answers.

I glide through the bubbles, feeling them caress my skin as my reflection dissipates around me.

After thirty minutes, Ajay points to the dive computer on his wrist. We need to head back up. We slowly ascend, passing ghostly pine trees, their branches tickling our skin. When I burst to the surface, for once I'm grateful for the feel of air on my skin. We wade out, remove our equipment and dry off, both quiet as we pack up, the low sun bouncing off the lake's surface before us.

The sound of people talking in the distance pierces the silence. I look up, see a couple walking through the trees up ahead. They have rucksacks slung over their backs, walking boots on their feet.

'Speak English?' Ajay calls out to them.

'Yes,' they reply.

Ajay takes the Polaroid photo of Niall that the kids let me have and strolls over to the couple. 'Seen this man?'

They look at it then nod. 'He was at a hut we passed,' the woman said.

'When?' I ask, joining them, my heart thumping in anticipation.

'Twenty minutes ago,' she replies.

'Where is the hut?' Ajay asks.

She points towards a path weaving its way through the trees. 'Walk down the path, then you will see it.'

'Thank you,' I say.

We quickly get our stuff together and start heading towards the hut, walking between the glimmering lake and the green fir trees that line it. Above us the setting sun winks between the branches, a soft breeze swirling around my bare neck.

Might I really be about to meet Niall Lane for the first time?

Soon, we come to a clearing, a small hut lying in the distance. But as we draw closer, I see it's empty, quiet.

'There's no one here,' I say, disappointed.

'Wait,' Ajay says. 'Look.'

I follow his gaze to see a man walking out from behind the hut. He's tall, tanned, grey beard, black tattoos.

I freeze, unable to breathe for a few moments.

'It's him, isn't it?' Ajay asks. I nod. 'Go to him, I'll just be here.'

I swallow. 'I'm not sure I want to now.'

'"There are only two mistakes one can make along the road to truth,"' Ajay quotes again. '"Not going all the way, and not starting." You've started. Now you must go all the way.'

I look at Ajay and he nods, brown eyes encouraging. I somehow place one foot in front of another. As I draw closer, Niall looks up. His blue eyes are striking against his lined, tanned skin; his hair longer than in his photos, peppered with grey. He's wearing a dark wetsuit, his camera in his hand. Behind him, I see a rolled out mattress in the hut, a book, some clothes.

I try to see something of me in him. But my heart's hammering so loud in my ears, I can barely focus.

This is the man Mum may have loved once.

The man who accidentally killed her sister.

He frowns, tilts his head like he might recognise me.

'Niall Lane?' I ask, surprised my voice isn't shaking.

'Yes.'

'I'm Willow North, Charity's daughter.'

Emotion floods his face. 'Jesus, you look just like her.'

I examine his face. Is he acting like a man who's seeing a ghost or who's talking to his estranged daughter for the first time? I can't tell.

'Did you send me an invite to your exhibition in Brighton?'

He nods.

'Why?' I ask.

He shrugs. 'It was an impulsive decision. I guess I wanted to meet you.'

'But you never replied to my email and messages.'

'I've been off the grid the past few weeks.' He smiles. 'Hasn't stopped you finding me though.'

'I have some questions.'

He gestures to a nearby log. 'Want to sit down?'

'Alright.'

I sit and he sits beside me.

'How can I help?' he asks.

'Were you having an affair with my mum?' The question just pops out.

He takes in a deep breath. 'I wouldn't call it an affair.'

'Did you come here together?' I say, gesturing around us. 'As lovers, I mean?'

'We didn't come here as lovers, no.'

'Okay, let me put this another way. You were here twenty-eight years ago with my mum, right? I'm twenty-seven.' I let that statement hang in the air as I watch his expression. It's unreadable.

'I know how old you are,' he says. 'I think the question you're trying to ask is, am I your father?'

I don't say anything, just wait.

He sighs. 'I'd like to know that myself. The truth is I have no idea.'

I feel my shoulders slump. I was hoping for some answers. 'Do you think my mum knew?'

He thinks about it for a moment. 'No, I don't think she did.'

'And my dad? Do you think he suspected?'

His face tenses. 'Who knows?'

'You didn't like him, did you?'

'He was no saint.'

'What's that supposed to mean?'

He looks away. 'It doesn't matter.'

I feel like I ought to defend my dad. 'You can hardly talk. You killed my aunt!'

He closes his eyes briefly, pinching the top of his tanned nose. 'It was an accident, Willow.'

'Really?' I dig her map out from my bag. 'I found something on her map.'

He peers at it, intrigued. 'What do you mean?'

I explain about the imprint and he sighs. 'I think I know what that's all about.'

'What?'

'Faith was pregnant when she died.'

'Oh. But why would she say she was scared?'

Niall shrugs. 'Maybe she was planning on having an abortion? There are risks if she'd kept it, it would have been a huge decision.'

'I'm not convinced.'

He looks like he's trying to figure out whether to tell me something.

'Is there something else?' I ask him. 'This is *my* family we're talking about.'

His face closes up. 'There are things best left unsaid.'

266

I shake my head, suddenly exhausted. 'I can't believe this, you sound just like my aunt. I've been visiting the places on this bloody map for answers but all I get are more questions.'

'Maybe you don't need answers. I've learnt over the years the truth doesn't always make you happy.' His face fills with emotion. 'I want you to be happy. It's very important to me. That's why I paid to have the ship salvaged. I knew you would want to see it.'

'You did that?' He nodded. 'Why? Because I might be your daughter?'

'Because your Charity's daughter.' His voice breaks and for a moment I want to give him a hug. But I stop myself and instead we both sit quietly for a moment, a breeze circling around us, the leaves of the pines above us fluttering.

Eventually, Niall turns back to me. 'If you want answers, maybe you need to look closer to home?'

'What do you mean?'

'I mean speak to your aunt.'

I laugh. 'You don't think I haven't tried to already? She won't tell me anything.'

'Maybe it's because she's trying to protect you. She was very close to your mother, she'll have more answers than I do. Prove to her you're not a kid that needs protecting. Show her you can cope with the truth.' He pauses, scrutinising my face. 'If that's what you're sure you want?'

Chapter Eighteen

Charity

Kazakhstan
July 1988

Charity stood in a busy street in Almaty, Kazakhstan's capital city, looking up at the hotel where Hope was staying. The sound of drilling echoed around her. The city seemed to be in the middle of a transition, new subways and hotels rising up, dust clogging the streets. And among it all Charity stood very still and very quiet as people jostled past her, clutching at the handle of her suitcase like it was an anchor.

'Charity!' She looked up to see her sister standing at the hotel's entrance, a huge smile on her face. Hope jogged down the steps of the hotel and pulled Charity into a hug. 'I'm so pleased you came. I couldn't believe it when I got the message yesterday.'

'I can't quite believe I'm here.'

'It's wonderful! Your boss is very good to let you have the time off.'

'I've worked enough unpaid overtime in the short time I've been there to make her feel guilty enough to say yes.'

Hope laughed. 'Well, I'm sorry the hotel isn't the most attractive of hotels. But it's the best one here for the price and there aren't any decent hotels next to the lake. Most people head out from Almaty. You must be starving. I know it's only five but shall we get some dinner after you check in?'

'Sounds good.'

Thirty minutes later they were sitting in the hotel's restaurant with its old-fashioned décor of beiges and creams that reflected the hotel's exterior.

'So what are you running away from this time?' Hope asked after they ordered their food.

'You know me too well.'

'I do.' Hope leant forward, face serious. 'What's wrong, Charity?'

Charity told her everything that had happened over the past few weeks.

'So Dan's been lying?' Hope asked when Charity had finished.

Charity nodded. 'I've seen a different side to him.'

'That's the way relationships work though, isn't it? You get to know people, see them for what they really are. The question is, do you trust him? And do you love him?'

'I do love him.'

'But you don't trust him?'

Charity sighed. 'I don't know.'

Hope's cheeks flushed pink as she watched a man in a tweed jacket walk towards them.

'Who's that dapper man?' Charity asked.

'My editor.'

'He's here too?'

'He offered to come at the last minute.'

Charity quirked an eyebrow. 'Is there a little romance developing here?'

270

'Shush!' Hope said as the editor came up to the table.

'Ah, so now I know why I was stood up for dinner,' the editor said. He was in his late thirties, tall and broad-shouldered with kind blue eyes and scruffy dark hair. He was just the sort of man Charity could imagine Hope ending up with. She smiled to herself. How wonderful would that be?

'This is Peter, my editor,' Hope said. 'Peter, this is my sister, Charity.'

'Ah, the psychiatrist.'

'Oh, nothing as glamorous as that, just a plain old counsellor. Why don't you join us?'

'Oh no,' Peter said, shaking his head. 'I couldn't intrude.'

'I insist,' Charity said, gesturing to the spare chair.

Hope frowned. 'Are you sure? Don't you want to talk?'

'I'm sure,' Charity said. 'I want to forget about what's happening in the UK and chatting to some literary types is ideal.'

Over the next two hours the three of them had dinner and talked. It was clear to Charity there was chemistry between Hope and Peter, who seemed enraptured whenever Hope talked. Hope wasn't so obvious about her feelings, but the little glances towards him as he talked, and the way she blushed when he complimented her poetry made it clear to Charity that she was developing feelings for him. It filled her with happiness. She loved the idea of Hope meeting someone, especially someone who seemed to share her interests.

But as she watched them together, she also started to regret making the decision to come out. It was clear she'd interrupted a budding romance.

'I think I'll head up now,' Charity said after a while.

'But it's only seven,' Hope said.

'I'm exhausted, Hope.'

'I'll head up too, then,' Hope said, going to stand up.

271

'No. Stay. It looks like you have a lot to chat about and really, I'm quite exhausted after the journey. We can catch up when we go to the vigil tomorrow evening.'

'You don't mind if Peter comes with us, do you?'

Charity smiled. 'Not at all.'

'I swear I'm all yours for the rest of the break.'

'Apart from the meeting I've set up with that Russian editor,' Peter said. 'We can always cancel it.'

'No, not at all,' Charity said. 'I'm here for ten days, Hope and I have plenty of time to catch up.

When Charity got to her room a few moments later she stared out at the darkening city, feeling incredibly lonely. It was wonderful seeing her sister so happy and on the brink of romance, but it also highlighted what a mess her own love life was in. Was Dan thinking of her right now? Or was she kidding herself? Maybe the simple truth was that he'd dumped her. He was a millionaire businessman after all. He probably had loads of flings. He was passionate, threw himself into things. He'd got excited about Charity but now the honeymoon period had worn off, he'd grown bored and was pleased to have found an excuse to get rid of her. Why else would he fly out to Germany without a word?

The reality of the situation really hit her then and she burst into tears. She loved him, she really did. She let herself cry for a bit and then dragged herself up, wiping her tears away. She just wanted to sleep. So without even unpacking or changing, she sank into bed.

The next afternoon, Hope, Charity and Peter hired a four-by-four to take them over the bumpy terrain that led to the lake. When they arrived a while later, the sun was setting over the dark lake, thin spruce trees rising majestically from its surface as water trickled down the surrounding cliffs.

Charity wondered what it would be like to dive under there. Maybe she'd get the chance if she could convince Hope to dive with her? When she'd broached the subject, Hope had looked pained. Maybe it was too hard for her, the memories of diving with Faith too difficult.

There were dozens of people gathered at the lake, the reflection of the flames from the candles they were holding dancing over the surface. A wizened old man stood in the middle of them, face sombre.

'Let's try to talk to him now,' Peter said to Hope.

'I'll wait for you here,' Charity said.

As they walked away, Charity contemplated the lake, remembering how Faith had described it with such passion.

A flashing light caught her eye. A man was taking photographs of the lake nearby, away from the crowds. He had dark hair, broad shoulders.

Charity frowned.

It couldn't be Niall, could it?

As she thought that, he turned and caught her eye.

It *was* Niall.

He slowly lowered his camera, surprise registering on his face. Then he strolled over. Charity peered over at Hope who was now talking to the earthquake survivor.

'What are you doing here?' Niall asked, voice incredulous.

'I came with Hope. She's been commissioned to write some poems about submerged forests, she's interviewing the earthquake survivor right now.'

Niall followed her gaze towards Hope.

'Why are *you* here?' she asked him, still not quite believing it.

'I read about the vigil, seemed like a good time to visit to take some more photos of submerged forests.'

273

Charity shook her head. 'This is just so weird.'

Niall smiled. 'It is, isn't it? But then how many other people in the world are as interested in submerged forests as the three of us?' he asked, gesturing towards Hope.

'I guess.'

He smoothed his hand over his stubble. 'So have you dived it yet?'

'Not yet. I'm not sure I'll get the chance, Hope seems reluctant.'

'I'm diving it tomorrow. I've hired a car.' He hesitated a moment, his eyes searching hers. 'You're welcome to join me?'

Charity laughed nervously. 'I don't have any equipment.'

'I know a place you can hire some from. It would be a shame for you to miss out.'

Charity looked at her sister. She would be out most of the next day meeting with the Russian editor Peter mentioned. What else would Charity do if she didn't go with Niall? Hide in her room until dinner time?

'Okay,' she said impulsively.

The next morning, Charity stared out of the window of the four-by-four Niall had hired, watching as city gave way to dirt tracks surrounded by hills and shrubs. They veered off into vast, sparse lands, farmers dressed head to toe in colourful outfits herded goats.

'So why hasn't Dan joined you?' Niall asked, jaw tensing.

'He's in Germany.' She didn't look at Niall, just continued staring out of the window, tears flooding her eyes. Then she felt his hand on her shoulder.

'Everything okay?' he asked softly.

'He just flew out there without saying a word. I think it's over between us.'

Niall glanced quickly at her, then away. 'Well, I can't say I'm upset to hear that.'

The car made a creaking noise as it bounced over the path. Charity thought of the night she lost her sister. The bump, the panic in her heart when she thought the car had knocked over a deer. How much worse it had been.

'Maybe you should slow down,' Charity said, grabbing on to the door handle.

'I'm trying to.'

As he said that, smoke started pluming from the car's bonnet. 'Shit,' Niall said as the car rolled to a stop. He jumped out and Charity quietly watched him as he opened the bonnet, leaning over it, one tanned and muscled arm holding it up. Her eyes travelled over the gleaming nape of his neck, his short dark hair, the hint of a tattoo peeking up from under his dark t-shirt. He looked up, caught her watching him and held her gaze, his look making heat coil inside her. She looked away and drank more water, trying to cool herself down as Niall walked around to her side of the car. He leant into her open window, so close she could smell the orange he'd just eaten on his breath. 'It's screwed.'

'Thought as much.'

He reached in and pulled out a map. Then he peered up, shielding his eyes from the sun as he pointed ahead. 'The canyon down to the lake's just there according to this. I reckon it's too hot to walk. Maybe we should camp out overnight, set off in the morning when it's cooler. I have a two-man tent in the back?'

She looked at him, horrified. How on earth could they sleep in such close proximity?

He laughed. 'The look on your face! Only kidding.'

'So what do we do?'

'I don't know, wait for someone to come by? There was that farmer earlier, maybe he'll come our way again.'

'And what, give us a lift on his goats?'

'Why not?'

They both burst out laughing.

'Here,' Niall said, reaching across to the side compartment and throwing her a chocolate. 'Keep yourself busy while I figure something out.'

'Oh, thank the Lord we have a man here to help figure things out,' Charity said. 'God forbid it's just me or, worse still, you were a woman. Can you imagine two women trying to figure things out?'

'Please share your tips on how we deal with this situation then,' Niall said, lips curling into a smile.

'The goat idea wasn't so far off.' She pointed at two men leading their horses along a patch of dry land nearby. 'Do you have any money?'

Ten minutes later Charity was behind Niall on the back of one of those horses, her arms slung around his waist, their diving gear hanging precariously out of the bags attached to either side of the horse's back.

She pressed herself against Niall, her fingers interlaced around his waist, the feel of his taut stomach sending rivulets through her.

He kicked his heel into the horse and it whinnied before galloping towards the mountains. Charity turned, saw the two men waving at her, the fifty dollars Niall had paid each of them tucked securely into their belts. Charity pressed her cheek against Niall's back, breathing in his familiar musky smell as the horse's hooves thundered on the ground. She focused on the sensations of wind in her hair, of the sun on her back, of her arms around Niall's waist. He shifted slightly, his body pressing against her inner thighs.

Soon, a glimmer appeared in the distance, the tops of fir trees trembling in the breeze. The horse slowed down as Niall pulled at the reins, eventually coming to a stop at the top of a huge canyon. And below, the lake.

'It's like paradise, isn't it?' Charity whispered.

'Let's get in there.'

Thirty minutes later they were heading beneath the surface in surprisingly cold water, the drowned pine trees rich and vibrant beneath the lake, branches heavy with leaves that hung like blue icicles in the glimmering water.

All sound disappeared, the misty ripples leaving her in a dream-like state. Ahead of her the trees shimmered in the haze, seeming to beckon her towards them. She glided over, fingers passing across the soft branches, the peacefulness she always felt when underwater spreading throughout her. The past few days she'd felt like she'd been standing in the middle of a sparse land, exposed and vulnerable. Here she felt safe; *here* she felt as though she could escape everything.

In the distance, Niall took photos, the flash from his camera lighting up the sunken trees, shrouding them in white, as though snow had fallen beneath the lake.

She found Niall floating in front of a particularly large tree, contemplating its bark, his camera at his side. She knew what he was thinking: this would be the ideal place to do an etching. She looked into his eyes, saw the question there. She nodded, so he lifted his knife and carved their initials into the tree.

When they returned to the surface, Niall thanked Charity.

'What for?' she asked.

'For letting me do the etching. I know my exhibition puts your name out there. I guess it's a tribute to what we once had.'

She avoided his gaze by reaching behind her to undo her tank.

'What we had was special though, wasn't it?' he persisted.

She looked up at him. 'It was.'

He smiled. 'And now we're here as friends. That makes it all even more special.'

She matched his smile. 'I agree.'

He peered at his watch. 'Fancy a snack before we set off?'

'You have snacks?'

He walked over to the horse and pulled two large triangle-shaped pastries from one of the bags. 'This is a *baursaki*, I got some at the airport.'

'That's so sweet of you to share, Niall. Thank you.'

They both perched on a large rock near the horse and ate the rich doughy treats. After they'd finished their snacks, Niall handed her a warm beer and they leant back, soaking up the evening sun.

Charity realised she'd been right to accept Niall's invitation to go diving. Yes, she couldn't help but feel slightly overwhelmed by his proximity. But if she could accept that she'd always feel this way, but not act on it, then that was progress. She liked the idea of a world where she could still have Niall in her life, without the drama of a relationship.

Was she hoping for too much?

As she said that, a rumble of thunder sounded in the distance.

'Uh-oh,' Niall said, sitting up. She followed his gaze towards a patch of dark clouds. 'Maybe we should head back.'

'Can the old boy over there outrun the rain?'

Niall shrugged. 'We need to try.'

'Okay, I'll just get changed and—'

'No time for that,' Niall said as they heard another rumble of thunder. 'Wind's blowing in our direction, the clouds will be here soon. Let's go now.'

Charity gathered up everything then jumped on to the back of the horse with Niall. The horse seemed tetchy, stamping from hoof to hoof as though it could sense the oncoming storm. Charity peered up at the amassing clouds, remembering the storm in Norfolk. Niall pressed his heel into the horse's flank and it cantered off, heading into the trees and travelling alongside the edge of the lake.

Charity felt pinpricks of rain on her head and held on tighter just as the heavens opened, rain pounding down on to them.

'Nightmare,' Niall shouted above the sound. 'We need to find cover somewhere. I saw a hut when we were standing on the canyon, we can try there?'

Charity nodded. The horse reared and they changed direction as the rain drenched Charity's hair and face. Eventually they came to a clearing and a small wooden hut that had been long abandoned, rotting wood hanging off the sides. But the metal roof seemed intact.

The horse slowed down and Niall carefully dismounted, helping Charity to do the same. They then led the horse inside. At the back of the hut was a pile of sacks, the rest of the floor was clear. Niall tied the horse to the handle of what remained of the door and then placed their bags down.

'I guess we just wait it out,' he said, sitting on the sacks and reaching into his bag for another beer. 'Want to share this? It's my last one.'

'Why not?' Charity said, joining him.

As the rain clattered down on to the metal roof, thunder and lightning exploding outside, Charity felt her head shimmer from the effect of the beer and the strangeness of the situation, being stuck in a hut in the middle of Kazakhstan with Niall.

'This is odd, isn't it?' Niall said. 'Us two stuck in a hut in the middle of Kazakhstan as a storm rages outside.' She laughed and he frowned. 'What?'

'I was just thinking the same.'

His face grew serious. 'That's always been the way with us, hasn't it? Like we're one person split into two people.'

'I guess that's what comes from being childhood sweethearts.'

Niall took a swig of beer, the tendons in his neck pulsing. 'I remember another time we sheltered from the rain.'

'Oh God, yes, in that cave.'

He nodded, eyes very intense. 'We were far from sweet then,' he murmured. She felt her body react and tried to normalise it, telling herself again it was just the way it would always be with Niall, this primal reaction. 'It was the first time I really saw you let go, just give in to what you were feeling. The way you looked, your eyes closed as you moved on top of me…'

'Niall, don't.' Charity looked away, not wanting him to see how flustered she was getting.

'What? We're just old friends sharing memories.'

'Friends don't share those kinds of memories.'

'You came for the first time that night, didn't you?'

'Jesus, Niall! You're going too far.'

'Am I? It's only too far if you don't want me to continue.'

Charity tried to push the memories away, tried to stop her body reacting. Niall moved even closer, his warm breath on her neck.

'I want to see that look on your face again,' he whispered into her ear. 'I miss that look.'

There was a sweet burning inside her, an uncoiling, a quickening of her heart and her pulse. She closed her eyes and felt his lips on her neck, his fingers dancing up her bare arms. She knew she ought to stop him, but she couldn't.

She let him push her back against the sacks, let him unzip her wetsuit and pull it off, let his lips travel down her to the place where the sweet ache was, let him make her come as he had all those years before. And then, as he moved on top of her, she opened her eyes, saw his blue ones blinking down at her as the storm raged outside.

'Please,' she whispered, her hips moving towards him.

He thrust himself into her and she felt that familiar frantic wave of feeling well up inside her as she rocked against him. When she saw Dan's face in her mind, his soft green eyes, she didn't push the thought away. Instead she closed her eyes, letting the memories of their gentle love-making clash against Niall's passionate urgency.

When they finished, she sobbed. Niall let her, understanding.

280

They stayed there all night, coiled up against each other, making love again. The next morning, as they emerged from the hut to a calm beautiful morning, the guilt overwhelmed Charity. Just a few days after Dan had walked out she was back in Niall's arms. Was the habit so ingrained she was destined to repeat it over and over?

As though sensing her mood, Niall grew quiet as the horse cantered gently up the hills and away from the glimmering lake that held their initials beneath its surface. Charity leant her cheek against Niall's back, the resignation of what she'd done, and was sure to do again, exhausting her.

'We did nothing wrong,' Niall said after a while, his eyes still ahead of him. 'You and Dan are separated, I'm single.'

'It's not about that.'

'Then what? It was inevitable, you can't deny that.'

She sighed. 'That's the problem, how inescapable it always is.'

He glanced around at her. 'There's a reason for that. We're meant to be together, you understand that, don't you? Every other relationship we have is doomed.'

She suddenly felt angry. 'And we're not doomed?'

'For God's sake, Charity,' Niall said, pulling the horse to a stop. He twisted around, looking intently into her eyes. 'We're meant to be. You know it, I know it, Dan knows it, your sister knows it.'

Maybe he was right? Maybe she was a fool for denying it?

When they returned to the hotel, they went straight to the room Niall had booked, Charity worried her sister would turn up at her own room. She felt as though she were drugged, the only certainty was the sweet mounting ache at the centre of her as Niall explored her body again with his lips and fingers.

But soon thoughts of Dan intruded. She couldn't help wondering where he was, if he really thought it was over…and if she was wrong to be here, with Niall.

'What's wrong?' Niall asked, tracing his fingers down the curve of her body.

'I can't help feeling guilty.'

Niall sighed. 'So you're thinking of Dan?'

'I can't help it.'

'You're here with me, Charity. That should be enough to tell you how you really feel.'

'It's not as clear cut as that.'

Niall sat up, staring at the ceiling in frustration. 'He lied to you. Then he disappeared to Germany without saying a word. That's *wrong*.'

'I'm worried I didn't try hard enough; that I've been too hasty. What if—'

'Jesus, Charity,' Niall said, shoving the covers off. 'He can't be that hard to get hold of. I'm going to have a shower. Call him, talk to him. And then if you still feel so torn, go back to him.' His face softened. 'I only want you to be with me if you're sure.' Then he walked into the bathroom.

Charity stayed where she was for a few minutes then she left Niall's room and headed back to her own. Once inside, she picked up the phone, dialling Dan's work number. Dan's PA Maxine answered. 'Hi, it's Charity.'

'Oh thank God you've called, Charity. Mr North is back and he's been desperately trying to track you down today after not finding you at the cottage. In fact, he's at your offices right now trying to discover where you've gone'

Charity's heart clamoured inside her chest. 'I'm in Kazakhstan with my sister. Can I give you the number to my hotel?' she said quickly. 'I'll wait by the phone until he calls.'

After Charity gave her the number, she lay back on the bed, staring up at the ceiling. If Dan was so desperately trying to find her then did that mean he regretted walking out like that? Had she ever really given him a chance to explain? And here she was, sleeping with Niall.

The phone rang. She instantly snatched it up.

'Charity?' It was Dan. He took a deep shuddery breath. 'Come home. I made a mistake walking out. I love you. Just come home.'

She closed her eyes, tears squeezing out between her lashes. 'Oh Dan, it's all such a mess.'

'I don't care,' he said passionately. 'All I care about is getting you home right now. I refuse to let you slip between my fingers. I've been a fool. I need to see you.'

Charity glanced at the door. Niall was waiting for her in his room right now. 'Why did you just leave like that?'

'My jealousy overwhelmed me.'

She swallowed. 'Of Niall?'

'Look, I don't want to talk about him, about my jealousy, it means nothing now. I can't be away from you, I've realised that the past few days. It's been torture.'

Then there was a knock on the door.

'I don't know what to do. I need time.'

'You've had time! Don't tell me the past couple of weeks haven't been torture for you too?'

'They have.'

Another knock.

'I'm due to fly back next week. We can meet then.'

He sighed. 'I'd rather not wait. I can hire a private jet.'

'No, Dan. Please, just a few more days. I'll see you at the cottage.'

'Fine. If that's what it takes. I'm not going to let you go this time, Charity.'

'I have to go.'

'I love you.'

283

'I love you too,' Charity whispered.

She put down the phone and took in a few deep breaths. Then she walked to the door and opened it to find Hope stood in the hallway.

'I got back early!' her sister declared. When she saw the look on Charity's face, her smile drifted away. 'What's wrong with you?'

'I'm so confused,' Charity said, moaning as she put her head in her hands.

Her sister put her arms around her. 'What's wrong?'

'Niall's here, I slept with him.'

Hope darted away from her like she was infectious. 'Please tell me you're joking?'

'I'm not.'

Hope flung her hands to the ceiling and let out a cry of frustration. 'What is *wrong* with you?'

Charity's stomach squirmed with guilt. 'I don't know. I was hurt. It was a mistake.'

Hope slumped down into a chair in the corner of the room. 'What about Dan?'

'That's the problem.' Charity explained the conversation she'd just had with him.

Hope shook her head. 'What a tangled web you weave. So you do love Dan?'

'Yes.'

'And Niall, you said it was a mistake?'

'It was but – but I love him too. Those old feelings just won't go away.'

'*Old* feelings. That's the problem, it's all steeped in the past, I keep telling you this.'

'And Dan? He lied to me.'

'Have you even tried to find out why?'

284

'He didn't give me the chance.'

'And what chance did you give him, flying out here as soon as you got the chance?'

Charity moaned. 'You're right.'

'You need to talk to Dan, really talk to him.'

'Yeah, maybe you should,' a voice hissed. She saw Niall walking down the hallway, his hair still wet, his angry eyes on Charity. 'I was about to come and apologise for being harsh. But turns out it's true, you really can't make up your mind.'

'Don't you think that speaks volumes?' Hope said, crossing her arms and looking Niall up and down. 'She can't drag herself away from the past, from *you*.'

Niall sighed. 'Hope, I—'

'I'm here, you know,' Charity shouted out in frustration. 'I don't need either of you telling me what to do.'

Hope and Niall grew silent, watching her.

'I need some time to figure things out,' she said, her voice softer.

'Fine,' Niall said. 'Take your fucking time. You can't keep messing with my feelings like this.'

Chapter Nineteen

Charity

Near Busby-on-Sea, UK
July 1988

Charity returned to the UK the next week to find Dan waiting for her at the cottage. They both contemplated each other for a few moments, then Dan strode over, pulling her into his arms.

'I've missed you,' he whispered. 'I'm sorry I let my jealousy overwhelm me.'

She looked up into his eyes. 'Of Niall?'

He nodded. 'It's hard seeing you two together. There's this spark between you that I just feel I can't compete with. I thought it just best I leave you to it. But I see that was a mistake now, I need to fight for you.'

She pulled away from him, turning away, worried he'd see what she'd done with Niall written all over her face. Niall had said she had to stop messing with his feelings. Wasn't she doing the same with Dan?

In the last few days of their holiday together, Hope had offered a solution: to stay with her in Busby-on-Sea for a couple of weeks, even more if she wanted, to get some space from both men. She could still commute to her job.

'I need some space to figure things out,' she said. Dan's face dropped. She quickly took his hand. 'I love you, that's one thing I'm sure of. But I need stability. I need everything to be sure and true. Will you give me more time?'

He took in a deep breath. 'If that's what you need.'

'I do.'

He gently kissed her lips. 'I'll be here waiting,' he said.

Charity returned to Busby-on-Sea that afternoon. Strange how the very place she wanted to escape from was now offering her shelter from the mess her love life was in. She took the time to reflect when she wasn't at work, sitting on the very rocks she once did with Faith and Hope, watching the sea and trying to find answers in it.

She loved Dan, there was no doubt about it. And she would always love Niall. But was it all too close for comfort? Would Dan always be jealous of Niall and would Niall always, somehow, crop up in her life and tempt her into his arms?

A month after arriving back from Kazakhstan, as she was tidying through Hope's messy bathroom cabinet one Saturday, she noticed sanitary towels on the bottom shelf. She ran through the dates in her mind and realised her period was late. It was never late, but then she did have a tumultuous few days in the lead up to going to Kazakhstan. Maybe she forgot?

The full horror of the situation dawned on her. If she were pregnant, how would she know who the father was? She and Dan had made love before they went out for dinner with Miles, the owner of the cruise liner. And then the night in the hut with Niall only happened a couple of days later.

She had to find out for sure whether she was pregnant or not so she drove a few towns away and went into a chemist's to find a home pregnancy test. When she got back home, she read and re-read the instructions. After taking the test, she waited anxiously for the result to appear. After a few moments, the tip turned to blue.

That evening over dinner, Charity played with her food as she stared out of the window. She'd been in shock all afternoon, grateful Hope was at the café so she could try to digest the news. Hope had arrived home full of stories about the customers, and Charity had let her talk, fingers grazing her stomach as she thought of the tiny mass of cells growing inside. She knew she wanted to be a mother one day but now? Is this how Faith had felt when she'd found out she was pregnant?

And then there was the fact Charity had no idea who the father was.

Hope frowned as she looked at Charity. 'Are you okay?'

Charity peered up. 'Fine.'

'No you're not. What is it?'

Charity bit her lip, tears flooding her eyes.

'Oh Christ, what now,' Hope said.

'I'm pregnant,' Charity blurted out.

Hope put her hand to her mouth. 'Charity! That's wonderful.' She frowned. 'Or is it?' She closed her eyes. 'You slept with Niall in Kazakhstan.'

'And Dan just a couple of days before. I don't know what to do.'

Hope slid her hand across to Charity's. 'Well, think about it logically. There's no question you're keeping it, is there? So you need to decide: do you really want an ex-con as your child's father? Every time you look at him, you'll know that he killed our sister? Plus he always said he never wanted kids, didn't he?'

Charity gnawed at her lip. Hope was right. Niall had always been so vehement about not wanting children. There was also the fact he didn't like being tied to one place. Her child would need security.

Her child. It felt so strange to think that.

'Then there's Dan,' Hope said softly. 'A good man, someone who can provide a stable loving environment for you and your child. And that beautiful cottage of yours, can you imagine bringing a family up there?'

She put her hand on her belly and imagined her child playing outside the cottage, kicking their little legs into the sea below, just as she had when she was a child. She could see a life there as a family. Deep down, hadn't she imagined that from the moment she saw the house? It had been early days with Dan but something inside had told her they'd have that one day, a beautiful house filled with a beautiful family.

Hope was right, Dan could be a good dad. She just couldn't see that in Niall. Niall loved her, deeply, but it was a turbulent kind of love. Not this soft, gentle kind – the kind of love a child needed.

She stood up. 'I'm going to call Dan.'

Chapter Twenty

Willow

Near Busby-on-Sea, UK
October 2016

I watch the sun begin to sink beneath the calm sea from the window seat in my room. My aunt Hope made the seat for me from old fabric. Funny the things you forget. All I've remembered lately is the bitterness between us, the anger and the arguments.

The cottage is quiet and dark. The walls press in around me, all the secrets I've discovered the past few weeks seeming to fill the space. In the distance, the homeless woman – Mad Shoe Lady – watches the sea, moonlight glinting off the trolley beside her.

I came straight here after arriving in the UK this morning. I'd hoped to find Aunt Hope tucked into her own window seat downstairs, notepad in hand as she stared wistfully out to sea. I planned to be calm; to be grown-up; to prove, as Niall had suggested, that I could handle the truth. But she wasn't here when I arrived, nor is she here now. So I went to my old room to wait for her, as I used to as a teenager.

I love this room. Knowing Mum grew up in it makes it special. Over the years, I'd stuck posters of various rock groups over the faded flowery wallpaper, lined Mum's shelves with diving books and atlases. But I'd kept her single bed, her floral duvet cover, now old and discoloured but hers all the same. Some of her clothes are still in the wardrobe now, stonewashed denim and colourful blouses. There are photos of her and Dad, clumsily stuck to the walls by me over the years. I get up now, find a picture of the two of them outside their cottage the year before I was born, wide smiles on their beautiful faces. Was Mum pregnant then?

I wonder if she missed being in her childhood house with the memories it held of Faith. Or maybe she preferred to avoid those memories. I peer up. There's an attic room above me that Aunt Hope always keeps locked, using the excuse that my feet would go through the fragile floorboards if I walked inside. Now I think about it, I realise that surely that must have been Aunt Faith's room?

I walk up the tiny flight of stairs that's hidden at the end of the hallway behind a door. They always used to fascinate me, these stairs. I'd sit on the bottom step and stare up at the locked door, wishing I could somehow get into that room.

When I walk up the stairs now, I hesitate before I put my hand on the doorknob. It feels sacred, somehow, to be back here, like I'm a child again. I take a deep breath and turn the knob.

The door opens.

My heartbeat quickens. I suppose Aunt Hope has had no need to keep it locked since I left. I find the light, turn it on.

I notice the wallpaper first, pale blue with colourful fish dotted all over it. Then the bed, a large bed with a thick cream duvet. It looks dusty but is perfectly made. Lying on two soft pillows is a doll with straw hair and blue dungarees. There's a pretty white dressing table where the two eaves of the roof meet. My reflection stares back at me from a large silver-edged mirror.

I walk carefully across the floorboards and over a white fur rug to get to the table. The floorboards creak but don't collapse under my weight. Clearly Aunt Hope exaggerated to keep me away from this room.

There isn't much on the table, not like in Mum's room where I found an array of hairsprays and perfumes and makeup when I moved in when I was seven. Here, there's just one bottle of perfume, a simple crystal bottle, and a tube of lip-gloss.

How unbearably sad, to think this room has been frozen in time all these years.

Stuck to the mirror is a photo of the three sisters together. Mum's about fourteen in it, her dark hair a mass of permed curls around her head, red pouty lips and stonewashed denim. Aunt Hope sits quietly, a book tucked under her arm, her red hair swept over one shoulder and trailing down her long purple dress.

Then my aunt Faith, soft blonde hair lifting slightly in the wind, a slim arm wrapped around her tummy, a pretty blue summer dress to her knees.

My heart aches as I look at her. She died so young, Mum too, leaving just Aunt Hope behind.

Poor Aunt Hope.

The three sisters all seem so different on first glance. But on closer inspection you can see they have the same shape to their faces: cherub cheeks, high foreheads, full lips. I catch sight of my face in the mirror. I look like them, too.

I want this photo. I *deserve* this photo. After years of not being told I had another aunt, of never seeing photos of her, I think it's only right. I pull it from the mirror. As I do so, another photo falls to the floor, hidden behind the photo of the sisters. I lean down and pick it up.

Then I let out a gasp.

He has dark hair instead of his normal blond, but I'd know that face anywhere.

It's Dad.

And his arms are wrapped around Aunt Faith's waist.

Chapter Twenty-One

Charity

Near Busby-on-Sea, UK
April 1996

Charity quickly shoved the overflowing bag of Dan's shredded paperwork down the side of the house with all the other bags, wiping the sweat from her forehead, cursing when she smeared jam over her skin. She licked her finger, wiping the stickiness away as she jogged up the garden, wind sweeping her hair up from her neck, the clip she'd painstakingly placed in the back of it tumbling out.

Oh well, she'd given up on looking perfect for special occasions the day Willow was born seven years ago.

'Come on, Tommy,' she cried out to their Labrador, patting her leg and realising too late that it meant she'd get jam on her dress too.

'I'll get him,' Hope said, appearing at the French doors that led out into the garden and grabbing Tommy's collar. She was wearing a long green dress, her red hair tied into a braid. Charity smiled, grateful. How would she cope without her sister here?

'I've done more sandwiches,' Hope called over her shoulder as she dragged Tommy up the garden by his collar, 'and found some more cakes, you must have put them in the pan cupboard by accident.'

'Oh, fantastic, you're a godsend.'

As they strode into the kitchen, Tommy took one look at the trays of food sitting on the side and shrugged Hope off before bombing towards the food. The two sisters took chase and as Charity reached for him her elbow caught the tray of cakes Hope had found, sending them flying on to the floor. Tommy's snout was in them before they could stop him.

The two sisters looked at each other then burst out laughing.

'Go,' Hope said, gently shoving Charity away. 'Finish doing your makeup before everyone arrives, I'll sort this all out.'

'I don't have time!'

Hope looked at her watch. 'You have twenty minutes. Now go!' She'd already started scooping the remains of the cakes up, throwing them into the bin. Charity reluctantly left the room. How could a kids' party be so bloody stressful? She walked down the cottage's hallway then jogged upstairs, worry with every step. What if there wasn't enough food? Was she wrong to have got wine for the adults? Had she arranged enough games?

As she passed the bathroom, she paused. Dan was brushing Willow's dark hair, telling her some story he'd made up about fairies who stole human hair because it was so soft to sleep on. Despite how busy he was with the imminent launch of his cruise ship, he still took time out to be with his daughter. Charity felt a swell of emotion. This was her family, her perfect little family. She and Dan had talked about having more children but things were so perfect as they were, it never quite happened.

'They can't have mine,' Willow said in her best indignant voice. 'I'd look silly without hair.'

Dan smiled. He looked so handsome in his white polo shirt and tan chinos. Charity was sure all the mums would be in love by the end of the party.

'I think you'd look beautiful whatever you had on your head, darling. There.' He put the brush down and stood back to look at Willow. She was wearing a bright green tutu over polka dot black leggings, and a t-shirt Dan had got her with a photo of their dog Tommy on the front. On the floor in a heap was the pretty red and black dress Charity had bought for Willow the week before. Clearly Willow had decided not to wear it and Dan had given in to her. Charity ought to be annoyed, she'd taken ages to find that dress, but instead she smiled, her stress dissipating as she watched them together.

All that mattered was that her beautiful daughter was turning seven today.

Dan caught her eye then looked towards the crumpled dress. 'The dress slipped from the hanger, didn't it, Willow?'

Willow nodded vigorously. 'And now the fairies need it to sleep on because they can't have my hair.'

'Quite,' Dan said, nodding with her. 'So Willow has *reluctantly* decided to wear her favourite tutu, leggings and t-shirt. Very heroic of her.'

'Very,' Willow said. Her serious face was replaced with a smile and she ran towards Charity, wrapping her arms around her mother's waist and staring up at her through her long dark eyelashes. 'Mummy, *please* can Tommy have some cake.'

'He already has, darling,' Charity said, kissing the top of her head and rolling her eyes at Dan.

'Oh no, really?' Dan asked, strolling over and pulling them both into a family hug. This was Charity's favourite thing, their ritual family hug carried out several times a day.

'Really,' Charity said, quickly kissing his neck. She wrapped her hand around his, felt his wedding ring. It still didn't feel real, that he was her husband and she his wife. They'd married in a quiet ceremony overlooking the sea five years ago with just Hope and a two-year-old Willow as guests.

'Tommy can have more cake though, can't he?' Willow asked. 'He'll be jealous watching everyone eat cake while he can't.'

'Of course, sweetheart,' Dan said.

'He's had enough,' Charity replied, giving Dan a look. How was Willow supposed to learn she couldn't get everything her way? 'He'll get a bad tummy,' she added. 'Do you want Tommy to have a bad tummy?'

Willow shook her head.

'Then keep the cake away from him, my gorgeous birthday girl.' Charity scooped Willow up, planting a kiss on her chubby cheek. 'Right, I really must finish getting ready, all I need is five minutes.'

'You look gorgeous,' Dan murmured, kissing her neck.

'Yuck,' Willow said.

Dan looked down at her. 'Race you downstairs?'

'No racing on the stairs!' Charity shouted after them as they darted down the hallway, completely ignoring her.

She laughed as she walked to the bedroom and sat at her dressing table, looking at the photo she kept on there of a tiny Willow curled in Dan's arms just after she'd been born. Charity thought back to the night when Willow arrived, a patch of black hair and punching fists, blue-eyed and purple-faced. She'd stared into her daughter's eyes and wondered if she'd got them from Niall. A few hours after the picture was taken, when Dan had gently handed Willow over to her aunt Hope, and aunt and niece had regarded each other for what seemed like an eternity, Hope had looked up at Charity. 'She has Faith's eyes,' she'd said.

'Faith's eyes,' Charity had repeated, almost laughing with relief. Yes, she had Faith's eyes.

'Ready?' Hope asked now, appearing at the bedroom door.

'Yes.' Charity stood up, taking her sister's hand and walking downstairs to celebrate Willow's birthday. No, she didn't have a moment of regret. Willow was the happiest child she knew and Dan was every bit as wonderful as she'd hoped he'd be.

Charity stepped out into the sunshine a few hours after the party ended with two bags of rubbish, a satisfied smile on her face. The party hadn't been perfect. Willow had had a tantrum when a little boy dared to try and pet Tommy, and Dan had burnt the sausage rolls. But it had been fun, a hectic stressful kind of fun.

Charity peered back inside to see Hope and Willow eating left-over birthday cake together. They had an interesting relationship, aunt and niece. It wasn't the kind where Willow would run to her aunt in delight each time she visited. Instead, Willow regarded Hope with the same look she'd given her aunt when she was born: serious and quizzical. But they had this strange bond, could sit for hours together in peaceful quiet. Charity found them out in the garden once, standing over a snail and watching as it painstakingly slid across the path with the same look on their faces. They stayed like that for half an hour. Willow seemed to be more like Hope than Charity sometimes. Charity didn't mind. Maybe she preferred that.

Charity walked around the side of the house, hauling both bags with her. As she did so, one of the bags snagged on the wall, a huge hole appearing in its side. Paper flew out, lifting in the breeze, evidence of the big clear-out Dan was doing in his home office in preparation for launching the new ship.

'Wonderful.' Charity sighed, grabbing the runaway paper, going to shove it back into the bag. But as she did so, a series of photos caught her eye.

They were all headshots of women who looked very similar to one another: blonde hair, blue eyes. With them was a fax, a modelling agency's contact details at the top. Someone had scrawled beneath it:

Dan,

Choose which one you want and I'll have
Georgia call you to make arrangements.

Thanks, Sasha

Charity flicked through the photos then let out a gasp. One of the girls looked just like Faith. In fact, wasn't it the same woman Charity had seen in the restaurant in India that had looked so much like her sister? She looked again, feeling sure of it. She tucked the photos into her pocket, walking back inside.

That night, with Willow in bed and Hope giving a talk to a local literary club about her third book of poetry, Charity brought the photo up with Dan as they snuggled on the sofa.

'These fell from the rubbish bags,' she said carefully, handing them to him.

'God, that was years ago,' he said, looking at the photos. 'Must have been for an advertising campaign.'

'This one looks just like my sister Faith, don't you think?' she asked, pointing to it.

He frowned. 'Can't see it myself.'

'Do you remember I told you about an argument Niall and I had in India?'

Niall. She'd not mentioned his name for seven years. She hadn't heard from him in that time either. But she'd read that he was doing even better with his photographs, travelling the world, taking photos of submerged forests and selling them for a fortune.

Dan's jaw tensed. 'And?'

'This is the girl I saw just before, I swear it is.' She pointed at the image.

'I don't understand what you're trying to get at, darling.'

Charity examined his face. 'Don't you think it's weird that it's the same woman?'

'How can it be? I suppose she might have gone on holiday to the same place as you. But it's all rather unlikely, don't you think?' He pulled her close to him, looking down at her. 'I suppose you've been thinking about your sister more recently, what with Willow's birthday?'

She sighed. 'Yes, it makes me sad to think Willow will never meet her aunt.'

'Or her cousin,' Dan said. 'Willow would have had an older cousin if Faith and the baby had lived.' Charity tensed. The thought had crossed her mind many times but it was hard hearing it spoken out loud. 'It'll be difficult explaining all that to Willow when she's older, won't it?' Dan continued. 'The fact your ex killed her cousin.'

Charity moved away from him, looking him in the face. 'Willow will never know. She doesn't *need* to know.'

'Why not?' he asked, face cold. 'She ought to know she had another aunt, surely? You can't just pretend Faith never existed.'

'I – I haven't thought about it properly.'

'But it's a no-brainer. We must tell Willow, surely?'

'M-maybe,' Charity stammered. 'She doesn't need to know about the accident though.'

'Why not?'

Charity peered up at the ceiling, imagining Willow sleeping in her little bed, arms wrapped tight around the old blanket she so loved. 'I haven't thought about it properly.'

'Now's the time then.'

She looked into Dan's eyes and then down at his glass of wine. He got like this when he drank sometimes, matter-of-fact and cold. It was even worse when he was stressed, as he was with the cruise ship launch fast approaching. 'I really don't think she needs to know about the accident, Dan.'

'She'll find out,' Dan replied. 'The internet's really flying, we'll be able to search archived articles online soon, enter someone's name and boom.'

The thought filled Charity with horror. 'Regardless, I'd rather not tell her. All she needs to know is her aunt passed away when she was young. If she asks how, we can say it was a car accident. No details.'

Dan shook his head. 'But that's not the truth. I'd feel more comfortable if she knew everything.'

'Dan,' she said softly. 'Faith was *my* sister, remember? I feel it's up to me to choose what to tell Willow about her.'

Dan held her gaze for a few moments and she could tell he was struggling with what to say next. Then he shrugged and turned back to the TV. 'Fine.'

She put her hand on his arm. 'It's just—'

He shrugged her hand off. 'It's *fine*, honestly.'

Charity leant back against the sofa. Was Dan right, should she tell Willow the truth?

'What's wrong with Dan?' Hope asked Charity in a low voice the next morning. They both glanced over at Dan who was angrily tearing at some toast with his teeth as he read his paper.

'No idea,' Charity replied. But she did know: it was that conversation from the night before. The first mention of Niall in over seven years seemed to have been enough to send him into one of his moods.

In the years Charity had spent with Dan, she'd seen more of his dark side; how he'd grow quiet for days. Often, she wouldn't know why and presumed it was work. Sometimes she knew it was her fault: something she'd said out of turn, like the time she'd brought up the flooding threat for the cottage again, another subject he'd wanted closed. She grew used to his moods, letting him be when she saw one approaching. Even Willow knew when to leave Daddy alone nowadays. But when he emerged from one of his moods, he'd shower them both with attention and affection, presents and trips away. It almost made up for the days when they lost him.

She could see he was sinking into such a mood now, all because of the conversation they'd had the night before. She wasn't sure she had the patience for it.

'I was wondering,' she asked, turning to Hope. 'How do you fancy *two* houseguests this week?'

Dan peered up from his paper, brow creased.

'But you need to be here for the launch,' Hope said.

'Not for a few days. I could visit with Willow then return the night before the launch.'

'You want to go to Busby-on-Sea?' Dan asked.

'It makes sense. It'll give you some space before the launch.'

'Sounds like your mind's made up,' Dan said, folding his newspaper up and standing. He walked around the table and kissed Charity on the lips. His lips felt hard. He pulled back to look her in the eye then his face softened. 'Just make sure you're back in time for the launch.'

'Why can't *I* go to the launch?' Willow asked for the hundredth time.

'You'll see the ship when we get back,' Dan explained to her. 'The cruise is for adults, darling, lots of boring wine and business talk. The best bit is the party when we get back. Now *that* you'll love.'

'The party with fireworks?' Willow asked.

Dan pulled Willow into a big hug. 'Yes, that's right, darling, and you'll be our most important guest.' He looked down at her, brushing her dark fringe from her eyes. 'I love you, Willow, my most precious beautiful girl.'

'Love you too, Daddy,' Willow replied, looking up at him with a huge smile on her face.

Charity watched them, her eyes filling with tears.

'Better get packed then,' she said, forcing her voice to be singsong for Willow. 'How exciting, an impromptu holiday!'

As Charity walked up the stairs to pack with Willow, she turned to see Dan standing at the front door, looking up at them both. He nodded once, like he knew why she was doing this – was grateful even – then let himself out.

Chapter Twenty-Two

Charity

Busby-on-Sea
April 1996

Charity stared out of the taxi window, watching the familiar sights of Busby-on-Sea flash past: the old abandoned ship in the middle of the town square, the art café that had been in her family for over thirty years; the cracked and filthy promenade.

Dan had called her, asking her to check in on the mansion. He'd not been able to sell it so it just sat there, empty and unused. She'd left Hope and Willow at the house playing a game of patience. Hope had taught Willow how to play it the night before and now Willow was obsessed, despite getting it wrong most of the time. It had been strange for Charity, arriving at her old childhood home the night before, peering up at the dark windows and remembering all the times she'd done the same after jumping out of Niall's car… including on the night Faith died, no idea it had been her sister on that road just a few moments before.

She didn't come to Busby-on-Sea much, desperate to avoid the memories. But when she did, they flooded back.

Charity pulled out the photo of Willow she kept in her purse. *Focus on your daughter, not the past*, she told herself. That's what she'd been doing for seven years, each time dark thoughts about the night Faith died crossed her mind, focusing on the future, on Willow.

The taxi turned into the long road leading up to Dan's house. It seemed smaller than she remembered, its white exterior now dirty, weeds poking through the once manicured lawns. It was being looked after by a local gardener and housekeeping couple. But it wasn't the same without people actually living there.

'This place has changed since I was here last,' the taxi driver observed. 'Dan North and his glamorous model wife.'

Charity couldn't help but smile to herself. If only the driver knew Dan's not-so-glamorous second wife was in the car now.

'My brother knew him well,' the taxi driver continued. 'Used to edit the local paper, passed away last year from a heart attack.'

'Oh, I'm sorry to hear that.'

'He was a good bloke, my brother. Had some interesting things to say about Dan North.'

'Really?' Charity asked, gripping the headrest to hear the driver better.

'Yeah, he leaked some good stories to my brother. My brother told me last year, before he died. Stories about local business, politicians…good photo of that hit-and-run bloke who killed that poor girl on Ashcroft Road. Probably before your time, all that.'

Charity's blood turned to ice as she thought of the photo of her and Niall that had appeared on the front of the local paper all those years ago on the day they found the submerged forest in Busby-on-Sea with Dan and Lana. The article had even revealed that she and Niall had been dating, something she thought only the three sisters knew.

'You said Dan North leaked it to the paper?' she asked.

'Yeah.'

The uncomfortable things she'd learnt about Dan all those years ago came back to her: the way he'd tried to wreck Niall's career, the methods he'd used to get the cottage. And now this? Plus Dan had implied he didn't know Charity had a sister who died until she told him on the boat the day the article came out. But he must have known if he'd leaked that article!

'You okay, love?' the taxi driver asked. 'I haven't just put my foot in it, have I?'

'No, it's fine.' She forced a smile and dug around in her bag for her purse, quickly handing the money over then stepping from the car. As the taxi drove away, she wrapped her arms around herself and stared up at the huge mansion her husband owned.

What games had Dan been playing?

That night, after dinner with Hope and Willow, she called Dan. The phone rang for a while before he answered, slightly out of breath. 'Oh, hello, darling. Just been watering the garden. Heard the phone and had to run for it.'

Charity imagined Dan standing beneath the willow at the end of their garden, absent-mindedly watering the grass as he stared out into the distance. He'd be wearing those paint-splattered old green shorts he liked to wear outside, a white t-shirt, sleeves rolled right up to reveal his tanned shoulders, his blond hair tousled. She wanted to be there to wrap her arms around him and look into his eyes, ask him what the hell he was playing at.

She sat on the bench, squeezing its edges with her hands to keep focus. 'I had a really disturbing chat with a taxi driver today.' She paused, took another deep breath. 'His brother edited the local paper here. He said *you* leaked that photo of me and Niall to him,

307

the one that was on the front page all those years back?' It came out in a jumble, words tripping over each other.

Dan didn't say anything. All she could hear was his breath down the other end of the phone.

'He's lying,' he said eventually.

'I don't believe you.'

Dan sighed. She imagined him putting his hand to his head, massaging his temple as he closed his eyes. Maybe the sun would be setting in the distance, dipping over the hills as it did, casting the kitchen in a soft orange glow. 'Who do you believe more, a random taxi driver or me?'

'I'm sorry, Dan, but the truth is, I don't know. Once the launch is out of the way tomorrow, we need to talk.'

Then she put the phone down and walked back into the kitchen. 'Everything okay?' Hope asked her.

'I just need some fresh air,' Charity said. 'Go get your bucket and spade, Willow sweetheart.'

An hour later, as Willow occupied herself digging up pebbles and transferring them to her bucket, Charity thought about the times she'd come here with Faith, Hope and Niall, all three lying on the pebbles, exhausted from an afternoon searching for the forest.

'Come on,' she said to Willow. 'Let's walk farther up, there's a rock pool, we might see some fish. You can pick some shells up on the way to make Daddy a special gift later.'

Willow's eyes lit up and she jumped up with her bucket, pebbles clanging against the sides as she ran down the beach ahead of Charity, picking up shells and examining them.

As Charity strolled along the beach, a dark figure appeared in the distance. As he drew closer, she recognised him. It was Niall. She felt a sense of panic, heart faltering. She glanced at her daughter who was crouched down and examined a pile of shells a few metres ahead.

She knew there was always a chance she'd bump into him when visiting her sister here, his father was still alive after all and surely Niall visited him, despite their difficult relationship. But after years of not seeing him, she'd grown secure in the hope that she never would.

But now here he was and he was quickening his steps towards her. Her breath caught in her chest at the sight of him after so long apart. His dark hair was cropped again, hints of grey in it. He looked leaner, his facial features more defined. His blue eyes looked tired.

'Charity,' was all he said.

'How are you?'

He stared at her, blinking. Then he seemed to compose himself. 'Good.'

'What are you doing here?'

'I'm back to take more photos of the forest, a kind of retrospective.' Charity smiled. 'I hear you're quite a success now.'

'I hear you married Dan North. Are you happy?'

'Very.'

Charity quickly peered at Willow. She was now sitting on the pebbles putting a large shell up to the sun and squinting at it. She caught her eye and smiled. 'Mummy, *look* at this shell!'

Niall frowned as Willow ran towards them, arm outstretched, a large shell in her hand.

'I didn't know you had a kid,' he said.

Charity took Willow's shell, her heart thumping horribly in her chest. 'How beautiful, darling. Look, there's a whole pile there,' she said, pointing to a collection of shells and pebbles nearby. 'Maybe you can find some more? Then we can get some ice cream from Aunt Hope's café.'

Willow nodded then jogged towards the shells, looking back over her shoulder again and frowning at Niall.

'She's beautiful. How old is she?' Niall asked as he watched Willow sit cross-legged on the side of the promenade, leaning over to examine the shells.

'Five,' she lied.

'Her eyes, they're very blue, aren't they?' Realisation dawned on his face. 'My friend has a five-year-old. Your daughter looks older than five.'

'She's got Dan's height. So tell me more about—'

'Jesus, Charity. Is she seven? Could she be mine?'

'Of course not!' Charity snapped.

He took a step towards her. 'If there's a chance she's mine, Charity…'

'She isn't. Okay? She *isn't*.'

'You're lying. I can tell. You don't know, do you? You don't know whose she is. Just tell me the truth,' he said, his face pained.

'Okay,' Charity said, sick of carrying this secret around each day. 'I have no idea whose she is.'

'Then why the hell didn't you just tell me?'

Charity didn't say anything.

'I see,' Niall said. 'You thought Dan would be the better father because of his money.'

'It wasn't just the money, Niall. You always said you didn't want kids. And you're always travelling.'

'I said that when I was seventeen, for Christ's sake. If I knew I had a daughter, I'd have given all the travelling up, you realise that, don't you?'

'I don't,' Charity whispered.

'I can't believe this,' Niall said. 'Can you get a test done?'

'No,' Charity said, shaking her head. 'Willow loves Dan, I couldn't do that to her.'

310

'And what about me?' Niall said, tears welling in his blue eyes as he grabbed her arm. 'Do you know what it's going to do to me knowing I might have a daughter with you?'

There was a loud clang as Willow's bucket fell to the ground, pebbles and shells scattering everywhere. 'Mummy?' she asked in a scared voice. Niall let Charity's arm fall to her side, face flooding with emotion as he looked at Willow. Charity took one last desperate look at him then jogged over to her daughter, leaning down to pick up the pebbles and shells she'd dropped. 'It's okay, darling,' she said. 'Shall we go and get that ice cream?'

'Why did that man grab you, Mummy?'

Niall flinched, turning away.

'I nearly tripped over!' Charity said, trying her best not to cry in front of her daughter. 'You know how clumsy I am. It was very nice of him to help me. Now, let's go, shall we?' She took her daughter's hand and led her towards the café in the distance, turning just once to contemplate Niall. He was standing in the same spot, watching them with a tortured look on his face. She felt sick to her stomach and full of guilt. He had every right to be upset, what a thing to keep from him! But she'd had no choice.

She rushed into the café and ordered two strawberry ice cream sundaes from the pretty teenager behind the till, then took them to a small table by the window, peering back out towards the spot where Niall had been.

He'd gone.

Their ice creams were brought over and Willow tucked right into hers as Charity continued staring out of the window. She looked at Willow, her pretty face smeared with ice cream. Had she made a mistake cutting Niall out of her life when she found out she was pregnant?

'Come here,' she said to Willow, reaching into her bag for some wet wipes.

'Daddy's ship,' Willow said, pulling the brochure Dan had produced for the launch from Charity's bag. She'd heard Dan reading from it to Willow as he'd tucked her into bed a few nights before.

Willow flicked through it as Charity watched her. She couldn't disrupt her life. She was happy in the cottage, with Dan. And so was Charity. She just wished she didn't keep discovering these strange things about her husband.

'Grandma,' Willow said, pointing to a photograph of Dan's mother, an attractive grey-haired woman with Dan's green eyes. She was sitting on an opulent red chair, hands crossed delicately on her lap, a distant smile on her face.

'Ah, yes,' Charity said as she looked at it. 'That painting's going to be hung up inside the ship.'

'Daddy says I look like her.'

Charity smoothed her finger over the woman's face. Maybe she did, a bit. Then she noticed something, a necklace hanging from his mother's neck. She picked the brochure up, peering closer.

A distinctive anchor pendant hung from it covered in sparkling jewels.

Faith's pendant.

How did Faith get Dan's mother's pendant?

There was only one explanation. He must have given it to her. Her stomach dropped. No, that wasn't possible. Surely he would have told her if he knew Faith? What if he sold it when he was young and Faith bought it?

She thought of the way Faith used to fiddle with it over dinner each evening, staring wistfully out of the window. Or the careful way she clasped it around her neck in the mornings, tilting her head to look at it in the mirror.

It meant something to her. It wasn't just some cheap trinket she'd found in a shop.

312

Could Dan have given it to her?

That night, as she kissed Willow goodnight, Charity remembered what Hope had said all those years ago: all that mattered was her daughter.

'I love you, darling,' she whispered to Willow. 'See you in a week.'

She took one last look at her beautiful daughter and then walked out of the room, going downstairs.

'I hope you have some armour packed in there,' Hope said as she looked at Charity's bags in the hallway. 'Sounds like you and Dan have a lot to spar about.'

Charity hadn't told Hope about the necklace, she needed to get the facts first. But she had told her about the taxi driver's revelations.

Hope sighed. 'Look, all I want is for you to have a normal relationship, Charity. If you're not with the man who killed our sister, you're with a prolific millionaire liar. Can't you just settle down with an accountant or something?'

'Or no man at all,' Charity said.

Hope looked away, no doubt thinking of Peter, her editor. Things had seemed to fizzle out with Peter after Hope decided to forgo their plans to spend more time with Charity when they were in Kazakhstan. Charity always wondered whether, if Charity hadn't flown out there, things would have worked out between them. At least Hope had a poetry book coming out soon, something she'd wanted for years.

'Whatever happens between you and Dan,' Hope said, her face serious all of a sudden, 'I'm here for you and Willow. This house is yours too, remember. You'll never be alone.'

Charity felt a glimmer of hope in her heart. If she left Dan, it wouldn't feel so terrifying with her sister by her side, would it?

Hope looked out of the window. 'Your car's here.'

Charity gave her sister a hug. 'You're wonderful, you know,' she whispered in her ear.

'Oh, stop being so soppy,' Hope said, shooing her away. But not before Charity saw her grey eyes glimmer with emotion.

Just before Charity stepped into the taxi, she glanced up at her old room, the room Willow was now sleeping in. She was already missing her before she'd even left. 'Love you, darling,' she whispered. Then she stepped into the taxi.

Chapter Twenty-Three

Charity

In the middle of the Aegean Sea, Greece
May 1996

Charity wrapped her red shawl around her shoulders. She could still smell Willow on it, that soft sweet scent of hers, baby powder and strawberries. She missed her desperately and yearned to be with her right now, pointing at the seagulls swooping down towards the sparkling waves. Instead, she was on her own, standing on the small balcony outside her large cabin, watching as the sea lapped against the vast white side of the cruise ship. It was as though she were travelling in a colossal whale. She felt tiny, insubstantial, completely at its mercy.

She'd hardly seen Dan since embarking. He was whisked away by his marketing people. She was fine with that. She needed time to pull herself together and figure out what to say.

The wind whipped her hair about her head so she stepped back into the cabin. It was opulent and romantic, with plush taupe chairs and bronze silk blankets draped across a large king-size bed. She ought to be excited about sharing that bed with Dan tonight.

But instead, all she could think about was the possibility that he'd shared a bed with her sister too.

She peered into the tall gilded mirror. She was wearing the long black silk dress with plunging neckline she'd always planned to wear to this. The idea had been to blow Dan's mind. But now she wished she was wearing something more appropriate for the confrontation she was planning. Maybe a suit of armour, like Hope had suggested. She looked down at the silver bag Willow had got her for her birthday. She'd be back with her daughter in a few days and everything would be fine. It *had* to be fine.

She took a deep breath, then let herself out of the cabin, tummy tingling with nerves as she walked down the corridor towards the bar. She pushed open the glass doors to get inside. The bar itself was made from polished rosewood with gold-topped stools lining it. Several round tables sat nearby where other elegantly dressed passengers were enjoying drinks. Beyond them, a large balcony graced the length of the room, protected by glass sliding doors. The ocean spread out wide and blue into the distance, the setting sun giving it a pink hue.

Charity sat at the bar and ordered a glass of wine. A peel of laughter rang out from nearby and a throng of dancers dressed in glitzy silver dresses passed outside. She felt out of place here, foolish. Everyone was happy and full of celebration.

'Charity?' Charity turned to see Dan strolling over, his hands in his pockets. He was wearing a tuxedo, his face unbearably handsome. Her stomach lurched as she thought about the possibility that he had known Faith, had *given* her that necklace.

He frowned. 'Darling, what's wrong? Have you been crying?'

Charity put her hand to her cheeks. They were wet. She didn't even know she'd been crying.

'Got hit by some spray from a wave outside,' she lied.

'Come here,' Dan said, pulling a handkerchief out from his pocket. He gently wiped it across her cheeks. 'There, perfect. Shall we go through to the dining area?' He put his hand out to her. She stared at it for a few moments and then took it, letting him steer her back inside and towards the dining area, past the photo of his mother. Charity stared at the necklace. It was definitely the one Faith wore. They passed more paintings including one depicting a voluptuous raven-haired Eve plucking an apple from a tree as a green-eyed snake looked on.

Was Dan a snake?

They entered the dining room and Charity felt overwhelmed. More Garden of Eden murals covered the walls, round tables and gold-leafed chairs decking the marble floor. In the middle was a circular glass viewing area offering views of the ocean floor below. A huge balcony curled up in the distance, a stage shrouded by gold curtains to their right. And above, a large crystal chandelier, colours from the beautiful dresses the passengers were wearing glimmering in the crystals' reflections. A woman dressed in green played a piano, the sound of laughter and chatter rising and falling.

Charity let Dan lead her to the table in the middle of the room overlooking the viewing area. She let him pull her chair out for her and pour her some wine. She smiled and she nodded yes, and all the time she was staring into the ocean's depths she was thinking, *Dan and Faith. My God, Dan and Faith.*

More people joined their table. When the food was brought out – a truffle omelette for starters, no expense spared, and a main course of steak – Charity barely tasted it at all.

'Time for my speech,' Dan said, patting his pocket. 'Wish me luck.'

'Good luck,' she whispered.

He gave her a quick kiss then walked away, holding on to chairs as the boat swayed slightly. Charity looked outside to see that the weather had rapidly changed, rain lashing down, the sea becoming increasingly violent, waves crashing against the side of the ship.

A few moments later, the golden curtains swept open and Dan appeared on the stage to rapturous applause. He looked larger than life, tall and broad shouldered and gorgeous. He bowed like a performer and delivered a welcome speech that sounded to Charity as though it was being delivered from the bottom of the ocean.

The boat shuddered slightly, cutlery and glasses clinking as people grabbed at them. A woman nearby put her hand to her mouth, clearly unable to handle the rough seas. But she remained where she was.

Dan laughed. 'Lucky we have the best cruise ship in the world to master these waves, hey?'

The crowd laughed nervously.

'So, now we have a treat for you all,' he said. 'Please take a moment to look towards our ocean viewing area. There are also screens around the room for your viewing pleasure.'

As he spoke, television screens fixed to the walls blinked to life, showing close-ups of the ocean floor. Charity peered over the rails at the viewing area, taking in the turquoise waters and seabed rocks. Shoals of fish shimmied by as people gasped and clapped.

All she could see was her sister's face.

Nausea worked its way up inside her. She scraped her chair back from the table and ran out into the corridor, towards the bar and out on to the balcony. She slid the glass door open and stumbled out, leaning over the balcony, not even noticing the driving rain, to take in large gulps of air.

'Oh God,' she whispered. 'Oh Jesus Christ.'

'Charity, what on earth's the matter?' She turned to see Dan step out on to the balcony, the wind buffeting his hair.

She turned to him. 'You gave Faith a necklace, didn't you? It was your mother's.'

Dan's whole body stilled, his face whitening.

'You did,' she said, putting her hand to her mouth. 'My God, you really did.'

His green eyes lifted to meet Charity's. They were devoid of emotion. 'I loved her.'

Charity closed her eyes, struggling to take in this confirmation of all her fears. 'How long?'

'Seven months.'

'How did you meet?'

'Her first week at university. I came in to do a talk for business studies students about starting up a business. We bumped into each other in the canteen, literally.' He got a faraway look in his eyes. 'Her smile did something to me. She saw my label, realised I worked in the shipping business. We got talking and—' He swallowed, face pained. 'It went on from there.'

Charity thought about it for a moment. 'You were already married to Lana then, weren't you?'

Dan nodded.

'So that's why you both kept it a secret. And you were the father of her baby?'

'I was,' he said, his voice breaking. Charity shook her head, feeling sick to her very core.

'I can't believe what I'm hearing.'

He started pacing up and down the balcony, his face twisted with rage. Charity barely recognised him. 'I was there the night Faith died you know. I was the witness who took Niall's licence plate number down.'

'You were there?' Charity felt her legs go weak. She remembered someone had testified but she'd never been allowed to attend court. 'What about Faith?' she whispered. 'Did you see it happen?'

319

Dan placed his hand against a pillar, looking down at the floor as he took deep breaths. 'No. I got there just after.'

'Why on earth was she walking on the road in the early hours?'

'We argued about the baby. She wanted to keep it but – but I wanted her to get an abortion.'

'How could you!' Charity shook her head. 'Poor Faith.'

'She jumped out of my car and hurried down the road. I stayed in the car for a while, trying to calm myself down. Then I went after her but by the time I got there, it was too late.' He looked up at Charity, face distraught. 'I heard her moaning at the bottom of the slope.'

Charity let out a sob. 'Oh God.'

'She kept saying her head hurt, that she was dizzy. When I felt it, her hair was matted with blood but it was so dark, I couldn't see it. I learnt later she'd hit her head on a rock. She told me she'd dropped her bag and was leaning down to get it when Niall's car glanced her, knocking her down the slope.' He let out a sob.

'She was still alive when you found her?' Charity asked.

He nodded, face contorted with grief.

Charity felt her legs give way and she slumped down on to the floor. It was all too unbearable.

'I held her as she died.' Dan shook his head, taking in a shuddering breath.

Charity was quiet for a moment, then she said: 'So you were the witness who found her?'

'Yes. But I didn't tell the police I knew her, I said I'd just been walking along the road. I couldn't have Lana finding out.' He shook his head. 'All that beauty and talent extinguished in a few moments. All because of *him*.' He curled his hands into fists. 'But all he got was two years. Two years for taking my love and our baby away from me! So I had to take something away from him too, something he loved deeply.'

320

Charity stared up at him. 'Revenge? This has all been about revenge?'

Dan nodded. 'I remembered the licence plate and the make of the car so I reported him. I embellished the truth a little, said he'd seen her fall down the slope but didn't stop for her. I was patient. I knew you'd eventually return to Busby-on-Sea, Niall too once he found out you were back. Then I did all I could to get you back together so I could pull you apart again.'

'I don't understand, how did you get Lana to drive into a tree?'

He shook his head. 'Of course I didn't make her do that. But it worked out rather conveniently, didn't it?' Dan seemed more together now, almost proud of his plan. 'I didn't like using you as a pawn, I know Faith wouldn't have approved of that part of my plan. But it was all I had. And when you really think about it, I was doing you a favour. How could Niall ever be good for you? What on earth were you thinking?'

'So you were responsible for the lookalike model in India. The newspaper article. Sabotaging Niall's job prospects,' Charity said. 'My God, it all makes sense now. And then what? Did you seduce me to hurt Niall, *marry* me to add insult to injury?' She let out a sob. 'You never truly loved me, did you? It was all about getting revenge on Niall.'

His face softened. 'That's the problem, Charity. I *did* fall in love with you.'

'I don't believe you. You can't possibly be capable of love after what you did to me, to Niall. It was an *accident*, Dan. All this for an accident. There was no intention to kill Faith, you understand that, don't you?'

He shook his head. 'This is what I've never understood about you, the way you continue to defend Niall despite what he did to Faith. He *killed* your sister. You can't see him for what he is, a murderer.'

She felt anger build inside. 'But he isn't, for God's sake! Maybe I'd understand all this if he'd actually intended to kill Faith. But he didn't.' She shook her head, backing away. 'I can't let you have anything to do with me and Willow after this.'

He laughed. 'Really? You think you can take her away from *me*?'

'I can if she isn't yours,' she spat.

He sighed. 'So it's true then, you did fuck Niall in Kazakhstan.'

She looked at Dan in surprise. 'You knew?'

'I knew he followed you out there, yes, of course I suspected.'

'And yet despite that, you've loved and cared for Willow.'

'I was happy to once again take something that belonged to Niall and keep her from him.' His face softened. 'Turns out my love for Willow quickly outweighed my hatred for Niall.'

Charity walked to the edge of the balcony and looked out at the turbulent sea. 'You don't know anything about love.'

'And you do, Charity? Aren't you the woman who has never been able to make up her mind between two men?'

'Love isn't about revenge,' she said without looking at him. 'It's about *protecting* the person you love, no matter what.'

'Like you've done for Niall all these years?'

'No,' she said, turning towards hm. 'Like he has protected *me* all these years. *That's* true love.'

'Protected you from what? What are you talking about?'

The sea roared in her ears, rain now lashing down on her. Her mind spun, her whole body trembled, her hatred for Dan and the way he'd manipulated her, taken Niall from her, made a *fool* of her, boiling inside.

'*I* was driving,' she shouted. '*I* killed Faith.'

It felt shockingly wonderful to say it out loud. She never thought it would feel this way after all these years of keeping the secret – the secrets of all secrets – deep inside her. So many times she'd wanted to confess, to tell Hope, even Dan. But fear had stopped her.

But now it was out in the open and she felt free.

Dan looked at her, face stricken. 'No,' he whispered.

'Yes, Dan,' Charity said. 'Niall's been covering for me all these years. He loves me so much, he went to prison for *me*. All your hard work to get revenge has been a waste. *I* killed Faith, Dan.' She put her hand to her mouth, stifling her sobs. 'I – I killed my sister. Oh God, Faith, my poor darling Faith.' She crouched down, hand to mouth as she saw the wet road as it was that day, felt her feet on the pedals, the gear stick in her hand.

'Not too fast,' Niall had said. She'd ignored him, pressing her foot on the accelerator, adrenaline rushing through her.

'Practise makes perfect, remember,' she said. 'And now you have this car, we can do *lots* of practising.' Then she'd turned to him, searching out his lips. It had just been the briefest of moments, mere seconds, but it was enough.

The car swerved as they reached the bend, and Charity felt a soft bump on the car. Niall grabbed the steering wheel, shouting at Charity to put her foot on the brake.

'What was that?' she'd asked, voice trembling as they came to a stop.

'A deer or something. We better check.'

They'd both got out, Charity pulling her coat around herself, terrified at the thought she'd hurt an animal.

Would it still be alive? Could they take it to the vet's?

Would she get into trouble?

They'd scoured the road but found nothing. When they'd got back into the car, Niall took over the driving. 'Don't worry,' he said. 'It was probably nothing.'

And the thing was, she hadn't worried. The incident evaporated from her mind as she'd put her hand on Niall's knee, sad another night with him was drawing to an end. Then they'd driven away.

Was that when Dan had seen them? If he'd turned up a few moments before, or if Niall hadn't insisted on taking the blame, how different would things have been?

'We're not so different, are we, Charity?' Dan said now, bringing Charity sharply back to the wet deck and tumultuous waves below. 'Lives filled to the brim with terrible secrets and lies.'

There was a sound of footsteps on the deck. Charity looked up to see one of the deckhands running towards them, a terrified look on his face.

'The captain needs you, sir,' he said.

Dan frowned. 'What's wrong?'

'There's a wave coming, it—'

The ship jolted violently. Charity stumbled, falling against a set of sun loungers as Dan slid across the deck, grabbing on to a pillar to steady himself.

Screams rang out from inside.

Charity looked out at the sea to see a huge wave curling up into the air. There was a loud creaking sound and the ship jerked again. Dan tried to grab for her, their fingers grazing.

'Willow,' she whispered.

Then the wave engulfed the ship.

Chapter Twenty-Four

Willow

Near Busby-on-Sea
October 2016

I hear the creak of a floorboard and look up to see Aunt Hope watching me from the door. Her eyes drop to the photo I'm holding and she sighs.

'Dad knew Faith?' I ask, holding the photo up.

'So it appears.'

'And you knew?'

'Not until after your parents passed away when I found that same photo. That's when I put two and two together.'

I don't even bother asking her why she didn't tell me. That doesn't matter now. All that matters is this photo I'm holding. 'Didn't Mum feel odd dating someone who'd gone out with her dead sister?'

Aunt Hope's eyes lift to meet mine. 'I don't think she knew. Faith never told us and I don't think your father told your mother. She would have told me if he had.'

I stare at the photo of Dad. 'Jesus,' I whisper. 'Why would Dad keep such a thing from Mum? And why would Aunt Faith keep such a thing from her sisters?'

My aunt sits on the bed, gliding her hand along the duvet cover, dust puffing into the air. 'He was married.'

'Oh.'

She sighed, grey eyes emotional. 'As for why Dan kept it a secret from your mum, I've asked myself the same thing all these years. I often wonder if he sought your mother out because she was the closest he could get to Faith.'

I digest what she's just told me. 'Poor Mum. If she ever did find out, that would have been so painful.'

The doorbell goes. We both look at each other. No one visits Aunt Hope here, they always track her down at the café if they need to. She gets up and, for the first time, I notice what an effort it is for her. Maybe working at the café is too much for her now.

'I'll come with you,' I say.

We both walk downstairs and before Aunt Hope even opens the door, I know who it is: Niall Lane. I can tell from the height, the dark hair. My aunt knows it's him too because she pauses in the hallway, hand going to her chest. It must be difficult, seeing the man who caused her sister's death.

She opens the door and there he is, dressed in dark jeans and a leather jacket.

'Hope,' he says. 'It's been a long time.'

My aunt doesn't say anything at first, just stares at him. Then she crosses her arms, looking him up and down. 'Yes?'

He peers over her shoulder towards me. 'I wanted to talk to Willow.'

'Why?' my aunt asks, all bravado.

'It's alright, Aunt Hope,' I say, taking my jacket from the coat stand. 'Shall we go for a walk?' I ask Niall.

He nods. 'Okay.'

I walk past Aunt Hope and impulsively give her arm a quick squeeze to reassure her. The gesture shocks both of us. We rarely touch.

'Don't be long,' she calls out like I'm a teenager again as I step outside with Niall.

I smile to myself.

Aunt Hope watches us as we stroll down the lane together then she closes the door, a pensive look on her face. I imagine her going to her window seat, craning to see where we are. I thrust my hands into my pockets. It's really cold today, the sea sending up a fine mist which hovers over the pebbles.

'Your aunt hasn't changed,' Niall says.

'And she never will.'

He smiles. 'No, she won't, will she? She's been good to you, taking you in. I was worried for you when I found out your mother died.'

'How did you find out?'

He looks around him, face pained. 'I was in Busby-on-Sea actually. I'd just gone for a dive and saw people gathered at the café. I didn't even know the cruise ship had gone down the day before. I overheard some tourist saying the sister of the café's owner had died on the ship. When I saw the news, I realised it was Charity.' He takes in a deep breath. 'I felt like I'd died too. I wanted to be angry, at Dan, at the *world* for taking Charity from me. But there was just gut-wrenching pain. *Physical* pain. I actually doubled over with it.' He looks at me as though just realising I'm there. 'Sorry. She was your mother. I can't possibly know what you must have felt. The last time I saw her she was with you. It was the day before she died.'

'I remember. It was by the café, right?'

He nods. 'She'd have liked the idea of Hope taking you in.'

'And what about you possibly being my father?' I ask. 'How would she have felt about that?'

'That's why I came actually. Turns out I can't possibly be your father.'

'What do you mean?'

'I'm infertile. I've suspected it for years. One girlfriend a few years back couldn't get pregnant. I got some tests done last week. They confirmed it. There's no chance I could ever have conceived a child.'

'But what about Luki?' I ask.

'Judy was sleeping with others when I was staying at the commune. I think Luki just likes the idea his father is a British photographer.'

I feel a heady mixture of disappointment and relief. Disappointment because part of me wanted to have a father who was alive…and who hadn't lied to my mum.

But there's relief too. The fact is my father was there for me for seven years, held me when I cried.

'Are you surprised?' Niall asks.

'I think so. You can't help but see the similarities between you and me, can you? There's the diving. I like travelling, I'm a bit of a nomad, I'm blunt as hell, not charming like my dad.'

Niall smiles slightly. 'You're a spiky little thing, that's for sure. But you probably got that from your aunt Hope.'

I shake my head. 'I'm nothing like her.'

He laughs. 'You're just like her, it's as clear as day. Even the way you hold yourself,' he says, gesturing towards my crossed arms. 'And that look in your eye.'

'What look?' I say, uncrossing my arms.

'Like you're looking right into my soul. Your aunt may have always hated me but I've always admired her. She spoke the truth when others didn't.'

I laugh. 'The truth? You wouldn't believe the stuff she's kept from me.'

'Maybe it's been for your own good.'

'No, I have a right to know about my parents. The things I've discovered today…' I shake my head.

He frowns. 'What have you discovered?'

I contemplate his face a few moments. The fact is, he loved my mum and he went out of his way to get his fertility tested for me. He deserves to know the truth. 'Well, turns out my dad was seeing Faith.'

Niall's face goes white. '*Seeing* her?'

'Yes.'

I hand him the photo of my aunt with my dad. He blinks, clearly shocked. 'This must've been taken the year she died, I remember her hair was really long then.'

'Yep.'

He stares out at the sea, a look of deep concentration on his face, like he's trying to figure something out. Then he shakes his head. 'Jesus. Revenge, that was what it was all about.'

'Woah, wait, slow down!' I say. 'What are you talking about?'

He's quiet for a few moments then nods to himself. 'Dan was the main witness against me during the trial for Faith's death. Different name, different hair colour. But I found out later that it was him who testified to seeing my car drive away from the scene.' His blue eyes spark with anger. 'And yet he never let on all the time your mother and I knew him...all the time your mother was *with* him.'

I think of the dad I knew, the handsome, charismatic man everybody loved. He didn't seem the type to tell such a huge lie.

'Why would he do that?' I ask.

'Revenge?'

I think of my dad's kind face, his all-encompassing smile. Was he really that bitter about Faith's death that he was willing to lie to Mum?

'Niall?' a croaky voice asks from behind us.

Niall looks over my shoulder, a confused expression on his face. I follow his gaze to see Mad Shoe Lady watching us with narrowed eyes. Her wild white-grey hair is static around her head, her face grubby, a long man's coat swathed around her thin body, the bottom trailing the ground.

'Do I know you?' he asks her.

She smiles, revealing gaps in her brown teeth. 'You know who I am.'

'I really don't,' he says.

'We slept together, you and I.' She smacks her lips together at him, laughing.

I look between them both, incredulous.

Niall peers closer then realisation dawns over his face. 'Lana?'

'Bingo!' she says, clapping her hands.

Niall clutches on to her trolley, looking her in the eye. 'It's really you, isn't it?'

She pulls the trolley away from him, wheels rattling along the path. 'Maybe. Maybe not.'

'Who's Lana?' I ask.

'Willow, this is your dad's ex-wife.'

Mad Shoe Lady – or Lana, as I know her now – frowns, the dirt in the wrinkles of her forehead crackling. 'Dan was your dad?' she asks me.

'Yes,' I say, finally being able to mean it, too.

Pain registers in her eyes for a moment. Then she looks at Niall. 'She's *Charity's* daughter?'

'She is,' Niall says sadly.

She turns to me, scrutinising my face. 'Yes, I can see it. Same hair and you have Dan's nose too.' Her eyes harden. 'Are you evil like them two as well?'

'That's not very nice, Lana.'

'You know I'm right,' Lana says. 'Are you going to tell this girl what her mother did?'

Panic floods Niall's face.

'What's she talking about?' I ask.

'It's nothing, let's head back.' Niall softly grasps my arm and tries to steer me away.

I pull away from him and look at Lana. 'What are you talking about?'

330

'That second time – you remember, Niall – after Charity found out about the first time.' Lana turns to me. 'While Niall was sleeping, I did a bit of rifling around in his rucksack. I've always been a bit nosy. I found some rather enlightening letters your mother had written to him.'

She opens her mouth but Niall grabs her arm. 'Don't, Lana. Let me tell her.'

Lana shrugs. 'I don't care what you do.' She turns her back to us and shuffles her trolley along the path, her long matted hair swinging behind her.

I turn to Niall. 'Tell me what?'

Niall takes a deep shuddery breath and I feel sick to my stomach. What's so bad that it makes him react like this? He looks me in the eye, his own eyes filled with sadness. I brace myself.

'You need to know that your mother loved Faith very, very much,' Niall says.

'For God's sake, just tell me!'

'Charity was driving the car the night Faith died, not me. I covered for her.'

There's a sound of a bump behind us. I turn just in time to see my aunt collapsing to the ground.

Chapter Twenty-Five

Willow

Busby-on-Sea, UK
October 2016

The heart monitor beeps are driving me crazy. I pace Aunt Hope's hospital room, looking back at her every now and again. She seems so tiny and fragile hooked up to those monitors. I can't bear to look. Sure, she's always been small. But she's always struck me as being as strong as an ox too.

Ajay's face appears between the curtains. I called him when I arrived at the hospital. I guess I needed a friend.

'Come in,' I say.

He steps into the small cubicle and gives me a big hug before looking at my aunt. 'How is she?'

'Not great.' I try to hold the tears at bay. 'They say she had a heart attack. She's only fifty-seven!'

'I'm so sorry.'

'There's a history of heart disease in my family. It could be a combination of that, the shock of hearing what Lana said…and exhaustion.' I shake my head. 'She does run that café on her own.

Sure, she gets help but still.' I chew at my lip. 'I haven't paid enough attention. If only I'd just—'

'Oh stop whinging,' a small voice says from the bed. Ajay and I turn to see Aunt Hope struggling to sit up, her greying red hair spilling over the white covers.

'I'll leave you two alone,' Ajay says, stepping outside.

I rush to my aunt's side, helping her sit up. 'How are you feeling?'

'How do you think? Like I've been run over by a tank.'

My eyes fill with tears. 'You had a heart attack, Aunt Hope.'

Fear flickers in her eyes, then she composes herself and shrugs. 'Well, at least I'm still here.'

'You're exhausted, Aunt Hope,' I say. 'And there's the shock at hearing what Lana said,' I add carefully.

'Shock can't cause heart attacks. They've got it wrong, I've just not been sleeping much lately.'

'It is possible, actually, Aunt Hope. I read somewhere that stress hormones can narrow the main arteries supplying blood to the heart.'

'Oh for God's sake, do you—' She stops talking then laughs. 'Only we could argue about the cause of a heart attack.'

I can't help but smile too. 'Yeah, only us.'

She grows serious. 'I did get quite a shock though,' she says quietly. 'I heard Niall right, didn't I?'

'Let's not talk about that,' I say, scared the shock will trigger another heart attack.

She looks me in the eye. 'I think we've had enough of not talking about things, haven't we, Willow?'

I sigh. 'We have. We really have.'

Her face softens. 'I've only kept things from you to protect you.'

'I know that.'

'But this – this I had no clue about.' She shakes her head. '*Charity* was driving the car? My God. How could she have not told me?'

'Same reason you haven't told me things. To protect you.'

'Maybe. But to let Niall take the blame all these years…to go to prison.' She grabs my hand. 'I don't want to speak badly of your mother, Willow. But it's so out of character, to do something so cold. Charity was always so compassionate, so caring.'

I look at my aunt Hope, really look at her. I've made myself think she's distant, uncaring. But the truth is, she's the opposite. Everything she's ever done was for her family, including me, never for *her*. She's probably the most selfless person I know. How could I have not seen it all these years? How could I not have cared more for her?

'You can never really know people,' I say. 'All we see is the persona they present to people, not what's really inside. Maybe the truth is Mum was selfish and Dad was vindictive.'

'Vindictive?'

I explain what Niall told me. 'I think he was trying to get revenge on Niall all those years for Faith's death. Maybe Mum and Dad deserved each other.'

I try to absorb that fact, two selfish damaged people finding each other and conceiving me. I was born of lies and self-interest, guilt and revenge. We inherit our parents' traits, don't we? I suppose I've been selfish all these years, not truly recognising what Aunt Hope has done for me, putting my parents on a pedestal they didn't deserve to be on.

Maybe, now I know they weren't as perfect, I can stop imagining the life I never had with them? Maybe, in the end, all these secrets and lies would have seeped out and hurt me more than they have done now. At least I have the buffer of Aunt Hope to protect me from them.

I feel a strange unburdening. No more living in limbo in the shadow of a 'what if?' life. Time to start living *my* life, my *real* life where I accept my aunt as my real family, not a made-up one.

I look at her. How must *she* feel to know all this now? 'Do you hate my mum now?' I ask her.

She shakes her head. 'Of course not. She must have felt horribly guilty. That's why she probably became a counsellor, to atone somehow.'

'It must be hard, learning all this though?'

She shrugs. 'Such is life. And anyway, something good came from all this, didn't it?'

I frown. 'What?'

She surprises me by taking my hand. 'You, Willow! If Dan hadn't been so intent on getting revenge, he'd have never met your mum, and they would never have had you. I'm not sure what I would have done without you over the years.'

I feel tears well up in my eyes. 'But I've never really been here for you.'

'You've kept in touch, sent me letters and photos, haven't you? And when you lived with me, you were my little companion. My favourite memories are of staying up late into the night playing patience with you. Or watching you swim, you've always been such a strong swimmer. Or how about that time at Christmas when the bird got into the living room and we ran around trying to get it? I've never laughed so much.'

I think of those moments too. She's right, they *are* good memories. I just grew so bitter and twisted from our arguments, those memories were tainted. At least I had a chance of a family with my aunt, a chance I've squandered.

Not any longer.

The curtains open then and the doctor walks in with Ajay. Ajay hovers behind him as the doctor explains very gently to Aunt Hope that her ECG test confirmed she'd had a heart attack but that there was only minor damage to the muscles of her heart. 'You will need to slow down a bit and improve your diet,' he says. 'Your BMI is extremely low and it's clear to me you're not eating enough.'

Aunt Hope rolls her eyes.

'Listen to him,' I say to her. 'You *are* too thin.'

'Just because I don't have three sugars in my tea,' she says with a raised eyebrow.

'Maybe that's exactly what you need,' I say sternly.

'I wouldn't recommend sugar,' the doctor says with a small smile. His buzzer starts going off. He frowns as he looks at it. 'I need to attend to someone but I'll be back to explain the next steps.' He leans forward, squeezing her shoulder. 'You're very lucky you had your daughter with you when it happened. The CPR she performed more than likely saved your life.'

For once, I don't correct someone for saying I'm Aunt Hope's daughter because in a way, I'm exactly that, aren't I? It's like Luki said, someone doesn't have to give birth to you to be your mother.

As he leaves the cubicle, Aunt Hope narrows her eyes at me. 'You didn't tell me you knew CPR.'

'All divers get first aid training on their courses.'

'So you don't just swim around looking for pretty fish?' Aunt Hope asks, winking at Ajay.

'Ignore her,' I tell him. 'She knows we do more than that.'

My aunt looks towards Niall's outline through the curtain. 'Niall Lane, I can see you out there, you might as well come in!'

He walks in, looking uncomfortable.

'So, I presume you came to tell Willow you're not her father?' she says.

He nods. 'Yes.'

'Thought so. Doesn't mean you can't keep in touch though, does it?'

I look at Niall and he smiles.

'I've seen your photos too,' my aunt continues. 'Very impressive. Any chance I could have a couple for the café?'

Niall and I exchange a look. This is the closest he'll get to an apology from my aunt for blaming him for Faith's death all these years.

'Of course,' he says 'Charity would have liked that.'

'She would,' Aunt Hope says. 'She loved your photos...and she loved you. You were always the one, weren't you? I tried to tell myself she was more in love with the past than with you. But it was more than that.'

His face flushes, his eyes watering. He turns away, trying to compose himself and my heart goes out to him.

'And you,' she says, looking at Ajay. 'Where are you going to drag my niece to next?'

'Maybe not so far this time,' Ajay says, looking out of the window. 'Niall was telling me about the abandoned building next to your café?'

'What about it?' I say.

He looks at me, smiling. 'I think I might have found that dive centre I've always dreamt of opening.'

I laugh. 'Are you kidding? *Here*, in Busby-on-Sea?'

'I don't know why you're so down about this town, Willow,' he says. 'There were a bunch of divers on the beach earlier, looks pretty up and coming to me.'

'He's right,' Niall says. 'The council's ploughed loads of money into the place over the past year after the submerged forest started getting more attention.'

'Have you even *looked* at the place properly since you got here?' Aunt Hope asks me.

I realise I haven't.

'There's even a Starbucks here now,' she continues. 'And that building Ajay's referring to is like the TARDIS inside.'

'Maybe you can help me run the place?' Ajay asks me. 'Doesn't mean you have to stop travelling. You can base yourself here then go off when you want, maybe even finish that tour of all the submerged forests your Aunt Faith wanted to visit?'

Aunt Hope smiles sadly then squeezes my hand. 'I used to talk about that building a lot with your mum and Faith, you know. They wanted to buy it and turn it into a gift shop. I think they'd like the idea of you being involved with something like that. You could live in the cottage, it's only ten minutes' drive away.' She looks into my eyes. 'It'd be nice for you to come home, Willow.'

Home.

I follow her gaze out to sea, imagining the submerged trees beneath the waves, their soft mossy branches reaching up to the surface. I close my eyes, see Mum and my aunt Faith swimming through the forest, limbs graceful, fingers interlaced.

I smile down at my aunt. 'Yes, it would, wouldn't it?'

THE END

Acknowledgements

I started writing *My Sister's Secret* not long after giving birth to my daughter. It was an intense time helped, as ever, by the support and love of my wonderful husband, Rob, and our parents: the Fountains, the Buchanans and the Archbolds.

You'll find one name that will always appear in my acknowledgments: Elizabeth Richards, my constant literary soul sister, a shoulder to cry on and a soundboard to sling ideas at.

Thank you to Jenny Ashcroft too, who was kind enough to offer invaluable insights – including advice on how to juggle writing with motherhood!

To my uncle Glenn Archbold, thank you for helping me with the dive scenes, you're an absolute star.

I must give a shout-out to the lovely Charlie, whose Urban Writers' Retreat allowed me to reach my deadline: three days of quiet writing time in beautiful Devonshire countryside…oh, and cake too!

A huge thanks as ever to my agent Caroline Hardman whose honest, no-nonsense critiques and unwavering support help me to be the best writer I can be.

And finally, my editor, Eli Dryden, whose insightful and brilliant editorial notes and constant enthusiasm and support have been a godsend.

How far would you go for the one you
love the most?

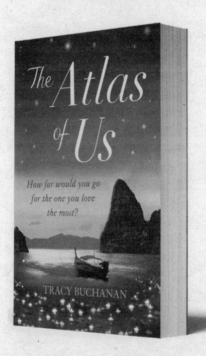

Read an extract from the acclaimed The Atlas of Us,
available in all good retailers.

Prologue

Everyone runs except her. Their movements are panicked, eyes wide, arms flailing. But she can't move, legs frozen as she takes in the ferocity of the wave eating up the beach ahead of her. She takes a deep breath and wraps her arms tight around the atlas, her heart beating a strange beat against its cover: slow then fast then slow again.

Just a few moments before, she'd been walking along the shoreline, toes sinking into the warm sand. The soft beach had stretched out vast and gold before her, the walk to the bungalows seeming to take longer than usual.

Now the sea is buffeting against the bungalow three rows in front. It blasts around the sides, its bamboo walls rattling then breaking apart before disappearing into the watery depths.

Someone to her right screams. She turns, sees a long-tail boat thrashing about on top of the oncoming wave. It smashes into a palm tree, its wood splintering as the tree bends back. A man she'd seen swimming in the sea moments before is clinging to it. His eyes catch hers just before he tumbles into the whirlpool of water below, spinning around among deckchairs, beach bags and God knows what else.

Her legs find traction and she stumbles back, breath stuttering as the water surges towards her.

She peers behind her. There's nowhere to run, just more flat ground, more palm trees.

The wave engulfs a small palm tree in front of her, its roar filling her ears. A food stall topples over in its path and careens towards her, fruit churning in the relentless gush of water.

The sharp smell of brine and seaweed fills her nostrils.

It's so close now.

She suddenly feels a strange kind of serenity. She refuses to live what might be her last moments in a state of hopeless panic. This is what she has learned lately, a calm acceptance of what must be. It wasn't always like this. She once fought against her fate, twisted out of its grasp, stumbled on regardless.

Not now.

She tries to face the wave, stand tall and strong, the atlas held against her like it might somehow protect her. But it's no use, fear prevails. She runs into the tiny bathroom, slamming the door shut behind her and sliding down the wall until she feels the cool of the tiles against her thighs.

Maybe she'll survive? She can swim, kick her way to the surface, see the sun and think how lucky she was. She'll go back home, hold tight to the people she let down and never let them go.

Tears flood her eyes as she thinks of all she is leaving behind; of mistakes that may never be remedied.

Thank God she sent the letter.

There's a creaking sound followed by a loud thud. The bathroom door quakes and she realises something has fallen against it.

She's trapped. No chance now.

She quickly scours the room, eyes settling on the plastic bag used to line the bin. She grabs it, wraps the atlas in it then shoves the atlas into the bag slung around her chest, yanking at the adjustments until they're so tight they hurt. She won't let the atlas get destroyed, not after what she went through to get it back. The walls around her vibrate as objects are flung against them. She thinks of the man on the palm tree. That might be her soon, another piece of flotsam on the tide.

Dread overwhelms her.

There's a thunderous rushing noise and someone screams, someone close enough to be heard over the roar.

It's here.

The wall in front of her begins to crack, water tracing a long line down it, finding its path towards her. She pulls her knees up to her chest, pressing the bag against her stomach, taking comfort from the feel of the atlas's bumpy cover against her skin. She closes her eyes and sucks in an urgent breath.

This is it.

As she hears the walls start to tumble, feels specks of water on her cheeks, an unbearable sadness takes over her.

Did she do enough for those she loves?

She closes her eyes as the wall in front of her smashes apart, water ploughing over her. She's lifted with the wave and flung against the sink. The porcelain cracks against her shoulder, pain slicing through her.

The bamboo walls around her crash apart and she's propelled outside with the wave, her body spinning with the force of it as it gallops towards the line of palm trees nearby.

She manages to keep her head above water, gasping for air, and tries desperately to grasp at something, anything, her dark hair blurring her vision as it lashes around her face.

Her fingers graze what she thinks must be the branch of a palm tree and, for a moment, she thinks she might have a chance. But the strength of the wave whips it away from her, thrusting her underwater and spinning her so erratically, she can't tell what is sky and what is ground.

Water gritty with sand and debris rushes into her mouth. She snaps her lips shut, desperately trying to hold her breath as she's pulled deeper and deeper, her chest bursting with the effort.

But the need to breathe is overpowering, every part of her yearning to exhale. Her chest expands, her head ringing. And then she's giving in, mouth opening as she takes one last blissful breath, the faces of all those she loves strong in her mind.

For a brief moment, she thinks she sees red hair, green eyes. She reaches her hand out, but then everything is gone.

Chapter One

Krabi, Thailand
2004

When I close my eyes, the water comes: the violent thud of waves, the tart smell of salty dampness seeping through the cracks of my dreams. But when I look out of the bus window, it's nothing but mangled cars again; boats that have somehow found their way onto the roofs of two-storey buildings; suitcases flung open, their innards spilling out onto the dusty pavements below.

The bus takes a turn and I'm facing the sea again. It looks calm, ebbing and flowing like it's forgotten the devastation it caused a few days ago.

My phone buzzes, a text from Will. I force myself to look at it.

Did you get my voicemail? You shouldn't have gone.
Call me.

'British, love?' There's a woman watching me from across the aisle. Stark white lines dart up from the strapless top she's wearing, disappearing over the fleshy mounds of her shoulders. I feel the urge to tell her about my friend Simone who nearly died of skin cancer.

Instead I nod. 'Yes.'

'Thought so. I saw you at the airport earlier. We're going to see about our son, he's eighteen.'

My heart goes out to her. How would I feel if it were one of my girls missing? 'I'm sorry. I hope he's okay.'

'We hope so too, don't we, Roy?' The woman peers at the man next to her, but he just continues staring bleakly out of the window. 'His friends say he met a girl, spent the night with her. Now he's missing.'

Missing.

That's the word I've been using to describe Mum's status too since getting a call from her friend Jane on Boxing Day. But now that I'm heading to the temple – the endgame – *missing* seems too optimistic.

'What about you?' the woman asks. I can see she's desperate for the comfort blanket of talk her husband obviously can't offer. He's probably like Will, always telling me I talk too much. Even after I'd got the phone call about Mum, he was too engrossed in his new iPod to listen properly as I tried to tell him how desperately worried I felt.

'My mum's been travelling around the islands over Christmas,' I say to the woman now. 'She's not tried to call anyone to let us know she's okay. We're really worried.'

'Oh, poor luv. You've come out here all alone?'

'Yes. I'm all my mum has. We're very close.' I don't know why I lie.

'That's lovely. You're very good to come out here for her.'

Or stupid. That's what Will had called me when I'd woken him in the early hours to tell him I wanted to fly out here to find Mum.

Maybe he was right. Maybe I am bloody stupid to leave

the girls with their dad and come alone to a country more alien than I've ever known. I can smell the foreignness in the scorched spicy air drifting in through the windows; see it in the wires that hang precariously from the pylons; hear it in the strange urgent accents of the Thai people outside.

I feel my chest start to fill with apprehension but quickly swallow it away.

'Have you been putting photos of your mum up on the notice boards?' the woman asks.

I nod. 'Yes.'

'Strange, isn't it? All those smiling faces?'

She doesn't say why. I know what she means though. Strange to think half of them might be dead now, bloated corpses laid out in a temple like the very one we're heading to now.

What if Mum's one of those corpses? Oh God.

'Did you check the patient list at the hospital?' the woman asks.

I clear my throat, trying not to show the fear building inside. 'Yes, I did.' I'd gone *into* the hospital too, waving my mum's photo in the faces of harassed-looking staff whose accents made my head buzz with confusion, the phrase book I'd bought in a hurry at the airport useless.

'You never know, someone might call,' the woman says, looking down at her mobile clutched in her plump hand. 'The embassy photocopied the picture we brought of our son. So nice of them. I'm sure it'll all be fine.' Her hand flutters to the small cross around her neck. 'I'm sure we'll . . .'

Her voice trails off, her eyes losing focus as the bus slows down. A large spiky roof with gold spires comes into view, a mountain shrouded in trees behind it. As the bus draws closer, the whole temple appears before us, curved and ornate with tiered icing-sugar walls and arched windows fringed with gold. Two painted tiger statues adorn its entrance, looking ready to pounce on the frantic relatives and tired-looking officials hurrying around the busy area in front of it. This must be where the foreign embassies are: white canopies, rows and rows of photo boards, lines of desks weighed down with paperwork and flags. I try to find the Union Jack among all the other flags, as if it might blur the strangeness of this place a little. But all I can see is a tiny beige monkey that is weaving in and out of the table legs. I make a mental note to tell the girls about it. They'll want to know things like that when I get back. They don't need to know about the bodies I've seen floating in the sea, nor the turned-over cars. Just this little sprite of a monkey and the bright green lizards I noticed while waiting for the bus.

I think of their faces when I'd told them I'd be leaving them for a couple of days to find their nanna. My youngest, Olivia, had got that look, like she might cry any minute, and it had made my heart ache. They've not spent more than one night away from me and even then it felt like a small kind of torture for them – and me. To make them feel better, I'd told them Daddy was taking them to the show they'd been going on about; the same show he's made every excuse under the sun *not* to go to.

I hope he takes them, I really do. He needs to spend more time with them. He can make their breakfast and ferry them from one friend to another like I do each day, wash their clothes, clean the house, pick up the dog muck in the garden . . . the list goes on. Maybe he'll understand life isn't such a breeze as a stay-at-home mum?

Oh God, what was I thinking? How on earth will he cope? I really was stupid coming here.

We pass under a square blue archway, the red globe lanterns hanging from its ceiling trembling in the breeze.

The woman sitting across from me clutches at her husband's arm. But he ignores her just like Will would ignore me. I want to shake him, tell him his wife needs him. Instead, I reach over and place my hand on the woman's plump arm. The woman nods, her eyes swimming with thanks. But she doesn't speak any more.

The bus comes to a stop beneath a lush green tree, and I try to recognise Jane's son Sam among the crowds from the photo she sent. A man approaches the bus.

It's him.

His tanned face speaks of exhaustion, of sadness and unknown horrors. People stand, blocking my view of him. I rise with them, smoothing my fringe down, checking the collar of my neat blossom-coloured blouse. Despite it being early evening, the heat's a nightmare, sweat making the thin material of my blouse cling to all the wrong curves, curves I usually cover with tailored tops and trousers; strands of my fine hair already escaping from the ponytail I'd crafted so carefully a few hours before. I'm pleased I inherited Dad's height and blond hair, but combine that with my mum's curves and I'm in trouble.

I catch myself mid-moan. How can I worry about my weight when Mum's missing?

The bus driver hauls open the door and I step out, blinking up at the sun and trying not to think about what it must be doing to all those bodies. The other passengers hesitate too, faces white with worry as they take in the temple in the distance. A woman leans her face into her husband's chest and sobs while two young men next to me take frantic gulps of water, the nervous energy throbbing off them.

I feel even more alone now, watching all these people. They're all terrified of what they might find, but at least they're not alone. I look at Sam. Maybe I'm not so alone. I shrug my bag strap over my shoulder, heading towards him.

He turns as I approach, frowns a little like he's trying to figure out if it's the same person in the photo his mum sent. Then he smiles. 'Louise?' he asks, a Northern lilt to his voice.

He's in his late twenties, a few years younger than me, and is wearing a white linen shirt and cut-off blue jeans. This close, I can see the light stubble on his cheeks and chin, the small jewel in his nose, the wheel pattern of the pendant hanging from his neck. He has tanned skin, fair hair, a mole on his cheek. Will would call him a hippy, like the man with long hair who was renting the house a few doors down with his Chinese wife and two children last year. I'd been desperate to invite them over for dinner; they'd seemed so interesting. But Will had always found some excuse or other not to. Six months later, they'd moved away. I wasn't surprised. They didn't look the type to be happy in an estate full of expensive new builds and gas-guzzling family cars.

'Yes, I'm Louise,' I say to Sam. I note a hint of surprise in his eyes. Maybe he was expecting someone like my mum, all bronzed and arty with floaty skirts and flowing scarves, instead of a pale, blouse-wearing, stay-at-home mum from Kent. 'Thanks so much for offering to help,' I say. 'Your mum said you'd been helping out? I'll try not to take up too much of your time.'

'Take up as much time as you want. I promised Mum I'd do everything I can to help you.' He examined my face. 'How are you holding up?'

'The paperwork's a nightmare but—'

'I mean about your mum missing. Must be tough?'

'I – I'm not sure really. It's been a bit of a blur since your mum called. I'm sure everything'll be fine, I'm sure we'll find her . . .' My voice trails off. The truth is, I'm terrified. Terrified I've lost my mum before I've even had the chance to patch things up with her. 'Jane says you live in Bangkok.

Did you travel over here to help out?' I ask, trying to change the subject. Small talk seems out of place here, but it's a type of anchor for us Brits, isn't it?

He shakes his head. 'I came to Ao Nang to visit a friend for Christmas. Luckily, we were staying further inland. As soon as we heard what had happened, we started helping out and I ended up volunteering here,' he says, gesturing around him.

'It must be difficult.'

He swallows, his Adam's apple bobbing up and down. 'Very. But at least I'm doing something to help. Have you done all the form-filling and DNA stuff?'

'Yes, twice. No sign.' I peer towards the temple. 'So, do we go in there then?'

'Not yet. The bodies are back there.' He flinches slightly, like it physically hurts him to say that. 'I'd recommend the boards first, there's photos of each body on there. People find that easier.'

'Yes, that makes sense.' My voice sounds strong, considering.

'Why don't you show me a photo of your mum and I'll go look at the boards for you?'

'You don't have to, really. I can do it.'

This time, my voice breaks as I imagine seeing a photo of Mum up there. Sam gently places his fingers on my bare arm. They feel cool, dry. 'I'm here to help, Louise.'

The woman from the bus approaches from the direction of the photo boards, her face pressed against her husband's chest as he stares ahead, tears streaming down his cheeks.

I look back at Sam. 'If you're sure?'

'Of course. You've probably been asked this already, but are there any distinguishing marks, jewellery, anything that will help me identify your mum?'

'Just a bracelet she always wears. She's wearing it in this photo.' I start digging around in my bag. 'Thing is, I haven't seen her for over two years so I'm not sure if she still looks . . .' My voice trails off. Why did I say that?

'Two years?'

'It's a long story.'

Sam scrutinises my face then nods. 'Understood. So, the photo?'

I pull the photo out and hand it over. Mum looks happy in it, tanned, smiling, her dark hair whipping about her face. Slung over her shoulder is a pink bag with the smiling face of a child embroidered into its front. I can just about make out her precious bracelet, a rusty old charm bracelet with bronze teapots and spoons attached to it. She's wearing the yellow cardigan with red hearts I got her a few years ago too. That did something to me when Jane emailed the photo to me after they'd both gone to some Greek island together last year, made my heart clench to see her wearing the cardigan I got her – like maybe Mum *did* care for me.

Something changes in Sam's face as he looks at the photo. 'That's an unusual bag. I think I saw it last night.'

I try to keep my voice steady. 'With a body?'

He looks pained. 'Yes, I'm sorry. It was wrapped around the woman quite securely. It came in late so if there's any ID with it, it won't have filtered down to any lists yet.'

I sway slightly, vision blurring. Sam takes my elbow, helping me steady myself.

'I'll go out back and check for you,' he says softly. 'Is it okay if I take this photo?'

'Yes.' My voice is barely above a whisper.

'Why don't you sit down?' He steers me to a nearby seat, an oddly shaped bamboo chair that feels rough under my calves. He then runs towards the temple, his flip-flops slapping on the sandy concrete as he weaves between the tables and photo boards, apologising to people as he bumps into them.

I put my head in my shaking hands. Is this what it comes to in the end? I feel a rush of regret and anger. Regret at not working hard enough to rebuild my relationship with my mum again when she stopped talking to me, anger at the fact I'd had to even *try* to rebuild it. It had only been a stupid argument; I'd never dreamt it would have led to her not contacting me for such a long time.

'Oh, Mum,' I mumble into my palms.

I stay like that for a while, trying to grapple with the idea of Mum being gone forever. When Jane had called saying how concerned she was, I knew, quite suddenly, that I had to come out here to find Mum. It wasn't just about finding her, it was about starting over with her, making amends. I'd brewed on it all of Boxing Day as I'd watched the news unfold on TV until I'd had to wake Will to tell him what I'd decided. I could tell he didn't believe I'd go through with it, even when I started packing my suitcase.

I sit up straight when I notice Sam jogging towards me again. He's holding a bag to his chest like it's a newborn baby and there's this look on his face that makes something inside me falter. He places the bag on the dusty ground and crouches down in front of me, placing his hands over mine. I pull my hands away, stifling the growing panic inside.

'There was a passport in the bag,' he says very softly.

He pulls it from the bag and hands it to me. I open it, see Mum's face, her name. I put my hand to my mouth and blink, keep blinking. It feels like there's a wave inside, flattening everything in its path.

'You said the bag was found with a body,' I say. 'Have you seen it?'

Sam nods, face crunched with pain. 'There's a lot of . . .'

He sighs. 'A lot of damage to the face. But she has dark hair like your mum's.'

The edges of the world smudge.

I close my eyes and smell Mum's scent: floral perfume, mints and paint oils. With it comes a memory of her smiling down at me, her paintbrush caught mid-sweep, a blot of black ink smudging the eye she'd been painting – her own eye. The ink crawls down the canvas, distorting her painted face. I was eight at the time and had just got back from a disastrous day at school.

'What's with you, grumpy face?' she'd asked me.

I'd hesitated a moment before stepping into the spare room she was using as a studio. Our house was just a small three-bed semi but my father had insisted on turning the largest room into a studio for Mum. It had always felt off-limits to me. But she'd beckoned me in that day, gesturing towards her paint-splattered chair, a bright blue leather one she'd found in the local charity shop.

'Tell me everything,' she'd said, kneeling in front of me and taking my hands, getting green paint all over them.

'I don't want to go into school tomorrow,' I'd said, resisting the urge to pull away from her and clean the paint off my hands. I'd never got on well at the private school Dad had been so keen to scrimp and save to get me into, the teachers always seemed to regard me as inferior to the other, richer kids. Mum had warned him it would happen. 'There's nothing worse for a snooty bourgeois than an aspiring bourgeois,' she'd said. Is that what she'd thought of me when I married a company director – a snooty bourgeois?

'Why not, darling?' she'd asked.

'My teacher told me off today.'

She'd raised an eyebrow, smiling slightly. I remember

thinking that mums aren't supposed to smile about things like that and part of me was annoyed. Why couldn't she be like other mums?

'Why'd your teacher tell you off, Lou?' she'd asked.

'I told the truth.' Her smile had widened. 'She read out a poem she'd written to help us with our poems and I said it was rubbish.'

Mum had laughed then, those big white teeth of hers gleaming under the light. 'You told the truth, that's wonderful! "Beauty is truth, truth beauty. That is all ye know on earth and all ye need to know",' she'd added, quoting her favourite Keats poem.

'But she hates me now.' I'd crossed my arms, turning away. 'I can't go into school.'

'Of course you can! You can't let fear rule you, Lou. You have to fight against fear, stare it right in the face.'

'You okay?' Sam asks, pulling me from the memory.

I open my eyes, Mum's words echoing in my mind like she's right there with me.

You can't let fear rule you, Lou.

'Can I see the bag please?' I ask Sam.

'Of course.'

He hands it to me. It's dirtier than in the photo, caked with dried mud, and there's a grotesque tear across the child's face. I imagine Mum shopping in one of Thailand's markets with it, reaching into it for a purse to buy some odd Buddhist ornament, half a smile on her tanned face.

I take a deep breath then unzip it, peering in. There's a hairbrush in there, a bright red lipstick and something wrapped in a plastic bag. I pull the brush out first, examining the hair on it. It looks dark, just like Mum's.

But then lots of people have dark hair, right?

I place the brush gently to one side and look at the lipstick.

Mum sometimes wears red lipstick. She's not alone in that though, plenty of women do.

But what about her passport? That can only belong to one woman.

I clench my fists, driving the surge of grief away. It's not over until it's over.

I reach into the bag again for the item wrapped in plastic. It's square-shaped and feels heavy, its surface rough beneath the material of the plastic. I pull it out and lay it on top of Mum's bag. Its front cover is made from strips of thin wood interweaved with each other and an image of the earth is etched in bright turquoise into it with four words painted in gold over it.

The Atlas of Us.